Whump! The ground shook and reports of the guns on the hills kept up, explosions slamming against the hill in front of them. Save the equipment. Save their shelter. Protect themselves against the chance that some enemy up there had something to answer the tanks: a general in Hell never assumed anything, and lasers and disruptors and tactical nukes were always a possibility. Get themselves and their equipment out of here, and discover why later—that was Julius Caesar's priority.

Cleopatra was shouting orders of her own, snatching up equipage and personal belongings and wreckage and shoving them at an orderly while legionaries struck the tent they had been sleeping in. That sudden flattening of the canvas as Julius glanced back showed him the chopper on the field beyond the camp, all aglare with its landing lights and making a target out of itself—till it roared back into the air and beat directly overhead, throwing unwelcome lights on the camp.

Achilles was taking a recon or deserting them, it was a tossup which.

KINGS
IN HELL

C.J. Cherryh
and
Janet Morris

KINGS IN HELL

This is a work of fiction. All the characters and events portrayed in this book are fictional, and any resemblance to real people or incidents is purely coincidental.

A Baen Books Original

Baen Publishing Enterprises
260 Fifth Avenue
New York, N.Y. 10001

First printing, February 1987

ISBN: 0-671-65614-7

Cover art by David Mattingly

Printed in the United States of America

Distributed by
SIMON & SCHUSTER
1230 Avenue of the Americas
New York, N.Y. 10020

CONTENTS

Knight's Move

The house was all too quiet since Julius had gone away. Young Brutus lounged in his room, played his records, did his studies (Augustus was merciless) swam in the pool, and did his fencing practice alone, partnerless, because Sargon was busy, had been busy, continued to be busy; and Dante Alighieri was no fun at all, locked in his room with his computers.

Mostly Brutus pitied himself. His father Julius had gone away with Mouse and Hatshepsut and Kleopatra (the *women* had gone off on some great and dangerous adventure and he, seventeen, almost a man, languished on his bed, chin on arms) and Antonius and mysterious and foreign Germans and even Niccolo, of the stinging wit and the frightening stares—Brutus even missed Niccolo Machiavelli, and sighed and sighed and sulked even to the point of tears because he had lost the world all on a summer's day near Baiae—he never even remembered dying; and he had found Julius Caesar here in Hell and gotten Julius to say what he had known, oh, for at least two years, that he was Julius' son. Better, Julius had taken him, the bastard, into his arms and hugged him and *called* him son in a way that made up for all the whispers (almost) and all the misery of a boy about whom there had been plenty of whispering in his life. His fierce, his handsome, his clever father had acknowledged him and shown him wonders like

1

jeeps and telephones and installed him in this gloriously beautiful villa where Augustus claimed to be Commandant of all Roman Territories or something like that . . . the world had certainly gotten very strange just after his little span of life, and something had changed the Rome he knew, but he did not know what. And did not presently care. He had spent all his life treading around the mystery of his own existence with his mother wincing and looking terrified at this remark and that (oh, a boy could pick up such subtle things that his elders never knew he saw or sensed) and living in general with a nagging pain like glass in his gut—just so he sensed another pit which might swallow him and spoil all this wonderful life: and his father stood on the edge of it and Augustus in the midst of it, so he did not ask, not at all, he was good at not asking things. He only wanted Julius to love him and call him son as his father Junius had never been able to do . . . *boy* and *lad* and *youngster* and every endearment but son.

So now Julius was off in some danger with the women and he was too much the baby to be with his father. He struck chips out of the practice pole, he begged to be allowed onto the firing range, he was afire to get his hands on weapons and prove himself a marksman and a fencer to be reckoned with, to show such brilliance that Sargon would be awed (if Sargon ever came near him, if Sargon ever had the time) and would go off with him to join Julius and show him what a man his son had become and what a mistake it had been for Julius to go off without him.

Julius would be in some great danger with hordes of barbarians pouring down on him and Mouse and the others and he, Brutus, would come roaring over the hill with Sargon driving the jeep, firing as they came; the barbarians would all run in terror and Julius would jump down from his jeep and stand there looking so proud of his son—

Brutus sniffed and wiped his eyes and his nose and wished he had something to eat, because his stomach hurt, and he was tired of the stupid records. "Off," he said. And a sycophant, one of the cloud of invisible servants that infested the house, materialized enough to cut the stereo off. "Food," he said. "I want a sandwich." He was not supposed to use the sycophants like that. *Don't get lazy*, Augustus would say. *Do it yourself.* But no one knew and no one cared. Sniff. "Ham and cheese. Glass of milk." The Emperor himself had food brought in when he was busy. So he was entitled. It was a mansion, after all. They were rich. There were no slaves, Julius and Augustus both hated them, so they had to use the sycophants you could never look at and never talk to (some of the slaves he had liked, at home, and some were kind to him and stole him tidbits out of the kitchen when his father sent him to his room without supper, which was what this felt like. And old Melanippe had told him stories while she would sit and peel apples. But the sycophants had no such stories.) Sniff. Sargon had, and even Augustus, and Dante wrote them even, but none of them had time for him.

He could run away and join the army. Julius would be in dire trouble and he would spot the enemy sneaking up on him and slip through enemy lines and warn Julius, rescuing the whole Roman army and becoming a hero. Even Mouse would be impressed. Fathers were easier, having an investment at stake.

A door closed in the hall. His ears pricked up. Sniff. Someone was up here? He had lost track of Dante, then. He had thought Dante was in his office with his damned old computer. That was who it had to be.

But he heard no footsteps, just a moving out there. Stealthy-like. And someone brushed heavily against the wall.

Brutus' heart began to pound, as if somehow he had gotten across that line from his vivid imaginings to something wrong in the house that was not exciting and interesting, it was scary, and he was seventeen and not up to the kind of trouble that tended to come down on this house.

Viet Cong? he wondered, had some Cong assassin gotten in an upstairs window or something and was there some barefoot black-clad man going down the hall with a machine-gun, ready to mow them all down? He gathered himself up off the bed, careful not to make a sound, his tennies silent as he could make them on the floor as he cast about him desperately hunting a weapon, any weapon, and finding only the *rudus*, his stick-sword, there in the corner.

Psst! he said, and quietly snapped his fingers, hoping for a sycophant; but they were *never* there when trouble came, and that desertion made him sure that it was real trouble, there was danger, o gods, and he was all alone up here, the Cong might murder them all and it was all his fault if they got to Dante and to the downstairs.

He gathered up the foil and slipped to the door, listened at it, tried to nerve himself to yell out and raise the house and not be a fool and not open that door at all, but just to yell and hide under the bed the way a boy ought with a hall full of machine-gun-wielding Viet Cong outside and Sargon of Akkad downstairs—Sargon would come charging up there with his gun and mow them all down—

—Sargon would come rushing up into their fire and get killed and they would all be butchered by hordes of Cong, even poor scholarly Dante, slain like Archimedes at his papers—

"*Haaaiiiii!*" Brutus yelled, and jerked the door open, and rushed out to kill the intruders one and all, and frighten them down to Sargon and ambush if he could.

But it was a lone and naked man out there, who turned round and stared at him in shock—it was a one-handed man, Mucius Scaevola, his father's friend who had gone off with him, who stared at him as if he had seen the most bewildering sight in his life, and who then lost his balance and staggered and went down on his side in a heap.

"*Sargon!*" Brutus cried. Of all his seniors in the house, it seemed more Sargon's department than anyone else's, that one of the bravest soldiers of Caesar's army turned up stark naked in the upstairs hall and fainted on the floor.

Deep in the uncharted bowels of Hell, Achilles piloted three mad Old Dead in his chopper, chasing a horse Alexander of Macedon thought to be Bucephalus along a beach as treacherous as the Devil himself, a beach that sometimes resembled Ilion, sometimes not.

In search of what, had these passengers come? —Alexander, Judah Maccabee, and Diomedes who'd fought with Achilles on the beach until Diomedes had been wounded and Achilles slain by Paris? In search of an omen taken from the flight of a wild beast? In search of redemption?

If the steed with flagged mane and tail running below them in a spray of lather and sand was Bucephalus, then the beast wasn't wild and any omen taken from it was suspect.

If redemption was the goal—some way out of Hell through guile or force of arms—then Achilles' passengers were more than fools, they were pawns: just the sight of Paradise rising, "down here" at the end of tunnels running deep below Hell's "surface," should have taught them that topography was little more than mythography where the Devil's way was law.

Achilles ought to know. Achilles had flown this black, Hughes-built bird through tunnels barely a hand's breadth wider than his rotor blades to get here. Achilles had embraced Hell's multi-temporality, learned what he could and kept learning from the Americans, the Russians, even the Asians.

None of these Old Dead he ferried had learned even Hell's simplest lesson: that omens were the Devil's work, like the weather and the very lay of the land here—not to be trusted. In fact, none of Achilles' passengers had learned a damned thing about Hell, long as they'd been here. They clung to the old ways and suffered mortally because of it.

He thought, while pulling up out of a dive meant to herd the horse into a box canyon so that he could put the chopper down on the sand (even fusion turbines had limits) and capture it, that Diomedes, at least, should have realized that they had greater troubles than Bucephalus.

If the chopper was not Hughes-built, and the co-pilot an automated black box, it might have been possible to discuss matters with his fellow veteran. But the decibel level in the cockpit was 120dB and Achilles hadn't a headset to spare for Diomedes.

Who probably wouldn't have known what to do with one, although Alexander of Macedon had come aboard with a thirty-two shot Uzi 7.62 slung over his shoulder. Come aboard with it and referred to it as his "slingshot."

They were hopeless, these ancients, so much more ancient than he.

He banked, pulling up on the stick by his knee, his other hand on the wheel. Diomedes, surely, would have considered what it meant to have taken Ilion from Agamemnon, an Atreidês.

Achilles might have facilitated the second sack of Ilion with his chopper, but it was Diomedes who'd overpowered Agamemnon, son of Atreus, king of Mykenai and brother of Menelaos.

Had ten years on Troy's beach taught Diomedes nothing about the Atreidês? Ten years because Menelaos' wife, Helen, had run off with Paris?

He shook off a shudder as Paris' name sounded in his head. Paris, a coward who shot arrows from cover, had killed him, and Paris' war name was Alexander.

That was the sort of omen you could count on in Hell. Correspondence divided by catastrophe math.

The great black horse was nearly gray with froth, dappled and rearing in the box canyon, ears flattened to the chopper settling to block its only escape route.

Achilles felt a soft thrill of satisfaction run along his nerves. Do the job in front of you. Don't reach. That was what the American who had come to him with orders (presumably from the Pentagram) had said.

Take this chopper down to help Julius' people. Co-ordinates're already laid in. Somebody named Welch is there, with a commo truck. You'll get further orders presently. For now, just help some old friends of yours.

Americans tended to be secretive. Achilles liked them. If he'd known then that he was being sent to a stronghold in which Agamemnon was preparing to refight the Trojan War, he'd have asked which "friends" the American meant.

He had no friends among the Achaeans present. None of his Myrmidons were here. The Argive Diomedes was a rival; Agamemnon was madder than he'd ever been.

So it had been a judgment call, factoring in the datum that Diomedes was allied with Julius Caesar and Agamemnon was on the other side.

Beyond the windscreen, clouds of dust were beginning to settle. Somewhere down the canyon, a stallion's angry scream could be heard as the rotors died.

Achilles, son of a river-priestess, took off his com helmet and turned into the body of the chopper, past the automated flight deck to where his passengers were struggling with their harnesses.

"Diomedes, come here a minute," said the prince of Thessalia to his contemporary, as the boyish Macedonian and his big Israelite bodyguard opened the cargo door and jumped to the sand.

The Argive came forward, stooping as he entered the flight deck's close confines.

"So, Myrmidon? What is it? The horse-augury waits."

"Have you thought about the omen we left behind? The citadel? What you've done? Revenge is an Atreidês art-form."

"He's not a woman," Diomedes shrugged, clever eyes cold in a Zeus-proud face.

Women had started much trouble; Helen, Clytemnaistra's sister and wife of Menelaos, had begun the war, but Clytemnaistra had finished it, murdering Agamemnon in good ritual fashion with a labrys-axe. And the father of Agamemnon and Menelaos, Atreus, had raped the daughter of his brother king who lived down the road, after serving him his sons for dinner in revenge for what liberties that king, Thyestes, had taken with Atreus' wife. Then the bastard of Atreus' union had seduced Agamemnon's wife and probably prompted the ritual murder. Following that, Electra did what she did. . . . Atreidês and women were a combination to warm the Devil's heart.

Diomedes had had his own troubles with women, Achilles knew. Still, it wasn't the response he'd hoped for. He pressed: "Look, Diomedes. We've left that citadel full of Atreidês and Achaeans who've been on ice for centuries with only Caesar's forces and some Germans to make sense of it. We shouldn't be away too long. Unless you don't care what we come back to . . . ?"

Again, the man who somehow had come into possession of the shield of Herakles shrugged. "Alexander loves that horse. And you. A bird came to me, a great black bird with your head and told me what to do, to bring you two together. He thinks your souls are somehow linked . . . you must have realized that."

"And Caesar does, too? Whoopee. That and a ticket out of here will still get you nowhere." Achilles was snapping his helmet on its hook and belting on a side arm as he spoke. "Is that what you really think you're after? A way out? There isn't any, you know. Those rumors just make the Devil grin . . . gets mortal hopes up, keeps people from settling down and trying to make something out of—"

"Out of what?" Diomedes had always been, like Odysseus, complex and unpredictable . . . too smart, perhaps, for his own good. "I've no burning desire to find more than I have." Diomedes waved a hand to encompass what lay behind, whence they'd come: a citadel like the beach at Ilion, Achaeans and familiar surroundings. "All I wanted was to feel at home, to keep busy. I follow the *basileus*—Alexander—because it amuses me."

"Atreidês revenge won't amuse you. You didn't do that well with your own wife; his is freed from her prison of stone, and all manner of mischief and strife will—"

"Achilles, spare me. Leave here, if you can. It seems to me you can't. You're here on the Devil's business, and though I'm not happy to see you, or pleased that such business includes me, I can't think what harm it will do if Alexander gets his horse back." Those last words were choked with a horseman's emotion.

"You accusing me of something?" Achilles said slowly, settling the Colt officer ACP on his hip. "I'm nobody's boy. Not the Pentagram's, not Authority, not. . . ."

"Not your American friends? Then you're the only man in Hell who can say that. Look, fool. . . ." Diomedes retreated until he could stand upright.

Backlit in the chopper's wide-open side door, he

continued, "Fool. But you always were one. Go, stay. It matters not to me. For all I know, even if we fly back in your bird, we may never find that same spit of beach, or those people we left there. You didn't see that coastline writhe and change, or hear the wails coming from the Mourning Fields. Accept that you're in Hell, Achilles, and that you can't win even a point of honor when you don't know the rules of the game."

With that, Diomedes scooped up the shield of Herakles and strode down the canyon to where Alexander, a lithe, slight figure in the waning light, held his hand out to a great steed whose foreleg pawed the ground and whose muzzle was extended toward him in disbelief.

And Achilles thought, watching Diomedes stride toward the Israelite and the little Macedonian who hoped his horse would remember him after thousands of years, that Diomedes was kidding himself if the Argive believed what he'd said.

Diomedes was entangled emotionally here. Achilles had learned before he died there on the beach something Diomedes had not. Or perhaps because he'd died there, and Diomedes had not. You can't let yourself have anything to lose.

It was the single rule that had kept him on the right side of Authority in Hell and kept him from suffering like those around him.

Achilles cared about nothing but Achilles. It was the only way to go. It had gotten him this chopper and this assignment and countless other perks over endless time. There was only a tiny voice in the back of his mind that whispered, *But this is different. These are vets, compatriots, equals. It's special. It's dangerous. It's beginning to hurt.*

He ignored the little voice, as he'd ignored oracles and shrugged off Caesar's weird looks and erudite innuendo. Anybody who believed Homer would believe in anything.

Achilles didn't believe in anything at all.

"Sargon!"

Brutus had no experience dealing with unconscious people or dying ones. He hesitated in that doubt, afraid of touching the man, afraid of moving him and hurting him and almost as vividly . . . of being a fool and wrong and deserving blame for stupidity; but it was a cold floor and hard and no one ought to lie there with a fool staring at him. *"Sargon!"* Down the hall Dante's door opened. And Brutus came and got down on his knees and tried to pick up Scaevola's head and shoulders, finding out how heavy a dead weight was. He gave a great heave and got his knees under, and saw Dante hurrying down the hall. "He's hurt!" he yelled at the poet. "Dante, get Sargon!"

A glass of milk and a ham and cheese sandwich materialized and fell and shattered.

"Fool!" Brutus yelled, cradling Scaevola against his own warmth; Dante had run, the sycophant had fled, leaving the mess behind. He was terrified. He felt Scaevola breathing, he patted the man's face and gathered up his limp left hand and shook at him. "Please, *Muci*, please wake up, please, please, please, come on, wake up."

A racket in the downstairs hall now, Dante yelling after help, and sycophants chittering about. "Get a blanket!" Brutus snapped at the servant-ghosts. "Find Augustus!" Because everything was sliding into chaos and the Emperor could make them all do what they

ought. He felt a stir in the body he was holding, felt
Scaevola draw a little gasp of a breath, and he patted
at Scaevola's cheek again. "Oh, please."

Scaevola's eyes opened, blue eyes, faded blue, a
little slit of color in a white face. Brutus could see it,
felt the sudden difference in Scaevola's body as muscle came back to life, so slight a change, but over the
edge toward living. Scaevola's eyes wandered in that
half-open state, opened further, as if he did not know
where he was, or did not recognize Brutus upside
down.

"It's me," Brutus said, trying to twist round so that
Scaevola could see him more rightside up. "It's
Brutus."

"Am I home?" Scaevola's lips trembled. O gods,
Brutus thought, a grown man was going to cry, he
had thought a man must never cry, and he had never
dealt with a situation like this, which terrified him as
much as death did, that Scaevola was going to em-
barrass them both forever. Tears ran a crooked trail
down Scaevola's face when he blinked, his eyes rolled
glistening and desperate, but he got his mouth to a
hard line and got several large breaths. There was
more noise belowstairs; heavy sandals were headed
up, Sargon was on his way, and likely Augustus, and
Scaevola was trying to hold it. Brutus took his fingers
and swiped the tears off Scaevola's cheek, and looked
up at arriving help with a defiant scowl, for both
their sakes.

"Dammit," he said to Sargon, and the Emperor of
Rome and the poet Dante, "I've been yelling half an
hour! He's hurt—" He caught his breath, held tight
to the young soldier who was hardly older than himself, and who had given up his right hand once and

long ago to show his enemies he was not afraid. Such
a hero as this could never give way, Brutus would
not permit it. "He's all right, I think, he's going to
be all right, he's freezing to death and I can't get the
damn sycophants to get a blanket!"

One settled out of midair and floated down over
Scaevola soft as a wish. A baby blue one.

"Here." Sargon, Lion of Akkad, squatted down
and shifted his sword out of the way—Sargon stuck
to his kilt and his sandals and looked more like the
Assyrians than otherwise, but he was not. His huge
arms gathered Scaevola up blanket and all, and got
him to help himself a little; Sargon stood up, and
Brutus did, trying to help and knowing he was in the
way now.

"I died," Scaevola murmured. "Trouble—trouble
down there." His head came up, nodding with weakness, and his eyes wandered as if they still saw
something terrible. "O gods. Lion—"

"*Were you with Julius?*" the Emperor demanded,
and Scaevola turned his face that way, leaning heavily against Sargon's support.

"I was just with him—" Scaevola blinked and tried
again to focus. "Mycenae. It's Mycenae. The damned
Trojan war—"

"Get him downstairs, get him a robe," Augustus
shouted at Sargon and the air about them, which was
suddenly thick with nervous sycophants all chittering
and anxious to please.

Sargon drew Scaevola toward the stairs. Brutus
hesitated, then hurried and got up against Scaevola's
other side, holding onto his handless right arm, as
Scaevola tried the stairs and worked his way down
them, step by difficult step.

"Get me a drink," Scaevola muttered under his breath. And managed to walk, with their help, all the way to the bottom.

Alexander was weeping freely when Diomedes joined Maccabee, a few feet away from the boy-sized man who leaned against the great horse, his arms thrown around its neck.

Bucephalus—if it *was* Bucephalus and not some demon in disguise—took time from nuzzling Alexander every now and again to bare its teeth in their direction.

"The horse is in his prime," said the tall, fair Israelite who'd just been resurrected and lost patches of memory, but not his guerrilla's instinct. "And Alexander is past the age at which he watched his pet die. This is not right."

"Not unusual, either, Mac," Achilles said, but his hackles rose.

"And the omen?" the Israelite asked, turning a suicide commando's eyes on him, eyes like the Undertaker's, from whose tender ministrations he'd just returned. "The omen of driving the horse into a blind canyon? Of trapping it so?"

There'd been no way to discuss things in the chopper, but the Old Dead didn't understand technology. Gods knew they should have been able to assess the evidence of their senses.

Achilles took a step backwards. Men just returned from the Undertaker's table were always weird. This one was weird as Diomedes with his obsession about women and his fears about the citadel not being there when they got back.

Then he realized that the horse was going to make

it impossible to get everybody back. He said, "Screw the omens," to Maccabee and called out, "Alexander, we can't get that horse aboard the chopper. What are—"

As if by magic or curse, upon the uttering of those words, the stallion with his roman-nosed head and great arched crest and rock-hard hooves disappeared.

Alexander, with a cry like a man mortally wounded, stumbled forward into the wisps of mist that were all that remained of Bucephalus.

Maccabee rushed to his aid, calling on his God, who surely couldn't hear him here.

Suddenly, from the canyon's rim, an ear-splitting whinny sounded, and resounded in the canyon below.

Alexander dropped to his knees, hand to his eyes.

And Bucephalus pawed the ground once, reared against the dusky vault of Hell, and turned to prance away across the plateau as if saying, "Well, come on, let's go, let's play 'catch the horse' some more."

Maccabee was at Alexander's side and Diomedes turned pointedly away from the shaken king and approached Achilles, who was now leaning against the chopper with is arms folded.

"Don't say it," Achilles warned before Diomedes could propose any further wild-horse-chases. "That's no real horse and I'm not going to be lured into anything. I'm not a horseboy. I'm taking this bird back to the citadel before Paradise rises."

Flying at night over this terrain, without any ground control, wasn't Achilles' idea of a real good time.

He started to suit his actions to his words and Diomedes followed him into the chopper saying, "Maccabee was murdered, you know."

"No kidding?" Achilles' sarcasm made Diomedes

frown. "I saw Mac when he was busted up, buddy. You didn't. And what's the big deal? Goes around, comes around, in Hell."

"No big deal," Diomedes replied softly. "It can happen to any of us. We're going to follow the horse until Alexander says we're not. And you're going to help us."

Achilles stopped moving, conscious of the big Argive, who'd been Odysseus' choice for the night hunt, behind him.

Very slowly Achilles turned, one hand resting on the butt of his pistol. "Are you threatening me, friend?"

"Me? I'm just trying to put matters in terms I'm sure you'll understand."

The pause in which Achilles floundered for words was altogether too long. And all he could come up with at the end of it was, "I'm not flying into unknown conditions, over uncharted territory, in the dark. And you can tell your Great King that."

But since Alexander himself was scrambling aboard as Achilles spoke, Fate intervened in the form of the Macedonian, who said, "I wouldn't ask it. Bucephalus is free, alive, well in his glory. We'll find each other again. Let us rejoin the army."

Which almost drowned out Diomedes' muttered, "Just like old times, you sulky bastard."

Almost, but not quite.

In a warm robe and sitting in a big easy chair in Augustus' own study, Scaevola was a little steadier. A sycophant showed up with a bottle of wine, the first Citizen's best chilled white, and when Sargon had opened it and poured, Scaevola took the longed-for drink, incredible luxury, when for the last terrible night he had been fighting a losing battle for his life and the lives of the men with him, first on ground he knew and then in a surreal stairwell full of fire and smoke and endless enemies. And finally bleeding to death of a careless step, that had let a fallen enemy thrust his blade up under his armor—

He shuddered and took another drink, washing the dust and the taste of the Undertaker's antiseptics down, and drew a panting breath, looking at Augustus and Sargon and Julius' newly-found son, and the poet Dante Alighieri, who stood and sat in a solemn half-ring, waiting and staring at him in a way that made him altogether nervous, and sent his mind scattering this way and that with worry for the men in his command who were *not* with him—and those who had been, and those—

—but he had left them in Caesar's charge, Julius would see to them, he would not have left them in any peril on that hill.

Don't go in there, he had tried to warn Caesar of that citadel, when he knew that he was not going to have any more time to explain, but his life had already been leaking away from him, and perhaps he had said that and perhaps not. He felt that he had failed Julius if he had not said that, and he had to face Julius' two sons, the adopted and grown one, and this desperate boy, and tell them—

"Julius was all right when I left him," Scaevola said hoarsely. He shivered from the chill of the wine glass and had nowhere to set it, so he simply tried not to shiver. "We—Agamemnon sent us below—"

"Back up," Augustus said, all calm, all patient. "You had command of the cohorts, first and second."

"Alternate with Antonius," Scaevola said. Thoughts wanted to scatter. Augustus' calm voice encouraged organization. They had set out on a night maneuver, going out from the New Hell West Armory, two cohorts of the 10th Legion; six of the groundeffect battle tanks, six jeeps, seven, counting Mettius Curtius who had lagged far back: communications, supply train . . . and after that, stranger and stranger things. Alexander of Macedon had showed up, the first time in all Hell that anyone Romanside had ever *seen* the Macedonians, with part of the Macedonian cavalry and some easterners, a couple of oddly assorted Jews, one Judah Maccabee and a New Dead named plain Zaki, point, no other name. Who wormed his way into the com truck with Machiavelli.

Maybe that was the beginning of their troubles. Maybe he should leave nothing out.

"You've been getting our transmissions," Scaevola said to the Emperor and to Sargon, reckoning they were both back-up to Julius, in whatever was going on, that the whole business was *not* the training maneuvers they had been told at the outset. "I don't know where we went wrong or what happened, but I think there's something rotten inside our ranks. The Macedonians are still with us. Hatshepsut was in charge of the tanks. This fellow from the Lebanon showed up, Gemayel, guerrilla types, there and not there all along the route: Caesar knows him, I think; this Zaki seems to know him—" He took another sip of the wine. Caught his breath and tried not to let the voice wobble. "We stopped by New Cumae, got this damned eight ball—"

"What?"

A one-handed man with a drink had a hell of a time

with gestures. "Black ball," Scaevola said, " 'bout fist
size. It's an oracle. Ask it questions and answers
float up out of the black stuff inside. The men got it
bet one way and the other whether it's real, I don't
know what Caesar thinks, but he kind of has that
look I think he's not real sure. The Old, Old Dead—
the Macedonians: they're impressed." Gods. So much
had happened. "Tydidês is with them. Diomedes
himself, five foot shield and all. It's a real sight,
Auguste, I tell you. Then we got these two New
Dead, Welch and Nichols, Americans, with Machiavelli in the com truck, and I don't trust them worth
turning my back. We've got the Germans Tiberius
lent Kleopatra, but she gave them to Alexander,
then, then this damn Macedonian king raids the
quartermaster's rig and takes the biggest tent he can
find, at gunpoint, him and that Maccabee. I tell you,
Auguste—" He had the shakes just thinking about it,
and took another sip of the wine. The last. But
Brutus scrambled up and filled the glass from the
bottle sitting there, quick and earnest.

"Thanks." Another drink. His head swam. And the
anger was more distant. "Right then, right then,
Auguste, we would have carved him up for roast, but
Caesar said we should let him have his way. So we
did. We were running into the damned liches, out
by Phlegethon, and they nearly got Mouse. Should
have warned us. Should have warned us. But we had
that damned Oracle. Leaning too much on it."

"The eight ball," Augustus said.

"That thing. And the damned Macedonian. We—"

"Steady," Augustus said.

He had caught himself. Leaned his head back, and
took his breath again. One of the ghost-servants had

gotten to the glass and restored it to his hand. "I'm all right." He had said that before he died. Before he had fallen into Julius' arms, making a liar of himself. He had been terrified, then, not knowing where he was bound. Where the Administration of Hell would put him this time, and he loved them so much, his people, Julius and the rest. He was home again. He had waked on the Undertaker's table, gone through that awful place for the second time in his existence, and against all odds, they had sent him here. Someone had pulled strings. It was the only answer. There were too many enemies, some of them in high places, but he had come back to another life in the place he most wanted. Augustus . . . they had been in radio contact. "Thank the gods," Scaevola said, "and whoever got me back—"

"We'd like to know that."

"It wasn't you, then."

"Curtius radioed back that something was wrong. That he was going to the camp. After that we lost everything."

Mysteries upon mysteries. Not to know—*whose* piece he was in this game—that bothered him, that fact swam around in his consciousness and sent ripples through all the facts he knew. He hated to be used. He suddenly doubted everything. "*Auguste*, don't rely on me if it wasn't you. I woke up on that table, that's all I know, there's no knowing how many gaps there are in what I know. Or what I've seen or what I've dreamed—" Panic beckoned. He rested his head back to keep it clear and wished only for a bed and sleep. The wine was hitting him hard and it was hard to keep his eyes open.

"How did you die?" Sargon asked, a deep and

harsh voice, foreign to the dream that wanted to take him. "What happened?"

"I fell—The liches—the ground was breaking up, the whole camp under attack—they were racing the damned tanks—"

"Racing the tanks?"

"Something went wrong. The ground turned unstable, just came to pieces, fire everywhere—" He shivered, muscles twitching without his wishing it, and remembered a dais and a brazier and Etruscans, a sea of watching faces. Remembered pain and the stench of burning flesh. His own. But that was very long ago. Two deaths ago. "I went under, that's all, and I woke up in the fog, on this riverbank. Stumbled around till I ran into this—"

—ghosts on the riverbank. Ghosts had seized on him, dazed as he was. And he had fought them, such as he could, there beside a tree where infants hung like fruit, on a river of black reeds and endless mist. But they came at him out of the fog, too damned many of them, everlastingly too many—

"—damn lot of Greeks," he said. His heartbeat had picked up again, strong and angry. "Hauled me off to this place like—like—"

—paintings on the walls, that much he remembered. Bulls. Axes. A king sat on the throne, wearing a golden mask, soldiers beside him, in helmets of ivory and leather, leaning on their spears. Upside down columns, bright red and stark black.

"—like nothing I ever saw. And this masked king—he said he was Agamemnon. He said he was a judge and I was going to the hells below. Said—he was collecting forces. I'd join the rest. Wait there till he had the omens—the omens, he said. Then he was going to show everyone . . . show everyone . . . win the Trojan War, he said."

"Trojan war?"

"I don't know. He said it was Achilles' fault. He said it was the gods. But he was going to change his omens. He raved and he asked me where I'd come from—I didn't tell him. I tried to get at him, I figured then he wasn't any friend of anybody, but he— "

—guards moving, spears lowering; he had thought then he was going to die in that attack—

"—he just stamped his staff on the ground and the stones just opened up under my feet."

—More fire, fire and a pit in which shadows of his own troops had moved, had fought there, desperately, against endless other shadows. And he was one of them. There was a stairs—

"This pit then—we were all in it, me, thirty odd of the legion—and these damned shadows, these *things*—we just kept climbing; like you dream, and there isn't any end to it, but those stairs led *up* and that was all we cared about, getting out of there. We were all lost, I think—all of us the same. I never had time to ask them. We just kept killing those damned shadows, and the fire kept burning higher and higher up the stairs, so there was no choice. Sometimes we could hear that crazy king laughing. Sometimes we heard—gods, I don't know what. Like a thumping. It was like those sounds in a bad dream, I don't know why it was terrible, but it was, and it was behind us . . . we just kept coming up those stairs forever, till the whole place shook, and we came up into the light. We came out . . . came out into open air, and this ruin of the king's house . . . but I'd stepped on this man, I knew I was hit, I didn't think it was that bad, I just kept walking—"

—all a great valley laid out before them. And Caesar and all the rest of the legionaries arriving on the crest of it, walking into ambush. . . .

"Saw Caesar down there. On the hill. Getting shot at. So we took the archers out. And I guess it was all right. I walked down the hill, I guess I was bleeding, I know I was, but I didn't want to think it was bad, I guess you never do—Next thing I knew I was back with the Undertaker."

"Was there anyone else?" Augustus asked.

He tried to think. Nothing came clear. There was white light. There was—was the old man himself. Was everything he recalled from so long ago. Perhaps there had been other things. Perhaps he was muddling everything from that first time. His wits hazed. His eyes were shut and he struggled to keep them open. "*Auguste,* there could have been. I don't know. It's hard—hard—" A moment of gray then. Of panic. "Don't let them take me out of here. Don't let them—"

A hand seized his arm, painfully hard. "You're safe." A gentle hand touched his face. "It's the wine, lad. It's just the wine. Let go. Sleep, it's all right."

"Caesar," he said. "Got to get there. Got to—" But the fog was back around him, and he did not know where he was, whether he was dreaming or whether he was lying on the sand again, there in the fog. In this place anything was possible. He thought that someone was holding him by the arm, that someone was picking him up, and talking about bed. He was afraid, caught between realities. Perhaps he had only dreamed this, perhaps he was still lying on

that table, with the palsied old man leaning over him
and asking him questions. . . .

. . . asking him questions.

"*Auguste,*" he tried to say. "They—asked me—asked
me the same questions. I think—think I might have
told them—"

For a young man who had given up so much *not* to
have talked to an Etruscan king, the realization that
he had yielded to a doddering old man and spilled
his guts, that he had talked now, caught in a dream
and no longer sure where he was—that cut deeply at
his self-esteem.

Damned Macedonian. That was the beginning of
things. Alexander of Macedon and his foreigners,
and Caesar listening to them and not to those who
loved him.

"Send me back to him," he asked the fates, asked
whoever ruled this place. "He needs me."

Alexander sat with his nose pressed to the window
of the chopper as it roared through the night, staring
out and down at Hell below.

There was little to see, yet; just the phosphores-
cent ripples of Cocytus or whatever sea it fed, the
occasional pastoral fires of hilltop citadels and shore
settlements.

Or so he read the lay of the land, much more
casual than he pretended to be. He wasn't worried,
as Maccabee was, that they would be denied a reunion with Caesar, Kleopatra, Hatshepsut, Zaki and
the rest.

Separation from the others would be a kindness,
and Hell was not kind.

Separation from Bucephalus had been a javelin in

the heart, but only transiently. If Alexander could put any stock in omens, here, he'd count Bucephalus' appearance as an auspicious one: he'd been able to bury his head in that sweet-smelling mane once more. And Bucephalus had promised him a future as the horse pranced on the bluff, free of all encumbrance. Free at last.

So Alexander took the omen to be that no trap is ineluctable, no Fate final, no situation hopeless. It was an omen consonant with his nature, suited to the needs of Alexander the Great.

Thus the return to Mykenai (as Diomedes had nicknamed Agamemnon's citadel) was something he faced with less trepidation than did Maccabee . . . with less trepidation than he faced with just-resurrected Maccabee, if the truth be known.

He wanted only to stare into the dark and remember the velvet of Bucephalus' nose against his cheek, the miraculous smell of horse in his nostrils—to hold the good thoughts.

And all thoughts of Maccabee were tainted. Maccabee, his dear friend, his acknowledged Hephaistion in this underworld of make-do, had been murdered and returned to the Undertaker.

Now Maccabee claimed not to know how much he'd told to whom of Alexander's faring.

Not that it should matter, riding in a helicopter sent from New Hell, what Maccabee might have said. But it mattered that Maccabee hid behind protestations of faulty memory. Alexander needed total loyalty, must have complete trust.

So he stared silently out the window, rather than talking to his friend who was somehow different after his sojourn through Death's door, and tried to think only of Bucephalus and rejoice that, even in Hell, his genius had given him such a marvelous gift.

Even in Hell, Alexander had managed a moment of unspoiled joy. A complete win. A total triumph beyond even his dreams. Thus, triumph and joy were possible. Thus, Alexander would wrest from Hell every secret joy it held.

Surely, while he stood with his arms around Bucephalus' neck, Alexander had beaten the Devil. For a moment, he had conquered Satan and the army of the damned. Therefore, he could do so again. And again.

Having won this clandestine triumph, all other triumphs were winnable. He'd even find a way to trust Maccabee once more, not an easy task when the man didn't trust himself.

He reached out, never looking away from the window, and touched the knee of his first and best friend in Hell.

"Companion," he said quietly, "look there, below. The citadel. Your fears are groundless."

Maccabee, beside him on the bench, scrambled to look.

And Diomedes, stretched out opposite, came up on one elbow.

The bird angled, making each passenger grab for purchase.

"The citadel?" Maccabee squinted into the night, uncertainty making his accent surface so that his voice had an Oriental lilt. "It's my memory that can't be trusted, then."

The Israelite sat back, rubbing his eyes with his palms.

Diomedes grunted, "Your memory? And mine,

then. There was not so much water around it, when
we left—not so wide a harbor, nor so many beached
craft."

Alexander looked again, peering so hard that he
could feel his eyes sting as he demanded more detail
than they could provide.

What he saw was, and was not, the place they'd
left. But the tanks were there, the great physeters of
war with their deadly snouts. And the campfires of
Julius' 10th legionaries were there.

And if other things were there, things foreign and
things whispering of wide dark seas and Cretan ar-
chitects, then Alexander would overlook these incon-
sistencies, for the moment: Caesar and his Egyptians,
Germans, Jews, Maronites, and Americans were still
in control of Mykenai.

The oracle of conquest that he'd taken from
Bucephalus suited him far better than the oracle
they'd taken from Kleopatra's eight ball, which had
told them, "See Minos," but he'd never doubted that
he would.

Had he not met Diomedes? Come face to face
with Achilles? Found Bucephalus? Distinguished himself in the second assault on Troy?

Was he not Alexander?

Kings and Castles

"Damn," Hatshepsut murmured, rousing herself from her sleep—an uncomfortable sleep in the back seat of a jeep on a hillside—as the chopper came beating in over the hills. But that was not the thing she damned, waking Mettius Curtius from his even less comfortable post slumped over the center-well in front—("Sleep," she had told him, trusting the legionary sentries she had borrowed from Julius, and installed on the heights to guard the tanks that guarded the valley and hill of Mykenai, at the foot of which Julius was camped, in what might be a long and dangerous night.) That helicopter was, she hoped, Achilles returning, overdue. But what else was happening—that thumping and pounding of the earth—sent her lurching up with one knee on the cushion as Mettius Curtius scrambled for the radio and put in an urgent call.

The thumping resounded through the hills as the copter came, but it separated itself from the noise of the machine—grew louder and louder, vibrating through the earth, the same regular pulses which had shaken the land and toppled the stones of the citadel in the previous night. Now in this afterglow that passed for night, the outlines of Mykenai's shattered hill retreated into dimness like a trick of the eyes, blurred and spread and reared higher and higher. Lights gleamed on slanted and massive walls.

The lamps of houses and citadel and temples glowed within those perimeters.

"Isis and Set," Hatshepsut breathed, seeing that. The prevailing wind blew off the river Cocytus with a stench of rotten sands and damnation, a mire of ambitions and intentions. She shivered, who was not accustomed to shivers, no, not at the worst sights in Hell.

But the persistence of this one—the damnable persistence of this abomination that kept reasserting itself: the Hellene king of Mykenai, the king in the mask, had conjured them his private obsession and shaped them the image of fabled Troy, risen like a fever dream out of Cocytus' mists and stench—

It was sure that Agamemnon was loose again. The thumping of his staff somewhere applied to stone, shook the hills as if some god's artillery were at work; and even these present outlines might blur and shift if his lunatic obsession gained headway.

"Fire," she yelled over that noise. "*Curti*, get them the hell concentrated on that citadel, dammit, before these hills shift—*fire! Titan One, target the citadel!*" She was yelling, near admitting the pickups in her jewelry, which she never owned to.

"Pharaoh," Curtius objected, turning half about, "the Macedonians—"

There were men of their own side up there: Alexander's. They were the Macedonian guards Alexander had set over Agamemnon, and damned little good they were doing. "Fortunes of war," she said. While on the hill above them came a roar as one of the sleeping battle tanks woke, the sound of ground-effect fans thrumming under the beat-beat-beat of the chopper landing down there on the edge of Julius' camp in a sweep of lights and dust. The tanks on the hills on this side and that of the valley returned a crackle of acknowledgements to her orders, and went into operation using no lights but their own nightsight: turrets were turning, guns seeking a new elevation. Fire blasted out, like momentary thunder and lightning, one discharge near at hand, deafening; others cut loose in their own time from across the valley, redoubling echoes and distance-delayed reports off the hills, redoubling again as multiple shells slammed into the hill of Mykenai, and flared in brief fire. The citadel darkened.

Then the ground under them heaved like a restive horse, shivered and shook its skin and jolted them sideways. The jeep motor coughed to life, Curtius' own estimation of the situation; and the pharaoh of Egypt slapped her driver on the shoulder and hurled herself over to the front seat on the passenger side, whumped into place and got her legs sorted out. "Go!" she yelled as another shock hit amid that renewed and uncanny thumping, and Mettius Curtius, who had jumped his horse straight to hell in his first death, slammed the jeep into motion in full flight from what was happening around them. Hatshepsut grabbed the mike and ordered her six tanks to seek stable ground.

Julius waved his arm, shouting orders of his own, while officers ran for jeeps and the camp boiled into activity. *Hell* of a way to be jolted out of bed, himself and Kleopatra, with Antonius rushing in—gods, Antonius had done that more than once in their lives—to yell that the landscape was going berserk and that the whole of Hell was rising against them.

How much of Hell was actually involved Julius did not at the moment know; but it was more than he wanted. Scaevola had gone to the Undertaker, and whether Scaevola had talked none of them knew, but Scaevola was not the only one: Maccabee had taken the Trip and had come back to them, Maccabee was in that chopper that was settling down amid the quake and the renewed upheaval of a promontory against a grayed and misty night.

Of a sudden the Pharaoh's guns cut loose from the hills and shells whumped into the citadel heights above them—"Damn!" Julius yelled, and at the man with the field phone: "We've got men up there, dammit, stop that shelling up there!"

All about him jeep and truck motors whined and roared, and tents were billowing down throughout the camp as the line soldiers of the two cohorts prepared themselves against the chance of a fire assault: canvas burned too well, and would make them silhouetted targets. As long as they had time and until the centurions should start yelling orders to run for formation, the legionaries were arming, then knocking down their tents, getting those stakes and guyropes out of the way of maneuverings, and rolling that canvas into bundles the quartermaster and his men would snatch up into the trucks if they had the time.

Save the equipment. Save their shelter. Protect themselves against the chance that some enemy up there had something to answer the tanks: a general in Hell never assumed anything, and lasers and disruptors and tactical nukes were always a possibility. Get their equipment and get out of here, and discover why later—that was Julius' priority.

Whump! The ground shook and the reports of the guns on the heights kept up, explosions slamming against the hill in front of them. Klea was shouting orders of her own, snatching up equipage and personal belongings and records and shoving them at an orderly while legionaries struck the tent they had been sleeping in. That sudden flattening of the canvas as Julius glanced back showed him the chopper on the field beyond the camp, all aglare with its landing lights and making a target out of itself—till it roared back into the air and beat directly overhead, throwing unwelcome lights on the camp: then it went totally dark, speeding toward the newly risen hill.

Achilles was taking a recon or deserting them, it was a toss-up which.

The ground shook in worse spasms. Julius staggered on his feet, heard an explosion of yells and curses across the camp. Klea reached him and grabbed at his shoulder as the ground heaved and bucked.

Quiet then. The thumping that had rolled like thunder—ceased, leaving behind it only the sounds of motors whining in the dark, the stunned murmurs of the troops that died away into silence so profound the copter sounds came back, echoing off the hills, and the noise of the tank-fans wove back across that pulse, deceptively serene.

"Zeus," Klea breathed.

"Agamemnon," Julius said. "Where in hell is he, that's what I want to know." Dead Macedonians, overwhelmed by their prisoner up there on the hill, was his inmost thought; Alexander's guards dead of some treachery of the Mycenaean king, or blown to the winds by Hatshepsut's shells, either was possible—

and Julius was already thinking (being Caesar) just
how much of the blame for that eventuality to take
and how much to cast to the Egyptian—or if it turned
out to have saved their collective hides while it cost
them Macedonian lives, how to get the best out of
that, too.

Brakes squealed. A jeep arrived out of the dark
and found them both in its headlights. Mouse had
reached the motor pool and come back again. But
there was nowhere to escape to, no action evident
. . . just a hill up there which had settled in some
form different than it had held before, and a wind
that carried the mingled stench of blasted earth and
explosives and rotten sands. They were blind, he and
Klea, with the glare of the headlights in front of
them.

About them, the flattened camp and the stunned
ranks of the legion, murmuring with wonder and
dismay and the knowledge of men whose City was
earthquake-prone, first that it was nothing natural
that had overtaken them so suddenly in this nether
level of Hell, and then that if it was anything like an
earthquake they were due the aftershocks.

"Pro di," Mouse said, looking up and about him
like the others in this sudden hush; and Mouse swore
very seldom.

"Kill the lights," Julius said; and blinked in the
ensuing dark, straining his eyes toward that distant
shadow of the hill.

The thing that had happened once on this plain,
that had loomed like illusion, had reshaped itself
right in front of them, shells and guards and all their
efforts notwithstanding. On the summit a city glowed,

raising flat roofs in tiers above the vast and slanted walls.

Not Mykenai, not the hill-fortress, on its conical hill, surrounded by its dome-tombs. It was Troy which Agamemnon had purposed, and Julius had no doubt what had just birthed itself out of fire and confusion. He had seen its latterday ghost once, in his service in Asia; had seen Roman Troy among its clustered hills, white marble, a town built on the ruins of cities and crowned with temples; and when he thought of that, it was as if the years rolled back and he was a lieutenant again, with too much of civil war behind him and an unguessed future ahead of him.

Had that Roman lead with too much to prove— stood here once before, in Asia, dreaming of Achilles, whose tomb was there, beyond the citadel? Dreaming of Alexander, who had exchanged shields in that tomb and left his own, *hubris* beyond *hubris* for a mortal man. So that famous shield which had been Achilles', had also been Alexander's, and Alexander's had rested untouched in all the wars and bloody scrabblings for power of all his heirs, for a Roman youth to see and long for.

And more than thirty years later he had stood at Kleopatra's side in Alexandria, before Alexander's glass-faced sarcophagus, and seen that ancient gold and ivory shield Achilles and Alexander both had carried—had touched it before he destroyed Alexander's mummified body with his own hands . . . for that gold-haired, taxidermied travesty on life seemed somehow like a prison: unnatural that it should continue to exist, a husk which had once held *him*, himself, his essence, his soul. He had not taken up

that shield either, though by then he could have
taken what he pleased in Alexandria or anywhere
else in the known world. He had left it for a grave-
gift. To Alexander. To his own youth. Recalling a
night at Troy, the hush of the tomb, the ground they
all three had walked, though centuries apart.

A man—he had said it gravely to Kleopatra, on the
Tiberside before his death, and once again, and lately,
in Hell—a man has three souls, the ancestor-soul,
the tomb-soul, and his personal one. One life for
each. And in all of Hell they had never met before,
he and his incarnations—the prince of the Myrmidons, the Macedonian conqueror, and the Roman
dictator descended of kings and gods. Aeneas of Troy
was Julius' personal ancestor, Aphrodite's son, sire of
Iulus, sire of the kings of Rome.

But into the Julians, out of Latin blood, something
foreign had come, implacable and terrible. He had
recognized himself here, in a like geography on Earth,
on such a night; he had suffered the same mortal
chill, knowing then that by his presence on this land
he had walked in two lives before, the life-thread of
the world itself was drawn tight and near to snapping, and that his would fray every thread it crossed.

So he had not touched the shield then or later. His
other Aspects had carried it twice to war. And at that
advanced stage in his life and in the world's weari-
ness he had hoped to let it lie, bury it, be done with
wars and blood. As in Achilles' tomb he had let
Alexander's lie, knowing he was not ready to die
young.

"*Cai*," Klea whispered, her hands on his bare arm.
"*Cai, mi Iuli—*"

The hills of Troy. The battle plain and the whole of

his life in front of him. *O my gods, goddess-mother,* *You existed then. I was so damned young and I knew* *so little.*

"It's one of his spells," someone said. And Mouse's voice: "Let him be."

All Hell trembles. It has not wanted us together. *Now by our presence this place is compelled to exist* *and all other places are in jeopardy.*

"*Cai*—O Mouse, go, find Antonius. Please, quickly."

"No." Julius drew a deep breath and let it go, tore his eyes from the vision and the dark and sought something on which they could fasten, some touch of reality and color. Klea's face, dim in the gray night, was all that offered itself. He put his hand on her shoulder. "I'm fine. No problem." And because he knew there was no choice and no forestalling it: "Mouse, find Alexander. And Achilles when he gets back."

Not *if*. There was no doubt in him at all. His Luck had betrayed him. There was no hope of failing that meeting.

The great machine had let them out as the earth shook, tents came billowing down and the whole of the huge camp vanished while the hill of Mykenai withdrew from them and began to become another thing. . . .

Then suddenly the world was quiet, except for the sounds of machines and the isolated cries of frightened horses. Alexander stopped in his course through the aisle of the camp, looking skyward for some sight of the helicopter which had deserted them, and scanning the hill which had risen in front of them.

If the eagle-view from the machine had confounded

him, the view from this angle found its counterpart
in memory and jolted him like a wound.

I was here, that memory said first, and said that
whatever this place was it had meant something profound to him, and something terrible and glorious. *I
was here. I know this place.*

Then: *Troia,* that memory said. *Ilion. Achilles.*

"Damn," breathed a voice beside him, and louder:
"Damn him to Hades! he's finally done it—"

And Diomedes left him and Maccabee, running,
running, before Alexander had known it, down the
aisles of flattened tents and bewildered Romans.

"Alexander," Maccabee said, and gripped his
shoulder— Maccabee, who sounded lost and frightened—*Can the baneful dead love at all? Perhaps they
do. This is a place of curses, and he suffers, perhaps
most of all, knowing he is ill-omened.*

I should run after Diomedes and stop him.

*I should be honest with Maccabee. But I cannot
touch him. I cannot tell him what I suspect.*

"It's Troy," he half-whispered to Maccabee, thinking at once of Agamemnon, and of the men he had
left to guard him: dead, surely dead. More of blood
and debts on him. Rage shook him, terrible in its
quietness. "It's Troy. Diomedes has gone hunting."

"Enemies?"

"And friends. What has Caesar done here? What
has he let happen?"

The physeters came on in black anonymity, showing no lights, toward a camp which showed none but
the lights of the jeeps. The fans of the nearest machine roared and kicked up a stinging wind laden
with dust and grass and pebbles. It passed like a
creature out of myth, black and massive, while they

shielded their faces and legionaries near them cursed the night and a driver's carelessness. It threatened them a moment, then passed harmless, avoiding them somehow, even blind. "Judah—" Alexander began to say, having finally gotten the words he wanted, words describing destructive loyalties—and Diomedes. *Go after Diomedes,* he would say to Maccabee. *Reason with him like a friend.* And when Maccabee should object it would do no good—

We must let the past go, he would say then, recalling Bucephalus. *We are harmless to each other if we do not follow old patterns. We must not fall into them. You and I, Judah, we must not fall into them—*

But men came up about them, men smelling of furs and sweat, and oil and machinery—giants, breathless and muttering at him in their strange tongue. "Alreich," they called him: or "Tyr." It was the only thing he could understand of their babble, these giant, strange men the queen of Egypt had given him.

"Alreich," they said now, and one seized him and flung arms about him, one and the next and the next, slapping him on the back and holding him by the shoulders while a light swung by them, showing tears running down into their beards and their faces all aggrieved with love.

Hell take them, Alexander wished, trembling with anger for their intervention, and felt their hands and felt the force of that possessive love of theirs, that love which he had had all too much of in his life, that love which he used and knew he used in his men; and hated himself for using in his friends. Even Hephaistion. Even Judah. And Kleitos. It foreboded calamities. It bruised him like their hands, their strength which he hated and could not overcome. *Lamiai and vampires. It is my soul you have your hands on. No more deaths. No more. Let me go.*

He pushed away from them, from Perfidy and Murder and all of them—was that Famine? Had Famine come back to them, having died once? Like Maccabee?

"Alreich," they called him, touching him with their hands as if he were a carven god.

"Alexander," Maccabee said, touching him from the other side. The man inside him would have turned and fled. But the muscles which had held him steady in a hundred battles did not know how to do that. "Let be," Alexander said quietly, and took possession of them all with a breath that inhaled their souls and tangled them all with his fate. There was a light on them, bouncing and blinding, glinting off German spears and rifles and the faces of curious legionaries and casting Maccabee's face in gaunt shadows. He turned and faced the double lights of an oncoming jeep, and swept a gesture to take them all out of its way.

But it stopped beside them. The driver was the man they called Mouse, Caesar's herald.

". . . *thing's looking damned solid.*" The voice came back into the narrow confines of the com truck, spitting with static— Achilles, from an airborne vantage further down the valley. "*There's sea out there. Ships. A camp. Hell, it's a flat plain to the first hill, mile and a half, a mile past that to the citadel, as the road runs, river on right and left, the highest overlook's from the wall on this side. I can draw you a damn map. I'm coming back.*"

"He doesn't need to look at it," Niccolo Machiavelli said to Welch and Nichols, and got a curious stare from them. "It's Achilles. He doesn't need to look at it."

Welch caught it then, and gave him a second stare. "Yeah," Welch said; and Niccolo got up and went out the back of the truck for another look at the situation, in the wind that had begun to blow, a cooler wind, such as came off the sea, fighting with the mist-laden airs off the swamp. He blinked. There were lights on the hill, the lights of habitations. The shapes of the hills about them were changed. It was a naked feeling, with the com truck bulking large here on the flat with the tents down and nothing between them and the scrutiny of whatever watched from that height.

The copter came beating back, its noise echoing off the hills as it came toward them and passed overhead.

The lonely sound of a horse at a gallop echoed against the same hills. One of theirs, bolting in panic, it might be. There was enough insanity this night.

Niccolo leaned there against the side of the truck and stared up at the hill which bulked indeed solid and black and ominous.

Up there, when it had been Mykenai's hill, a small number of men had held a garrison in tumbled ruins. Now that hill did not exist in the same aspect. So someone had made a mistake. And if he knew Julius, Julius was not one to call charge and go up there in the dark. Not against a power that could rearrange the landscape.

There was death up there. And Niccolo so hated dying—even with special dispensations and assurances. There was the indignity of it. There was the knowledge that he had infringed upon certain understandings that made him safer than others in Hell. Most of all there was the pain; and Julius knew this, when he had looked him straight in the eye and made him understand he wanted Scaevola cared for, whatever strings had to be pulled. Wanted one young soldier safe in his passage home and out of this nether hell which they had followed the courses of Phlegethon and Lethe to find—And later, when Niccolo had reported to Julius that he had done his best but did not know the outcome, Julius had looked up, fixed him coldly with his eyes, and said—*you know the penalty for treason, little Niko? Do I need to tell you that?*

Not I, he had said, honestly appalled.

And Julius had risen, stood very close to him and murmured the word *crucified,* among others, which, no, Niccolo had not seen, not in all his time in Hell, nor wished to see, and least of all wished to experience personally. He had stared right into Julius' eyes when he said it, his friend, his civilized and modern friend, and discovered that there was something in Hell that could still give him nightmares.

Niccolo had often kept poison near him in his career in Hell, but to carry it constantly on him—he had not done that in a long time. He had it now. He did not want to be without that alternative either day or night.

The copter settled in its original place beyond the peripheries of the flattened camp, showing lights at the last, which illumined a cloud of dust. He watched it. And turned, startled, as he was aware of someone at his back, where he had not heard so much as a step.

Zaki stood there looking at him—a Israeli Jew, Zaki, small of stature; a little man of shadows and varying substance: now soldier, now spy, now technician, now staring at him with cold and narrow eyes and now sweeping off that shapeless hat of his to crush it further in one hand and to scratch at his neck as he came closer. "This whole place is crazy."

"*Perdio*, more than crazy, my friend. *Stubborn*." For a reason Niccolo could not name he thought again of the poison, the little darkness, the surety that his connections could rescue him from this place. He would face the Devil rather than Julius. At the moment the thought of that office in New Hell was even comforting.

But Julius was a tenacious enemy, maddeningly deliberate and appallingly sudden by turns he could not even yet predict. And that very quality both advised Niccolo Machiavelli that to desert Caesar might be to desert the wrong side and to damn himself, Caesar rising to new influences in the hierarchies of Hell; and it tugged at strings in Niccolo that led places Niccolo did not acknowledge: to have Julius look at him that way had *hurt*, in a way few things got to him. He had not deserved it; and he smarted under Julius' suspicion with the righteous anger of a man who so rarely was innocent, and who therefore thought his loyalty a rare and precious gift—*perdio*, spurned by some flaw of perception in a man he had so regarded as to give it. Double wound—which cast his judgment in doubt, yet another hurt, and gnawed at his self-esteem.

Now, troubled, he cast another look toward the

hill, where enigma had posed itself. "We have made a mistake, my friend. We had Agamemnon and we had a garrison on the hill. Now I think things are very different up there. We should have killed him. Now—" He gazed into the dark, toward the hill, and suddenly, like a thunderstroke, saw redemption. "Now we have our job, do we not? Where is Gemayel?"

Zaki scratched at his head, replaced the hat. "Where is he ever? Somewhere. Somewhere close."

Zaki scratched at his head, replaced the hat. "Where is he ever? Somewhere. Somewhere close."

"Position," Niccolo said. "We need a field phone out there. We need information."

"Where are you going?"

"Information," he said. "And Caesar." Figuring it was going to be quickly one and the same location. "Get the rest of it set up."

There was silence at his back. Resentment. But he calculated that the little man would do what he was told, because it was the logical thing, the thing he would have done without Niccolo Machiavelli to give orders, because they were all in this and Zaki had no wish to die.

So, likewise, would Nichols and Welch cooperate, like it or not.

Niccolo knew more of Hell than most, knew the theory and the mechanisms of Hell, and the most basic law, which was to avoid blame and seize advantage. Someone had erred. Someone had made a grievous mistake up there tonight or someone had been outstandingly clever: in either case, the blame in this was not his, and therefore the advantage might be.

"Hold it, hold it!" Pharaoh discovered a vantage

point from which it was possible to see all the citadel again, and Curtius swerved their jeep to a stop, over a rough spot in the grass; a bush went down under the jeep, and scraped the underside even while they rolled to a level halt. There were no roads hereabouts—none, at least, that they had found. The chopper was back from its foray off across the valley, the com truck was talking, and she answered and confirmed the instructions it gave her, for the tanks to target on the access to that citadel, hold their fire and wait it out.

That sounded like Julius, who had no fondness for night actions or precipitate, unreconnoitered attacks, given any choice at all. She had had no direct contact with any of the command, only the English speaking voice of the American, Nichols, who called her *ma'am* and used too little diplomacy; Americans made her nervous, a multifarious and hybrid lot, like Romans for shouting their opinions and like Greeks for having ten thousand of them. Set only knew what they were up to in the com truck, but so far she trusted it was indeed Julius' order and did what the barbarian Nichols said.

Everything they knew about the land was up for revision, that much was certain, and the rules were not what they were used to in civilized New Hell. A landscape that so rearranged itself might do it again. The copter had reported ships and sea, and that wind which blew in their faces smelled of other than the swamp. What, she wondered, if some power shifted Cocytus out of its bed, inundated the flat, and set them back in that black bog, from which they had scarcely extricated the jeeps and the trucks, thank gods for the pontoons and the groundeffect tanks.

Or what if some malign power rearranged the coast, poured sea on them, or opened the ground beneath them?

Lob a few shells up there unannounced, drive for that gate in the confusion and blast the heart of the place: that was the immediate strategy that suggested itself. The Macedonians up there probably had had their throats cut, by Agamemnon's orders or by someone or something else, something that could change the rules, or around whom the rules shifted. There was a Power loose. And *that* might not be affected by shells and mortars and disruptors, but its minions might: and that might gain them something.

Damn, wander around this nether hell looking for a way out and they discovered nothing as stable or as reasonable as the villa back in New Hell. But there was no trap as secure as comfort, either.

Negotiate with it? Discover it and use it and take advantage from it? Julius was Niccolo's teacher, posthumously and in Hell's own time. And he and Niccolo were still hers. She owned that much.

So she waited, tracing Julius' own thoughts: *It hasn't destroyed us, therefore: it can't at all; it can't without cost; it doesn't want to; it doesn't want to yet; we have something it wants; it's waiting on its own instructions: is that all the possibilities? Damn, no. Maybe it's just crazy.*

Somebody has to get a look at it. It's challenged us or we've challenged it and in any case we can't turn our backs on it, can we?

It'll find us, won't it?

She turned her jewelry off. It was a light they did

not need, she and Curtius, parked on the slight slope, within shot of the hill itself. And on a trick of wind she heard the distant sound of a rider, going hard.

"Who would that be?" she murmured.

"No idea," Mettius Curtius answered, who was a cavalryman, but they had mostly Macedonian horse with them; the Roman cav nowadays was mostly mechanized. Then: "Damn. *Troy.*"

"Is that significant?" She discovered awe in the young Roman's voice and frowned. "Let me tell you, Roman, my damned successors let the north slip their control. I heard about it."

"In your time?"

"In my time! In my time, Troy was a sheepcot with ambitions and the Hellenes were barbarians north of the Cretans." She gazed at the shadowy outlines, the gleam of lights. "Some damn pile they made out of it. Looks like Ophet."

"Where, Pharaoh?"

"Thebes. Thebes, you called it." She shifted in her seat and used the field glasses again, saw a light dim as some sentry walked past it on the walls of Troy. "*Can't* have gotten this rich off sheep. Damn walls are slant-sided, like Ophet, rubble and fill, I'd say, damn thick, and the gates are side-set—Set and Typhon! it wasn't any sheepherder designed a wall like that. Or he was a genius." She passed him the glasses. "Damn Cretan navy."

"Cretans?"

"We were river-sailors. Never any good at sea. I tried, gods know. Hired shipbuilders, built sea-going ships. My damned successor let it all go. And the Cretans managed the north sea like a Cretan lake. So

this sprang up, outside our reach. Damn, if we'd
seen it—if my successors had seen it coming, more
to the point: *I* was exploring Hell while this was
going on, and my damn fool successors spread exiles
from shore to shore, gods know, and some of them to
Crete and further. Isis and Set, we did spread what
we knew." She sank down in the seat and stared at
it, thinking again of a shell landing at those gates,
shells within the walls. No. "But it's *not* Troy, hear
me. No more than this is Asia. Expect this and
expect that—that's what they want. That's the dangerous thing. It *looks* like what it isn't." Uneasier
and uneasier. "This place is your illusion, not mine.
Important to you. Isn't it?"

"It was important," Curtius said.

"Get me down there."

"Where?"

"Caesar, dammit, *somebody* had better be down
there who can see straight."

The staff had wanted to set the tent up again.
"Then *you* sit in it," Julius had said shortly, thinking
of possible artillery mounted on the citadel heights,
and the kind of target one tent standing and lit would
make—no greater a target than the whole citadel
made to their guns, but there was never a guarantee
that an enemy was not prepared to be foolhardy.
Antonius arrived, in a jeep with the Amurrite king
Aziru: "Find anything?" Julius asked, and:

"No," Antonius said. "You want us to try the road?"

"Is there a road?"

"There's got to be a road," Antonius said. "There's
a gate, isn't there?"

"We're taking care of that," another voice said,

and Niccolo Machiavelli showed up like a wraith, black on black, white face and pale hands. "Zaki and Nichols are on it. Do you want otherwise?"

Machiavelli, arriving with dutiful efficiency. He should not have been so direct with this man of twists and turns. Julius knew that. And he worried about it, giving a glance at Machiavelli's carefully composed face. Not a flicker of resentment either open or concealed, but Machiavelli was breathing hard: he had been running, and his eyes were bright and anxious as if all his thoughts were up there on that hill.

"They'd better be damned careful," Julius said. "We're a sitting target." And turning his face from Machiavelli, which raised the hairs on him as it would have to turn his back to an armed enemy: "*Antoni*. Get down the rows. File the cohorts out of here, up under the lee of that hill." They had lost their high gun positions, withdrawing the tanks to the camp. Four of the tanks would have been settled safely on the flat, the way the topology had revised itself; but two would have been perched embarrassingly high on a wooded and rocky height, and maybe not able to get down at all: it was as well to have pulled them fast. But it was a disadvantage at the moment, with the damned plain at their backs open to gods knew what. Get the men under as much cover as they could in good order, that was first priority. *Where the hell's Gemayel and his lot?* Klea! Go with Antonius! If you find Gemayel, tell him answer his damn phone."

"I—"

"Get!"

Kleopatra scrambled for the jeep, climbed in past

Aziru, fell into the back as it sped off. Julius turned a
flat stare on Machiavelli as a flare of headlights caught
them both. Brakes squealed; another jeep pulled up
from the other side, narrowly evading collision with
a running officer, and Alexander vaulted the side.

"Julius," Alexander shouted.

About the time another jeep pulled in, squealed to
a halt, and Hatshepsut climbed down.

"Agamemnon's loose," Julius answered. "That's Troy
up there."

"I know," Alexander said, shouting over the jeep
motors. And with a furious wave of his hand. "Silence these damned things!"

Motors died. Instantly. Men in wolf-furs came panting up, pale braids flying, weapons rattling: the German Guard had arrived, out of breath and anxious,
behind Alexander and Maccabee.

"We are being challenged," Alexander said.

"That's fine," Julius said. "Question is, *which* of us
is being challenged. And whether it's worth the answer or whether there's any percentage in it."

"We go in," Alexander said, with a wave of his
hand at the citadel. "Otherwise we leave an enemy
at our backs as we go."

"We don't know which damn way we have to go in
the first place!"

"That!—Zeus Thunderer! how clear do you want
the way? The omens are there!"

"They look about as good for a turn south. There's
a fleet sitting out there in the harbor and we don't
know how it's armed: for all we know they've got
cannon or worse."

"I saw it. From up there. And I know the way.
Don't you?" Alexander looked about him, as legion-

aries hurried past. "Where are you directing these men?"

"Under the hill yonder till we sort this out." *Gods. He doesn't follow it.* "We've got reconnaissance—spies. Radios. We can watch the area from the sky. We're putting the information together as fast as we can, but we can't assume there aren't any guns up there that can reach to here."

Alexander bit his lip. His nostrils flared. But he glanced again to the black mass of the hill and his eyes were flickering with thought when he looked Julius' way again. "Meanwhile our enemies have no need to ask where we are. That is an open plain at our backs, the sea and a citadel barring us before, the mountains and rivers to either side."

"Makes me nervous as hell. I agree. It's not a good position. But there are damn sure worse ones. That's two and three armies that might turn up. One from the sea, Basileus, and we don't have ships. What in hell are we going to do with a sea-going enemy? Move out there when we know Troy's at our backs? They're *our* relatives, and I sure as hell don't trust Father Aeneas to recognize us with open arms."

"You think they can't move a hill," Hatshepsut said. "You think they can't fold it down on us. And whatever city that looks to be, is *meaningless*."

Female and uninvited voice in an already touchy matter. Alexander's back went stiff; Julius felt his own hackles rising, and drew a breath and swallowed it. "The pharaoh is right," he said. Use the title, gods, the Macedonian would respect that, and not go off in a rage to his own side—*pro di,* the *Greek* side, the fleet, while his own ancestry lay in Troy.

"So we take the high ground," Hatshepsut said, at

which Julius took in another breath and wished he had not played peacemaker. "Never mind who's sitting where. The tanks can reach it. Knock the gate out, put one tank inside the walls, let the chopper put a handful of our people on the citadel roof, and then we talk with whoever owns that place—get control of that citadel, get our guns up there and by Set we'll dictate the terms."

Alexander looked her way, interest and offense in plain conflict on his face. The Macedonian turned toward Egypt like a fish to a lure; but she was not, plainly, an adviser he knew how to take, not in matters he understood. And assuredly not from a quarter he understood.

"Damn expensive probe," Julius said, coolly—play it very cool, he thought; defuse this. Fast. And don't set Hatshepsut off, either. "Too damned expensive."

"No," Alexander said. "Zeus! Land on the roof! Can your physeters take down the gates, woman?"

"Damned right they can."

"Hold it," Julius snapped, as Hatshepsut headed for the jeep. "Curti!"

"Caesar!" Curtius looked his way, sitting tight in the jeep, not about to budge. And Hatshepsut turned, jewelry flashing to life with a mauve and red balefire, lighting an imperial scowl.

"So do we wait?" she asked.

"Julius," Alexander said, with a narrow, measuring look. "Do we wait?"

"Damn, we don't overrun our reconnaissance!" The jeeps were his. So was the com truck and the communications links. That meant the tanks were his. And the chopper. He stared at two fools. No. Three. Maccabee stood with Alexander, dogged as the

Macedonian. And the German Guard was looking ominously confused.

"We," said Alexander, "are in a trap. You talk about guns on the hill. Will it be better tomorrow? Do we lay seige? Wait out we know not what arriving at our backs or against our faces? These guns are better at height, like any catapult, am I in error? And best to take this height. Deal with both sides. *I have men of mine up there, Roman,* and night and speed are the best allies we have, am I in error? How many men will we lose by daylight? Am I in error?"

Well, young Caesar would have done it the quick way. Young lieutenant Julius the fool had gone over an Asian wall headlong into the enemy and won himself a decoration. Middle-aged Julius had gotten himself in a mess in the Vercingetorix Affair and narrowly pulled it out of the fire, beating a young hothead who had been very like himself. A damn great deal like himself, and the kind of man who might have brought all the north down on Rome.

So later, quietly, he had executed him. And stopped his intrigues from his Roman prison. He, *he,* Caesar, knew the danger in rebels. Having been one.

"*Pol,*" he muttered. It was inversely Young Caesar he stared at, a piece of himself he was arguing with; and he must take the conservative position, Crassus-like. Like damnfool Bibulus, whom he despised in Rome and in Hell.

It was fear that gnawed him; fear for the men. Faces he knew. Names he knew. Men he might not get back from the Undertaker. Gods knew what had happened to Scaevola or what hell he was in now, if Niccolo had failed him. Fear for the house, and all

his interests, and all the too-many people who put
their lives in his hands.

Or perhaps it was age. He had lived to die old.
And he remembered those years. He was thirty-five
for all eternity, but his mind, his habits—

"Mouse!" he said.

"Caesar," Mouse said, no more leaving his post
than Curtius had.

"We're going to need some volunteers," Julius
said. And when Alexander muttered something about
his own men: "No, dammit, they'll break their fool
necks bailing out of the chopper. Curtius—" He
looked at his watch. If it was a dependable night,
they had a lot of it left. "Run ferry service for our
friends here and *you* stay the hell out of the volunteers. Find the quartermaster, tell him I want all the
tents up again. No lights. Just set the tents up." He
prepared to climb into the jeep with Mouse. "You
want this so damn bad, Egypt, you explain it to
Achilles. Niccolo!"

"Cesare."

"Get over to the com truck, move, man. Tell them
what's going on. I don't want this on the air."

Machiavelli turned and went, broke into a run—no
hesitation from him, no saunter and no bow. Gods.

Does he agree with this lunacy?

*Is this Macedonian and this woman with her nov-
elties and her gadgetries—more sensible than the
Old Man? Does Niccolo think so?*

Dare I trust him?

"You," he said to the two kings, and the Israelite
general, and their suicidal German Guard, "you stay
on the ground. Leave it to experts. I'll pick you up
here when we go. Mouse—" He got into Mouse's

jeep and hit the seat, signal to start them moving. He grabbed for the radio himself, to locate Antonius.

He was not going to cross open ground with the infantry, that was damned sure: no suicide charges. The cohorts were not like the phalanx, incapable of maneuvering except on flat ground. It was a hill they had to take, and the Tenth, which ordered itself in the old maniples on the march, had learned a few other things in Hell.

Achilles stared at his petitioners, there in the headlamps of the jeep, carefully took the grass stem from his mouth and straightened from where he leaned against the copter, took a slow, analytical look up toward the hill of Troy, beyond the camp, black shadow beyond the few lights that showed. Lunatic. First the Romans knocked down their tents. Now they were starting to set them up again. And the Egyptian woman in the glowing jewelry and the fuschia jumpsuit was standing there with the king of Macedon proposing a raid on the citadel.

"Just drop it on the roof, huh?"

"Set it down, unload and out," the woman said. "Three part move. They're going to have all their attention on ground level when the tanks break that gate."

Achilles walked out away from them, drew in a breath of the stinking air, and gnawed at his lip.

"Can you do it?" the Macedonian asked.

He turned a sharp look back. "Who's going in?"

"Picked force," the Roman said. "Tenth Legion. They'll know what they're doing."

"Goodness of my heart, huh?" He spat, and looked yet again at that view, that hove up there like a decade-long nightmare. He shrugged off the prickling between his shoulders, and went back to the helicopter, skipped up to the deck and leaned out. "You got a landing picked out? You know what we got up there, whether they got anything modern? You know if a damn timber roof is going to take it? You know damn well where you're going after you get in there or who the hell we're going after?"

"No," the woman said. "But we're not going to know till we do it, are we?"

"Get Diomedes on this," Achilles said. "That son of a bitch was inside the palace. I wasn't."

Which was all he intended to say on the matter. He left them there outside, went forward and settled himself into the seat, turned on the work-light and went through checks, ignoring the view forward, where what had eluded him in life sat there mocking him with disasters.

The jeep left. Presumably it took the lot of them away. He made his contact with the com truck, listened to an American voice talk jargon at him, and code words he understood. "Yeah," he answered back, taking notes with a grease pencil; and: "Yeah."

And felt the shocks of one set of footsteps and two landing on the deck behind him. He turned around, yanking the pistol from its holster by his seat.

Maccabee and Alexander, in the dim light from behind him. He kept the pistol in hand. They stopped.

"The *basileus* and I are going in with you," Maccabee said. "When the Romans come—say that we are part of this."

"Fond of the Undertaker?"

Maccabee flinched, a drawing of his mouth. Alexander frowned.

"Your funeral," Achilles said. And got back to work.

The camp lay behind a ditch and earthen wall, a barricade lit by torches that curled orange smoke aloft into the unnatural night. Tents showed beyond, sprawling wide, unlike the orderly aisles of the Romans: tents and brushwood shelters, and beyond them would lie the black-prowed ships, their masts unstepped and their sails stowed, like a pod of black, wide-eyed dolphins beached and stranded in the dark—Diomedes knew what was there to see as he rode the single track toward the brush and timber gate, the torches, the sentinels.

Agamemnon would hear him out. If not, his old comrades would—Odysseus and old Nestor, Sthenelos and Euryalos, a hundred others who were dear as brothers to him, gathered here, ready to repeat their disaster, held helpless in Agamemnon's damned and damnable madness. The High King's unwholesomeness tainted everything, his disease spread through the souls of all who followed him and made them mad, that was what had drawn them here and stranded them on this shore.

But Diomedes was not snared. His vision was still clear, his counsel still sound; and he could wake them from this dream, he knew well that he could. He had only to confront them and seize them and shake them to sanity; and all this illusion would fall away.

The brave horse ran exhausted now: four, nearly five miles lay between him and the Romans, as he drew near the Hellene gates. Somewhere behind that barrier a horse called out a challenge, while the sentries on the outside of the gates stood to, shadow-figures marked by the white ivory of one helm, a white plume on the other. They moved the barricade back as he came, and shouted aloud as he rode through, into the enclosure of the camp, into the mazy aisles there by the horse-pens and the chariots that rested on their shafts. He slid down, gave the sweating horse a pat on the neck, before he should hand it over to the men who were coming from all sides to receive him.

A rough hand landed on his shoulder. He whirled in alarm and indignation, the blood still rushing in his ears and half deafening him as he blinked in amazement at the men in front of him and the men who rushed up in the torchlight, causing his horse to shy up away from him: he held to the reins in profoundest shock, and let them go to grab after his sword as he found himself among strangers and assaulted from all sides. Someone grabbed him from behind and another about the waist and another about the legs as the wave of bodies went over him with shouts at once familiar and strange to his ears. He hit the ground, cracked his skull in doing it and struggled in dazed desperation as they weighed him down. Pain exploded across his jaw; the night went blacker and crazier still; pain again; and he was deeper in it, still trying to fight, but getting nowhere at it. His feet were held, and dirt got into his mouth when they shoved his face against the ground and slammed his head down by the hair.

Dark after that. He came back to a throbbing in his skull and an ache in all his ribs. His legs were held. He could not decide why his arms would not move, until a rough grip hauled him over to face torches and shadows and he felt the cords that held him. Someone grabbed his hair, another pair of hands took his arms, and dragged him up to his feet, on a level with the largest of these shadows, at which he blinked and spat dirt and tried to focus.

"It *is* Diomedes," that one said in English, a voice, an accent, and a shadow-form which nagged at memory across thousands of years of Hell. "And what brings you to us, Hellene, with no truce and no challenge? Is it another raid, another murder?"

He knew the man then. And the man beside him—a torchbearer held aloft a light and the shadows acquired faces. It was Hektor, son of Priam; and his brother Paris. And they were all Trojans in the camp.

Faded Gods

"You watch out for all these faded gods, Zaki—they've as many hidden agendas as there are 'heroes' in Hell," Welch warned the little Jew he was dispatching to aid Achilles on the night assault over the slanted walls of Troy.

"Faded gods?" The hairy little Jew was all teeth and eye-whites, leaning against the black com truck in the black dark.

Beyond Zaki, inside the truck, Nichols was trying to pierce Ilion's countermeasures and take readings on men and weapons within the stronghold. *Ilion's countermeasures.* The thought bothered Welch more than the communications blackout Caesar had imposed, more than the sudden reversion of the terrain to an ancient Asian battle plain, more than anything but the planned assault itself and the way the citadel sat there, daring him, taunting him. If it could speak, it would have said, *Anything you can do, we can do better.*

But the citadel couldn't speak. It was an inanimate. A stubborn ghost. A ghost none of the Old Dead, to whom Welch had been assigned, could resist. And it shouldn't have had countermeasures. It shouldn't have had anything—it shouldn't be there. It shouldn't, most especially, be there *again*.

Welch understood too much of Hell to miss the real problem the citadel of Troy symbolized: things

were out of control on a systemic, not just phenomenal, level. The Devil himself couldn't have predicted
that Ilion would manifest ECM—electronic countermeasures. If Old Nick knew, he was probably mad
as Hell.

Welch sighed and answered Zaki, trying to warn
the little Jew without scaring him half to death.
"That's right, Zaki—faded gods. Caesar, Alexander,
Achilles: they all were cult figures, in their day.
Makes some kind of difference here. . . ."

"What kind? Hatshepsut and Kleopatra called themselves 'living gods,' too." Zaki's voice illuminated his
face as Paradise rising couldn't have: it carried all the
hatred of thousands of years for the Egypt which had
oppressed his ancestors.

"What kind, I can't say. But there're lots of souls
hereabouts who believe in those old myths, and in
the men who personified them. Unless we come
upon any talking horses, we might as well hang up
the com network until we've penetrated the citadel
and found out who and what's jamming us. That's
what I want out of this little jaunt. Tell Achilles that.
And tell him he's on his own until he sends up a
flare."

The little Jew struck a match: Achilles had brought
cigarettes in the chopper.

Welch's mouth watered and his nostrils flared as
Zaki lit one and the hook-nosed face of the Israeli
agent was transformed into a burial mask from antiq-
uity by the capricious dancing of the flame: deep
dark sockets with sunken gleaming eyes like eyes of
cowrie shell; cavernous nostrils up which hooks had
been thrust to clean out the brain cavity for mummi-
fication; lips as red as blood coral on some inlaid
funeral mask.

"Smoke?" said those lips, and the spell was broken.

Welch reached out gratefully to take the cigarette Zaki offered and the Israeli added, "So what if the com truck is useless? We have our eyes and ears. So what if the citadel is more—or less—than it seems? Nothing is as advertised in Hell. So what if we lose these god-kings of whom you speak? Where will they go, but to the Undertaker's table?"

It was Semitic wisdom. And yet Zaki's final question hung in the air between them, voicing all Welch's own doubts.

"Yeah," said the American who'd been station chief in Athens in the 1970's and who had, consequently, a grasp of the mythological and historical complexities involved in the operation before them that none of the others—Old or New Dead—could match. "That's the question, isn't it: where will they go? Is it still the same rules, down here? Or is this actually, not just putatively, a deeper Hell, with deeper traps and different laws? When Troy shivers into something else, it looks like Mykenai. So what's that indicate? Minos was a Judge, lord of the Underworld. In his own right. If we lose these Old Dead down here, I wouldn't want to be the guy the Devil decides is responsible for something he'd as soon not admit is a problem."

"So you're saying we dare not take casualties?" Zaki's voice was sharp, a hiss on the wind. "That, with our backs to the battle plain, the ships of a barbarian armada on one side, a baited trap before, and the forest of the Unborn Dead on the other side, we dare not venture forth?"

"Forth, shit. It'll come to us, if we don't go to it. No, I'm saying cover your ass, is all. First and foremost. There's no guarantees in this. Pretend like you're alive, okay?"

"Okay," said the Israeli, the cigarette held between pursed lips, one eye squeezed shut to keep out its smoke, his cap a shapeless mass between his hands. And turned to go, when Welch stopped him:

"Zaki, what I want is—" It was going to sound fey to another of the moderns. Welch knew it. He hated to risk credibility but hated more to risk lives. "Look, there's the shield of Herakles that we took. There's the legend of the shield of Achilles—what Alexander and Caesar did about it. There's the mask of Agamemnon, and whatever's behind it. . . . Zaki, stay right by Achilles. Whatever happens, don't lose him in there. The Macedonian troops aren't important by my reckoning. Something else is: Get a fix on Agamemnon. If we can take him prisoner and bring him back here, we might have a chance to get out of this thing with our butts intact."

"Out?" Zaki, halting in mid-step, said over his shoulder. "Out of Hell, you mean? Or just out of this predicament?"

"Out of this fucking mess, is all," Welch snapped, and wheeled on his heel, taking the com truck steps in a single vault and sliding the door shut with a harsh metallic slam of finality.

There was no "out" of Hell, everybody ought to have realized that by now. This whole thing was a charade, Welch had thought, until the damned hills started turning into myths and the waters taking the sides of his party's enemies. Now Welch was beginning to wonder whether there wasn't more at stake here than the egos of a bunch of antique, crazy kings.

If the Devil had a problem and Welch was somehow stuck in the middle of its resolution, then things made a different kind of sense.

Of course, nobody ever told you what you were *really* supposed to be doing in an operation like this—that rule, true in life, was holding true in afterlife.

Welch could accept it, but he didn't have to like it. The least Authority could have done was put him in the picture.

"What's up?" Nichols said, reaching for the pack of cigarettes folded in the sleeve of his black t-shirt as he stretched in his ergonomic chair before the truck's main console.

"What's *up?* Nothing, not a damned thing except the chopper and my blood pressure. You want a goddamned explanation, go consult that bitch with the eight ball. Have your fortune told. Get out of that chair, now. Let me work."

"Awright, awright," Nichols said softly, palms toward Welch, his face carefully neutral, offering no threat or resistance. "Don't get your skirt wrinkled. I'll be up front when you want me."

When. Not if.

Welch sat down before the blind-jammed eyes of the com truck's mapping screens, which should have been able to count the bronze nails in Troy's famous gates, and began looking over Nichols' careful, brief notes.

Nichols knew his place. And knew that sooner or later Welch was going to find use for the ex-Ranger's unique talents.

Among this bunch of fruity Old Dead, Nichols was Welch's secret weapon. When and if Welch dared use him, Nichols would air drop behind enemy lines or assassinate a given target dependably, no fuss, no mess, no regrets.

Early retirement programs were looking more and more tempting, not only for the enemies out there on the beach and in the citadel, but for the kings Welch was escorting on this weird journey.

If he'd been sure that they'd end up back in New Hell, Welch would have started that program tonight, with the Roman and Egyptian kings.

But he wasn't sure, damn it. He wasn't sure at all.

Achilles had started his rotors when the little Israeli came running up to the chopper's side and waved.

What was one more? He had Alexander and the Macedonian's Israelite boyfriend and two berserker German guards; he had a twelve-man strike force from the 10th; he had about as much use for Zaki as for those sixteen others.

He waved the New Dead Jew aboard, and wasn't surprised when, despite the "Fasten seat belts" order he'd given through his com mike, the little fellow came onto the flight deck, feeling his way in the near-dark, and slid into the co-pilot's vacant seat.

They were running without lights and with everything but fuel and attitude gauges dimmed.

"Mind?" said the Jew who was just Achilles' size, reaching for the shoulder harness and the secondary headset, leaning forward to put his lips to the headset's mike.

"Nope. Just don't touch the black box—that's my co-pilot."

The black box was above the co-pilot's instrumentation, mounted forward where a heads-up display would have read. Green and amber lights chased themselves across its otherwise featureless face, lights Achilles was reasonably sure Zaki couldn't read.

Settling the headset over his ears, Zaki said, "Right. Thanks," into his mike.

They were lifting steadily into the night. At a thousand feet, Achilles leveled off and put the chopper in "surveillance" mode, which quieted by half the racket that the rotors made and brought infrared landscapes to life on a monitor between Zaki's legs.

The Jew grunted in surprise as Achilles touched toggles and the screen split, adding a view of the city and the citadel they were approaching.

The citadel pictures weren't anywhere near as edifying as they should have been: Troy had more ECM than Achilles had ever encountered in Hell. All he could get was the fortress's outline, black and squat, and basic topographics.

He didn't say a word about the lack, thinking that Zaki probably hadn't seen anything like what Achilles' bird could do, even so, when the little Jew started telling him what Welch had said about priorities.

". . . and we're not to concern ourselves with the Macedonians in there. We're to take Agamemnon hostage, if we can't take the citadel. If we can knock out its countermeasures—"

"*Take* the *citadel?*" Achilles interrupted acidly. "With a dozen Roman legionaries, two berserker Germans who don't understand Greek or English, one Israelite suicide commando, and the Macedonian boy-king? You've got to be joking. Your boss has got to be. Or you're both deluded."

Achilles was breathing deeply and, for the first time in this entire sortie, felt fear.

He'd been calm and capable, negotiating tunnels barely inches wider than the spread of his rotor blades to get here. He'd been laconic during his first flight over Ilion's slanted walls. He'd been taciturn when he'd ferried Alexander on a wild horse chase.

Now he was not. And the anger that rose in his gullet frightened him the way nothing in Hell that was phenomenal could do.

Achilles had a temper. His temper was a beast with whom he did eternal battle, a wild and ravening thing that, when it broke loose, slaughtered indiscriminately and gave no quarter. It recognized no law and it had killed many the last time, on this battle plain, once Agamemnon had taken the girl Briseis from him.

Until then, on the beach, he had been the staunchest of Agamemnon's supporters—there by choice, the choice of an independent ally, not of a vassal.

But Agamemnon had taken the girl from him and his furious and ungovernable anger had got loose. What followed was history.

Finally, on that short flight up to the citadel, Achilles was rocked with remembrance. Of the sacrifices, human and animal, he had made to hungry gods while the "civilized" Achaeans looked down their noses at him.

Of the lying Greeks and all their perfidy. Of the compassion he'd felt for Priam, the Trojan king, in the beginning; of the pity washed away by his fury. And of all the blame for all the deaths on this beach centuries ago. Blame that he knew was his.

He'd come to Troy on his own and taken twenty-three towns along the way, including Lyrnessos. He'd found the girl, Briseis, there. She'd been his and none of Agamemnon's to take.

But Agamemnon had more men on the beach, and had taken the girl. Wrath had blinded Achilles then and he'd prayed to his mother, the goddess Thetis, to punish the Achaean lord.

And so down to Agamemnon had come the wrath of the gods and a false dream which had precipitated an untimely assault upon the citadel.

An assault which Achilles at first refused to join, even when Agamemnon offered fine gifts to assuage his temper and restore honor between them.

At the last, Patroklos had prevailed upon Achilles to lead his Myrmidons forth and prevent the Trojans from putting the entire Greek camp to flame.

But Achilles did not reconcile himself with Agamemnon until Patroklos was killed in battle. And then, his mighty anger loose upon the Trojans, Achilles went into battle and routed the enemy, killing even Hektor, the great Trojan champion.

Achilles had worn the armor made for him by Hephaistos that day, for Patroklos had died wearing Achilles' customary battle gear.

Deep in his soul, Achilles still wondered if the gods had not mistaken Patroklos for him, because of the armor. If Patroklos had died in his stead, the gods' hunger was appeased soon after, when Apollo took a hand.

Apollo had helped Paris to kill Achilles—Paris, the pretty boy, idiot boy and coward, a lover not a fighter, a man who shot arrows from the cover of bushes.

Achilles shook his head and growled, his mouth beginning to dry with anger.

So long ago. He seldom let himself think of it.

He'd done what he could, before the arrow a god had guided killed him, to blunt the sword of his anger; but it had been useless.

In its wake, sick among his carnage, he'd found pity in his heart and let old Priam ransom back the body of Hektor.

He'd done that by the code of honor that was his, so different than that of the "civilized" Achaeans among whom he fought.

They'd sneered at his offerings to the gods, because they were too citified for human sacrifice, not knowing that all men were sacrifices to the gods.

Well, they'd know it now, those who'd come to Hell.

And Hell looked to him tonight, with the Israeli from the unimaginable future beside him and Alexander the Great in his chopper's cargo bay, altogether too much like the glimpse his departing soul had gotten of the strand on which he'd died.

Below, he saw the beached ships, the hollow ships of the camp.

And he stared, his autopilot engaged in taking him to the roof of the citadel, down at the camp by the sea and the ships and it looked wrong to him.

It was wrong in the way the ships were positioned, wrong in the placement of the earthen wall and mud gates. Wrong in style, in some indefinable manner of defense and tent and fire-build that told him it was not his Myrmidons, nor his Achaean allies, on that beach, but some imposters.

He almost told this to Zaki, but what did it matter? This was Hell, not a return to his past.

He understood it as Alexander, in the cargo bay,

did not. As Caesar, who talked of shields and consonances forced on thousands of years, did not.

Achilles did not know who might be in those long ships, those hollow ships beached below the citadel, but he did know that his soul was his own, that no part of it belonged to Julius Caesar.

Not to a Roman who traced his lineage to Tros, to the Trojan princes—to the enemies who had killed him. No, no part of him was Caesar. Achilles owed no allegiance there.

But the part of him that bred anger before which even mighty Ilion had toppled in a day—that part of him knew that his wisdom wasn't shared by those about him.

Alexander must be warned of Caesar, whom Achilles now saw in the role Agamemnon once played.

Alexander must realize that, should blood become the telling factor, Caesar might well come down on the side of Priam's tribe, since he traced his ancestry to it.

For Achilles—the man who'd been educated by Chiron and hidden from his fate by a goddess; who'd grown up disguised as a girl and then fallen into his destiny, quarreling with Agamemnon at Tenedos; the man who'd made love to Helen in a dream and been made invulnerable except for a small spot on his heel (where his mother held him when she dipped him into the Styx)—this very man, who'd been gods' pawn and sport, who'd been the mechanism by which the oracle had proven true when she'd told Agamemnon his fate . . . *this* man that Achilles had been, who had been able even to make an accomodation with his fate in Hell, was not a man to take treachery lightly.

If Caesar came down on the side of Priam's Trojans, if treachery was even sniffed, Achilles would simply kill him.

Likewise, if Agamemnon gave him cause, the Atreidês chieftain's death would follow.

What Achilles would do was in his nature. As he had always done, when the gods decreed that his wrath be waked, Achilles would demand honor's price.

And this time he had not only his fury, but also the chopper's cannon and more modern skills of war than any but Welch's New Dead.

This time, if treachery and dishonor walked abroad, Achilles would not need to call on Thetis, the mother-goddess of his heart.

For not even the Devil incarnate had more fury than Achilles. And in the Devil's name he would gladly balance honor's scales.

He glanced over at the Jew beside him, who looked at him quizzically out of the corner of one long almond eye, who'd seen the quickened rise and fall of his heroic chest and the white knuckles of his hands on his controls.

Then Achilles bared his teeth in the vaguest simile of a smile and said, "What if it ain't Greeks on the beach? What if ain't Agamemnon in the citadel?"

"What if things aren't what they seem?" Zaki responded smoothly in a soothing voice, slouched in the co-pilot's seat as if he were round a cozy fire and not flying into battle. He shrugged a thin shoulder. "Then we do the best we can, my friend. As we have always done, your people and mine."

"Yeah. Okay," said Achilles. "The Undertaker's a personal friend of mine."

*   *   *

On the beach, amid Trojans, Diomedes was lashed to a chariot's centerpole.

The horses traced on either side of him were wild to run.

"So, Diomedes, breaker of horses," said Hektor, whom Achilles had dragged by thongs through his heels around the citadel during the war, "think you can break these?"

Old Priam was tugging at his giant son's arm and Helen, slumped against Paris' side, was weeping softly close by: "Oh gods, oh gods, you'll start it all again. Again, by Zeus, again! Please, Paris, stop them!"

And the fey youth was whispering back, "Now dear, don't worry. It's just negotiations, you see. Nothing for you or me to worry about. And you know Hektor when he's like this. . . ."

But Priam, beloved of Zeus, son of Laomedon and king of Troy, a man whose name had become synonymous with the ups and downs of fortune's whimsy, tried harder to reason with his son: "A death, such a death, now, will bring us all disaster. Hektor! Hektor! Look at your father. By Hermes who helped me once before, you must listen now!"

And the huge fighter put his foot on the centerpole where Diomedes' head was lashed to it and said, "Listen? To what? An old and frightened man?"

"If you had listened during the last war, you spoiled Trojan brat, you'd not have perished so ignominiously! If you'd come back within the walls when I begged you, the city might not have—"

"Phaw!" Hektor spat, and the spittle landed in Diomedes' hair.

Diomedes could do nothing: he was gagged and bound and dizzy from blows to the head. He strug-

gled reflexively against his bonds as the wild horses
stamped and kicked, occasionally hitting him, or bit
at their traces, once in a while biting him.

But this farce would be perpetrated within wise
counsel; Hektor had made sure of that with the gag
in Diomedes' mouth.

"If, if, *if,*" the son said to the father, towering over
him and glowering down at him. "*If* my fool of a
brother hadn't taken up with this slut, we'd all be in
a different place."

Helen began to protest.

Paris quieted her and Diomedes saw, as the Trojan led the woman away, the profile that had launched
so many ships and begun the ten-year war.

Priam didn't back away from his huge offspring,
but said, "My son, listen. Despite your pride and
wrath, listen. The Greeks have our citadel, and we
must, I agree, take it back. But making a sacrifice of
this man, when the Fates have provided us with a
hostage, is a pure waste of Fortune. Let us send
emissaries to the citadel, and arrange an exchange."

"An exchange? This man for the whole city? Why
should they? We must send him back, terrible in his
death, a sign of what we will do to them when we
have our city back." And Hektor's square jaw jutted
as he brought his face down, so that his prowlike
nose nearly touched his father's. "Remember, the
forces are positioned in reverse. Therefore, by the
logic of Hera, we will win the battle this time."

"This time it will be you who drags Achilles round
the citadel? This I've got to see," Paris hooted from
where he was comforting Helen, who wept freely
and kept volunteering her services as a go-between
in a quavering voice everyone ignored.

"*This* time," Priam broke in, "all my sons will listen to the wisdom of their father and behave like men, not like animals."

And there was something in the quiet, deadly tone of the father that made Hektor straighten up and seem to shrink.

Perhaps, Diomedes thought, watching all from his vantage lashed to the chariot, it was the memories, the same memories that threatened to flood his own reason from time to time.

But whatever it was, Hektor mumbled, "Fine, send an emissary with ransom demands for this Diomedes, breaker of horses. Perhaps, if his counsel has been truly wise, they'll want him back enough to negotiate in good faith."

There was a silence then. *Greeks never negotiate in good faith,* it said. *Greeks lie. Greeks build great horses, gift horses with death lurking within.*

For an interval all the Trojans stared at one another and at Helen, sobbing softly. Finally Priam said, "The woman will take the message. It is only fitting."

"What?" Paris strode forward, his face working. "You can't let them have her. We'll never get her back."

"And good riddance," said Agelaos, a Trojan killed by Diomedes in the war, who stood with Abas and Adrestos, men also dispatched by the Argive in the war.

Here, captive of the Trojans, surrounded by men who had died at his hands and kings and princes who had suffered from his cleverness, Diomedes had long ago given up all hope.

He fully expected a slow and agonizing death or, worse, unending servitude and degradation.

The one thing he wished was that horses not be used against him, drafted against their will into the service of his enemies. His affinity for horses was a special thing, one no mere man had the right to sully.

So as the wild horses kicked and bit him, considering him only part of their torture as they plunged in unfamiliar traces, he strove to forgive them.

They were just as afraid and just as helpless as he.

Any moment, the whips would crack, the horses bolt, and he would be dragged to a bone-crushing death.

Or not. Nothing he could do would change any of what was about to occur.

He had been foolish. He had rushed in, thinking it was home—the Achaean camp, all his compatriots on the beach. He had been fooled by the Devil and foolish.

Where had his wisdom gone when he needed it? What had he thought to gain here, even were it the Achaean camp?

Full of self-recrimination, he lost track of the conversation around him; concentrating on facing death and the Undertaker without flinching, or worse fates as best he could.

He only barely heard the decision of Priam and his sons:

"Then, it is settled. Paris, you will escort Helen to negotiate at the citadel, but not venture in the gates. Hektor, you will treat your captive well enough, until we hear back their word, yes or no, that we can give this Diomedes back without shame."

Hektor was coming close, a knife in hand, as he said over his shoulder to his father, "Your idea, father. And your blame, if it goes wrong. But have any of you considered the force on the plain? Perhaps it is them with whom we should treat."

The knife was coming near, and Diomedes' ears were ringing.

He hadn't really understood what was said but he understood the knife, coming toward his throat, his eyes.

He squeezed his eyes shut and heard the Trojan laugh at his cowardice.

Then the gag was loose.

And gone.

There was an interval in which the Trojans talked but their words were like the buzzing of bees in his ears, half-audible over his own breathing.

Then Hektor was leaning over him, garlicky breath bearing words he could understand: "What do you say about it, horse breaker? Who's in command on the plain? What have they to do with Agamemnon in the citadel? What wise counsel have you got for us, that might keep you one with your limbs and eyes until sunrise?"

Diomedes said nothing.

Hektor leaned very close now, adding: "Come on, night hunter, or I'll give you to those ghosts whose souls you sent here. You don't have to be in one piece when we send you back—*if* we do—just breathing."

And then as the three men Diomedes had killed in battle edged closer and more faces he recognized from the Trojan War popped up behind, Diomedes said hoarsely: "Caesar. Send word to Caesar, on the plain. And to Alexander, who will ransom me."

Once the word "ransom" had been said and not

denied, a ray of hope shone in Diomedes' inner sight. It was a solemn right, that of being ransomed.

Or it had been, in simpler days, fighting a simpler war.

As the Trojans whom he'd killed in battle began roughly to unhitch the wild horses and raucously to talk of what they'd do to him that he might survive, Diomedes began to think of death as a refuge he hadn't recognized.

Then hands were rough on his bound arms and legs and it was too late to think of anything at all.

But he did hear Priam protesting loudly that honor demanded the prisoner be treated righteously.

It was the definition of those words which was in dispute in the Trojan camp.

The first question on Achilles' mind was whether to put down on the citadel roof, but archers and spear chuckers on the ramparts answered that for him.

He set the autopilot to hover five feet above the roofline, stared at the timbers below while caulk blew away like snow under the chopper's gale, and called through his intercom: "Okay, Tenth, give 'em Hell."

The side door was opened and the chopper bucked.

He augmented the autopilot and cursed the Hughes-crafted black box that should have been able to keep their attitude steady despite the sixteen men who didn't know enough not to line up on one side of the door.

He yelled into his mike: "Stay in your seats until you jump," and better than a ton of live weight redistributed itself.

Arrows were flying but Achilles stuck his head out
the side window to see who was on the roof and saw
Alexander, first on the timber, calling his men forth
with gestures and open mouth, even though the
wind from the rotors whipped away his words.

"Get down, you fool," Achilles muttered and, as if
Maccabee had heard him, the tall Israelite grabbed
Alexander by the waist and slung him unceremoni-
ously under one arm like a sacrificial statue, skidding
down the roof along the rappelling line none of the
Tenth, let alone the Germans, really understood how
to use.

At least they had their automatic weapons out and
were returning fire, Achilles noticed, watching ap-
provingly as the flash-suppressed muzzles blinked
softly in the dark, the chatter of the fire inaudible,
but the lessening of spears and arrows proving that
the shooters were doing some good.

Crack! Ping! A round hit the chopper's under-
belly, where she was armored.

Three feet higher and Achilles wouldn't have been
in any shape to swear at Zaki, still sitting in the
co-pilot's seat: "Assholes! Friendly fire is all we need."

"Are you so sure it's friendly?" Zaki wanted to
know, unbuckling his seatbelt and, standing, instinctively checking the laser-sighted pistol at his hip.
"Any reason they can't have weaponry as good as
ours?"

Another round convinced Achilles that Zaki might
be right. He started to lift the chopper from the
rooftop, out of range of whatever artillery the adver-
sary had.

"Wait up. I'm going with them."

"It's your funeral."

The Jew grinned at him like a jackal. And stopped, hardly stooped in the low hatchway between flight deck and cargo bay. "But what about you, the chopper? Where will you be when we're done?"

"I'll be wherever I can do the most good. Don't sweat it. If you need pulled out, just get into the open—in the court, back up here, wherever. I've got enough electronics to babysit the guys I brought in here, you included."

"And if you are shot down? This helicopter is invaluable. Enemies might claim her. . . ."

"Let 'em try it," Achilles grinned, and his fingers flew over the sequencing panel, telling the autopilot to use a recognition function to keep tabs on the commandos he'd just landed and, in case of emergency, to keep out invaders by pulsing electric charges through the titanium plating—until she blew herself up, in the event that he wasn't producing any brainwaves the ship could detect.

"Y'all have fun, now," Achilles said to Zaki, then turned back to his instrumentation, readying his cannon for strafing runs and his area-denial mines for the front court and putting his electronic warfare gear on notice that he expected it to pinpoint the counter-jamming system that was somewhere in this citadel, or blow a circuit trying.

When Zaki hit the roof, a beep sounded in Achilles' ear and the chopper spun skyward.

As he reached for his infrared goggles, freed at last to begin taking out the positions that were firing on him, Achilles cursed beneath his breath. "Damn you, Jew, the least you could have done was close the damned door on your way out."

*   *   *

Alexander had not only command, enforced by tiny boxes like miniature field phones strung on the leathers of his troops, but experience: he'd been in this palace before.

Or he'd been in a very similar palace, the last time it had manifested as Ilion on this spot.

But he'd not been on the roof, nor on the upper-most floor.

The troops had been warned not to eat or drink anything, and under no circumstances to let the tainted water hereabouts touch their lips.

Maccabee had been warned not to leave his side.

He wasn't sure if he was willing to forgive the big Israelite for lifting him off his feet, but this was no time to argue about it.

He hadn't really expected this much fighting on the upper floors. He didn't remember so many minions.

But at least there were no pink-marble statues to come to life before their eyes.

There were only hostile fighters, some with modern weapons, some with bows and javelins.

And there was blood aplenty, and screaming in the torchlit dark.

He wished the night would end, in this evil place. It was too full of shadows and from each shadow, it seemed, men coalesced to bar their path with heavy fighting.

Every time they encountered Achaean soldiers, Maccabee would yell in Greek: "Bring us Agamemnon! Produce your lord!"

But this produced only curses and dying and soon Alexander's sandals were sticky with blood and blisters were raised on his ankles and the soles of his feet.

His sword arm ached, even though Maccabee was beside him, doing so much of his fighting for him that, had Alexander the strength, he would have protested.

As he would have protested that the Germans should not force their way in front of him, every time an enemy sought to engage him in battle, if he could have made them understand.

Through it all, Zaki was on his right, small and quick with his modern weapon that placed a red dot on the chests of men a moment before they died.

Thus, they fought their way down two flights of stairs and things began to resemble the palace with which Alexander was familiar.

He let out a deep sigh when they made the main floor landing: Agamemnon must be close by.

And in his ear, spitting from the box laced on his cuirass' shoulder strap, came a voice saying, "In the basement—Agamemnon."

He didn't recognize the voice, but that didn't trouble him. He'd only recently come to realize that these boxes weren't miniature oracles, with men inside, but communications devices.

Maccabee, beside him, was looking his way. They were about to leave the relative safety of the staircase, between whose walls his sixteen men could battle and even triumph against scores of enemies, and venture out in the open.

They had an alternative, however—to continue down, as the shoulder oracle suggested, into the basement.

It was a moment, as sometimes comes in battle, of heady quietude. No men crossed swords; no enemies ran forward screaming battle cries and brandishing weapons.

It was as if they existed in a different place, like an audience watching a play, or dreamers suddenly aware that they dreamed.

In that eddy of calm which, in Alexander's experience, always broke abruptly into the din of renewed assaults, Maccabee said softly: "Achilles, probably—he must have found the demon suppressing the box magics."

And Zaki, on Alexander's other side, groused, "Found the jamming center? He ought to be clearing the court, but yes, it's possible. Listen."

And listen they did, in that calm through which no warring penetrated.

And heard, from outside, a dull chatter like distant drums or the cascade of missiles from a unit of sling-shot soldiers. Which, of course, Achilles approximated with the "cannon" he commanded.

And then a sharper, louder, horrible sound blocked out all other sounds.

It rent the air and made the stones of the citadel tremble.

It rocked the flags beneath their feet and set the roof to swaying, so that they were showered with caulk and plaster and powdered timbers from above.

"Jehovah, the gates!" Zaki yelled as the entire great hall before them seemed to sway and the troops Alexander had been expecting began pouring out of shadowed corridors.

Sconced torches shivered in time to the pounding of the thunder from outside.

Zaki grabbed his arm and Maccabee leaned close to mime: "The basement. Let us hasten!"

They didn't just hasten, they ran.

They ran not from the Achaean enemy, but from the death Hatshepsut's physeters could spout, a death which made no distinction between soldiers, but only slew.

And as they did so, they were joined by others of the 10th, behind them, and also by men of Agamemnon's army, panicked and intent upon preserving their own lives so that no fighting broke out between the enemies on the stairs until one man shoved another. And then progress became chaos on those steps to a deeper Hell.

The light here, when Alexander knew more than battle lust and exhaustion, was reddish.

He didn't remember gaining the ground floor landing, or how many or what men he'd slain to get here.

His sword arm was dripping with blood and aching with tetanus so that it trembled. Spent brass skittered under his feet and his Uzi was empty, all its spare clips expended and discarded.

Beside him, Maccabee's big chest heaved with effort and the man so recently returned from the Undertaker's table was intent on keeping his bulk between Alexander and whatever the taller man had seen in the center of the room.

All around were the men of the 10th, mingling with the defenders of the citadel and with—Zeus be praised!—Alexander's own Macedonian cavalrymen.

Yet none were fighting, not even his Germans.

All were still again, weapons at ready, as if some agreement had passed between them that it was time to rest.

Every eye of every man taller than Alexander—all

but Zaki—was fastened on something in the middle of the room.

People sidled slowly about, unconsciously regrouping into their ranks.

And from without, above ground, the world still trembled under the assault of Hatshepsut and her physeters and Caesar's mighty army.

Down here, it was still as a grave and as red as the Devil's eye.

The columns were red and gilded.

The ashlar was red as blood.

The wall murals above had a reddish cast, showing bloody bulls goring bloody bull leapers amid friezes of rufous dolphins and bare-breasted, red-skinned women with snakes curling on their arms.

Alexander shouldered Maccabee aside as if the big Israelite were no larger than Achilles and no more formidable than Zaki.

And he saw then what had stopped the fighting and the troops in their tracks.

In the middle of the far wall, amid a dizzying array of red and gilded pillars, sat Agamemnon on his throne, his golden mask upon his head, his scepter that could shake the world and remake its contours held firmly in one hand.

Achilles was strafing the ramparts, where he could be of some help to Caesar's oncoming foot.

Hatshepsut's tanks had blasted the side-set gates to splinters and were maneuvering by zigs and zags into the central court of the citadel while, around them, footsoldiers fought.

Once or twice he'd thought he'd seen inhuman

heads on tall and muscled forms—goat-headed men, men with lions' manes, men with falcons' beaks.

But the ground support could handle whatever it found, he told himself.

And though his ancient soul remembered all its superstitious awe at the thought of quasi-human enemies, he kept his chopper circling.

There was nothing supernatural about the .30 millimeter slugs his chain gun was spitting down on Ilion.

He was tempted to forget that Achaeans, even if led by treacherous Atreidês, were his targets, and pretend he was killing Trojans.

One way or the other, his wrath was loose.

He'd found the countermeasures station and blown it—it had been in a grain magazine, discernable by the heat signature and infrared it threw.

They hadn't bothered to disguise it, thinking, he was sure, that it was invulnerable.

It hadn't been.

And now he could talk to the com truck, or to the tank drivers, or to those among the crazy Old Dead who didn't insist on referring to field phones as "Oracles of Litton."

He could talk, but everybody was too damned busy to listen.

Everyone except Welch, who'd been troubled that Achilles had laid enough area-denial munitions in the central courtyard to blow both contesting armies, tanks and all, back to New Hell.

"Hold your fucking fire, Achilles—don't detonate any—repeat, *any*—of the mines." There was a pause. "You *do* have them on remote detonators, don't you?"

"Yeah, yeah. Timers can't handle a change of plan.

You think I'd lay a minefield and get our own guys stuck in it?"

Welch's deep sigh had been audible even over the chatter of Achilles' gun and cannon. "Great. Thanks. Over."

And it would *be* over soon, if the progress of the interdiction force was half as good inside as it was where Achilles could see it.

He pulled the chopper up for a better look: recon and tac air was his job, nothing more.

So he was swooping high over the walls, now deserted of living men and only occasionally festooned with corpses who'd balanced on ramparts as they died, when he saw the single chariot racing toward the rear of the assault force where the com truck and the resupply vehicles were.

"Hey, Welch! Patch me through to Caesar," Achilles demanded.

"Why?" Welch's voice was burping with static.

"There's a chariot approaching the left flank—from the beach camp, looks like."

"Caesar's got enough on his mind, Achilles. One chariot—"

"Welch, don't argue. There's something weird about this, you can't see what I—"

"Something weird about *that?* What about the rest of this mess? I can't raise any of that strike force you landed. Thought you took out the ECM. . . ?"

"I did, you mother. You can't make contact, it's your problem. Over."

And Achilles, full once more with his wrath, broke contact and whirled the chopper into a full vertical circle (something it was not designed to handle) as he headed, chain gun blazing, down into the citadel's central court. There he'd damned well find out for himself where the party he'd brought here was, and what sort of help they needed.

Paris was driving like a madman.

The chariot horses of Troy were screaming as they ran, eyes wild and terrified, their ears flat against the deafening chaos into which Paris was driving them.

Helen had given up screaming: she couldn't be heard above the din of battle or the horses' louder cries.

She crouched low, her hands grasping the curving wall of the chariot's car, her fair skin so white her lips showed like a bloody slash in Paradise's rising light.

They'd finally gotten back at her, had Hektor and Priam, for finding her way out of Achaean misery by seducing Paris and arranging her own "kidnapping."

Finally. They'd been trying for centuries.

Now she was sorry, although she'd never been in all these years.

Paris was grim as he struggled with his team's reins.

It occurred to her that the horses might well be choosing their course, out of control and bolting.

Paris would never admit it, were it the case.

But the wide leather reins were so taut they blurred in his hands, and his leg muscles were corded, and she was about to give in to tears when, at last, the chariot jolted to a halt.

Hands over her ears, she came up on her knees and looked out at the battle plain for the first time.

She'd hoped never to see such a sight again. She'd

told herself she didn't have to look—she'd seen it all before, from inside Ilion's walls.

But here, the corpses were not butchered in the dirt. Here, there was no chorus of groans and darkening of mortal sight.

Here there was no battle plain.

They had crossed it, left it behind.

Paris had brought her not to the tents of this "Caesar" who crouched with his army on the plain, but right up to the gates of beloved Ilion.

And those gates were smashed and rent.

And bloody. Blood dripped in streams, marring the whitewash and coursing the stones.

Blood soaked the mud brick and men hanging from the walls.

Ahead was a noise like she'd never heard as, within those gates, chimeras the size of her father's palace quested through the courtyard, rolling over the wounded and the dying with a thousand weighty feet.

For a time the chariot and its occupants went unnoticed, but not for long enough.

She might have prevailed, given longer, upon Paris to drive away.

They could have told a tale to Priam, lied and said the enemies would not treat. They could have come back another time, when people weren't so busy. She could have found a way.

But now it was too late: magical chariots with burning eyes roared through the gloom to surround them and horrid men in weird battledress jumped out and grabbed their horses' bridles.

She stood up, terrified now, and whirled to run out the car's sloping back, and saw others behind:

There stood men in clothes of many colors, men with curious weapons and helmets the more fearful for having no horsetail crests.

And other men, with leather breastplates, men who'd obviously been at war so long that they'd shortened their cloaks and lost the burnish of their helms. And these had crested helmets, but of a sort she'd never seen: blood-red crests that stuck up straight like cocks' combs.

Through these men, encircling her chariot, came a slight form who held at its hip a metal sword with no edge.

Its face was awful, leathery and foul, with bulging eyes that had no pupils. Its pate was bald and horrid, brown and shiny. Its stature was slight and yet men gave back from it on either side, even bowed.

It looked at her, one hand on its hip. Then in a muffled, accented voice, it said, "Here to join the fray, are we, dearie? Win the day for someone? Whom, may I ask?"

The Greek it spoke was classical, weirdly phrased.

Helen wailed, "Paris! *Paris!*" and her husband turned around, that look on him he had when he was thwarted, his lips a thin line, his small chin jutting like his big brother's.

From the horses' heads, a man's voice shouted, "Where the fuck did *they* come from?"

But everyone ignored it.

The figure confronting Helen was taking off its face.

And under the bulging eyes were painted eyes, wider than a human's, and slanted.

Under the leather jaw was another jaw, firm and round, with rosy lips that curled.

The lips said, "Some decorum, please. I am Pharaoh, Egypt—Kleopatra. And you are, I must assume, the fabled Helen, if that boy's Paris . . . ?"

"Yes," she heard herself answering. "Yes, we are. Prince and princess, and not accustomed, lady, to such treatment. We come to treat with you in the matter of—"

"Right, right. Whatever it is, dear, we're a trifle busy at the moment. Aziru, would you take these two to the rear of the train and put the German guard to seeing that they're comfortable—and secure—in my tents under my protection . . . until we get time for them?"

"Yes, Pharaoh," said the man at the horses' head and, with that, two men vaulted into the chariot, men with weapons Helen understood.

At the urging of the men with naked daggers, she and Paris dismounted and were led away among the baggage train.

Agamemnon wanted to have a dinner party and the whole thing was giving Alexander a déjà vu.

"Look, lord Atreidês," he said once he'd taken the supplementary throne that Agamemnon had ordered brought for him and he sat beside the man potentate. "There's a war going on up there. If you want to have dinner, then surrender the citadel to Caesar's forces and we kings can discuss matters properly."

"Surrender?" The golden mask turned toward him slowly. "You wish to surrender. I assure you, it is not necessary. What is necessary is that matters take their destined course. Helen must be returned to us. We will fight until our honor is bright under the sun once more—"

"There's no sun out there, old fool," Zaki called from the nearest pillar where he and the Germans were lounging with Maccabee, pretending to relax but ready to intervene. "There's just Paradise, rising. Remember where you are? Where all this got you and yours the last time? You're dead, buddy. Dead as door nails. Dead as . . . dead."

Maccabee put a hand on Zaki's thin shoulder and the little man subsided, his eyes cast heavenward, where they encountered a ceiling decorated to the glory of forgotten gods.

"We're going to have a good meal and discuss your surrender," Agamemnon said implacably. "It's only fitting, between kings."

"Sir," Maccabee said in turn. "Surely you realize you can't hold out down here, not with Caesar's army in control of the storage magazines, the ground floor, the ramparts. . . ."

"With you as my guests? Come now, man." The mask turned to Maccabee; the eyeholes showed only shadow. "Let's not be impolite and discuss things such as hostages and relative costs. And too, you must realize that the doors are barred. Down here, all things are mine—you and your troops included. Don't take my word. Look about you."

Alexander did, if surreptitiously. There were no windows, just corridors leading off in every direction—or in no direction.

Men could be seen lounging in the dimness there. Alexander's force was substantially outnumbered.

Agamemnon was right—there was no sense in pushing matters.

Caesar would be along to get them presently.

Until then, humoring the mad Achaean chieftain seemed the only prudent course.

But to be on the safe side, he said into his shoulder-mounted box, "We're in the cellar enjoying Agamemnon's hospitality—me, Zaki, Maccabee, all of mine. We think you ought to join us."

"What?" Agamemnon sat bolt upright so that his brocaded robe fell away from his scarred and bony knees. "You overstep, Macedonian. If you're inviting your ill-mannered friends to dinner, the least you could do is ask my leave."

"Ah . . . well, may they join us, King Agamemnon?"

The mask seemed to smile. It couldn't have—it was solid gold, stiff as a corpse. But it seemed to smile. "Oh, surely," Agamemnon giggled, a burbling sound that resounded before it issued from the hole in the mask's mouth. "Invite them. There's more than enough for all. Invite—"

"*Basileus! Where the fuck are you?*" came Achilles' demand on a blast of static from Alexander's shoulder.

Agamemnon's hands flew up to his ears. He shot bolt upright and he howled. Still howling, he wrenched the little box from Alexander's shoulder and crushed it beneath his sandaled foot.

The Germans rushed the dais. Maccabee was one leap ahead of them. Zaki alone held back, and thus was not brought up short at swords' point as a dozen Achaeans interposed themselves between the men below and the kings on the dais.

"All right, all right. It's okay," Alexander said in English. "Nobody's hurt. Just don't use the boxes. Not where he can see—or hear."

By then Agamemnon was seated again, humming

softly to himself and motioning servants from the shadows.

The servants were, of course, bearing fruit.

Alexander was just about to remind his men not to eat anything when Agamemnon leaned close, in kingly fashion, and murmured in a voice only Alexander was meant to hear, "Brother monarch, please don't offend my majesty by speaking in foreign tongues. And please partake of these humble victuals. After all, you're going to be my guests for a long, long time."

"Let me get this straight," said Caesar, toying with a commando knife as he walked along the impromptu line made by Achilles, Welch, Aziru and Machiavelli as they stood at attention. "We've lost Alexander, Maccabee, and all his crew down some crack in this benighted rabbit warren and you can't even talk to them on the field phones?"

"Yeah, but we can locate them with telltales . . . sir. We know where they are," Achilles said, pointing at his feet, planted firmly on the flags of the ground floor throne room. "We just can't figure out how to get there from here."

Caesar shook his head. "This is so, Welch?"

"Ah, yes sir, it is. We did get a message from Agamemnon's brother, Menelaos, that they'd consider some sort of deal, sir, but. . . ." Welch's mouth turned down and he shook his head.

"*But what?*" Caesar thundered.

"But you can't trust Greeks," Machiavelli said softly, with a quick glance toward Achilles. "Especially Atreidês—the revenge motive, you know, sir."

"But what is it they *want?*"

Silence along the line of men.

Caesar slapped his knife blade in his palm. "You, Niccolo, are always quick with answers. Answer me."

"I believe they want, ah . . . your surrender, sir. Ours, that is."

"Impossible," Caesar fairly growled.

"Of course it is, sir. If I could just have some time alone with Menelaos. . . ."

"Not yet," replied Julius Caesar with ill-disguised disgust in his tone. "Not yet. I've a mind to leave this matter in your hands, but not yet. What, exactly, did Menelaos say Agamemnon wants? His exact words. The specifics of this 'deal?' "

No one spoke. But then, Caesar had directed his inquiry to no one in particular.

"Welch, can you answer that?"

The man whose ears were the keenest in Caesar's army said, "Surrender does seem to be a part of it, sir, but it's more like Helen of Troy that he wants."

Caesar strove to remain expressionless. "Continue," he said at last, hoping Welch had something more to say.

"That's why we brought Aziru, sir," the American said. "He says Helen and Paris turned up on the left flank during the battle, and that Kleopatra took them."

"*Took them!*" Caesar repeated, realizing that he'd have heard this bit of news straight off, if these men hadn't been so afraid of telling it to him. "Well, *get* them from her. Bring them to me. In my tent. As soon as possible."

Queen's Play

The eye-patched Roman in khaki took a turn before the window in Augustus' study . . . worried guests tended to do this, so many years of them, in fact, that the carpet showed a certain wear.

It was Julius' habit, that floor-pacing. For a moment, Horatius' back being turned, Augustus suffered a vision of Julius returned: tall, dark-haired figure in khaki—till Horatius turned round again and showed that frowning, piratical visage. Thinking of New Hell, doubtless: the skyscraping Hall of Injustice towered all too ominously beyond, and dominated thinking in this room.

Beyond that, the Pentagram, where Rameses II held power—or danced to Mithradates' string-pulling, now that Hadrian was deposed from command in Hell.

Augustus had Hadrian. Or at least, Augustus' operatives had moved into Hadrian's uptown apartment, booted out the Egyptians and Assyrians who so sollicitously watched the convalescent ex-commander, and quietly moved Hadrian to a location Augustus knew; which Horatius and Sargon knew; and which frustrated the hell out of Rameses. It was a measure of that frustration that no word had leaked of Hadrian's *second* abduction, which meant that Rameses was working very hard on finding him, and wished to do it quietly. Or that Mithradates did.

Certainly the Pentagram's inner circles knew that they had been challenged and they were embarrassed. Dangerous. Most of all they had to dread the prospect of a recovered ex-commander surfacing with charges to level; and with troops loyal to him.

So did Augustus dread it. And intended that should not happen. Which, in the tangled ways of the Silent War in Hell's administration, the opposition knew and knew Augustus knew they knew. All of which tended to keep things low-key and moderately sane. It was the counterpoint to the larger moves—like the Egyptian colonel who had moved bag and baggage into Assurbanipal's villa; like Assyrian money recruiting mere officers and insinuating them into the rebel cause—all the while the Pentagram was both fighting the rebels *and* supplying the Assyrians the money they supplied the rebels. . . .

Meanwhile Tiberius the lunatic grew friendlier and friendlier with the Assyrians, Julius' natural son and murderer Brutus had shown up, amnesiac and innocent as they came, Julius' and Klea's son Caesarion had deserted Tiberius to the rebel side, all at the very time that Julius had gone off and vanished himself and half the household with a timing that might make Rameses as nervous as it made Augustus himself—Augustus himself fervently hoped that such was the case.

Or Julius had fallen into a trap. And they were never, ever going to see him again, or Klea, or Hatshepsut; or perhaps even Niccolo; any of which prospects singly was enough to keep Augustus awake of nights, and all of which collectively—

"He will keep trying," Horatius said, meaning

Scaevola; and Horatius gave a helpless move of his hands. "He *is* still trying."

Meaning at recon. Meaning Scaevola out there with a century of the Tenth, a truck and a jeep, and his own knowledge what the territory around the juncture of Phlegethon and Lethe *had* looked like, the night it drank him down to wherever he had been—if he had not hallucinated half of it. Scaevola was trying to get back to his commander, trying to re-establish communications with him if nothing else.

"On blind luck," Augustus muttered. "We've got to do better than that for him, *Horati*."

Horatius One-eye slipped his hands into his pockets and regarded the Emperor with his one-sided sight, his mouth settling into its accustomed grim lines. "Uptown?"

"We have Hadrian," Augustus said. "We have lines into the Pentagram."

"Dangerous to use them," Horatius said. "We've used them too often as it is."

"*Di superi!* dangerous, the man says." Augustus leaned fists on his littered desk, staring across it at his own spy chief. "Dear *Horati*, I find us in some danger as we are."

"I mean," said Horatius, "that it is possible to choose our moment to provoke Rameses, but we are far from ready."

"Readiness is your department."

Horatius did not so much as twitch. "And I am telling you we are not ready."

Augustus slammed his fists onto the desktop. "I am telling you I want to know what connection the Pentagram has to Julius' disappearance. I want to know whether the Pentagram knows the route out there."

"Then we can ask Hadrian. But it will betray things to him as well. Do we want that?"

"We want it." The imperial we. It was not, of course, what Horatius had meant. "We want it, *Horati.*" For the hundredth time Augustus longed for Niccolo, for Machiavelli's trimly elegant insolence lounging in the chair yonder, in the stead of Horatius and his modernity, his ciphers and his damned military mind, which kept thinking in patterns that made Augustus very nervous.

This was, after all, the man from the Tiber bridge. The one who got himself out there and let it go down under him, because he reckoned himself an expendable. And if Niccolo was hard to handle, Niccolo was a political mind, one Augustus understood with his own intuition; Horatius was entirely a military one, who thought in terms of expendables and diversions, and who might (another thought that gave Augustus nightmares) be more Julius' man than he was his. There remained the possibility that Julius had not confided all he knew—to him, or to Horatius Cocles either, before he went off with Alexander of Macedon; there even remained the possibility that these events or some portion of them were Julius' own doing, which one had always to take into account when dealing with Julius Caesar; none of which thoughts helped Augustus' peace of mind when he looked Horatius in his single eye and wondered how much of the intelligence Horatius gathered was going to him and how much was being stored up in Horatius' own head, preparatory to some move of his own— had not Scaevola asked to be sent back to Caesar?

But who had affirmed it as a good idea and scoured up the equipment and named the men to go with Scaevola?

Augustus had ruled too long not to keep a ready mental file of proponents and opponents of every policy which came out from his bureaus. It was, he thought, precisely *why* he had reigned long.

He smiled now at Horatius. "*Ask* Hadrian what he knows about the geography out there. More to the point, ask him who else knows. And then ask him what connections Agamemnon has to anyone."

"That opens a can of—"

"Snakes. Yes. But we'd better know as much as he knows, hadn't we? Mention the name Agamemnon. Shake the tree and see what falls out."

Horatius did not object to that. He had one of his thoughtful looks, the brow above the patched eye arching a little, the mouth quirking tight at the corners. "Yes," Horatius said, "majesty."

". . . you're going to be my guests," Agamemnon said, leaning close to Alexander, "for a long, long time."

The while drawn swords threatened his Macedonians, his Germans, and Judah Maccabee, held in the center of the throne room. The little man, Zaki, who had been there among the red and black pillars when the others made that aborted rush to defend Alexander's person—was not there now. Just the pillars.

And the servants who arrived from one of the ten of corridors that led from this hall approached behind the lines of armed Achaeans, bearing wine and fruit and moveable tables, Agamemnon's hospitality.

Maccabee's eyes shifted that way, the rest of him

motionless, the way they all were, even the Germans, with their swords and spears opposed to Achaean weapons . . . their guns were empty. It was the ancient weapons they had now. But those were not the only weapons in the room. There was, for instance, Agamemnon's staff. There was the poison in the gifts Agamemnon offered, that stilled the blood and left a man living and trapped. *Don't drink or eat,* Alexander had warned his men. And tried to warn the Germans, gods knew.

What do we do? that look of Maccabee's said; and Alexander caught his eyes and stared back with a bland and thoughtful calm that surely baffled the Israelite. Smiled at him then, and turned and took the rhyton that a servant offered him, still smiling when he looked the gold-masked Atreidês in the face.

"Brother," he hailed this walking affliction, and walked away from him, down the steps to the center of the hall, the rhyton in hand. "Let us not forget amenities." He spilled a little of the wine on the floor. "To the earth and the shades which we are." Another spill. "To the vine and the god of madness—" *—who has blighted you, you atrocity.* A third spill. "Not forgetting the sea and the winds and the rivers and the daughters of rivers—"

A king and a priest-king had a great store of prayers and invocations. And time was what they needed. He had other things in reserve, which sent a prickle of fear over him: there was, for instance, a pretense of the holy sickness—he had had it, when he was drunk, enough to feign it when he was not; which blasphemy sent the wind down his back, but a son of the Rites had some privilege, and such a man he was—Olympias had gotten him the ancient way, Philippos his putative father not the wiser. She had gotten Philippos drunk on wine and the god and mixed his seed in her with that of the sacrifice, so there might have been twins, one mortal, one not; but since there was one, there was no doubt that he was the god's. So Olympias had sworn, her young son's face caught between hands strong as brass, her eyes like the eyes of the snake that peered through the black veil of her hair beside her cheek, its tongue darting and flickering: *The god is in you, the god-who-dies and the god-reborn.* Meaning cycles and the old rites and the knife which Zeus himself had escaped, castrating his father Kronos and replacing Rhea with his own wife-priestess Hera. . . .

". . . Zeus Thunderer, father." Another spill of wine. They said he, Alexander, had suborned the assassin who killed his father, or they said that Olympias had done it, and that it was one and the same. It was true there was no love lost between him and Philippos. It was very true. For a moment the masked king transformed in his eyes and the hall was Macedonian Pella, with Kleitos there, alive—and Hephaistion—

—*Hephaistion*—

The figure standing by him offered another cup, gold and figured with bulls; it blurred and blurred again.

"Alexander," it said, most horribly, most gently. It had no face at all. "Do you blaspheme? Drink and endure the god you have invoked. It is your *moira*, your pattern, son."

It was his mother, Olympias, with the housesnake twined all black and brown among the amber and jet jewelry she wore, with amber beads in black hair, and kohl about brown eyes as ophidian as her god's. They were the colors he remembered of her, it was the touch he remembered, when she took him along with the women—all at once he knew, if he turned, where she would lead him, it would be a cave, flickering with torchlight, and the priestesses—

He had not rushed screaming away. His drugged limbs could not accomplish it and his pride had restrained him. Only in his dreams he saw the pillar that impaled the earth, saw the earth convulse and heard the echoing cry the victim had made, whereafter his personal nightmares were of such women, and his only trust was in men.

Slim, cool fingers brushed his arm and kohl-rimmed eyes stared into his, hypnotic. There was a sharp pain in his forearm, and he saw the snake about her wrist, felt the numbness spreading from its bite. But housesnakes were never venomous.

"Thou art god," she whispered, giving him all power (but who gave, could take away) and all worship (but who worshipped could deny). "Come and meet the god."

The rhyton fell from his hand. Red wine spattered and stained his feet and her gown, amid the puddle of wine in which they stood. Her gown was flounced in red and gold and blue, gold trimmed; her wasp-waist was girdled with a gold serpent. Her breasts were bare and the nipples were rouged like her lips and her cheeks, her eyes enormous with kohl.

Not Olympias. A young woman. She led him up the steps. He heard someone call out *Alexander!* but the voices were like the humming of bees, distant and quite unimportant. The golden mask blurred like the sun and the room spun about him while the young woman left his arm to cling to the king's.

Alexander, the voice said again. He half-turned, furrowing his brow, trying to understand why anyone should call his name, but:

"Alexander," the king in the mask said sternly, recalling his attention, and beside him the woman's amber-and-jet serpent entwined with her black and curling hair: "He is our guest," the woman said, and smiled with rouged lips and rouged cheeks. She clapped her hands and light voices rang, feminine laughter; women appeared in flounces and bangles, bare-breasted, bringing more wine and more food.

"No," Alexander said then. It seemed wrong, in a way he could not, through the haze, fathom, as the cave had seemed wrong, and the man screaming in his nightmares. He tried to walk away, stumbled on the steps and caught himself, but the wound was aching now. "King," he said faintly, his voice lost in his own ears like the buzzing of the others voices. Hard hands closed on his arms. Men drew him back among them, into what seemed safety.

While Agamemnon turned and walked away like a king in the plays, masked and robed and carrying his staff, hand in hand with the woman.

"Alexander!" Hands shook at him. He turned and blinked into Maccabee's face, feeling keen pain in his arm, as if it were fire from fingertips to shoulder.

"I think," he said, cold and afraid, and feeling failure worst of all, failure to have protected his men, or to have bettered this place after all, "I think that I am dying, Judah."

"No," said a female voice. "Not dying. Let us have him. He will not die."

He tried to protest this. Maccabee held him closely, was holding him on his feet, while the whole room spun and the bulldancers of the fresco danced indeed. "Beware," he said, or hoped he said, "beware them."

"The bull is garlanded," a woman said, screamed, raved, near at hand. And he knew the rest of it. It echoed ominously in his skull. *The bull is garlanded. His slayer draws nigh.*

Nigh . . . nigh . . . nigh. . . .

So the seer had said of Philippos his father.

"Father-slayer," they had whispered of him. It was not true. It was truly Olympias who had suborned the assassin. But he had foreknown it all his life that she would do this and make him king. In that much he had guilt. His father had foreknown it and feared him.

With patricide a man served the goddess and became the god.

He tried to tell his friend these things. He was a king and he was in mortal danger. But Judah let him down on the cold stone and abandoned him to the women, whose voices echoed in his skull like voices in a cave. There was a sharp sting like the other, and the figures on the walls danced with the bull they would slay. Others marched with the moon-shaped axe, and brought water for the ritual bath, round and round the walls, while he lost himself in the drug and the touches of their hands.

"What are you doing?" someone asked, clear and sensible. It must be a god it was so lucid amid this sanity. But he did not hear the answer.

And again, leaning over him, himself lying naked on a soft bed, with the soft light of oil lamps and painted fish and dolphins on the walls, the woman of his illusion whispered: "My love, wake up."

She had shed the skirts and the jacket and the serpent that clasped her waist. Her hair hung in ringlets, black as night, her breasts still were rouged and honey-colored in the lamplight. Her mouth curved in a smile and lowered to his, tasting of wine and spices; her skin when it met his was oiled and warm, and when they lay together (Where did he gain the strength for this? But it was the god, or he was dreaming, he did not know—) her body slid freely over his, warm and perfumed, so elusive that he could not tell at first that it was not some movement of her hands that insinuated itself between them and crept upward with undulations at once powerful and rasping against his belly and his chest and twining around his neck and shoulder. At this he should have panicked, but the fear was very far away, the creature was a daimon, and numinous as the woman who whispered in his ear:

"Thou art Aigistheos, Aigistheos, Aigistheos—"

Alexander, he whispered, but his body betrayed him, the serpent wound now tightly about his neck and the blood roared in him.

"This night," the woman whispered, and the serpent's tongue flickered around the tender inside of his ear, "thou art *Aigistheos*."

Sistra chirred and drums beat. He was a woman's vengeance. He understood this role. For a moment it was Olympias who held him, and it was crime beyond crime they committed. In the next it was an Erinys, whose teeth were sharp against his tongue, whose unbound hair of live serpents licked about his

face and whose wings beat with a noise like thunder
in his ears while his body spasmed. But:

"I am Klytemnaistra," the woman said, "the queen."

There was still occasional fire coming from the
sector Menelaos held, which was not an enviable
position, Caesar reckoned from his vantage across
from those lines: Paradise rising in a smoky, stench-
filled dawn . . . showed body after body burning
down to ash as bodies would in Hell: the source of
some of the smoke. Burning buildings was another,
cookfires, whatever else: a good part of the town was
flattened along the major avenues where the tanks
had come uphill. Now one of the groundeffect tanks
held that approach up from the gates while a second
was busy maneuvering itself into a position on the
height, a great deal of roaring and whining of fans,
but from that spot they had a sighting on the Trojan
camp *and* height to use. If they had to use it.

Meanwhile, if that had left anything uncovered, he
had told Hatshepsut to take the third tank back down
and join the three holding the flat approach, down
which any Trojan advance had to come from the sea.
So much for reverence to the ancestors.

Meanwhile Welch and his truckful of marvels was
attempting to sound out the hill sideways as well as
top to bottom.

"The men," Mouse said quietly, arriving at his
shoulder, "would prefer you took cover, *Cai Iuli.*"

It was an exposed position here at the doors of
what was left of the palace. There were snipers, true
enough. "Damn palace might as well be mined,"
Julius said. "If we can't get at Agamemnon he can
collapse the whole damned thing around us. Take

the hill out. Raise one up. Fold the damn ground over on us or bring the sea in. What in *hell's* Klea waiting on, and why in hell doesn't Agamemnon just roll the sea in on the Trojans? Tell me that one, *Deci.*"

"I," said Mouse, "would prefer you took cover. *I* would prefer you got off this hill. They may take offense at the tanks."

Julius chuckled softly, dark humor that Mouse could draw out of him. "There's some reason for this." He gazed off down the hill, beyond the courtyard that was littered with Achilles' mines, toward that still-standing quarter where Menelaos was holed up. Some-where. Maybe even underneath. Which he did not at all find amusing. "More to this than meets the eye, Mouse, indeed there is. Menelaos says they'll cut our people's throats below if we don't do every-thing they ask, but how are they to get out, mmmmm? once we've done what they ask—without relying on our word; which I wouldn't: they don't know us at all. Menelaos with a handful of snipers demanding we give up hostages, Trojans out there demanding their city back for Diomedes—do you know, we could go on at this hostage-snatching for a week, theirs and ours to demand theirs and theirs to demand theirs and ours: the damned thing's endless, you know, and I'm not sure either of them's got what he claims."

"Please," said Mouse, "get out of the open."

"Ah," Julius said. "But if it were the power that shapes this land that demands we surrender his brother's wife—do you think he needs hostages? I wonder at him. I do wonder, Mouse. And what do you imagine they send us Helen for? What—?"

"*Iuli?*"

Mouse's voice came distantly. Of a sudden the sky seemed to go red in Julius' sight, the whole world to go hot and cold, and the sound of his own heart to ring in his ears. He blinked and the courtyard was clear again, his breath coming harshly still, as if he had been with a woman, as if he had hallucinated—

"Come inside," Mouse said. "Get inside."

A sweat had broken out on his skin. The falling sickness, he thought, with a little touch of fear. He was thirty five. It was not due to afflict him yet—not the way it did at the last. He caught his breath, leaned with one hand against the stucco wall, blinked as he caught the sound of a truck motor, one of the quartermaster's rigs coming up the hill. "What's that?" he breathed; and winced as a shot spanged off the truck and another went through the door. *"Dis et omnes perditi!"* he yelled at their own snipers, stationed up on the roof to pin down Menelaos' snipers. *"Protegite carrum, vos matribus ignominia!"*

Fire dutifully spattered back into Menelaos' section as the truck made the last part of the climb and turned the corner of the palace, squealing to a halt that coincidentally presented its backside and covered the doorway.

The passenger-side door opened. Antonius slid aside from the driver's post and out in the cover the slanted park provided that side; and the rear flap went up as a blond-braided German bailed out, rifle swinging wildly over his shoulders. Another followed, the Germans growling to each other in their own language; and that one put up his hands as Klea appeared at the back of the truck and jumped.

The German set her down as if she and her gear weighed nothing, which was damn near the truth.

"Klea!" Julius snarled, waving her and Antonius to cover in his doorway. More Germans were coming down off the truck; and of a sudden two more blonds, male and female, in white garments soiled and mud-spattered. Their hands were bound and the Germans handled them as if they were toys, passing them down to the next as the last Germans vacated the truck and Kleopatra came striding over dusting her hands and taking her time.

"You called?" she asked like the prostitute in the play, and tilted her head up and regarded him with that don't-get-pushy look that was not what he was prepared to meet up here, under fire, and with half of Hell gone lunatic. "I made it."

"You damned well could have couriered them up!"

"Ttttt." Klea walked past him and signed with rapid finger-movements to the Germans, who faced the prisoners about. "But which fox do I trust the geese to?"

He saw. And took in his breath.

"I'm not sure which one's virtue's more in danger," Klea said, in that dim haze that hammered away at his senses. And that was true too. If there was a couple the gods had made perfect, it was this ivory and gilt set of pieces, the man and the woman standing so anxiously one against the other. "I got them here. They keep protesting they're under truce. They say they've got Diomedes." She had the eight ball in one hand, and turned it up to the light. "And they want Troy for him."

"They will kill him," Helen said, tears shining in those remarkable eyes.

"Ransom," Paris said like an echo. "For Troy."

There was not much hope in either face.

"You know," Julius said in the oldest Greek he knew, and slowly, "your husband is over there. Menelaos. He wants you back. You've got one of our people. He's got twenty. And he doesn't want a city. Just you. After which those machines can take your camp out."

Helen hid her face against Paris' shoulder. Paris looked away, cheek against hers. That was all.

Julius folded his arms, looked from them to Klea to Antonius. "Damn fools," he said. Thinking of the disturbance a pair like that was in reach of an army; and that Trojan horses came twolegged as well as four.

"Well, well," a voice said then, and Achilles walked out from the doorway to stand beside him, Achilles in his dark fatigues, helmet in hand. His red hair had come loose from its knot and hung over his shoulders like so may snakes. "I saw this from the roof. I thought I'd just drop down."

His almost-fiancee and the man who had killed him. Julius drew a quick breath and frowned, moving instinctively off the step to put himself between Achilles and the prisoners. And there was that giddiness again. *Gods, not now*, he thought, looking back, standing still for fear of his balance going. But Achilles had a strange look as well, as if he had heard something troubling—or felt a sudden weakness. Julius stared at him. On the step as Achilles was they were eye to eye—suddenly it was as if some contact were opened into Achilles' soul, as if whatever barriers the man had were down and he was staring into some stormy sea—

Oceanid, Julius recalled. Elemental.

Then the moment was past and the dizziness had

passed. He tasted blood in his mouth. He felt the fool, trying as he had tried in life to reorient himself and recall where he had been and what he had been saying when the moment came on him. The Old Dead called such fits prophetic. He called them a damned nuisance. But he and Achilles had had it in synch; had it—till now, that Achilles stood there wide-legged, glaring at the pair that had caused him so much of grief.

"They're mine," Achilles said.

"Wrong," Klea said, her hand on her pistol; eight giant Germans came to instant attention, rifles ready; Achilles looked her way; and Julius, who had seen that look smouldering in Achilles' eyes before now, and now found it unmasked, found his heart beating hard and his hands sweating.

"Let's don't start *that* again," Julius said.

"Do you deny them to me?"

"They're Klea's damn prisoners—*listen* to me, they've got Diomedes."

"Whoopee. Good riddance. You got a damned screwed up mess, *general*, sir, you got half your staff gone missing, you got another one out on the beach, what else are you looking to do before lunch?"

"You damned thickskulled—" The Thessalian infuriated him. The cocky, belligerent stance and the moves maddened him, got at his own temper in ways that no one had gotten to him since he *was* that age, since he had stood glowering at the dictator Sulla and cursed him to hell over a woman, his wife, his first wife, the love of his youth and the woman he never talked of with Klea, who was the love of his wiser years. It was mirror into mirror. And the pulse was hammering in his ears, and the rage shivering in his limbs. "Where was recon on that camp out there, and how in hell'd you lose twenty men you were damned well supposed to support up here? All the fuckup here *you* had a hand in, you damned—"

Achilles' hand came up. His did, countering the move, if a weight had not hit his shoulder, flinging him back, if a hard hand had not held him and Mouse's voice hissed: *"Iuli!"* A woman was yelling, another was yelling: *"Shut up!"* and Antonius was spitting the two words of German most of the army knew. None of this was important. Julius stared at Achilles at close range and finished his sentence: *"—incompetent lunatic. Make good. Or keep your mouth shut."*

Achilles' face was transformed with rage. The pulse in his cheek had become a regular tic. There were two large Germans holding him back and they seemed precariously few.

"They're Klea's prisoners," Antonius said. "You want to repeat it all, man, with *you* playing Agamemnon this round?"

That scored. Achilles' mouth went harder still, white around the edges. "You just put your price tag on them." Modern English. Not a modern mind, not behind that gas-flame stare. "You got a buyer, *general,* sir. I have your leave, *sir?*"

"Get the hell out of here."

Achilles spun on his heel and stalked back inside, black, slight figure, red hair streaming down his back—he grabbed it as he went, twisted it into a tail at the nape and jammed the helmet on before he vanished in the hall.

The cold and the roaring that came and went were back again, like madness. Julius turned and stared at the prisoners, the gold and ivory pair in the hands of the Germans, who stared back at him. And Klea, whose mouth was drawn taut and whose eyes were starkly afraid. Not a word from Klea, not since she had challenged Achilles.

"Dammit," Julius said to her, "you *know* what kind of man that is."

"I know," Klea snapped back, "I *live* with one. *I was defending your damn property, what do you think I was doing?*"

Kleo-patra, Patro-klos, Hephaistion. She had her own illusions. Or they were not illusions and they all were helpless. Julius felt an unwelcome twinge of terror, a sense of menace that had nothing to do with guns or the shifting topography: a sense of menace inside, in the soul, the mind, whatever it was that made a man unique, even in Hell—*that* was at hazard, that was being pried at and loosened, and its foundations eroded.

We are in deadly danger, do you know it, Klea? I had to get him apart from us. We're on a downward slide to a pit of our own making and the weight of Correspondences here is greater and greater, that is the madness, that is what turns our swords on ourselves—We are fighting for our existence, Klea, and poor, damned Agamemnon is the soul central to this hell—

"He—Agamemnon—has power on us through Achilles. Through what began here. The foundations are going, Klea. Rome. Everything—founded here."

"He's having a seizure," Antonius murmured, and a light hand touched him, closed on his rigid arm.

"The god," Helen's faint voice said. "It's the god in him."

"Damn, no," Julius muttered. But then the structure, so logical, was unbuilt, the image and the clarity irretrievable. Like dreams, evaporated to nonsense in the waking. He felt only weak then, as he would when one of the attacks left him. "Damn nonsense. Where's Achilles gone?"

Then he knew that he had been insane, that his reason had gone patchy and vague and he had offended the Thessalian in a moment of unreason, an act of temper affronting his own intellect. If he had humiliated Achilles he had done as much for himself, in front of Klea and Antonius and Mouse, Mouse who had no nerves and gazed at him now with not-quite-wonder, having seen him fail before: *So what will you do now, Cai Iuli, how will you get back our honor?*—for Mouse trusted him that much, in Mouse's way. It was unbearable.

He walked away from them, giving no orders.

The suffocation went away. It was a woman who lay with him, the woman with the honeyed skin, the smell of spice and wine, and the delirious touch of her mouth while sleep came and went.

Maenad. He was in danger of his life. He was the man in the cave. He was the dancer in the Maze of the Goddess' bowels, where the pillar met the womb of the Earth and the stream ran down to join the dance, the ripple of torchlight on flesh, the smell of earth and stone and age—

His arm ached from fingertips to shoulder. His heart thudded against his ribs.

He was in bed. With the queen of Mykenai. His brother's wife, in his brother's hall. His name was Thyestes: he ruled in Tiryns; he guested in Mykenai, rolled this lusty Cretan woman in his arms—this foreigner whose two sons denied him inheritance from his brother Atreus, all oaths broken. But he had his revenge. Atreus abed asleep with the slave he, Thyestes, had brought from Tiryns; himself abed and not asleep with Aerope of the soft breasts and the wide thighs . . . then quietly, quietly, Aerope his willing partner, he crept down the hall to the Great Hall of Mykenai and the Fleece that hung behind the throne, the holy symbol that would bring the kingship to Tiryns, not Mykenai. . . .

But there was outcry. He fled emptyhanded, Aerope falling behind in their panic flight, in the desperate rush for the gates and the drowsing guards—and, truth, without the Fleece he could not have helped her. He made it away, and escaped the search, reaching the walls of his own fortress of Tiryns . . . to hear later that Aerope had paid the price for them both. In a dream he saw her flung from the cliff, from Atreus' hands. In that dream Agamemnon and Menelaos watched Atreus kill their mother, stolid-faced images of Thyestes' own two sons, his dark-eyed daughter.

Dancers on another night, years hence—whirled about a torchlit hall, abandoned before the solemn processional of priests and prietesses in fresco; the banquet in Mykenai proceeded with glitter of fire on gold, cups and plates and bowls. Mykenai again. Quarrel resolved. He feasted with his brother, laughed to the bawdy jokes. Menelaos was there. Agamemnon. Young lions, like his own sons. Handsome. He said as much to his brother.

Till they brought in the platter that should have held the goats' heads; and he saw the faces of his two sons, heads on that plate, the dish from which he had eaten.

A rush of dark then. Madness in which someone screamed. He remembered later rushing from the gates, remembered his daughter Pelopia, alive, trying to stay with him—he, trying the escape route he had used before—madness then, a tangle of woods and madness, of female body which he took by ambush and used like an animal until he remembered that he was a king, and left her all he had, his sword, wiping away her tears and bidding her come to him with that token should it be a son—

Then: son, son, son, the madness echoed in his skull, and he ran and killed and ran again, that was all, till strangers hunted him down . . . but not altogether strangers. They bound him and smiled wolfish smiles and called him uncle. They were Atreus' two sons; and Pelopia, they said, was their father's whore, mother to their half-brother Aigistheos. So Atreus had won it all.

After that, long misery. He was alone, chained mostly in the dark—he had been a king, he remembered. But they kept him from the light. And finally they sent a murderer to him.

He smiled at this man, this young man, having no throne left, and no house, and no friends left but this, who came to deliver him from life. But he saw the sword then, and knew the mark on it, and laughed hysterically. *My son*, he said, remembering that sword, *My son, is this the token?*—

The young man cried out and fled.

"Hush," the woman said, when his body convulsed and the venom came on him like fever, his senses reeling. "You have not seen it all. You are that boy. You are the son now—Aigistheos."

. . . up the stairs, where Pelopia span, the spindle whirling in her fingers, the thread going down and round and round from the calloused, work-worn fingers. *Son*, she said, his mother. And he held out the sword in a shaking hand and said that he had found the man of the token.

No, a voice protested, not wanting to see the rest. But:

Give it here, his mother said. And calmly when he had done that, she told him the old story, their secret story, that he was not Atreus' son, that she had refused to nurse him when he was born, so Atreus would command her to mother him: whatever she had wished he would have done contrarily. By that cleverness she saved him, her revenge on Atreus, for she had found herself a man in the dark, in the woods, when she failed to find her father and knew the pursuers close. She had cheated Atreus of herself; and given him a stranger's son; and made him believe it his by rejecting it.

Not a stranger, the boy says, the words echoing as if they came out of some cave. *Not a stranger. I am your son. And by this token, I am also your brother.*

Blood then. A great deal of blood. Perhaps his mother/sister killed herself. Perhaps it was his hand. Certainly it was the sword, in both their hands: he could never remember how it was.

But he and his father slew Atreus.

And Agamemnon and Menelaos, away bride-seeking in Sparta, marched north for vengeance. But Thyestes cheated them with his death.

Only the forest after that. The wild things. Agamemnon ruled in Mykenai; Menelaos in Sparta—till Menelaos lost his bride, and the kings all went to war in Troy.

The queen Klytemnaistra of Mykenai, Agamemnon's wife and Helen's sister, came to speak with her shepherds, and stopped at a spring, the summer day being warm.

And saw a young god, a satyr, a man to cure her loneliness.

In her bed, in high Mykenai, Aigistheos laughed, Pan's dark laughter, and used the talents the god gave him, fearing nothing, not the jaded priestess, the maenad, the elder sister who was always overshadowed by golden Helen. Klytemnaistra had no reasons such as his, only a sister who stole everything, most of all the love of everyone Klytemnaistra loved. Her hate was the sum only of one lifetime.

She hated. He simply *was* hate. And the force of him excited her, like the possession of the god.

"Aigistheos," she whispered in his ear. "My husband is home. Agamemnon is home. . . ."

"I don't know," Maccabee said in despair. It was the second time through the corridors, himself and the Romans and the Macedonians, and the two silent Germans, named Perfidy and Murder. They had tried line-of-sight this time, stationing themselves out along the corridors within view of each other so that they could quickly explore the alternatives of the branching ways that went out from this throne room. But there were not enough of them. They ran out of men before they ran out of corners. They ventured a staircase, and two more turns, and were back, insanely, maddeningly, in the throne room from which they had left. They had seen Agamemnon led away. They had let the women aid Alexander, and seen them melt into a haze—

—which became a confusion of bodies and motion and shadow, confused with the painted figures on the walls, or the figures hypnotized and held them all paralysed and beclouded.

How could such shadows bear a man away? And they had let it happen, their limbs and their wits betraying them. Minions of Agamemnon, Maccabee was sure. Alexander was snakebitten and raving, they had seen it, and one of Agamemnon's women, these witches with their snakes—had cast a net of confusion on all of them. They had not found him, nor Agamemnon, and Zaki was missing as well: Maccabee, twice through the maze, cast about him wildly, desperate in the tenuous loyalty of a Roman band and Alexander's irate Macedonians and two Germans who stared at all of them with iceblue eyes and silent rage. They had been fools and still were made fools. Maccabee raked his hair back and stared from point to point of the room which was the juncture of so many corridors. Nothing was left but the throne and the painted figures. The tables. A small smashed box, lying on the floor. The boxes had spoken once, and died when the Achaean broke that one.

"We have to bring help," Maccabee said. A man was indeed a fool, who for pride kept doing a hopeless thing. "Try again to talk to them."

"I *been* trying," a Roman said, a hook-nosed, scar-faced man missing an index finger—he rattled at the small box he wore. "*Heus! Heus! Audi me.*"

Nothing. Nothing, and again nothing. A way out. A way to Alexander. Either one he would settle for.

"We cut one transmitter off," the Roman said suddenly. One did not expect wit from a face like that, but the eyes lighted, the whole face took on a wolfish delight. Faces like that Maccabee hardly trusted. But: "We unscrew this mother and just keep cutting her on and off. If they got anything on us, they'll read it."

It hardly seemed to follow, but the Roman started taking the equipment off and apart. He thought it broken? Maccabee wondered. It was a way of fixing it? He watched while the Roman took the guts out of the box, stood clear when the Roman waved off all the help offered him and walked over to the middle of the room, to stand there and meddle with the thing in absolute concentration.

"Does it work?" Maccabee asked.

"Nesci'," the Roman muttered, tapping away at it. "Fellow named Morse got this system. Damsight better'n the old signal fires. I give 'em the SOS, and hope to hell they got shovels. Sir."

Maccabee came closer and looked at it, and at the plastered, seamless ceiling, and back at the Romans. "Signal flashes."

"Yessir."

For the first time he felt an affinity to this bluff, sullen kind—the curious shy look the legionary gave him, a plain man, a farmer or a shepherd, maybe, by birth: big fingers quick and skilled with the tiny parts of the oracle. He had twelve of this sort, men quiet as this one, men like the Macedonians, who bickered and seethed with fury at losing their leader, and the two Germans—God knew what they were thinking, fingering their guns and talking seldom even to each other, but looking, he saw, to him for orders. He was still weak from his murder; desperate, from his loss of the friend who had trusted him; but he was calmer, suddenly, knowing the measure of the men with him, that they were not enemies. *Sir.*

They must chart this place. There were ten exits. A certain number of turns be it up or down, led back again. There had been an entrance. Somewhere nearby Alexander was—

A groaning came, as if the very earth shifted. Or had a voice, somewhere deep in unguessed caverns.

"Damn," the legionary said, his signaling forgotten. One of the Germans said: "Tyr," which was the name they called Alexander.

The other one said another word, at which his fellow drew in a deep breath and made some kind of sign.

Maccabee clamped his jaw tight and refused to guess what it was. The timbers of an old fortress could sound like that. Or bending bronze, if distance and depth distorted the sound. It was not, at least, a human voice.

"I don't know," Welch said. "What the hell—" The signal had stopped. *Help*, the interrupt pattern had spelled out. SOS SOS SOS SOS till it stopped. So it was not Zaki. Zaki could have told them more, if Zaki were talking, which Zaki was not. They were short on moderns down there. He did not trust it, and looked at Nichols in the dim light of the consoles. While the pattern resumed again. SOS SOS SOS.

"We know *where* it is." Welch tapped a pencil on his sketch. "Question is how they are. One man we know might know a way down there. For all we know it fell in on them. Maybe it didn't."

"They worth it?" Nichols wondered.

The pavings were cold beneath his feet, the winding halls were acrawl with painted figures that moved and flickered in the olive-oil light of the lamp Klytemnaistra carried. Her back was dusky shadow, her naked body and dark, curling hair was limned in gold as she walked before him, carrying the only light. Dolphins leaped on the painted walls, small fish darted. They moved beneath a magic sea, among reefs and weeds, and reached a painted shore, where vines grew, upon a stairway that led down and down, a processional of priestesses and at last the titanic figure of a bull, which leaped down into the earth, into shadow, where the steps ended.

He was naked too. So one was, who served the earth, who followed the priestesses. The frescoes gave way to a large room, a water-filled bowl the size of a man on the floor; a throne on which sat the masked king, between the upright posts of the labrys-axes.

He hated. He had no question what he should do. "Come," he said to the king, to Agamemnon. "It's time. Give *me* the staff."

"Do you take my place?" the king asked. "Is that what you wish?"

It was a magical question. He shuddered at it. For a moment the room wavered, shimmered, became a cavern, a pillar. A scream ran through the dark, and out of that dark Klytemnaistra was handing him a bronze, heavy axe. Mirror-imaged, moon-shaped blades. Labrys. The ancient, the forbidden thing. The women's axe.

"Treachery," the king said. "It is treachery. We are Achaeans. We do not kill our kings."

It was wrong. A man knew his own blood. He was not Achaean.

"Heraclid," he said, and saw the woman retreat from him. "Damn you, I am Tirynthian! I am—"

The staff rang against the floor. The walls shivered. "—Herakles, Heraklidês, son of the god. I am Zeus-Ammon. Already king, of Macedon, of Egypt, of Persia and of Hellas." He felt a pain behind his eyes and in his arm, and pressed the fingers of one hand against his eyes until red light flashed amid the dark, and the cold grew greater. He felt menace in his blindness. He heard the earth groan, and the hair rose on his neck. There was no longer the hate. Whatever he had been, he could not recover. Whatever he was he could not remember. He felt a cold wind brush his shoulder and whirled and swung the axe til it shocked against something, till he freed it and swung again, the dark rage coming on him.

When it was done there was no more sound. He staggered away and somewhere had left the axe. He found stone under his feet, and under his hands and knees when he fell, stunning himself. When he opened his eyes he could not see. The blackness was absolute.

"Judah!" he called out. "Judah!"

A voice came back to him. He could not name it. He knew who he was now, and that he was cold and in a great deal of difficulty, a damnable great deal of difficulty, and that somewhere he had killed someone—

—Kleitos? Could he have killed his old friend, his teacher, the man who had taught him the weapons that he used? Could a Great King do such a thing?

A Great King *is* the law, Persian voices whispered. You stand above mere right and wrong. You had no choice. He affronted the dignity of the King.

He squeezed his eyes tight, tears rolling out and down his face. It *was* Hell, blackest Tartaros, and he was in it, the spear that he had aimed for his own heart had gone in, nothing else could hurt so much, but guilt.

It was the wine, Kleitos, it was the god, I do not deserve this.

I do not deserve to be alone. It was never my choice. The god chose. I meant to miss, Kleitos!

A spear, not an axe. Images tumbled, bright behind his eyelids, hell within his skull, the world all shrunken to that night, that drunken, repeated night—

"Alexander!"

There was a light. The least gleam of a light, which played on rock walls and set his heart to thudding in his chest as if he had been running. He had his sight. There was a world, be it a cave, wherever he had come.

"Alexander!"

A nightmare shambled into view, a rumpled figure, a waxen, hairy face underlit, its eyes all hollow and the whole vision suddenly exploding into glare as light swung into his face and blinded him again. He flung up his arm, scrambled for his feet as cold flesh betrayed him and he sat down again, cracking the back of his head against the stone wall and jolting the arm down so that the light hit his eyes again and blinded him.

"It's me," the voice said. "Zaki." Quick, strong hands probed his head, his ribs, his arms and legs and feet. "You're cold as ice."

"I can walk," he said. He. Alexander. He drew in a large breath and tried to get to his feet. Zaki heaved on him and braced him up, leaned him against a rock wall.

"Stand there," Zaki said; and let the light down,

and fussed with belts and rattled his equipment, and got his jacket off. "Put it on," Zaki said.

It smelled of sweat. Was warm from Zaki's body. "I don't need— "

"Put it on!" Zaki was still stripping clothes. "Damn, take these."

Undergarments. They were warm, at least. Zaki started dressing again, fast, his breath frosting in the light. Alexander put on the shorts and hugged the shirt about him, beginning to shiver as Zaki, clothed again, swept the beam of the electric torch about the cavern.

"Where is Maccabee?" Alexander asked. "Where are the others?"

"You tell me," Zaki said. "I've been trying to find a way out of here."

He leaned against the stone, remembering insane scenes. He had lost his clothes somewhere, he had lost hours in some kind of fog, out of which he could bring scattered images to focus, like a dream. But this was not his concern. Maccabee was. His Macedonians. The Romans and the Germans who had followed him and whom, somehow, he had lost. The Great King did not lose himself; it was assuredly the others who were lost. But the Great King did not intend to let it rest at that.

"Labyrinthos," he said hoarsely. A mirrored-crescent image flashed through his mind, bronze and gold. The king in the mask. Painted dancers with a painted bull. "Minos."

"English," Zaki said.

"Minos. The king is the bull. The god in the maze. You don't dance with the women."

"You hit your head," Zaki said.

Alexander fingered the knot. His arm was fevered. It was the only part of him that felt warm. The heat in the clothes had fled. "The Oracle," he said. "We are following the omens."

"Yeah." Zaki took his arm and led him.

His legs tried to betray him. It was the cold. The ground was uneven and he felt nothing in his feet. "Where?" he asked. "Where are we going?"

"Damn if I know," the Jew muttered, this little man of Maccabee's choosing. "But you got to move. We walk in circles if we have to, to keep you warm."

"Find Minos," Alexander said. "We have to find Minos."

"Fine. Maybe he's got a map and a pair of pants. Where did you leave your clothes?"

"I don't know." He did know. It was too insane. Perhaps in fact he had taken them off himself. At the least he did not know the way back. "Go down. Find the pillar." He knew that there would be one. He knew the law of such places.

"Yeah," Zaki said. "Pillar. Sure." The light of the torch crossed stalagmites and stalactites of fantastical shape. "You got a specific one in mind?"

The Wrong Stuff

Aziru had been prince of Amurru too long to ever think of himself, here in the Underworld among a surfeit of potentates, as "king."

He'd been a pirate prince of his seaboard nation for all of his prime years, kneeling to the Hittites and the Egyptians and trying to keep his father united with his kingdom and his head. It was only in his later years, years he remembered as a wine-fogged dream now, when his alliance with the Hittites grew strong and their mighty ruler grew to depend on his counsel, that Aziru had acceded to the throne.

But this body that he wore in Hell, this frame of knotted muscle, this head and beard of thick black hair, this temper as athletic as his sinews and joints— this body remembered the old days best, days when he'd gone raiding on the Mediterranean, a shadow of doom the mighty nations feared.

Even in the com truck, with Bashir Gemayel on one side and Machiavelli on the other, listening to the American called Welch apportion manly deeds and heroic quests among them, his flesh remembered what it did best: the feel of a choppy sea under him, grappling hooks in his hands, raping and pillaging among the fire and smoke. And disappearing in good time, to live to sail and to fight again. . . .

And his mind remembered the old songs of his earthly life: *"Tablet, sing the manly deeds of Suppilu-*

129

liumas, Great King of the Hittites, the hero . . ." "I proclaim to the universe the deeds of Gilgamesh. . . ."

But of Aziru, prince, then king, of a little-known nation called Amurru, no one had ever sung. His valor had not been made known to the people, his valiant struggle to preserve Amurru as an independent state had died as he had died.

So when Welch, the New Dead's wizard, said, "Nichols, Diomedes is yours. I don't care how you do it, but get him out of the Trojan camp, take whoever you think's got the right stuff and—" Aziru interrupted the American:

"I will accompany Nichols, and from the sea we will strike the Trojans' ships. We will set them afire and when they run to save their long ships, my friend Bashir will steal into the camp and rescue the hostage, Diomedes."

Finished, Aziru crossed his arms, conscious of the eyes of Welch and Nichols, and of Gemayel and Machiavelli, that rested upon him.

Machiavelli frowned, his narrow, well-trained lips preparing to argue.

But Welch said first, scratching his head and staring at Aziru as if he stood before the sun, "Yeah, maybe. What think, Nichols—take the Zodiacs, make it an amphibious assault?"

Aziru noticed that, the whole time Welch spoke, he kept watching Machiavelli out of the corner of one eye—not so difficult to do in the close quarters of the com truck, but noteworthy, nonetheless.

The man called Nichols, in his turn, scratched at one bicep, where an eagle tattoo quivered. The New Dead were plagued by fleas, though Aziru was never bitten: fleas did not like the smell of him, it was a gift of blood, of his desert heritage, that Authority had not thought to strip from him.

"I think," said the taciturn Nichols, who reminded Aziru of assassins he'd employed during his kingship, "that we're talking about the *wrong* stuff. . . . I don't know these guys, what they'll do, what they *can* do. I'd rather go on my own, chief, like I know how. I don't need to be worrying what these guys'll do if—"

Machiavelli said unctuously, "My sentiments, exactly, *signore* Welch," and Aziru remembered Aye, advisor to the Amarna pharaohs, and Ribadi, governor of Byblos, and every other snake who'd crawled the palaces of his day, giving false counsel and playing realms and regents to their own advantage. And stiffened.

Welch flicked a glance past him, to Gemayel, who had not yet said one word. "Well, Bashir? Which side are you going to come down on? Without you, the argument's academic. No team is going anywhere without Maronite support troops—yours are the only men we've got with enough guerrilla training not to fall all over each other in the bushes and alert the whole Trojan camp."

Nichols muttered, "Fuck all, Welch, didn't you hear what I said? *Alone* is the name of this game."

Then Gemayel said quietly, with a lilt to his English that somehow reminded Aziru of home, of the sun glinting off the Mediterranean and of the Lebanon, of the Niblani mountains scraping the sky with their peaks, "We will fight with our brother, Aziru—on land or sea, it matters not to us. As for the hostage," Gemayel shrugged in an immemorial gesture; "one man to the rescue or a hundred, it makes no difference: all hostages have their salvation in God's hands."

"Great," Nichols groaned. "I need these guys like I need a day-glow wet-suit and bells on my toes."

"It's settled, then," said Welch smoothly, as if his American compatriot had not spoken, "Nichols takes Aziru and Gemayel, and whatever Maronites Gemayel wants to kick in. That's the command order, in case of casualties, okay? Everybody understand? If Nichols is out of play, Aziru, it's your ball. If you lose touch with both of them, Gemayel, you're on your own recognizance. We'd like Diomedes back—at least, Caesar would—but not enough to lose the retrieval team we're sending out. Understand? Get your own butts clear, if it's not do-able, and I'll be satisfied."

Gemayel nodded stolidly: "As God wills."

"Not here, buddy," Nichols corrected. "Here, it's the Devil who's calling the shots."

Aziru was barely listening. He was watching Niccolo Machiavelli, and wondering why Welch was so carefully excluding Machiavelli from the foray, but not from its planning.

And Machiavelli, in turn, corrected Nichols, his eyes meeting Aziru's for the first time that day, "Not entirely the Devil, here where the Anunnaki dwell in the mountains."

Gooseflesh rose on Aziru's arms and he clasped them, one with each hand. Behind Machiavelli, Aziru could see the ghostly circles of Welch's magic, green maps which spun and spoke in arcane tongues to their master, maps which purported to show even where the lost Macedonian and his party were, far below the palace on the hill upslope from the com truck that was parked below Troy's side-set, ruined gate.

In this mobile citadel of New Dead magic, a man

no one trusted had just uttered the names of the Seven Judges of Hell, judges from a religion ancient even in Aziru's day, judges who had meted out justice to Gilgamesh, seven torches in their seven right hands.

Machiavelli's words spooked Aziru like nothing since the night Phlegethon, the moving river of fire, had tried to swallow him whole, spooked him so that all he wanted was to get out of this foul-smelling metal wagon, into the clean air where no shadows lurked under Paradise's ruddy light.

Spooked him so that Aziru paid no attention when Welch, dismissing the rest of them, asked Machiavelli to stay behind, saying, "Niccolo, I need you to help with this Menelaos person, as soon as Achilles brings him in."

Aziru was no longer concerned with the hostages held by rival factions, or even the rescue effort under way, but with the survival of his eternal soul.

The Anunnaki. The Seven Judges of Hell.

A meeting with them could rewrite a man's destiny, even here. If that man survived it.

Zaki was beginning to wonder if the Macedonian was going to die on him.

Here—wherever here was—among the caverns hewn from living rock, in the light from Zaki's halogen torch, the *basileus* wasn't looking like Great King of anything. He was waxy and pale, lighter than he ought to have been. He was, in short, looking like a man about to die.

Find Minos. Find the pillar. Alexander was a king, would be to the last, giving senseless orders. A snake-bit king who'd been through something else, something which had left him bruised and weak and which, probably because of the bump on his head, was dogging his steps and dragging his spirit down.

And yet, there was hope. Zaki, whose parents had survived the Holocaust and whose wiry little body had survived three shooting wars and numerous Mossad excursions into PLO tunnels and PLO strongholds, knew that there was always hope. He'd been a founding member of Unit 1001, whose sole purpose was to extinguish the lives of those who tried to extinguish the light of hope that was Israel.

Zaki never gave up hope. He never gave up. But half-carrying the Macedonian, his size but so heavy, as if Alexander's very flesh resisted assistance, he was running out of strength.

He'd walked the Macedonian in circles and then he'd walked him through tunnels, looking for the damned pillar of Alexander's fixation. Or for Minos. Minos was a myth. Minos was a Judge. Minos had a Minotaur. *Labyrinthos,* Alexander had said.

Well, it was no worse than the '73 War or the aftermath of the Munich Games. But it felt worse, because Zaki didn't believe in the objective: Minos.

He said, finally, because the sweat rolling off their bodies was making his hold on the Macedonian king nearly impossible to maintain, "Look, Alexander, I've got to take a break."

And he let the king slide from his shoulder, a simple matter of letting go the wrist he'd been holding, the arm crooked round his neck.

Alexander slipped bonelessly to the floor, and Zaki let his own legs fold, assuming a cross-legged seat, and for the first time in hours, shone the flashlight in a wide circle around them, instead of directly and steadily training it on their path.

Stalagmites. Stalactites. *Pick a pillar, any pillar, friend.* "How's it going, King?"

Remind the monarch of his responsibilities. Of his identity. Of being Alexander. And then of the goal; getting the fuck out of here, wherever here was.

Somewhere up there, Agamemnon raged. Above him was the army, the tanks, the com truck.

The com truck. Memory struck Zaki like a jolt, so that he slapped his forehead with the flat of his hand.

Alexander was trying to answer Zaki's first question in halting English: "It is . . . going. She was making me a god, again. Gods are anathema here, no? And yet the god is in the maze. We're going to dance with the Mino—What is it? Zaki, what is it?"

The eyes of Alexander, eyes that could pull heroics out of men too tired to raise their heads, loyalty out of German barbarians who had only the rudiments of language, and love out of armies who subsisted on hate, stopped roving the columned cave and fixed on Zaki. "Zaki, tell me what."

"Your . . . earring, Alexander." Theoretically, the com truck should have been able to fix on them via the earring, even if the density and composition of the rock between them and the surface precluded two-way communication. But for some reason, it hadn't beeped or even bleeped static.

It might have been forgotten, in all the confusion above, that Alexander still wore it. They had issued it to him for the first sortie into Troy, before the battle . . . before so much that had gone wrong.

"Can I see it?" Zaki held out his hand, and there were beads of perspiration glittering on his palm. He should have been cold down here, with half his clothing given to the monarch, but he wasn't. He was hot.

And in his other hand, the halogen torch was wavering. So he set it down in the cradle of his crossed legs and that caused the shadows it threw to dance crazily, as if the rock formations about them were moving.

Alexander's fingers were clumsy at his ear, but the king didn't argue, or ask for help.

Zaki waited patiently until Alexander held out the earring in his palm, then said, "With your permission, I'd like to take it apart," as he plucked it with as much reverence as some men would have had for a diamond from Alexander's palm.

"Whatever," Alexander said dreamily, his attention on the dancing shadows. "The pillar, you know, is the place for sacrifices. Sacrifices are what we are. I'm sorry. . . ."

"Never mind sorry." Zaki had his pocket tool out and was working away at the earring with the screwdriver meant for gunsights and gun screws. "If this works, we'll have a beacon—they'll be able to find us."

"Find us? We must find them," Alexander said in a voice suddenly stronger, one of those kingly voices that Zaki had heard altogether too much of on this journey through Hell.

And then, just when he'd gotten the earring's back open and was tapping delicately at its innards, the Macedonian sprang to his feet with more energy than Zaki would had thought he had, and went stumbling off toward the shadows that danced near the limits of the halogen-thrown light, murmuring, "Come then, mother, let's do it all again, to the glory of the gods," his steps weirdly cadenced, as if he were dancing with thin air.

*   *   *

Achilles was willing to listen to Machiavelli, which was why he consented to get Menelaos and bring him back to treat with Caesar and his pack of trained monkeys.

He'd never have done it for that bastard Caesar, except that Menelaos was part of the damned problem, and Helen was in Kleopatra's hands.

The Atreidês were a nasty bunch of suckers, and that hadn't changed. The Atreidês camp, downslope from the palace, was in about the same condition as the rest of the ruined town—better off than the citadel, than the palace per se, but not by much.

He'd come in the chopper and he wasn't about to leave it.

It gave him a certain satisfaction to be hovering three feet above the soil of Ilion, waiting for Menelaos to come to him.

Most of the Old Dead were limited in their ability to adapt. The chopper was scaring the piss out of the Atreidês camp followers, who'd withstood everything else thrown at them.

Of course, Achilles was hedging his bets: his bullhorn was blaring Miles Davis' *Sketches of Spain,* as Hellish a tape as Achilles had on hand, and he had all his lights on, though it was daylight.

Which made it impossible for the naked eye to get a really good look at what was throwing up all the dust and gravel and making the horrendous racket in the middle of what should have been the Achaeans' last stronghold.

Achilles lit the cigarette he'd filched from Welch and grinned as, squinting, their hands at their brows to shield their eyes, three Achaeans came haltingly forward, Menelaos in the forefront.

"Yo, Menelaos—that's far enough for the rest of them. You're coming with me, alone," said Achilles into his mike, the signal overriding the music so that his voice blared out at 120dB, a sound pressure level that made the three hesitantly-approaching Achaeans clap their hands to their ears, whereupon their unprotected eyes began to tear.

"Who speaks to me?" bawled Menelaos, son of Atreus, brother of Agamemnon, lord of Lakedaimon, first husband of Helen.

"It's Achilles, you asshole. Just like I said. You *do* remember me, I hope? Come on, let's go." The words, spoken into the mike, rolled out over the Achaean camp. Achilles found that he was enjoying himself immensely. Still, he should be careful. He reached for his M-16 and settled it on his knees. If he had to, he'd clear the Atreidês decks, here and now. As a matter of fact, he half hoped he'd have to. These men represented scores unsettled for centuries.

"Go? With you? Why? Where?" Menelaos yelled back, unmoving now, ten yards from the chopper, his robes whipping against his musculature in the rotors' wash.

"Where?" came Achilles' reply, resounding to the very walls of Troy. "To Caesar's camp, where your wife is. You do remember Helen, don't you? It's a matter of honor, if an Atreidês knows the meaning of the word. And it's about your brother, who's slipped his wrappings. We want you to talk him out of doing something the Atreidês will never live down, no matter how long Hell lasts."

Menelaos' squinting face worked. The tears streaming down it were from the unbearable light, Achilles was nearly certain. But looking at the cuckold, a man as handsome of face as any Greek could be, a man whose wavy black locks were shot with gray and whose high cheekbones were sharp and withered from worry and travail, Achilles felt a moment of pity—and of kinship. Helen had made fools of them both.

Helen had, in fact, made fools of them all: every manjack of these Achaeans, and the Trojans who opposed them, were fighting for a wanton slut whose shadow fell over the honor of men.

Left to her own devices, she'd probably neuter the lot of them and burn their phalluses to the glory of her woman's gods.

He hoped the stamp of Hell didn't lie on him as heavily as it did on this stopped, tired hero, a man who once was taller and finer than Achilles, but whom life and death had worn frail.

Hell was what you made it, he thought, throwing off the unaccustomed moment of regret as the Atreidês leaned first to one side, then the other, and his bodyguards drew back.

"I will come with you, Achilles, son of Thetis, lord of the Myrmidons, but you must guarantee my safe return on the honor of Peleus, your father."

"Sure thing. You bet," Achilles said into his hand-held mike, and touched the button that dimmed the chopper's hellish lights so that Menelaos could see what awaited him. "Come aboard."

Diomedes was tied to his horse, staring at the sea rising about them and the shadows the hollow ships threw as they merged with nightfall.

Hektor had prevailed over cooler heads, and decreed this punishment: Diomedes was to drown upon the back of his faithful steed, the two of them staked in deep water, where they would die once the tide was high.

An anchor had been thrown out, and the horse's halter roped to a pulley thereon, and the two of them had been led seaward while the tide was low.

Diomedes had protested, for the horse's sake. The bright-maned steed was guilty of nothing. But Hektor's heart was hard, and Diomedes remained upon the horse, his wrists tied fast around its mighty neck, his ankles around its barrel.

First the water had been lapping at his toes, now it was up to his knees and the horse under him was beginning to quiver and snort.

Soon the water would reach the steed's nostrils and it would begin screaming.

He wasn't sure he could bear that.

He kept trying to find a way to free them. Ropes might become loose, or might be pulled loose, in water. He hoped and strained against his bonds and the horse under him did too.

But the tide was implacable, rising, and the hollow ships beached behind him threw long and angry shadows, so that dark was coming over him.

Finally, he began gnawing at the rope with his teeth, hoping he could bite his way through it as the water began to lap about his thighs and the bright-maned steed he loved began to neigh in fear—that horse who, up until then, had trusted him to find a way to save them.

Welch, alone in the com truck, was busier than a one-armed paperhanger.

And about as ineffective, trying to monitor everything: Achilles in the chopper with Menelaos, headed home; Nichols and his operations team of Gemayel and Co., sneaking around the Trojan coast in two Zodiacs; the weird SOS's that kept coming from what must be the Roman contingent, somewhere below ground in the Trojan palace; and, for good measure, a telltale on a sideband that he'd assigned to Alexander days ago, during the first assault on Troy.

It ought not to be there, but it was. And *where* it was—*that* was bothering Welch so much that he'd sent for Caesar.

He had no idea whether His Majesty would come in person, or send a representative, but Welch wasn't about to leave his post, or send a message, when what he had here was so sensitive.

He'd told the guard outside not, under any circumstances, to let Machiavelli in here, on pain of death to be inflicted by Welch, personally, a threat that might have had more clout with one of the New Dead, but which had been backed up by the look in Welch's eyes.

By the time a knock came on the metal sliding door, Welch was nearly past caring whether Caesar deigned to visit him, or not. He was in the middle of oversight of Gemayel and Aziru's boats, taking terse reports from Nichols, and generally having his idea of a real hard time.

It figured that Caesar would pick the worst possible moment to make an appearance.

When the Roman came in, wearing rumpled fatigues under one of his regulation red cloaks, Welch said without preamble: "Looks like the Macedonian is about two hundred feet below what we thought was the lowest excavated level of the palace, sir." He punched up a computer display and waved a hand at it, leaning back in his ergo chair, wondering whether those ancient eyes could make any sense of a computer-enhanced topographic display.

Caesar's reply, "Is he alive?" was inscrutable.

"If you mean moving, yes sir. If he's trapped, he's not physically impeded—not under a rockfall or immobilized. But there's no way I can find that he could get down there. I've been bombarding the area with—" Welch stopped. The intricacies of computer mapping by infrared and other waveforms wouldn't interest Caesar. You had to treat these Old Dead like very dangerous children. "—rays, invisible tracers that bounce off walls and tell me where there are large, empty spaces. And I can't find a way up to the surface from where he is."

"And the extent of these . . . passages?" Caesar tossed his head and fixed his intense gaze on Welch.

The com tech shrugged and tapped a button. Something like a maze replaced the more complicated diagram on his terminal screen. "Read 'em and weep . . . sir. Here's where he's been since I started tracking the signal." Tap. A red dotted line appeared in the left mid-section of the maze.

Caesar nodded as if it all made perfect sense. "The labyrinth. Of course, I should have known. Thank you, Welch. If you need me again, don't hesitate to call."

And Caesar turned on his heel in a whirl of red cloak and was gone before Welch could object.

" 'The labyrinth, of course,' " the American repeated savagely, tilting back his chair and slumping in it, chin propped on a fist. "*He* 'should have known.' Well, fucking good for him."

Not a word about getting those trapped men out, not the ones on "B level," as Welch had designated the place from which the primitive SOS kept coming, or the one or ones on C level, from which Alexander's earring-mounted telltale kept bleating like a lost lamb.

When Nichols got back, the two of them were going to have a heart-to-heart about ways of cutting this mission short.

These Old Dead, especially Julius Caesar, were getting on Welch's nerves.

Nichols was in the water, by himself, wishing he could swim his way back to the real world. If he'd had SEAL-issue gear, maybe the large, unidentified fish which brushed his legs occasionally as he swam wouldn't bother him. But he didn't and they did.

He didn't want to be a MacSnack for a MacShark. He just wanted to get his target and get out.

He had a com-link with the two Zodiacs, and the crazy Old Dead, Aziru, kept asking him dumb questions.

At least Gemayel was there to give answers from the other boat.

All the two Zodiacs full of Maronites were supposed to do was back him up, if he was showered with arrows. At least, he hoped to hell it would just be arrows. Welch swore up and down that no scan he'd taken had showed any heavy metal weapons—nothing more serious than a javelin.

But a javelin could kill you.

The Undertaker's table wasn't Nichols' idea of R&R.

But he wasn't averse to a little action, if it came his

way. Killing a few of these crazy antiques in good old
hand-to-hand might work some of the tension out of
him. He had an auto-pistol in a waterproof bag, a
combat knife, and a belt full of naughty little grenades which tended to maim, rather than kill, and
thus put three men out of play for every one you
fragged—wounded had to be carried.

But best intelligence (Welch's plus what Gemayel
was getting with his night-binoculars) said that
Diomedes, the target, was staked out in the water,
between two of the long black boats that the ancients
called "ships."

Most of the ships were beached at low tide, so
they'd be floating at anchor now.

Gemayel and Aziru had the diversion worked up,
if he called for it. Otherwise, the fun wasn't going to
start until after he'd gotten the hostage clear.

Night-sight goggles weren't really meant for un-
derwater. He kept worrying that they'd short, and
kept refusing to duck his head down to ID the big
fish. With luck, they were dolphins, or else they just
weren't hungry.

He kept swimming toward the green blotch that
was something living, something half out of the very
florescent-looking waves that kept breaking against
it.

He wished it was man-shaped, but it wasn't. He
wished it was moving, but it wasn't doing that either.

What the Trojans had done wasn't clear to him
until he came right up on it.

Then he saw the horse's wide-eyed head, its neck
straining, its nostrils thrust up out of the water, and
the bulk on its back that might, or might not, still be
alive.

"Shit," he muttered. These bastards weren't any-where near civilized.

But what did he expect? This was Hell, after all.

He swam faster, saying into the com unit on his shoulder. "Diomedes is tied to his horse and they're both out here. The horse, anyhow, is still alive. Over."

Aziru's voice beat Gemayel's back to him: "What-ever happens, you must save the horse if it lives. He would want—"

"Fuck you, buddy. If it's me or a horse, guess who wins?"

"Nichols," Gemayel's voice cut in, sounding like "Ichols" because the damned com units clipped like crazy, "we want the body, in any case. If the horse is alive, take its head and it will swim with you."

"Thanks, both of you. Now shut up before some-body aboard that boats trips to the noise."

And the boats were close, here. Close and black and big enough, now that Nichols was in the water below them, to rate the designation "ships."

He was just dog-paddling in between them when the horse noticed him and sent up a belly-shaking scream of terror and relief that made Nichols start.

He could hear movement above, on board the ships: men coming to see how the horse was doing. Men with torches came toward the stern of the closer boats.

"Awright, boys," Nichols whispered, paddling with his feet while with one hand he unclipped the first grenade from his belt, "time for that diversion you promised me."

Then he lobbed the first grenade, dove toward the sea bottom, and held his ears against the concussion that would surely follow.

It did, and he stayed under, watching the horse's legs churn closer and closer as he swam abreast through murky water, and judging as best he could what Diomedes' chances of still being alive might be.

Then he was close enough to get out his combat knife and slit the ropes binding the man's wrists to the horse's neck, and to sever the thicker rope binding the horse's halter to the anchor.

Without a pause, as his vision grew red-grained from oxygen starvation, he swam away from the concussions of ships taking hits on either side, his hand tight on the horse's halter-rope.

When he had to come up for air, the horse neighed at him, rolling its eyes, but the man still clutching its neck didn't move.

But Diomedes *was* clutching the horse's neck, his hands wound in its sodden mane.

Nichols took a chance and stopped trying to drag the horse away from the ships, now in flames and rocked occasionally with explosions as whatever flammables were on board—alcohol in sealed jars, grain in rhytons, oils—burst their containers, and men screamed and sought an enemy they couldn't seem to find in the fire-licked dark.

The horse had the idea now—it didn't want to be any closer to the fire than Nichols did; it didn't want anything to do with the occasional sailor who threw himself, aflame, into the water, either.

It swam steadily and he swam beside, touching the man still roped to its barrel, considering trying to give him artificial respiration or even a Heimlich manuever to clear the salt water out of him, talking softly: "Hey, Diomedes. Hey, man, come on, wake up. It's me, Nichols. You're safe, sort of. But you've got to wake up, man. We've got a boat out there. It'll take you, but probably not this horse. Hear me? You're going to lose your horsie if you don't start talking to me. I'm going to cut you loose and drag your ass—"

The man on the horse turned his head and opened swollen eyes a crack. Bruised lips formed words, but Nichols couldn't hear them. "Good man," he called, swimming toward the Zodiacs, pulling as strongly as he could on the horse's tether. "Good man."

And then, into his com unit. "Okay, Aziru, come get your buddy—and his horse. Over."

From the transceiver on his shoulder came only silence, until he called Aziru's name again, and Gemayel's voice reached him instead: "I'll be right there, Nichols. I thought Aziru would be with you by now."

"Well, he's not," said Nichols, trying to hold onto the horse and the semi-conscious man and still swim, trying to guide them away from the spreading, flaming slicks fanning out from the hollow ships as they went down. "I thought he was with you. Over."

But it wasn't over. Not by a long shot.

Maccabee was beginning to wonder if he was going to be able to hold them—his twelve Roman legionaries, his two Germans, and the exhausted remnants of the Macedonian cavalry they'd picked up somewhere along the way.

The way: They were lost in a maze and the maze kept growing—or seemed to: each time they marched through it, never strung farther than arm's length from one another, it took more turns to return to the centerpoint, the pillared room with its ten—then twelve, then fourteen, now sixteen—offset corridors.

And the man who was signalling, the single legionary still patient at his task, was the only touchstone they had with any certain reality, the only one who'd been in the room with the pillars and the mosaics the whole time, the only one who served as a point of continuity.

This time, when they returned, there was food about—lion-headed rhytons of wine and fresh fruit that couldn't be poisoned (his stomach said), and a glazed look in the legionary's eyes, even though he swore he'd eaten nothing.

"Heard sounds, sir. More groaning. And tapping," the legionary reported, while out of the corner of one eye, Maccabee watched the giant Germans, Perfidy and Murder, sidle close to the laden, legged tables of Agamemnon's hospitality.

"And the king—Agamemnon? Any sign of him?"

"Nah. Nothin'. Nobody," said the legionary without halting in his tapping.

"Then," Maccabee said as gently as he could, "how did all this food get here?"

The man looked up for an instant, puzzled. There was sweat on his swarthy brow and his pupils were pinned. "I—don't know, sir," said the man in a troubled voice.

"Never mind. It doesn't matter. Keep signalling. They'll dig us out." *If they can find us. If they can hear us. If we're anywhere that's contiguous to where they are. Basileus! Alexander, why hast thou forsaken me? It was the dying, must be the dying—I am tainted, still wearing the shroud of recent death. Alexander barely spoke a word to me; my touch has become the touch of death to my friend. And Alexander could not wait to shun me, to abandon me.*

Deep from the earth, down a passage Maccabee reckoned as due north, came the sound again, the scraping, groaning sound as if a giant waked, and stretched, and rolled.

Then it subsided, as if the giant had gone to sleep again.

The Germans said something to each other, Perfidy frozen with an apple halfway to his mouth, staring off in the direction of the sound.

Maccabee found himself striding up to them without deliberation. He knocked the apple from Perfidy's hand.

The huge blond hulk seemed barely to notice. His pale gaze was riveted on the shadowed distance, on the corridor behind the throne—a corridor Maccabee didn't think had been there before.

They should stay here, he knew. Wait for the inevitable rescue party. It was simple common sense. But there was nothing common or simple about matters here, below the Achaean palace floor, and nothing sensible.

Maccabee didn't want to die again. Suddenly the underground throne room became unbearably oppressive, the walls seeming to close in on him, the mosaics of bull leapers and dolphins beginning to quiver as if they might come to life.

"Let's go," he said in Greek, decided. "*Agite,*" he added, for the Germans' benefit, motioning toward the passage behind the throne.

If it was a maze, still, they'd come back here eventually. If it wasn't, he needed to know that too.

. . . Somewhere down one of those corridors, Zaki and Alexander had disappeared.

And Alexander, not the Roman army or the moderns who served it, was where Maccabee's first loyalty lay. A way out of Hell, by force of arms. No one had ever said it was going to be easy.

"Let's go," he repeated. "Macedonians, take the point. We'll find Alexander, or he'll find us—somewhere down there."

The Macedonians hustled to obey, but the Germans were quicker.

Perfidy's head had turned at the sound of the *basileus'* name. Now he unsheathed his sword in one fluid motion, calling, "Tyr! Tyr?" in a voice that made the red-painted timbers tremble, and he and Murder fairly ran into the tunnel, shouldering the Macedonian troops aside as if they were stripling boys.

Maccabee followed, behind the Macedonians but before the Romans, whose loyalty to him was tenuous at best. He didn't care even if they mutinied.

He sympathized with the Germans, running off their panic and their helplessness, running away from frustration as much as toward Alexander.

In a way, the two were much the same.

A goal, any goal, would do in a moment like this.

Even as the shadows enveloped him and a sharp turn cut off the central throneroom's light, Maccabee was reaffirming his faith, restating his litany, regaining his strength:

Faith was the key. Survival was the method. Life was the prize. Even in this hellish maze, a man must do what he could.

Achilles brought the chopper in over the Roman

camp in a wide circle that showed him Caesar's preparations for withstanding Trojan retaliation:

Four tanks were locked on the Trojan campsite, their deadly snouts questing back and forth in predetermined targeting arcs.

Decius Mus' jeep careened down a line of infantry reinforcing revetments—sandbags and trenches in a neat semicircle to hold the Trojans behind the line.

To the rear of the Trojan camp, ships were still burning bright.

He was tempted to sweep low, do a little extra recon, scare the piss out of Menelaos, who was blanched and drawn beside him and who'd already filled up the single airsickness bag Achilles had been able to find.

"Hold on, Hero, it's going to get a little rough," Achilles warned his passenger, the temptation of snapping a roll of surveillance film too strong for caution to override.

And as Menelaos' mouth opened and an involuntary *Aaiiieee!* came from deep in the Atreidês' throat, Achilles dived toward the shore camp, lights doused, his autopilot set to determine the audacity of his swoop.

Buzzing the Trojan camp was exhilarating, and Achilles whooped with joy, his fingers inching toward his chain-gun: nobody had told him *not* to strafe the enemy.

So absorbed was Achilles with his internal decision-making that he didn't realize that the autopilot had red lights shining on its face and was beeping quietly but insistently until the ground swooped up to meet him in a terrible rush and all fucking hell broke loose below:

Arrows, flying from crossbows. Javelins, cast at too-close range. A cracked windshield. Sand everywhere.

In the whine of overheated engines just before blackness descended, Achilles had time only to curse the malfunctioning autopilot as everything went completely and irretrievably wrong.

Nichols, wrapped in an army blanket, brought Diomedes to Caesar himself and then left, saying only, "Here's your man. Got his horse, too. Lost Aziru and five Maronites doing it. Hope it was worth it."

Diomedes blinked rapidly as he looked around the tent of the Roman commander, at the fine woolens and the soft bed on which Kleopatra lay, propped on one arm, in little more than a veil.

"Sit down, Diomedes," Caesar said quietly, and did so as an example.

The Roman chairs were strange, backless and curved.

Diomedes sat on the rug instead, pulling his own blanket tight, noticing for the first time the other man, deep in the shadows of the long tent: Antonius, with a look of dark wrath on his face.

"Tell us how you were treated by the Trojans," said Caesar in a voice too full of iron to be conversational.

The tale was told by his bruises and his weakness, Diomedes knew. He didn't want to be the cause of bloodshed—or the excuse for it. He said, "Hektor is impulsive, you know that from Homer's song. And Priam is old, his wisdom weary and not always heeded in the camp." He shrugged. There were black wings everywhere tonight. He knew now that none of the others saw them, or heard their terrible beat. But he did. They were the wings of war, the dark spirits that visited the battlefield. They were Achilles and his black bird of prey. They were Fate's wings.

And none of these Romans had seen men turned to birds in Italy, black wings flapping up into the horrid Italian sky.

These Italians were the mechanism of Hell, he knew—of greater wars than men should fight, of intolerance and carnage beyond measure. Maccabee had told him of the Romans' deeds. He saw their legacy in the lines of Caesar's face. He finished his report to Caesar with: "Don't use me as an excuse for what you'll do in any case. The Trojans on that beach are more my kin than you—or than yours."

"Even after what they tried to do to you?" purred the Egyptian slut from her velvet bed. "Even after what they tried to do to the horse Caesar gave you? To a poor dumb animal?"

"Animal, but not dumb. Not as dumb as the German guards, who know only slaughter and less words than any horse. And yes, even after what they did to me. You can't barge in and change the outcome of this, from your 'superior' vantage of hindsight's wisdom. You'll only make things worse. Let the little men fight their little wars. Don't read your glory-thirst and your mythic misunderstandings into this. There's a rhythm here that you disturb by your very presence. This ground is strong and willful. The gods of the hills and the gods of the sea will not take lightly to interference. Already, Aziru is gone, a sacrifice to your hubris. More will—"

The tentflap rustled. A Roman spoke Latin too formal for Diomedes' ears to decipher.

Caesar fired three words back and Niccolo Machiavelli entered.

Diomedes, exhausted from the effort of speech, turned to look: you didn't offer Machiavelli your unprotected back, even when he couldn't strike at it: you didn't give the man ideas.

The frail-faced Italian started to rattle in his native tongue.

Caesar interrupted: "In Greek. We have a guest."

"Then, Cesare, the news is this: Achilles in his helicopter, with Menelaos aboard, crashed into the no-man's-land between our defenses and the Trojan camp."

"Survivors?" Caesar demanded, as Kleopatra rose up in her near nakedness and, unconcerned, came to take Caesar's arm.

Diomedes averted his eyes, fastening them on Machiavelli's ferretlike face.

The face said: "It's too soon to tell. Welch says he gave Achilles specific instructions to come directly back. . . ."

"The fault, dear Nikko," said the Egyptian harlot with the painted breasts, "is not in question." Her voice was full of condemnation. "I'm sure Caesar wants only their safe return—Achilles, Menelaos *and* the helicopter."

The Roman looked at the woman beside him and shook his head minutely. Her lower lip blossomed petulantly, but she dropped her eyes.

Caesar said, "Niccolo, oversee a rescue party yourself. Take Antonius with you."

The young Roman at the back of the tent groaned theatrically, but came forward. "Lucky me, lucky me."

Hands up, he circled around his commander, blew a kiss toward the woman, and came abreast of Machiavelli: "Well, Niccolo, looks like you're going to get your hands dirty, after all. Let's go."

And they were gone, leaving only the three of them together in the Roman tent.

Caesar, back in his chair, looked broodingly at his booted feet. The woman sat beside him, as might a noble wife or a brother lord.

And Diomedes sat before them, crosslegged on the floor in his blanket, for far too long a time in silence.

At last he said, "I have a half-drowned horse to see to, Julius Caesar." He rose up.

"We'd like to talk to you further, Diomedes. About the Achaean stronghold. Did you know we've lost Alexander there, somewhere beneath the cellar floor?"

The woman tittered, a harsh laugh full of taunt: "Let's see, that makes it"—she raised spread hands and began counting off casualties on her fingers— "Achilles, in what better be the DMZ; Maccabee; two Germans; twelve of the legionaries; assorted Macedonian cavalrymen; Zaki; and of course, Alexander himself. Tell me, Diomedes, do you think Helen and Paris are worth the lot? Could you negotiate a trade?"

"A trade? With whom, Agamemnon? Priam? The both?" Diomedes shivered, in the silence that was his answer. The woman hadn't even bothered to count Aziru, lost at sea. "Better treat with the gods of the underworld, if you can find them. Or the Devil himself." Diomedes wanted only to get out of there, where the smell of woman and soldier was too strong, into the clean air, where his horse needed tending.

"Are you refusing," asked Caesar with studied in-
credulity, "to negotiate for the release of your fellow
hostages?"

"No. I didn't say that. I said, you can't control this,
only make it worse with your meddling. But I will do
what honor demands."

"Fine," said Kleopatra brightly, hopping up to
take him by the arm, "then let me take you to *our*
hostages."

Caesar called, as Kleopatra led him out, "Come
back when you've a plan—the wise counsel we've
heard so much about. We can use some."

He'd given them that. They hadn't listened. Now
they wanted foolishness equal to their own.

And the Egyptian wench who had him by the
arm wanted something else—something he wasn't
sure he understood.

But what she didn't understand was how volatile a
confrontation involving him, Paris, and Helen was
bound to be.

The sea had opened up and swallowed Aziru whole.

In the dark, a whirlpool had sucked his Zodiac
down, and around, and down some more.

And now it floated, rocking softly, in an underground river, or lake—neither he nor his Maronites
were certain which. They'd lost most of their gear in
the maelstrom; they'd been lucky they hadn't lost a
man.

Now, their flashlights burning, they paddled for a
distant shore.

And on that shore, lights blazed—seven torches in
the distance, a beacon.

An invitation to judgment, Aziru knew.

The Maronites around him, good Christians, didn't understand. He told them, "Wait here," when they reached the bank and went forward on his own.

The torches were back from the shore, up an incline of rock worn into steps by thousands of feet. He climbed it, feeling both exhilarated and afraid.

He was Aziru, prince, then king of Amurru. He was being summoned to judgment by the Anunnaki, the Seven Judges of Hell with their seven torches in their seven right hands. He was being granted an audience with the gods of the Underworld.

He was as much in awe as in fear as he gained the top step.

Before he proceeded, he looked back at the Maronites in their black Zodiac, bobbing by the rocky shore.

Then there was only what lay ahead, and Aziru faced the mystery squarely.

Before him were the seven Anunnaki, their faces terrible like the faces of gods, their sinews great like the sinews of gods, and their eyes blazing like the eyes of gods.

And they stood around a pillar, a pillar huge and wide, a pillar in which was a cavern and, from that cavern, a light glittered and a smell issued like that of a great bull in rut.

And also, before the Anunnaki, two men knelt, one supporting himself on stiff arms and the other with an arm about the first.

These were small men, puny mortals, tired and frayed and kneeling in the presence of the gods, directly before the cavern in the pillar from which stench, and now smoke, issued forth.

This smoke was smoke twice as pungent as the

smoke from the Anunnaki's torches, smoke that made Aziru's eyes tear and his nose close up.

In the smoke and before the Anunnaki, Aziru knew that he, too, must go on his knees and lower his eyes before the gods of the Underworld.

And when he did that, he looked to his right and saw that the two men beside him were none other than Zaki, the little Jew, and Alexander the Great.

And they were weeping before the Anunnaki, the Seven Judges of Hell.

"I *told* you," Nichols was saying to Welch, the two of them alone in the com truck, "that these guys were the *wrong* stuff for this sort of mission—don't blame losing that Philistine and his commandos on me."

"Amurrite," Welch corrected absently. "Look, Nichols, as long as you're all right, I really don't give a flying fuck about the others, okay? Now, *are* you all right?"

"Yeah, yeah, I guess." Nichols flopped down in his chair and slid it along its tracks, back and forth, back and forth.

Welch knew his operative—there was too much pent up energy in Nichols for his words to be the whole truth. "Come on, what's bothering you, Nichols?"

"This . . . the whole thing. Why don't we just dig those guys out of there, or nuke the palace and everybody in, and under, it back to the stone age? Or to the Undertaker's table, whichever comes first?"

"Against the rules, you know that," Welch said. Not that they didn't have a SADEM—Special Atomic Demolition Emergency Munition—with them: every unit like Welch's had one, fifty-three pounds, back-pack-portable, nice and neat and your mission was reduced to after-action reports.

But the guys below, way below, where they shouldn't have been, where no nuke would touch them, precluded a blow-off, even if Welch had been willing to admit that things were beyond salvage, which he wasn't.

"Nuking 'em? Yeah, I guess. But not digging 'em out. Want me to go steer those infantry onto the right track?"

"Yeah, okay."

The ranger started to leave. "And," Welch said, "Nichols—nice job. Sorry I didn't listen to you, but that's my fault."

"Yessir, it is," said Nichols, leaving Welch alone with his screens and terminals, artifacts of the complexity of this fuck-up.

He was beginning to wonder if the Devil really wanted to win this one, or if He could.

She was all she'd ever been, was Helen.

No less, no more, and the sight of her set Diomedes' head reeling, set him back thousands of years as nothing had done since he'd come out of that tunnel and seen the citadel on the beach for the first time.

His initial instinct was to kill Paris, there and then, take the woman and run.

It was crazy, but it was in his blood—in their blood, all of them.

She was an evil spirit, an impulsion to madness. Black wings beat round her like a velvet cloak.

He just stood there, his mouth open, while pretty Paris fondled her and said, "Diomedes, isn't it? I, ah

. . . I hope you don't hold Hektor's rashness against us. We need some"—Paris's eyes flashed to Kleopatra, to her guards behind, to the shabby tent among the baggage train where they were imprisoned—"assistance, someone who understands that *we* came here in good faith, that making us hostages only worsens—"

"Everything. I know." It was difficult not to be angry, not to take the handsome head in his hands and squash Paris like a ripe melon. But he refrained, not for Helen's sake—she deserved no courtesy—but for his own.

He thought dreamily, as he sat down with them and Kleopatra left him there to "do as you will to aid us, Argive, in a canny resolution to our dilemma," that he'd find a way out of this, for all of them.

And yet, looking at Helen's face, he couldn't think of a single ploy that would allow him to keep looking at her wide eyes and her inviting lips eternally.

That was the trouble with negotiating over Helen: no one who had her would willingly give her up. If she stayed here much longer, that sickness she put in men's minds would sweep the Roman camp and no one would listen to even the wisest of counsel.

Countermoves

It was as close as they dared take the jeep, the crumbling rim of the unstable land where burning Phlegethon plunged to meet the placid waters of Lethe. Beyond this was a land of hellfire, reeking of naptha and sulphur; below this were the holes down which (Scaevola suspected) his commander had gone; and Scaevola fretted back and forth between the reports of his scouts and the sputter which was all their single Litton and the patched-together com equipment they had in their truck could pick up.

No contact. They had met nothing alive out here, not even the halfliving, the liches, nothing of threat. And Scaevola, receiving yet more reports of no contact, here by Lethe's shore, gazed out over that flow where the river began to steam, and thought desperate thoughts.

"*Tertulle,*" he said to his driver, "it was near here. It was one of these places that must have brought them below. *A hole* they wanted; it was a hole they followed. I see no other choice. We're going to have to try it."

"*Vae,*" Tertullus murmured. "The Pit."

"A hole and a way down," Scaevola said. "You can tell the others. They can do what they like. The Undertaker sent me back once. Maybe he'll oblige me again. Or he won't. In any case, I'll take the field phone, I think it's worth the risk—" It was a matter

of style. Caesar was a master at it. Scaevola felt a
little diffident, more than self-conscious. The epi-
gram was the thing, the *dictum*, a bit of laconic
poesy at important moments. Roman armies were
notorious for sitting down on their rumps till they
saw the whys and whereofs of an action—even the
Tenth. Especially the Tenth. Leading it needed more
style than he felt he had. He had muffed it with old
Porsena—just froze up, no good word, just a gesture
of defiance: stuck his hand in the Etruscan's fire and
held it there, tongue-tied like a fool. So much for
epigrams.

"Might as well ride," his driver said, the same
game. Tertullus was always better at it.

Scaevola looked at him, appreciating the matter.
He had no doubt the legionaries could be talked into
hiking out there behind him—if he had the gift. It
was a matter of first explaining to the troops they had
a choice to make, which reverse logic he was not
good at: the mere prospect of speech-making filled
him with terror, and talking to the troops had to be
his job until it became—temporarily or permanently—
Tertullus'. "No," he said to Tertullus, "Not both of
us. I'll have the the phone. One of us two has got to
stay with the truck and keep ends together, right?
That's got to be your job."

"Dammit—"

"Hey. Name of the game, friend." He got out,
shrugged into his lightweight pack, took the Litton;
and a Galil, which he favored—the folding stock and
the reliability were a boon to a one-handed rifleman.
It was all familiar gear. He gave Tertullus' long face a
glance, hitched this and that strap to more comfortable spots. "Tell the guys—hell, I expect you'll want

a few, the rest, well—" So. He meandered off into uncomfortable silence. Tongue-tied again. He was better when he had the Old Man up front, that was all. Never short of words then. Just when it was on his shoulders. He felt his face hot, raw humiliation.

"You be careful out there," Tertullus said. "You know what it took to liberate that phone."

"You got it." He gave the Empire Roman a nod, the straps on his right shoulder another hitch, and started off, a long, lonely hike across increasingly unhealthy grass, toward that moonscape-desolation Phlegethon created.

Where's the lieutenant going? someone would ask next as Tertullus pulled the jeep up by the column.

On a hike, Tertullus would dutifully say, with all appropriate understatement.

And after a little to-doing and shouting, legionaries with the two centurions, the centurions with Tertullus, and most of them together, the men would swear him to Dis and follow within about fifteen minutes. It was just plain politics. An art. They were free citizens, even in Hell, and liked their *exempla*, their Public Moments, everyman's as well as the lieutenant's, that was all. Well a man understood that, who thought he commanded the legions.

A gout of fire came off Phlegethon, a wave of heat even at this range, blinding bright. A man acquired a sense of his own real size in this landscape, minute black dot toiling along in the face of a spew that dwarfed Tiber and all its ships. Scaevola hated fire. He saw it in his dreams. He discovered a particularly wicked poesy in the things his fate asked of him, which he thought might compose a tolerably good *dictum* if he were poetical, which, alas! he was not.

That river before him inspired only a case of *déja vu*, a ghostly pain in his missing hand, and a patient, gnawing terror.

Sors, his language called it. *Moira*, the Greeks said. The Americans invoked Murphy and his brother-god Finagle, and called it rotten luck.

Well, the hero-ing business took damn little courage once a man was launched; it was that first step that was the real killer; and after that, honest witnesses would keep him on the track, of whom he looked to have a hundred twenty-odd in short order, each one having launched himself. He only felt sorry for Tertullus, on whom he had settled the anchor job and, so far as Tertullus' own image, the worst end of it: but it was true, *someone* had to keep in touch on the surface or it was all for nothing; and it had to be someone who could handle things.

The job, it had to be remembered, was to get Julius help. And if the tunnels proved no good, there was one more way, Scaevola reckoned, the way he had gone down to Agamemnon's palace the first time, which he would take if he had to. *Sors* again. He could not just give up if he failed to find a useable hole, not after he had started away In Public like this: he could not be glib to excuse himself from a course the way Marcus Antonius could laugh a thing away, and somehow make the troops forgive him; he was not Antonius, not even Tertullus, so he just kept at a thing the best way he knew, and if men seemed apt to stay with him right into Phlegethon's plasma fires, well, at that point he would call them fools, tell them Julius needed them on the surface, and send them back from the brink. After which time they became Tertullus' business and he was his own.

The hellfire burned, thank the gods and the Divine Twins Murphy and Finagle—much hotter and quicker than Porsena's.

Stink of metal and insulation, stink of vomit and a spatter of blood onto the dead machinery in front of him—Achilles came to, hanging in the belts, lifted a half-limp arm and wiped at the drip of his nose. That was the blood, all right. He was *hurt*, damn dumb legends to the contrary. He bled, his head hurt, his spinal column felt as if it had been set down and all the vertebrae bounced into place, his left arm was numb, and his ribs and gut ached as if a horse had kicked him, that was the way he felt. Poison was what he had died of, poison of infection or the damn Trojan had smeared something lethal on his arrowheads—damn backshooting Trojan princeling had hamstrung him with a lucky shot and it had hardly mattered; he had not wanted to live when he knew the terms.

He was not sure what the terms were at the moment either. His legs would not move. But he got the belts released, and slipped sideways, which freed his legs and hurt like hell. Menelaos' damn airsickness bag had hit and spattered forward, misting the windshield from inside. Had to be that. It was impossible the man had had anything more in his gut.

"Shit," he breathed, bubbled, spat, and got upright enough to get a look out the fractured, spattered windshield. At smoke on the sea-rimmed horizon, at a veil of dust a damn sight nearer, a line that was coming inexorably toward them, while the chopper's guns were, by the fact that the chopper

had cracked itself up good and proper, useless.
"Oh, *shit!*"

The corridors turned and turned again and still the
Germans kept ahead of them. Maccabee ran, the
echo of the Germans' voice preceding them down
corridors and stairwells. "Tyr!" they cried, the name
that they called Alexander. The Macedonians understood well enough, and ran as best they could, string-
ing it out in front of him; and behind him the
Romans—he heard them following: he did not look
back to see. He thought of traps, and dodged around
a red-plastered column and down a stairwell in the
wake of the rest with his heart pounding and the dire
feeling that this all was preface to disaster of more
than physical kind. Death he had endured. There
were assuredly worse things in Hell. There was the
chance of losing Alexander in some irrevocable way.
There was the chance of failing him in some unfor-
givable way, of proving valid the furtive doubt he
had seen in the *basileus'* eyes—doubt the more terrible because it *was* furtive, was something that Alexander would not confront him with, not name, not
put words or shape to, a strange new geography like
the one which enveloped them and turned them this
way and that, multiplying possibilites each time
through the maze.

He redoubled his speed, gasping, shouldered past
the Macedonians, one and another. There was light
where they ran, the flare of torches and lamps, the
giant forms of blond-braided Perfidy and Murder
elusive before him as they rounded another corner,
their hulking shadows flaring and leaping in overlay
across the shapes of dolphins, down a stairway down

which the painted shape of a bull leaped, its horns aimed at the heart of the mystery.

The Germans plunged into shadow and into light again, into a throne room—

It was the same room. All exits were gone save two.

The legionary stood bewildered in the midst of it, with the Germans. With two bloodsoaked bodies, with gore spattered and puddled on the pale flooring, running down the frescoed walls, the steps and the throne itself.

"What am I to do?" Diomedes asked of Helen in the daylit tent—not of the Trojan prince, who stood glowering a few feet away—and looked into those remarkable eyes with a sense of desperation. He asked as a Calydonian, one of the River-born who, like Achilles, revered the Old Ways like—so few of Agamemnon's breed. *She* was River-born and Inachid. She was the nexus, the pin on which it all turned, hers and Klytemnaistra's the lineage which wove together all of Hellas—every royal line of all the River-born was mixed in her and Klytemnaistra, every single feud-ridden heritage.

O gods and great goddess, how they had hoped, the River-born princes, when they had come to win the heiresses of Sparta—after all the grief and calamity of Jason's years and the double tragedy of Thebes, after all the war and the betrayals, men heard the priestesshood of Sparta had passed from Queen Leda, to her daughters born one of the god and the other of a king remarkable only for his quietness. King Tyndareos was passing by the old Law, with the fading of Leda his queen; Leda the priestess had

named her successor; and of a sudden men were
reckoning the kinships and the lineages and seeing
the remarkable truth—the swan-queen's claim was
true and Fate laughed: the civil war was won, resolved, linked and bound and delivered, Leda's clever
victory over all the kings and the warriors and the
shattered towns. No warrior would unite the River-
born, but two priestess-queens: the swan-daughter,
the god-born, golden youngest to reign in Sparta as
the center of all Hellas, her dark sister Klytemnaistra
to reign allied to her in whatever citadel she chose.

Oh, they had hoped, each of them who had come
to contest—all the proud River-born princes; and the
damned interlopers, the Atreidês Agamemnon and
Menelaos, to whom no one had spoken. But then, so
few of the River-born had been speaking to each
other; gods, the joke of it, so many bloodfeuds, so
much war walking about on men's feet, courteous
and soft-spoken, and so, so careful of each others'
honor. Had it been the Atreidês who had urged
them take that fatal oath—binding all of them to
defend the priestesses' choice of husbands; and to
swear it with blood and great oaths, and upon the
peril of their souls, in those days before Helen chose?
Diomedes could not remember.

He had betaken himself and his wise counsel into
the shrine at Sparta in his own turn, had seen within
Klytemnaistra's eyes a thing he had seen only over
the shield's edge or a blade's bright point; and the
cold had run down his back. He had walked further
to the very *naos* of this temple by the Eurotas,
where the white-clad woman waited in the lamplight—
  —and o gods, the power in her and the power of
her. It blazed through her like light, it whispered

through the tread of her bare feet on the stones, it
shone in her beauty and the gentle sweetness of her
smile: it was Woman, was Promise, and all the things
which men court other than gold and fear, the true
deep power of heart and gentleness that a man knows
must exist, as he knows the gods must exist and that
justice must, and love, though he finds it nowhere.

Then she met his eyes, and that gentleness was
there, but—

—but, but, and but—

His own wise counsel had met that stare with
shock, as if he had discovered a crack in a holy
image, a flaw in pure Parian stone. It was not wisdom that he saw there. Not a goddess, not even a
woman. It was a young girl who looked back at him,
not wise, nor experienced, nor even deep of thought.
The flaw was there, was terrifying coupled with such
power and such god-presence.

We are doomed, he had thought then, of the princes
gathered outside, the kings-to-be of all Hellas.

And he had stood as Klytemnaistra came and whispered in her goddess-sister's ear, with furtive glances
of her long eyes toward him. No, Klytemnaistra had
surely said behind her hand, do not choose this one,
sister; beware most of all of Diomedes. He is far too
subtle and too clever to be ruled.

So Helen had looked doubtful and sent him away.
Helen—the great queen. The repository of all their
hopes. There had been a spark of something in Helen,
something of rebellion, even then. She dithered and
she delayed, she drove the suitors in distraction to
swear their oath lest she send them howling mad at
each others' throats, so much being at stake and so

much violence and so much ambition prowling the surrounds of Sparta.

She might have chosen his wise counsel; or Odysseus' guile; or Achilles' skill at war; any of these would have served Hellas well. She raged at Klytemnaistra, the whole camp heard her tempers and her tears; and certain princes' faces flamed red while the whispers went from eavesdroppers to the campfires round about the shrine on the Eurotas.

So what must a young girl do, high of pride and diffident toward her elder sister and at the same time determined to defy her in this husband-choosing?

What must a young girl do, whom the Fates had made their destroyer?

Why, choose the handsome one, the one in the shadows, the man who came only to press his brother's suit, not his own. She chose Menelaos, the weak, the shadow-king, the biddable one of the Atreidês. And set him in the place of power, the center-to-be of all Hellas.

In her rage Klytemnaistra chose the counter-piece, Menelaos' master, the Achaean prince Agamemnon, landless both; but she lent him the Spartan army to take Mykenai back and do murder on his uncle Thyestes. And the River-born went home in despair and disgust, hopes shattered but not yet knowing the worst.

Only Diomedes had foreseen it, had seen it in Achilles' anger and Odysseus' subtle hate, in the sundering of their uneasy fellowship and most of all in the binding that oath had set on them.

He gazed now into Helen's eyes—*Do you know even yet what you have done? What shall I do,*

*swan-daughter, Priestess? Tell a warrior what to
do—or this time will you listen to me?*

"I want to go home," she cried, like a little child,
and hurled herself all unexpected into his arms, her
arms about him—

—Paris looked at him and he looked at Paris over
her head. There was despair in Paris' face. Agony.
And hate. Perhaps there was the same in his own
look. There was, in his heart.

"Do you see your situation?" he asked of Paris.

"Damn you all," Paris said.

So Helen had escaped her shadow-king and found
herself another golden child like herself. Too much
like her. It was not wisdom that looked at him through
Paris' eyes either. Paris and Helen had risked so
much to come here. They were brave and they were
desperate. But Paris had never seen all the conse-
quences and did not understand even now what had
befallen him.

"Move, dammit!" Achilles gripped his passenger
under the arms and heaved, an effort that stabbed
fresh pain through his own elbow and through his
gut. Blood still poured from his nose and dripped on
him and on the man he was trying to pull to his feet
on the slanted deck, from where Menelaos had slid,
between the wall of the chopper and the corner of
the co-pilot's seat and a bank of dead electronics.
"Up!" He spat blood and threw a glance toward what
he could see out the dirt-spattered windshield: the
dust-veil was nearer and coming fast, and Menelaos
was making only disorganized efforts to get his legs
working and take his own weight. "Up, or you're

meat, you hear me! It's the whole damn Trojan army out there!"

Menelaos' legs started working, sandaled feet scrabbling on the deck mat; he flailed with his arms and pushed with his legs, and Achilles hauled him across another dead electronics console and let him fall on the downward side of the deck. Achilles braced his feet one way and the other and grunted with the pain of bruised ribs as he grabbed to steady himself.

Another look out the window. The hell with taking the helmet off. He found his flak jacket and heaved the thing on—good enough with high-velocity stuff: bad news with a spear coming at a man's gut. He grabbed up the Colt Officer ACP from its place by his seat and belted it on, staggered aft and bodily into Menelaos, who was staggering about trying to stand up in the dim insides. "Gun, damn you, can you use a gun?"

Menelaos muttered something and staggered again as Achilles got past him and into the locker. There was a noise in the far distance like building thunder, the sound of horses, of chariot wheels—

"Damn *fools!*" Achilles shouted to the air, the king of Sparta, and the too-distant Roman army. "Where's the guns, where's our cover, the damn tanks are fucking *waiting* on them! We're fucking sitting here and the fucking tanks are going to wait till we're the same fucking target before they get a fire order— shit, shit, *shit!*" The locker lid was bent. It stuck. He jerked it and gasped and sobbed for breath, working bent over to get at the munitions. "Fucking sitting on their asses . . . . *Get over here, dammit—*"

Menelaos grabbed the Galil that Achilles shoved at

him, and staggered, recovered to grab the belts and the grenades—

"You know what to do with those?"

"Bombs," Menelaos said.

"Oh, fucking hell." Tears ran down his face, he hurt so bad. He snuffled blood, wiped his nose and showed Menelaos the ring. "You clamp your hand down here, you pull this ring and you throw the damn thing as far as you can, not down my back, you hear me? There's another jacket in that locker, there! see? You go put that on." He buckled on his own belts and dragged himself up on the butt of the M-16— Man—"Damn!"—staggered back to the door, propped the gun up and heaved the latch over, working against the tilt. Blood ran down his nose and down his throat, and his breath tasted of copper. He heaved, failed, heaved again, blind angry and with red spots shooting through the dark. The door gave and creaked and slid, letting in the thunder and dusty fresh air. He heard Menelaos thumping about the other locker, and groped after his own seat again with the thunder growing in his ears and the dust growing in front of that dirt-specked, white-spattered windshield till there was no sky, just the brown dust and the ruddy glitter of Paradise-light on metal. "We've got to go!" he yelled back at Menelaos.

"I'm ready," Menelaos yelled back, jacketed and grabbing up his gear.

Achilles leaned over the seat and fished after a jar, gritted his teeth and sweated as his fingers slipped on the lid and he got it back. Unbroken in its cushy little nest there by his seat, or the Undertaker would be sorting him from his passenger in pieces. Five live grenades, pins pulled, nestled in against each other inside. The glass jar clamped the handles down. He hauled it up with the lid in his fingers, got a better grip on it and tucked it in his arm, exhaling a shaky breath. Another lean over the seat, a stab of pain, lips drawn back as he uncapped a red switch. Toggle switch and a red and a yellow button, one, one, and two. Battery-backup on that one, fucking right there was.

Then he shoved back from the seat and staggered back where Menelaos waited. He grabbed up the M-16 there by the door, stood poised with that glass jar of grenades clutched up against his ribs and a jump down from that tilted deck rim down to the grass looking farther than he wanted to take.

It was Menelaos that jumped, with the 10 pound Galil in its sling and a load of ammunition and grenades slung round his other shoulder—jumped and overbalanced and hit on his butt and the rifle's. A shot went straight up past the door.

"Damn!" Achilles yelled, flinching back and damned near losing the jar as his balance wavered. He recovered, tearing his ribs, yelled and swore and jumped, coming down on his feet and then one knee, sliding down the dust-slick grass into the trough the chopper had found with one of its skids, trying to stop himself with the butt of the M-16 in his right hand and with his left arm cradling the jar from rocks. "Oh, shit, oh, shit—"

It was a second more before he could get the butt planted, get his feet both under him and stand up, with the thunder nearer and nearer and the dust rolling up over all the sky. "Run," he yelled, and did, hard as he could, the glass jar still under his arm, and the king of Sparta hard behind him.

* * *

"When do we go?" Hatshepsut asked again, third repetition, pressing the earpiece tighter against her ear. Nothing, lately, made sense. Static riddled their communications, hissed and snapped, so that she winced. She had shed the florescent jumpsuit for plain khaki—let the Macedonians and the Ahhiyawans and the Luwian/Trojans make targets out of themselves. The way things were going she had a profound wish to look like part of the hillside—*Wait a fire order,* Julius had told her in no uncertain terms. And they had a chopper down out there, the Trojans had had time to put out the fire the sea attack had started in their ships, and presently the whole damned camp was on the move, right under their guns.

So, for much of their sweep, was the downed chopper, right where a stray shell could take it out; and the fact that the chopper was sitting there intact indicated the pilot might be alive . . . a damned attractive pilot and a damned sorry waste, that was what. She had one tank up on the citadel still, had *that* turret set to sweep the beach or anything shorter, but there were other options, like taking the rightmost, least useful tank from its position and going out there—

"Set and Osiris," she hissed, as a jeep went forward of their position, out from the revetments the Romans had made. She stood up beside Curtius, grabbed the field glasses and saw the pair in it, one in black and one in khaki.

"Hold fire," the order came to her over the earpiece, Republican Latin.

"What are they *doing?*" Pharaoh shouted into the mike.

* * *

"She asks," the legionary said, popping his head
out of the juggernaut poised in the position it and
the engineers had made for it, an earth and rubble
agger with a flat on which the monster could rest and
aim, " 'what are they doing?' Sir."

While the groundeffect tank rested still, except
the whine and adjustment of its turret; and Julius
Caesar, standing on its broad skirt, looked back at
the man. Titan One was his, presently, the most
useful of the tank positions and the one which
Hatshepsut only thought she had. The driver was
Roman.

He looked his most inscrutable at the legionary.
And said nothing, and looked back again over the
battle plain.

Fact one. Diomedes had said it. *A rhythm here
that you disturb by your very presence. This ground
is strong and willful.*

This ground does not like *modernity.*

This ground does not like iron. Or those who wield
it. Is one a fool to think that, Diomedes of the Wise
Counsel? Then both of us are fools.

Fact two. He knew men. He knew the look of a
man who held secrets, and Welch and Nichols were
not his, were not Alexander's either. He had come to
the truck, Welch's small kingdom. He had seen
Welch's face, seen the eyes, shadowy in the green
flare of the monitors, which met his only for a moment, cold and opaque as a man who belonged to
him would never look at him. A man worth the
having, but a man too difficult to gather quickly, or
without knowing his edges. A project, that one, like
Niccolo.

And himself, being Roman, he was a meticulous list-making bastard. He knew precisely what equipment he had "borrowed" from the Pentagram, what Klea and Antonius had liberated, had a tolerably precise idea what Hatshepsut had for equipment, including a list of the serial numbers. The com truck was not part of it. Nor did it come from Alexander. He was sure of that now, having run his own discreet investigations since the embarrassment of riches first showed up at the mission assembly point. He had, he hoped, accurately taken Maccabee's measure: about adequate for jeep or rifle . . . modern but not expert—though Reassignments *had* shipped him back damned conveniently when someone in camp put a knife in him. Zazki, then? But the little Jew worried too convincingly, too earnestly . . . to be Welch's control. The Pentagram was in the hands of Rameses: Rameses was a fool, but some of his associates were not, who used Rameses for a front. (Egyptians, Egyptians . . . Hatshepsut vowed she had no friends in Rameses' party, but that was yesterday: success might draw more and more Egyptians to Rameses' side, and the gods and Fortune knew, balances might shift—if she were not Hatshepsut, and a bastard and a bitch rolled into one: no, gods, he could not see her with *that* crowd, or as ruling Welch, no, no, and no. A problem, a bitch and a bastard, but not, he thought, playing two sides at the moment.)

Yet the com truck was with them; yet so, so inexorably, by such small increments of bad luck, his own communications were shorn away, his forces made increasingly reliant on New Dead and sophisticated equipment no one had ordered.

There was always, of course, Niccolo. Not to discount the possibility. Niccolo had been up to *something*: he would stake good money on that. There were all the small signals several centuries of sharing a house with a man could imbed at the level of instinct. Not mentioning Niccolo's recent and zealous reform. But all these things considered, he could still catch Niccolo's eye, still see now and again a glimmer of contact all the way to the depths—in a man whose normal glance was shadowed and reserved. Indeed, that Niccolo had somehow betrayed him he did not overmuch doubt. Small betrayals—he knew that Niccolo knew that he knew such things: the old game. But that Niccolo was under some extraordinary pressure seemed evident from all the signals. *Someone* had leaned on him, and leaned hard, either early or late in this mission. And that leaning was sabotage, the destabilization of one more of his resources.

Fact three. By such small and apparently unrelated steps he was being separated from trusted forces, made reliant on things and persons whose provenance he could not trace.

Like the com truck . . . the chopper, out of New Hell. MedEvac—the hell it was. Maccabee's ferry. Achilles playing Charon—on whose orders? Maccabee came back from the Undertaker in Achilles' care, then Alexander—at the very point when Julius began to reach accommodation with the Macedonian—vanished, and left him alone with that younger, most modern and maddening part of their tripartite soul.

Make good, he had said to that stranger with his stranger-still passport through Hell, Achilles Peliadês, who was *someone's* messenger, with his fancy chopper and his miracle electronics (which monitored gods-knew-what?); so forthwith, this errant fragment that was all he hated in himself—ran off with the chopper, picked up Menelaos, and dropped himself, the priceless chopper, and the possible key to Alexander's prison—right down where he, Caesar, would have to make a decisive move against the Trojans to get them out.

It smelled. Be it Achilles' choice or some agency's sabotage, it had a stench that reeked from one end of Hell to the other.

Moves on a board.

The first knight advanced, someone's rash move. Cracked himself up on the plain and was still alive out there . . . Welch said.

Black queen to the left, diagonal, with tanks. Hatshepsut was rash, but she *was* of the household, and remained an asset if he could rein her in.

Second black knight to the fore: visible threat. Mouse was in command down there on the lines, and in him there was no doubt.

Black bishop to the left, diagonal, on his own ingenuity. Niccolo . . . no one could ever be sure of Niccolo Machiavelli, but if there was a line to New Hell that did not go through that com truck, it was that one, who had reported one thing in Italian and another in Greek in front of Diomedes, and knew by the look that passed between them that he was still on the old job—and Antonius would fill him in on the rest of it. Rescue be damned. It was a feint out there, a deadly dangerous one, in the full view of that line that thundered toward the downed chopper.

Let's find out the rules, shall we, Niccolo? Find me the Trojans I want. Ones who will talk to us Romans. Where is that faction? Too smart to be here? Or with Priam on the beach and Greeks in the citadel, are other parts of the equation skewed?

The Dardani our ancestors were never state-enemies to Priam and his brood, but by Venus they were damned uneasy house-friends and in-laws.

And where's Hecuba? Where's Andromache and Cassandra and Creusa? Tented like campfollowers, or safe in some shadow-Hellas?

Gods, it's a question, isn't it? Where do those ships come from?

Closer and closer.

Far below, the chopper went up in a sudden fireball. In a moment more the noise of the explosion reached him.

He drew in his breath. It was possible, then, that Achilles was dead, gone back to whatever Agency sent him. Possibly he had suicided, helpless in that ship, betrayed by his Agency, seeing he had no more choices but capture by that oncoming Trojan line.

But he thought he would have felt that death.

Hell, no, that young bastard would have waited— till the chopper was enveloped and Hektor was looking in the door.

Luck to you, he thought, arms folded. And was quite earnest in it. Achilles at least was loose out there, well away from the blast, was alive and probably thinking fast—knowing Achilles knew the ground meant he himself had a good idea just where Achilles was going . . . without asking Welch.

Best use in the world for problems. Put them out in the front of the lines and let them figure out for themselves on which side their true interests lay.

The chopper blew with a shockwave edged with

particles, but they were far enough to keep running.
Choice of direction to run had been pure equation—
time and distance from the blast divided by time and
distance of the blast from the Trojans, and factored
by the likelihood at least part of the Trojan line
would sweep toward and around the chopper, hem-
ming them in—time and distance from the Roman
lines impossible, the river yonder the only hope they
had for a defense. Damned shame, Achilles thought
now, jogging along toward the riverside with the
taste of blood in his mouth and now and again a
glance over his shoulder. It was all against them, the
Trojans coming faster than he had wanted, and not
fast enough, dammit, to put them beside the chopper
when it blew. All that blast bought was a little time
and a little of their enemy's confidence, if that. But
subtract out those electronics, which no one was
going to get, including even the Romans and high-
and-mighty Caesar, damn him.

*Where's the fucking transport? Where's the tanks,
man? You know where I am.* Somewhere in the
distraction of the pain, he swore he'd as soon turn
the weapons he carried on Romans as on Trojans, on
the Romans so smug-damned-safe in their digs, behind the firepower of the groundeffect tanks, watching him die out here.

His nose had stopped bleeding. But the taste of it
was in his mouth, his heart was pounding and he felt
himself giddy, with the damned jar under his arm, if
he fell—if he fell—

He stopped, dropped down to one knee and set
the jar down. Menelaos caught up with him, reached
to grab the jar he had just positioned so carefully and
braced up in a gouge of dry sod.

"No," Achilles said. "I got that set, dammit, let it alone." He got up again with a shove of the rifle butt. "And come on."

There was a shallow streambed just beyond, dry in summer, but it filled in rainy seasons and ran down to Scamander. Day after day, year after year he had ridden across it to harass the Trojans and their allies. He and Patroklos, Patroklos riding at his side, Automedon with the reins and his Thessalian horses running the way only that team could—water splashing up from the chariot wheels . . . bright drops in a flash of sun, a break in gray clouds . . .

It was dry now. Gravel under his boots as he cut into it off the diagonal, and glanced back. It was a race—had been a race from the moment he had seen the line coming. Chariots had to slow, knowing that dip was ahead. But the charioteers, once they knew someone was out and loose and alive, had to know at once where he was trying to put himself—Scamander, the little river where one side or the other had so often fought for position, soft ground where the chariots were useless, treacherous land where a wrong move could mire a wing, force it against the river; or where a unit cut off could use the bends and meanders like a wall.

Not near going to make it. Not enough time. There where the seasonal stream had carved a rock clear of the ground, and a few bushes grew for cover—that was the best they were going to have. Pain rode his breaths. The landscape of grass and tilted rock and gravel was hazed in his sight and shot through with red. Rid of the damned jar, else the skid he took, that lanced pain his ribs, might have blown them all to Reassignments. He took in his breath, blind for a moment as Menelaos grabbed him.

". . . be all right," he said, and rested on his hip on the shallow slope facing the chariots, with Menelaos gasping and dripping sweat over him. Brush partially screened their left. The twice-mansized rock did better. From this position he crawled up on his elbows to get the jar in his view, right where a shot could take it. Right in front of the oncoming chariots.

It was gone. Gone. Out of sight. *The fucking jar fell over! Dammit, you screw-up!*

Menelaos got up on his knees and looked. Achilles jerked his arm.

"Get down," he hissed, "dammit, give me some of the ammunition. Even split."

While the thunder of the chariots came on, a wide-spaced line of teams running all out, a glitter of bronze-capped wheels and metaled harness in the Paradise-light. What happened next was hard to do. But the weapons he carried did not discriminate.

And Menelaos, damn him to the pit, did not hesitate. The Atreidês stood straight up and started firing. Horses died and fell, tangling wounded animals and broken wood and involving human flesh in the midst of it all. Achilles' heart ached. He had hoped the bomb would take a couple out, spook the teams it failed to hit, hoped the chariots would slow for the gully, veer when they came under fire and and give them human targets. But there was no choice. Menelaos took out the one chariot that might have bashed the jar and done worse than himself, damn him— made all that carrying and risking their necks useless as the charioteers spotted them clear and the line started bowing about them.

So he cleared his own sight, got up where he had a sweep and cut loose—killed a team outright, no butchery like the Atreidês.

Then the chariotry, losing one after another of their number and the drivers surely flinching from the slaughter of their horses, did what chariots were designed to do. They turned, having gotten the temperature of things, and drove away. They were only a screen for the infantry, a means to let the heavy-armed princes do their jobs, meet any chariots the other side might put out for similiar purpose, skirmish while the slower infantries caught up, let out their well-armored princes just as their commands caught up to them, and get the hell out of the way—to return only when their prince was doing the rest of his job, which was to stand last in a retreat, using his own shield, shieldman, and well-armored person to keep the enemy off his men's necks while they ran: the chariot would thunder in, sweep an arc between the prince and the enemy, sometimes with an archer aboard to help clear a spot, then get the prince aboard and do the screening job again while the infantry got the dead and wounded out.

This time the chariots pulled back to the advancing infantry to let their passengers off. And the princes had done their other job, which was recon.

"They'll come around us now," Menelaos said.

"Yeah," Achilles said back. "You screwed up, you fucked it up, you damn—" The rage deserted him for despair as he sank back to the slope. "That was our cover. If that thing had blown we might have had a fucking chance to get to the river. Hear?" Or it might not have worked. His strength was spent, and the shakes arrived, his legs and arms wanting to twitch, his gut knotting up as if he were in profoundest cold. In front of the Atreidês whose black stare sent the heat back to his face and claimed his limbs after a few spasms. *Bastard. Achaean filth. It's not fear, you mother-murdering pig.*

Hell gives me you for a partner. In Patroklos' place. Gives me lunatics who try to take pieces of me. Goddess-mother, is this the glory I traded my life for?

Shit. It's all shit. It's the Undertaker again, naked and alone and helpless. Again and again and again. And how many times have I been back here? A dozen? Two?

I'm buried here, mother. It's back again, has to be, my tomb's risen right over there, reshaped along with the rest of this damned plain. It's waiting for me.

Do you care? Or were you only a woman and a liar?

"They're coming," Menelaos said, on his knees by him.

"Get out of here."

"Where, for Zeus' sake?"

Give the Atreidês credit, he did not think of it right off. Achilles warmed toward the man. Laughed, a short breath which hurt his ribs. And gestured back, that way, toward Troy. "Romans," he said. "They'll take you in. Real friendly."

Menelaos looked at him a long, long beat, and things went on behind those black eyes—*Are you lying, Myrmidon, is it a trick, some subtle Inachid revenge?* An Atreidês always had to think that first. *But they'll kill you. Where's your profit in that?*

Achilles smiled, showed teeth. "Get. I won't shoot you in the back."

Menelaos' face went red. "The hell."

"The hell I won't shoot you?" Cancel the second thoughts on the Atreidês: as soon cuddle a viper. "Now, why would I do that?" Shouting came to them from over the plain, a different kind of sound than the rumble of chariots, a roar of voices, the armor-rattle of a full infantry charge punctuated with shrill, high yells, and the dust that went up colored everything beyond their trench—the units that met them would envelop them, if possible. "You watch my back, I'll watch yours. We get 'em stopped and whenever they get in spearcast they get the grenades. We tend off toward the riverside, if we get a breather. Most of all we keep those damn chariots and the bowmen behind the lines. Simple enough? You understand the load? You got it?" He ran a short demo with the Galil. The king nodded, sweating. His eyes showed white around the edges. As the howling, armor-heavy mob came down on them like a breaker on a beach.

Achilles stood up and cut loose at the bronze-gleaming line in a calm, well-reasoned sweep. DU rounds cut through shields, through bodies, and kept going; but there were more behind. Beside him Menelaos fired, while he reloaded, while he kept an eye to the lines and sweat ran on him under the flak jacket. He caught his breath and fired again while Menelaos fumbled his way through a reload.

Goddess, mother, no end to them. The fool could not get the Galil loaded—

"You're right, your right!" Achilles yelled, busy straight on while the line started coming round them on Menelaos' side. Menelaos got the Galil up, stumbling against him, fired and froze up on the trigger, the Galil emptying itself in a climbing arc that turned Achilles' way.

"Dammit!" he yelled on his way down, as Menelaos swung off his own balance and the Galil finished its clip. "Shit!" As the plastic stock of his M-16 hit the ground and shattered, his ribs met the ground and hurt like hell, and Menelaos was trying to fire on a human wave with an empty rifle.

The ground shook and the air hurt. He scrabbled to get his head up, seeing a hole in the middle of that Trojan rush as a debris-fall started, around a littered mess of a crater where the center of the Trojan line had been.

Shell from the tanks was his first thought. But not. It was the damned glass jar some Trojan foot had just knocked flying.

The lines hesitated in confusion. And he fired, while the broken stock battered hell out of his shoulder through the flak jacket. Menelaos came out of his freeze-up enough to try to load, dropping the box, swearing by Zeus Thunderer and invoking Hephaistos lord of things mechanical.

The Trojan line was split in two now, one part coming at them from the left, off Scamander, one from the right off the plain. The devastated middle was trying to regroup itself, was gaining its courage back, about to test whether the thunderbolt would fall twice. Coming into spearcast soon. If ancient weapons were all they had. Infantry could screen the chariots, turn-about—if whoever was in command had a thought in his skull, he would be calling for archers about now. That he had been lucky enough to get the prince with the grenades he did not believe.

"Hai" he yelled at them, the old Achilles rising up in him like strong wine, *"hai-ai-ai-aiiiii! it's me, you sons of bitches, Achilles son of Thetis the sea-born, grandson of the sea-daughter and greatgrandson of the Mother Herself!"*

He fired again, and cut a swath in the advancing lines.

The stairs fell away into dark, and even the Germans stopped. "Tyr," one cried, and: *Tyr—Tyr—Tyr—* the dark gave back.

Then the earth groaned, as if its substance grew restive again; and Maccabee caught himself as the stairs trembled. They had found Agamemnon, or the rag someone left of him. Had found a woman. *The* woman, maybe; or one of the other witches who had beguiled them. The Germans had muttered and one of them had cast some kind of lots and muttered and cast again as if he misliked his omens, which performance chilled Maccabee's blood.

So did the absence of the staff, the rod of power. Something walked this maze which had made bloody wreckage of two human bodies, stove ribs and spattered brains and split flesh, and it had walked out on bare human feet, tracks which they followed, bloody footprints which betrayed the killer.

Labyrinthos, Alexander had called this place. *The House of the Axe.* And Maccabee harked back to tales told round a rebel campfire, in the hills beyond New Hell.

Minotauros. Minotaur, monster in the maze, abroad

on human feet and having a bull's head and a taste for blood.

It was Alexander he tracked. He prayed that it was. But Alexander or monster or one become the other, it was the overkill that chilled his blood, the evidences of victims' panicked flight, the bloody handprints, the spatters here and spatters there and the grisly sight of bowels strung out and ribs sundered, part of a foot lying here, a severed feminine hand lying like a white, dead spider on the throne.

It was not an Alexander he had known in all their time together. Black rages he had seen. He had seen Alexander kill. But not the like of this.

A Roman shone an electric torch down the stairs. It lit up the dark ahead and showed the same bloody footprints, where the steps went down and met the stone of a cavern.

The Macedonians faltered then, talking among themselves in voices that carried and echoed; white faces turned up toward him, and one and the other of them started to retreat up the stairs.

Maccabee drew his sword. The foremost of the Macedonians stopped and the ones behind him did. And at Maccabee's own back Roman carbon-steel swords hissed out of sheaths, a sound that sent cold to his marrow. *Mutiny?* he wondered. But he had only a bluff to run, and he knew what the ones in front of him would do to his back if he panicked now. "If you're running," he said to the Macedonians, "try *down*. It's at least a chance that way."

Foreign eyes stared up at him. Roman still was at his back. Behind the Macedonians the Germans stood, shadowed as the Roman light had left them. At last the Macedonians gave back, and turned and went

on. Maccabee started on down the steps and the
swords behind him grated back into cover. Sweat ran
on him and his knees went weak as he remembered
the recent sensations of a blade in the back, and the
Undertaker's butcher-job.

They went down. All of them, into the dark. And
he did not even know whether the Romans behind
him had been backing him or standing ready to
carve him in pieces when the rebellion caved in.

It was chaos out there. Niccolo Machiavelli swore
and swerved the jeep violently to save them from a
hole, wrenched the wheel over again to keep them
on course. They were mad. Romans, Trojans, berserker Germans, Macedonians and all, and Julius
had gone mad as Agamemnon.

Farther, farther! Antonius had yelled, directing
them on against the Trojan line that filled the plain
at their left.

But the chariotry was coming on, horses full out,
charging against their jeep on its diagonal course.
They had the rifles, no one knew what the Trojans
had, and Antonius was telling him stop.

"This is mad!" Niccolo cried, veering for a U-turn,
and not stopping at all. "*Perdio*, find a single man in
the whole army—Julius has lost his senses! We've
already lost the helicopter! What more do we risk in
this confusion?"

"Turn and stop!" Antonius yelled, "or I'll blow
your head off."

Niccolo looked, stared down the barrel of a Colt in
a braceleted Roman fist, and let his foot off the gas.
He put the wheel over again, braked, and gave his
attention to the jolt and the dip of the left wheel in a

hole that sent a flash of sweat over him—an expectation of Antonius squeezing too hard and a bullet crashing through his brain, his most excellent, most valuable brain.

It did not happen. The jeep rocked to a halt with the chariots sweeping toward them in dustplumes, fronting a long battle-line strung out in lumps and bits and pieces, knots of men hardly distinguishable behind their huge shields and in the dust.

"Fool!" he said with a wild glance at Antonius, who had holstered the Colt and grabbed after the loudhailer on the floor. "Do you think they will listen now?"

But the Roman was scrambling up onto the seat, to stand there and shout in Mycenaean Greek: "I am Antonius son of Antonius, herald of Julius of the lineage of Anchises and Capys, prince of the Dardanians. Where is Aeneas?"

"Madness," Niccolo hissed.

But the chariots immediately in front of them veered and slowed, one and the other, and the hair rose up on his nape. In all of Hell there were sights he had seen, but this sudden quiet, this chaotic excuse for an army part of which simply halted itself and listened to a name out of fable . . . Agamemnon was a truth. Achilles was indisputable. But eponymous ancestors were not in the same class. He should throw the jeep into gear, fling the lunatic into his seat and take them out of this; the parts of the Trojan line that were still in motion were passing beyond them on either side, ignoring them as if they had ceased being part of the same world—allowing enemies at their flanks, at their backs if they kept going, as they themselves let enemies at their own. But the irrational held a perverse fascination. One watched, that was all, one prepared to take that Trip at least without predjudice this time (Cesare *must* forgive a desertion-through-demise if the demise was not his doing) though spears, God knew, would hurt. Arrows did. Cutting swords were a dreadful weapon.

"Do you fancy Tiberius?" he asked of Antonius. It was Antonius' peculiar fate to revert to the mad emperor's palace whenever he died: and Tiberius' mere name was an incantation to set Antonius on edge. "Dinner at the villa? Tonight, if the Undertaker makes schedule."

"Shut up!"

"White wine or red? Red, I think. Rare roast."

"Shut it up!"

"I thought it pleasant," he murmured, while the sounds of fire continued in the distance, above the thunder-mutter of armored masses moving past them at only a hundred yards distance in either direction, beclouding them with dust.

But out of that dust before them a figure walked, tall and bronze-shielded, white-plumed and seeming one with the haze and the light.

It stopped. It set its large shield square on the ground and shouted at them in that same if mangled Greek. "I am Aeneas son of Anchises and the goddess and I know no Julius for kin of mine!"

"Through your son Iulus," Antonius rose up to shout, thundering through the loudhailer. "In time yet to come! Do you think this is Troy, goddess-son, or that you have not died?"

Long silence, in which Niccolo tightened his grip on the wheel and held his breath to small movements.

"Why is your lord with the Ahhiyawaes?"

"My lord holds the hill for himself," Antonius

shouted back, pointing. "A Dardanian lord holds Troy, your descendant, goddess-son! the way it should have been—the way it is now! He offers you the city, goddess-son, and truce and alliance with your descendants. A way out of this madness!"

The bronze man reversed his spear and drove it point into the earth with a motion that sent the plume flying, that made the shield flash in the ruddy light of Paradise.

Niccolo stared, in the novelty of pure amazement. He saw a prince, an entire people, astonishingly lacking in guile. He saw a system of assumptions in which certain risks were not risks: a *keryx*, a herald, would not attack; the scattered line was many armies, not one, and each answered to individual interests, each choosing its fights as this one, now—untroubled by others—chose this time to listen. Had the Romans remembered this accurately?

Did Caesar send *Antonius* to treat with such, the man notorious for his failures and his lapses of honor—to treat with this paragon of Roman chivalry?

But Antonius had always won his best victories with oratory. And besides, Caesar had sent along Niccolo Machiavelli.

There were more and more of them, helmed and plumed and shielded in bronze and oxhide and leather, and they came on over the bodies of their own dead, came as if they could not believe that things so invisible could strike through bronze. Or it was the name he had shouted which had drawn them, it was the name that maddened them, their enemy, the man no weapon could touch.

Achilles just kept reloading and giving them burst after burst, firing while Menelaos loaded and turn about, raking whatever unit got closest, this side and that and straight on, till his arms wearied and his ribs hurt beyond anything reasonable to endure. Perhaps Menelaos was afraid. Personally he was most afraid now only that the damned jacket was going to save him too long. He was waiting, had been waiting since he knew they could not make the river—blinking sweat out of his eyes and killing enemies in heaps and piles and windrows, poor damned sods who went at this with such incredible persistence, because it was written down and true that they should win this one vengeance in their way.

"Damn you," he kept repeating to himself, muttering without a voice, and: "Damn, damn, damn—" —in a kind of tearful litany. Not the Trojans. His goddess-mother. "Lying bitch."

Not immune to pain. Nor wounds. Perhaps after all, it was the blood on his face that encouraged them, like so many wolves. Perhaps it was only habit and fate that kept them coming at him. The tomb was there. And they might well know it.

The rifle jammed, already gone beyond anything it ought to have to do. It died in his hands and it was Menelaos firing alone now. Last two reloads as it was; and the Trojans sent up a yell when he threw the rifle down and gave his last ammunition to the Spartan.

"Damn fools!" He caught his breath, blinked sweat and tears and panted open-mouthed, just watching while the Trojans surged forward into the DU rounds that consistently worked as much havoc in the second and third ranks as they did in the first. Another row of heroes fell and men poured over them—gotten their breath too, they had, and somehow they had gotten it all coordinated, damn primitives had discovered a rhythm of their own, coming forward on one side and the other, feint and draw back—He pulled the pin on a grenade and gave it to them.

So they lost a few. So that was chariotry coming up from the rear, and arrows flew about them from the limit of their range, damn nuisance—"Get that damn archer!" Achilles yelled at Menelaos, with the Galil fallen into a sudden and thundering silence.

"I'm jammed," the answer came.

"Bloody hell, it's moving up on us—" The charioteer had seen his chance, driving through for better vantage. One sharp-witted charioteer. One damned archer. Achilles pulled the pin on another grenade, lobbed it high, rib-stretching; and winced. Trojans were coming on all sides of them now, moving into spearcast under the distraction the bowman provided. He saw the charioteer, the prince, the archer—Saw the crest.

"*Peliadês!*" the opposing prince roared, brandishing his spear. It was Hecktor himself.

"Grenades, dammit—" Achilles flung another, staggered as an arrow whistled in and impacted his shoulder, as Menelaos staggered against him and the earth shuddered in thunder, as Trojans swept in on their left. He hurled another grenade, seeing that chariot trying to drive through the crowd of attackers. It fell short. He staggered as the earth heaved again, and stared in dismay as the ground split beneath his feet and softened, water boiling up in a soup of sand and froth, that took his feet from under him and drank him down still conscious.

Scamander! he raged at the inanimate, at a thing which had tried for him once when a Trojan trick tried to kill him, breaking the dike upstream. But god or devil, the old River took him now, cold and strong and irresistible—not Scamander at all, but sandy Cocytus-in-disguise, the truth under all the illusions. A man understood these things, whose lungs were aching and whose brain kept saying no, no, and no, to the urge to gasp once and relieve the pain.

Julius blinked, and gazed again through the field-glasses as the land shuddered and went quiet again. As a river arbitarily changed its course, looped like a vengeful snake, carrying glowing bodies with it in its course toward the sea.

The army was still there. But the wreckage of the chopper just—went down under the earth. Was not there. Only a round depression was left. And bodies left on dry ground glowed and vanished the way bodies did in Hell, when the Undertaker recalled them.

"Damn," he said to no one in particular, and caught his balance on the windy heights, there on the skirt of the monster tank, overlooking the battle plain. Alexander had gone. And perhaps now another part of them had gone.

One of them was left, the one of their triad who had not attacked, who had sat sphinx-quiet and watched the land shrug away its irritances. And that was either a vindication or a strategic disaster; but Achilles had at least proved Diomedes' counsel.

Juluis watched as the river corrected itself, sweeping back into its bed and leaving bewildered survivors, a Trojan army in disarray.

The Agency which had provided him such a wealth

of equipment and happenstance had either moved or now had to move. One or the other.

The pressure let up, sudden as a flight through air. Achilles flailed out, gasped mingled air and water amid a head over heels tumble that met a watery surface as if it had been a solid floor. He went under.

And slid feet-first on his back, a blindingly swift chute that flexed his body this way and that over slimy surfaces and slipped him gently as a ripple into a shallow pool.

He gasped and coughed, turned over on his elbows and coughed and heaved in spasms, helpless as another sodden body slid hard against his side—he was too busy breathing, and after a moment, his unseen companion started doing the same, choking and coughing and struggling.

He kept his face out of the shallow water, elbows on slick stone. He found the whole place lit in a dim gold glow, a cave awash in water-sounds above the hollow echoes of their coughing . . . as if the water kept going over the edges of this shallow bowl.

"O mother," he said through a throat raw with vomiting, "you are still a bitch."

Seeing Minos

Alexander didn't know how long he'd been kneeling on the stone floor, or even how he'd gotten there.

Then he remembered: it was all a bad dream, an evil omen, a fit of visions begun by the bite of a snake.

It wasn't real, he told himself, though his knees ached from the rough, cold stone.

Then Zaki touched his shoulder and that was real, the touch.

All too real, as were the tears his smarting eyes spouted to cleanse the evil smoke from them.

So the smoke was real too.

Beyond the smoke, he could see seven pairs of feet—horned and clawed with black claws that were sharp and clicked numinously upon the stone as they moved to and fro, as if their owners danced in place.

In the midst of all those feet there was another set of feet—a human pair, with cloven hooves behind. And these feet were in deeper shadows, and surrounded by a cavern or the walls of a hollow pillar.

The pillar was a stalagmite, he told himself; all else was hallucination, residue of the fit or the dream.

For the dreams had been of times that didn't matter now, filled with guilts that no longer applied. He'd long ago cleansed his conscious mind of those—

deaths he'd dealt weren't debts outstanding: Alexander was in Hell, paying a hero's price.

Yet his gut twisted with remembrance and he felt as if the Erinys had finally succeeded in turning him inside out.

How bad is it? he demanded of his shaken soul. What worse could happen now, than had already happened? Even should he even fail completely—fail Maccabee, on whose account all this had started, fail Diomedes and the rest . . . then what?

The Undertaker's table? Indignity, of course, but what was one more travail, these days? Lose a battle, give Authority a laugh? So they'd sing humbling songs of him; there'd be a legend for the bards to tell whose moral he, Alexander, would be: if he lost the title Great King, was no longer *basileus*, it would smart. But it wasn't worse than deserting your friends.

Who, of course, could always be refound. As a battle lost could be refought—everything happening above (he remembered that: he was below the ground, far below . . .) was subject to revision, if a man had the strength of will to joust with Fate.

So thinking, he straightened up to look eye-to-eye with whatever had those too-many feet and saw. . . .

Eyes awful to look upon, mouths born to speak dooms, faces as had been carved on Achilles' tomb that day . . . that day so long ago he'd traded shields there with the corpse of a hero he'd never thought to meet—or learn to disdain.

The mouths must have been waiting to speak to him; the eyes lit up at the sight of him.

And as words issued upon smoke from those orifices ringed with sharpest teeth, Alexander saw out of the corner of his eye the Amurrite prince, Aziru, motioning him urgently to look away, look away. . . .

But he was Alexander. He would not, *could* not, look away. In whatever state, under whatever curse, despite duress or penance decreed, he was and always would be that: heroism was no cloak to put on at leisure, then cast aside. A man's nature was born with his soul, tempered by his mind, and only manifested by his deeds.

As long as there was enough left of him to know who it was, he would be Alexander. And Alexander, to live at all—even live an afterlife—must live by his own rules.

It was the difference between a worthy life and a waste of soul; it was the spark that set men apart from the beasts of the field. If it was called arrogance, or insolence, then that was just the jagged fragment of a deep-riding iceberg—what hurt, what showed, what could be abraded by time and changed by the winds of fate.

The rest—what Alexander had brought with him to Hell and what Hell sought to destroy or alter— was his alone to guard or lose, to make or break. It was reborn on the Undertaker's table and as long as there was flesh enough left of him to twitch at the spoken name "Alexander," he would keep it unsullied.

That thing called his soul, his *animus*, that which Maccabee had accused of wearing out his breast, was the one thing Hell and all its demons would never take from him: he was the sum of his passions, his purpose, his rage and his deeds.

He said, a hand going to Zaki, kneeling beside him on that rough cold stone, to offer comfort: "Who are you, and what do you want with Alexander of Macedon?" in a voice that, though trembling, proclaimed his spirit well enough.

And as the smoke-words issued forth and this time turned to sound that cracked against his ears, Alexander also heard Aziru's shouted (from too far a distance, too faintly) warning: "They are the Anunnaki, the Seven Judges, the gods of the Underworld, Basileus. Beware!"

But he didn't want to beware. He'd "bewared" himself into this, spending too much care on those who followed him, and those who postured at only accompanying him.

Now, here, it was different: like meeting Darius on the battlefield, it was full of peril sought and wagers made.

And this time, he was somehow certain, his enemy would not be in any way unworthy.

If these were, as Aziru said, gods, then what was that to him? The Anunnaki were ancient gods, not his gods, not Zaki's, either.

Under his breath, as the smoke-words of the Anunnaki ceased to be indecipherable roars like angry seas, Alexander said to Zaki: "On your feet, Jew. What would Yahweh say, to see you bowing to decrepit spirits He long ago conquered in battle?"

And pulled on the Israeli, dragging them both to their feet with a strength in his shuddering limbs that came, as always, when he needed it, though no such strength had been there scant moments before.

Take care, miniscule monarch, roared the Annunaki with one voice. *We are the arbiters of your destiny. We have heard your every thought.*

"So?" Alexander gave back, weaving on his feet,

legs wide-spread, head raised with an effort that corded his neck as if he were trying to lift a horse with the top of his skull. "Arbitrate. I didn't ask to come here. I want nothing from you. I do not believe in you. Zeus is and always will by my—"

Silence, mortal! You fear not death, because you think yourself beyond it. Think again, think of what you've seen. Here, we are Authority. We can dissolve your precious self! Remember the dead in the throneroom, the Trojans on the walls of the citadel. How their corpses linger. Look not upon the Undertaker as a refuge, not when you die in our domain! For you may not have any easier time returning to your Dead self," warned the Anunnaki, *"than you had finding your way out of Our maze. Now, do you quake with fear, as is our due from men?*

Alexander held his ground and did not speak. The quaking was in his limbs and it was real enough: physical fear was something he couldn't deny, merely overcome or, at the last, ignore.

Zaki, his hand still grasping Alexander's outstretched arm for support, said, "Right on, Alex. By *my* God who art in Heaven, I never bowed my head on Earth, and now's no different." And then, louder: "You, hideous Judges: What you want from us, ask plainly. Or take it. I'm giving nothing else away."

Then the Anunnaki roared and that roar had no words in it; rather, it had the sound of tumultuous winds, of storms amid the mountains.

What response it was, or what it meant, Alexander couldn't fathom, just held firm against the mighty gale, which stirred his hair like the wind and stole the breath from his nostrils like the wind and pushed upon his chest like the wind did, too.

In the grip of that circumscribed maelstron, that storm issuing from the Seven Judges' mouths, Alexander could blurrily see Aziru the Amurrite come forward, put himself between Alexander and Zaki, and the seven beings with their seven blazing torches.

Though he barely heard the shouted words, those Akkadian words of old, Alexander could see Aziru's arms lift in supplication, see the Amurrite's hands rending his garments and his hair, and see a smile come over the seven mouths of the Seven Judges as if something clever had been said.

Thereupon, the wind died down and the smoke belched less, and what smoke their was wrapped itself around the slight, dark Amurrite as a mother wraps an errant child once she's found him.

And Aziru called to them, from the midst of that smoke, "Don't fret, don't weep for me—don't search for me, brothers. I have made my peace and won a better place. So can you, perhaps, so I leave you a gift: hope of forgiveness, of manumission, of finding your own way to Heaven!"

And, raising his hand in fairwell, Aziru was completely eaten up by the swirling smoke.

In a moment, he was gone.

There was nothing there of him, no scratch upon the floor, no sandal left behind.

And no Anunnaki either, just a sound like Olympian chuckling in the still, moist cavern air.

Alexander found his limbs weak and Zaki, shivering, leaning on him. When the Jew let go, both men sank to the floor, heedless of showing weakness.

Alexander, propped on stiff arms, shook his head repeatedly to clear it.

When he looked up, the Israeli was staring out

toward the black river that ran here, underground, saying, "Did you hear that?"

"What?" Alexander, with one more determined shake of his head to clear the blurriness from his vision and the ringing from his ears, forced himself to look in the direction that Zaki was staring.

And saw a little light, bobbing as if on a craft, somewhere out in the shadowy dark of the underground deeps, before he tapped the Jew upon the shoulder and said, "Never mind it, now. We've something else to deal with."

For now, inside the pillar which was flanked only by empty shadows, something was moving.

Stirring.

Glinting as if with gold.

Coming forth.

First came the head: a golden mask, the mask of Agamemnon, on prodigious shoulders too wide and broad to be the Achaean's, unless they were the shoulders of some transmuted ghost.

Then came the torso: broad and knotted with muscle as any hero's, with a golden torque upon its arm and a golden girdle around its hairy belly, while in its hand it grasped the accursed staff that changed everything when it struck the ground.

Behind that, in procession, came a ravaging bull of horrid aspect, a bull with painted eyes and gilded horns, a bull whose mouth was full of fangs, not molars, and whose nostrils flared as red as blood.

And the thing in the mask who was so much more than Agamemnon had ever dreamed of being, said, "Your turn, Alexander? Your judgment, I must assume, is what I'm here to render. Otherwise," said the masked face with its hollow, booming voice as it turned and gestured, "my friend here would be enough."

The bull was pawing the ground now, its cloven hooves shod with iron making sparks upon the stone, its little eyes glowing red.

"Your friend the bull? I must confess, you and your 'friend' have me at a disadvantage—you know my name; I don't know yours," said the king of Macedonia.

"Hah!" and: "Ho, ho! Ho, ho, ho!" laughed the man in the mask, a laugh that wracked his trunk and made his muscles writhe like snakes. "My name, is it? You do not recognize Minos, the Judge of the Underworld? Perhaps not . . ."

Minos. 'See Minos,' the oracullar eight ball had said. . . .

Minos' golden mask turned at a sound, out in the blackness where the tides washed past, carving the rock deeper as it flowed on and on. "Perhaps you'll recognize my friend, the Minotaur, when he chews upon your bones." He spread his hand and raised the other, the one with the staff held tight in jeweled fingers.

The Minotaur. *Minotaurus.* Why not? Alexander's hand went to his hip, where a sword should have been, but wasn't. He'd lost it somewhere.

Damn and all, he'd lost it.

But beside him, Zaki was reaching for something stuck down inside his pants, and when the Uzi came up, Alexander hadn't the time to warn of what might happen if the Jew riddled the Judge with bullets before the submachine gun began to chatter and everything went mad.

*   *   *

Bashir Gemayel's five Maronites, firing automatic weapons from the hip, rushed from their inflatable Zodiac boat onto the rocky shore at his command.

Zaki's gunfire must be supported, augmented. To Gemayel and his commandos, there was no doubt: they had seen the weird and awful enemy ensnare Aziru and whisk him away.

Now they saw the mad bull fall in mid-charge and the ground open up around the pillar which wasn't deep enough even to hold the two creatures which had come forth from it.

Their hail of bullets became a deadly swarm of wasps that ricocheted off stone and gave new meaning to the term "friendly fire" as men yelled, and fell, and became afraid to pull their triggers.

Alexander yelled at the top of his lungs: "Stop! Fools! It's Minos! It's a Judge! It's a way out of Hell you're destroying. Stop, I say!" with tears running down his face.

But by then it was too late.

The bellowing bull was on its knees, gnashing sharp fangs and spouting wine-dark blood which steamed when it hit the rocks. Its legs wouldn't hold it, and it scrabbled there, lunging, its eyes wild, its muzzle straining skyward.

Then it crashed to its side and the weight of it cracked the rock, cracked it so well and far that chasms opened between Bashir's own two feet and men on either side of him scrambled backward.

Arms pulled him from the abyss, an abyss out of which hollow keening sounded, keening like women above a grave.

When he looked up, it was all over: the great bull with the gilded horns and painted eyes was gone, down into the rock, which creaked and closed with satisfied snaps like shutting jaws.

And the man who'd been there, the single stranger Alexander had called Minos, was nowhere to be seen.

But Alexander was on one naked knee, bent down on the stone, and in the hand of the Macedonian, who wore only a shirt and dirty undershorts, was a golden mask. In the eyes of Alexander the Great was a rage such as Gemayel had seldom seen, even in Hell.

Alexander fixed him with a glare like a backhanded slap and said softly, "Didn't you hear me, Gemayel? The way out of Hell was here—through the man and bull and pillar that is no longer."

And that was true: behind Alexander, the pillar or stalagmite, or whatever it was, had disappeared.

The ground had closed up, the bull had sunk away, and there was nothing left, not even a slick of blood, to prove that anything had happened here. Nothing except the golden mask which looked exactly like the mask of Agamemnon.

"You've shut the door," Alexander continued when Gemayel just shook his head and spread his hands. "But it's not your fault."

Zaki, in baggy pants with an empty magazine in one hand and a Mini Uzi in the other, came forward, saying: "No, it's mine. When they took Aziru, I lost control. Demons, they were, for all we know. No god would send such creatures. And then that Minos-thing wanted to pull the same trick on you. . . . Alexander, if I was wrong, I'm sorry."

Took Aziru, had been Zaki's words, words that ran through Gemayel's five Maronite Christians like dropsy and would run through the Roman army the same way.

Even while Alexander was getting to his feet and telling Zaki, "Never mind it. The chance, if it was a chance of heaven, will come again. And if you're right that it was just one more Hellish plot, you've saved me. That Minotaur wasn't any Angel of God," the words were doing their work.

And though Zaki held his ground, the little man stiffening to his full height and looking the *basileus* in the eye while he told Alexander what fatted calves and bull-idols had meant to his people, and reminded him what the Minotaur's horrid jaws could have done to flesh and bone, and pointed out that Minos had promised no Heaven, only a rendered judgment in Alexander's case—all that time the Maronites were muttering among themselves, wandering around, their eyes on the ground, looking for the pillar that had been there and the way out of Hell that Alexander himself had said was here.

Maccabee (as well as the Germans before him, the Macedonians around him, and the Romans behind him) heard the sound of automatic weapons fire rip through the maze.

If before they had been nervous, now, in the deafening silence which magnified their footfalls on the stone as they ran toward the commotion, they were breathless with apprehension.

They were so little of an army now, so ragged with despair and disarrayed with dismay, that the Germans ran smack into a dead end of solid stone and were half-trampled by the Macedonians on their heels before Maccabee, with a bawled command, put a stop to it.

"Hold!" he demanded. "Listen!"

Everyone listened but there was only their heavy breathing, the creak of leather bound over laboring chests, the clink of metal-edged scabbards and D-rings—and silence.

Silence as deep and wide as eternity. Silence as complete as the wisdom of God.

And yet, as Maccabee tried to will away the pounding in his ears to better hear it, there was a texture to that silence; a soft, nearly inaudible rush like moving water.

Or the pulse of his blood in his ears.

He held up a hand as someone coughed, put his fingers to his eyes, and strained his every sense to find it.

And again it was there: the sound of rushing water.

Not an imagining, but a real sound. Beyond this dead end, somewhere.

"Tyr!" shouted one of the Germans into that hush with a voice that seemed to deafen. And the echo came back, "Tyr, tyr, yyr, rrr. . . ."

It was Perfidy who'd heard something, Perfidy who knelt now, his clawed hands digging at the stone. "Tyr!" he said again, this time with certainty, so that blond Murder and the Macedonians bent down to help him dig.

Maccabee watched these men, digging at the solid rock like dogs trying to dig a way to freedom under a fence, impassively.

And then he too heard more than water: the sound of men, not his own men but others, clearly there amid the chink of ax-blade and knife on stone.

"Hi! Dig, Romans, dig for freedom! For Alexander!" Maccabee commanded then, knowing that, wrong or right, it was time to give an order before he lost all semblance of command and was left, inert, like the bodies he'd seen on Troy's walls, a sacrifice to this hungry maze.

Kleopatra walked among the jumble of the baggage train, spread out before the the battle plain of Ilium where war's chaos had so recently reigned, her stride wide and her posture commanding as she sauntered toward Caesar's tent.

She had been summoned there, not politely. Abruptly. Through the mechanism of Mouse.

And Mouse now trailed behind, miserably or taciturnly—one never knew, with Mouse, what if anything besides Julius mattered, what besides command and order made sense.

Mouse was concerned that she watch her step. Mouse was concerned about the fey nature of this ground. Mouse did not want anyone falling into any pit that opened under foot or being swept away by the treacherous river Scamander, or any other river.

Mouse had said all that, in short declarative sentences that, of him, had been oratorial triumph. And Mouse had been at pains to make sure that Diomedes was not left alone with Helen—that Diomedes, too, would attend mighty Caesar's conference.

They had Aeneas to treat with now, Mouse had said, as if everyone understood.

Kleopatra did; but she understood, as well, the look in Diomedes' eye, and the way Helen had thrown her arms around the hero, and the quiver that coursed

Paris' flesh from head to toe whenever those two—Argive and much-coveted princess—so much as saw one another.

What Kleopatra understood, and feared that Caesar didn't (wouldn't, blinded by men's logic and men's pride) was that Helen might well be the cement that anchored the army here like plinths anchor statues. Helen was perhaps the most dangerous piece on this gameboard.

With the exception, of course, of Kleopatra herself.

The guards would hold the Spartan princess fast, unharmed and unharmful, until Menelaos and Achilles were returned by the sortie party sent to find them.

If they did. If they could.

Without Achilles to complete the pentagram of Julius/Alexander/Achilles, perhaps they'd find a way off this accursed battle plain. Or perhaps the key was meant to fit a keyhole between a pair of alabaster Spartan thighs.

But there was danger here, on this ground which shifted and reformed and became whatever place it willed, that none of their schemes would win out over Chaos.

She wanted to talk to Machiavelli, or spend some time alone with Welch in the com truck. Or both. Somebody had to do it and Caesar wasn't seeing what was before his face, only what he wished was there.

Men had that tendency, even the best of them. It was the handle by which women dragged them hither and thither; it was the advantage which, to Klea, had made up for being born female.

She'd never hated Osiris, or Isis, or even Horus, for the trick of making her a woman; she'd thought it a wondrous joke that she'd been given the element of surprise.

Now for the first time—as had never happened in life—her wiles would be truly tested, for another woman of power was on the scene.

Helen's childish spoiled-brat routine, Klea was sure, was only that: a ruse. Klea had played apparent weakness to advantage too often, too well, to credit Helen with only what lay on the surface.

Walking through what was left of the horse lines with Mouse behind, Kleopatra chanced to glance up at the citadel—so small, so unimposing, so primitive by the standards of one who'd strolled through Luxor.

It was too humbling, all of this, to be tolerated. They would win here. This was not their Hell, though it might be Diomedes'.

If worse came to worse, Klea would see the Achaeans and the Trojans left here, battling eternally, and the Roman army push on. If not a way out of Hell, then if they'd just find Thebes and the Great Green or even the Nile, Hatshepsut's tomb, perhaps . . . or Alexandria: if she was to be trapped in history, forced to repeat and replay until she got right past deeds and misdeeds, then she'd take her own, thank you very much.

If not a way out of Hell by force of arms, then a way back to Egypt would do. Suffice. Oh, yes.

It was this plan, this proposal, she wished to air before Machiavelli, and even Welch, to see what Authority, or Agency, if Caesar's innermost thoughts were right, would do.

There was no choice, however, but to put it off until she'd seen Julius and sat through whatever little show he was about to put on the Aeneas.

With Mouse trotting behind, close enough to grab her if the ground tried to swallow her, she hurried her pace. It was time to take control, keep these men from deepening their dooms, from choking on their pride.

She'd done it before, gods knew. By Isis and all the Adads of foreign Heavens, she'd do it again.

Antonius and Machiavelli had brought Aeneas to see Julius.

Was it success, or was it Machiavelli's worst sort of treachery?

As Klea and Mouse, then Diomedes, came into the audience tent (a fortuitous thing, to have brought the fancy tent along, here where primitives beguiled by bright baubles were everywhere), Julius wished he had told Antonius to give him more time alone with Klea and the Argive before bringing the ancestor in.

The ancestor. It was thus that Caesar found himself thinking of the man called Aeneas.

Direct-line ancestor. Oh, gods, what was he *doing* here?

The impulse to bury his face in his hands was so strong that Julius barely stifled it, but managed: Kleopatra mustn't see how deeply this meeting was affecting him.

The inclusion of Diomedes in their council was hint enough that even he, Caesar, was acknowledging the treachery in the very ground about them.

Klea's eyes were shining: a sign that something was brewing there. She had the accursed eight ball in one hand as she ducked under the tentflap Mouse held high for her.

She was more beautiful than ever: travail and danger became her; she was like a child again, like the young queen who'd mesmerized him. Who always would. . . .

He pulled his eyes away from her demurely-khakied form and said, "Sit, Klea. We haven't much time. Aeneas will be here shortly—"

Then Diomedes ducked through, his short, new beard full of dust and his eyes full of shadows.

Looking at him, Caesar saw the unexpected and it dried the prepared speech ready on his tongue.

For Julius had never expected to see Diomedes distracted, or uncertain, or holding himself on so tight a rein.

All of this was visible in the posture and the movements and the lowered head of the Argive Homer had credited with so much wisdom. The confusion of a smitten youth was on his face.

Klea's darting glance went between the two men, then rested in Caesar's. She said, "Don't mind our breaker of horses—he's in love, or as close to it as he'll ever be with a female who has only two legs and doesn't whinny."

Diomedes shot a stare at Klea, then said, "Caesar, women are poison on a venture such as this, I've long maintained. Two together, and it's nothing but a cat-fight. Give Helen and Paris—their care, their welfare, over to me. It's my place; they're my people. No good can come from letting this one hold the other's fate."

The manner of refering to women as if they were not present wasn't one that had survived into Julius' time.

He saw storm-clouds gathering on Klea's face.

But there were other considerations. First, Diomedes might simply be correct. Second, there were more questions, more parties, and more desires to satisfy than those of the Egyptian.

He said, "Let us leave it to the eight ball. That's fair. Then, no matter the answer, Diomedes, you'll give me your assessment of this Aeneas business before you leave."

"Fine." The Argive crossed massive arms.

"*Iuli!*" Klea protested, then said, "*Mi Iuli,*" as if humoring a dull-witted child, and turned the eight ball in her delicate, lovely fingers.

Diomedes got up and looked over her shoulder, his implication of treachery one Julius hoped that Klea could forgive.

The eight ball became still in her hands.

She read out loud: "Take the initiative," and before she could interpret that judgment, Diomedes crowed, "Before Athene, then, they're mine!" and returned to the curule chair opposite Caesar, where he sat awkwardly.

The son of Tydeus wasn't used to chairs, but he was used to winning: the grin on his face was well hidden from Klea.

"Done," said Caesar quickly. And: "Now, about Aeneas, do you think he can speak for the Trojans?"

"*All* of them?" Diomedes said in disbelief, then rubbed his jaw. "If anyone can . . . but it's not all of them you need on your side, is it? He'd be enough. If what you want is to return the Trojans to the citadel . . . ?"

The question hung in the air until Klea said, "Ha! Not bad for a Greek!"

Caesar hadn't expected Diomedes to see so deeply: it was one answer, one thing that might work. And he didn't understand why the Argive wasn't arguing—he was an enemy of the Trojans. Could it be that Diomedes, too, thought that the only way off this ground that held them like honey holds flies was to restore some previous balance?

He said, "That is what I want, if it leads to a way out of here . . . for all of us."

"There's been no luck yet, locating Achilles," Klea remarked.

Caesar could have strangled her, for Diomedes hadn't known that, not by the look on his face as the Argive rose to his full height in the tent.

"I'll be with the Spartan woman, if you need me. You shouldn't, until Menelaos can be found—if that's what you're saying, that he and Achilles never made it out of the chopper, then perhaps Aeneas *is* your only hope."

Your, not *our* hope, Julius noted silently.

Diomedes turned his back and was headed out before Julius had time to say, "Fine. Go, and have Antonius bring in Aeneas."

He really didn't want to be alone with Klea right now, not considering the look in Egypt's eyes.

Achilles had been in the wet sand and rock of the dark place so long that he was beginning to fear he'd been washed by Scamander into his own tomb.

His old tomb was here somewhere, perhaps around him.

He was shaking and he knew that Menelaos, in the dark beside him, was aware of that.

But it was cold and they'd decided to get out of the glowing, wet pit where the pool was.

So they'd trekked and trekked and come to more

water, a shore against which a dark sea seemed to lap.

And here they'd found spent brass—7.62 and 5.56mm shell casings from automatic weapons. And they'd found scratches on the rock, and a weird stalagmite which seemed to have a cave in it.

They'd shouted themselves hoarse and now they just sat, listening to scrabbling sounds as if something was tunneling through the wall behind them.

It wasn't his tomb, not with all this space and all this room to wander, to get lost.

They were very lost indeed.

Menelaos was afraid that the things scrabbling at the stone might get through and eat them.

Achilles was afraid of other things: of the earth closing in upon him, of being buried alive, of falling through or being washed away again, deeper this time. Of ending up in his own tomb.

It was here, above, on the battle plain. Someplace. Anything but that, he'd decided, would do.

But in that instance, he'd kill himself: he was holding his combat knife with its serrated curve so that he'd be ready. No hellish trick would pin his arms too soon for him to manage to pierce his heart.

Anything lesser, he'd deal with. He'd assessed his wounds, and Menelaos', and decided they were survivable.

Everything was survivable in Hell, of course, except madness: Achilles could handle whatever the Devil and all his horrid minions had to offer, except being buried alive.

So he waited, exhausted, listening to the scrabbling at the walls of this maze and watching the weird little cave in the middle of the stalagmite and counting the spent brass while his shoulder throbbed with pain and Menelaos kept telling him that everything would be all right, they couldn't die, that the very ground was native to their spirits.

He knew that. He just didn't want to *be* some disembodied spirit like those on the Tree of the Unborn Dead, or those in the Forest of the Damned, or any of the rest of it.

He wanted to strive with the living, not cavort with the shades—as much as any of them were living.

He wanted to keep his body, he wanted to make it to the surface once again. . . .

"Shut up, will you," he told Menelaos.

Even in the near-black dark (they were saving their flashlights), he could see the Atreidês wince.

"I mean, listen. Whatever it is, it's going to break through any minute. Get back."

He had three rounds in the Galil, which had been lying in the pool of the golden cave where they'd landed.

If it had been the M-16 that had been sitting in water and silt and sand, Achilles would have fired a test round, or stripped the gun and cleaned it. But Galils were like elephants, as tough as Odysseus, and more constant.

He'd cleared the jam with his Swiss Army knife and Menelaos' help.

Now he chambered a round and waited, legs spread wide, sighted on the area of wall through which something was obviously soon going to come.

"The flashlight, Menelaos. Shine it there."

"Are you certain?" said the cautious man, the prince who'd been chosen by Helen for qualities he lacked, rather than those he possessed, the handsome man who'd caused so much trouble and whose eyes were always mournful.

"Hell no, I'm not certain. But do it anyway. It's just light—and warning—we're wasting."

Back turned to the stalagmite that looked so much like a pillar, Achilles and Menelaos waited, flashlight scanning the bottommost section of rocky, featureless wall.

If Menelaos had given him any more trouble, Achilles would have wrenched the flashlight from his grasp, tied it onto the Galil, and that would have been the end of the discussion.

But Menelaos wasn't a coward. That had never been the problem. He was simply accursed, chosen by the Spartan bitch and the gods who worked through her.

When the chips were down, Achilles admitted to himself as the flashlight played steadily and without a waver over the daunting wall and the noise behind, Menelaos wasn't a bad guy to have around.

It was something to remember, here where saving himself might soon become a real possibility.

They both knew what horrors lived in the underworld.

They were both scared to death. But they were both veterans of the Trojan war—the first one—and suddenly that meant something positive to Achilles, though it hadn't for thousands of years.

A crack appeared, powdered rock drifting down from it, along the wall.

"Steady," Achilles said as the flashlight jerked a bit, talking to himself as much as to Menelaos.

"If it matters," Menelaos said through gritted teeth, "I never blamed you for anything that happened . . .

not in the real War, I mean—uh, many did, you know. But not me. Ever. I know my faults when I see them. And I know what was the gods' doing."

"Glad to hear it, friend," Achilles said absently, "Let's just watch that spot, okay? And get ready to dive in the water, if you have to—it may not be a great way out, but it is a way."

"A way?" Menelaos echoed, while from the wall in the flashlight's circle little chunks of rock and grunting noises began to issue. "How is that? I have no rocks tied on my feet to weigh me down, no rope to pull myself along, and I know not the current—whether it will wash me up on some farther shore, or give me to the River."

"Oh shit, I forgot. You can't swim, right? You don't even know what I'm talking about right? You stupid antiquated bastard, why didn't you learn when you had a chance?"

"I—" The flashlight wavered, then its beam zigzagged crazily across the wall. ". . . Swim?"

"Oh never mind. Get that flashlight into position. If I'm making for the water, I'll grab you and hold you. Just don't fight me, okay?"

"Yes, if you say so." The flashlight's beam steadied on the wall and now there was a hole big enough for a man to put his eye to—if he wasn't worried about having it plucked out of his skull.

Still furious that he hadn't remembered how relatively new a development swimming was, how men had not known the ways of the water and had dived with weights and trusted their fates to gods once they'd cut the stones from their feet, he said offhandedly, "Go take a look. I'll cover you."

And Menelaos did, his flashlight bobbing as he

inched toward the wall, then knelt down there and bent his head toward the hole.

"AAiieee!" shouted the Achaean. "By my mother and all the gods who—"

Achilles' hand tightened so quick and hard that he almost pulled through on the trigger and wasted one precious round.

"Menelaos, man, what is it? Are you hurt?" Prudence discarded, he bounded forward, throwing himself to his knees behind the other man, his Galil trained on the head and the hole to which it seemed glued.

"Hurt? Hurt?" Menelaos was giggling like a happy drunk, little chortles between his words. "It's your giant blond allies! We're saved!"

"Rescue? A rescue party?" Achilles sat back upon his haunches, the Galil's unfolded stock resting against his hipbone.

Calls were coming from the other side of the wall now: "Is Alexander with you?" Maccabee wanted to know, while the Germans kept yelling "Tyr! Tyr!" at the top of their lungs.

A rescue party, then, but not for him. Achilles swung his head to look behind, for some reason, and saw that weird stalagmite with the hole in it just as it was fading away into nothingness.

And in its center, something that looked very much like Hektor was coming into being.

Welch was trying to follow everything going on above and below ground with equipment strained to the limits of its capacity.

When Machiavelli appeared with Nichols (whom Welch had sent to get the ferret-faced Italian), Welch sat back in his ergo chair, fingers laced behind his head, and said, "Hey there, buddy, how's tricks?"

"Tricks?" said Machiavelli. "*Signore*, there are no tricks of mine here. None at all."

"Not here, maybe—not in this truck. Expecting any more messages from Higher Up, are we?"

Nichols wasn't exactly holding Machiavelli by the scruff of his skinny neck, but the implication of rough-house was clear: Nichols was hulking over Machiavelli, projecting all the bone-crushing psychosis that made Welch so fond of his operator.

"No, no messages. *Signore*. . . ." Machiavelli's hands wrung themselves; his face was pale: "We are trapped here, like the flies on fly-paper. You know it, I know it. Therefore, why suspect one another?"

"Because, you little rat-faced bastard, *I* didn't or-der that damned chopper and now it's fucking crashed and *I've* got to write it up—enter it in the debit column. You know what I mean?"

"No, *signore*, I do not." The Italian had velvet skin and limpid eyes and a razor-sharp mind, all of which were accentuated in the monitor-glow and chatter of humming components that filled the com truck.

"Come on, let me tweak this bastard," Nichols said pleadingly. Only half playing a part.

"Not yet, Nichols. Machiavelli, I'm going to ask you one more time, plain and simple: did you have anything to do with that chopper and Achilles being played down here? And if so, on whose orders were those components disbursed? Get the drift of the questions? *Who's fucking responsible for this sorry goddamn screwup?*" Welch's fist hit the padded arm of his ergo chair.

Machiavelli blinked but didn't shudder. Then he spread his hands: "*Mea non culpa.*"

"You-a-gonn-a suff-a," Nichols snarled from behind his hand clamping on Machiavelli's thin shoulder, "if the boss don't like your answers."

"Easy, Nichols. We've got all the time we need."

Welch had surprised himself, losing control like that. He tried again: "Look, Nicky, let's get something straight: we know you've got your own sources of communication—we saw a message come up for you—*here*—remember, on my own fucking data base. So it follows you've got other sources. And we know you requisitioned most of this stuff without Agency approval or even goddamn awareness. And now we need to know just who, or what, is fielding you. I don't want to step on some friggin' Pentagram operation because nobody bothered to tell me I shouldn't. You've got to remember, missions run in Hell, but like everything else, they don't run very well. So just tell us who's on the other end of your leash, how you're passing info and to whom, and we'll let you go—no sweat, no harm, no hard feelings. *Capiche?*"

"I do not," said Machiavelli carefully and very slowly, enunciating his English, "understand what you are talking about, *signore* Welch. What 'Agency' you refer to, I have no idea. As far as the rest . . ." Spread hands again. ". . . I am merely a humble servant of the Great Machine, as are we all. I have no special—"

"Welch," Nichols fairly moaned with incipient pleasure, "come *on*. Gimme this guy. I'll have him telling you whatever you want to hear in fifteen minutes."

"Yeah, but that's not what I want: I want the truth. You know that word, Nicky—'truth'? You heard it lately? You're telling me something by not telling me, you know? You're telling me maybe you scammed all this stuff, maybe you don't have squat for authorization, or maybe whoever tried to contact you through me and mine isn't on the same team we are. And you don't dare tell me that. Because if I get pissed at you, I'm going to let it be known around camp that you're responsible for Maccabee's recent trip to the Undertaker . . . maybe not the hand that struck the blow, but definitely the perpetrator. Caesar, I've heard, has a real horror of assassins and assassination plotters."

"No, no, *signore*," Machiavelli said miserably. "You don't understand."

"Say again?" Welch said softly, looking fondly at Machiavelli. "I didn't hear you."

"You do not understand . . . what I risk. What we all risk."

"That's fine, maybe I don't. So you explain it to me."

And Welch saw the cloud of disappointment settle on Nichols' face as Machiavelli began trying to talk his way out of what he'd talked his way into.

It was Paradise-set, or at least the ruddy glow was darkening to the tone of candlelight seen through mountain wine.

It hadn't been easy, convincing the Roman guards that he, Diomedes, had Caesar's permission to move the prisoners.

Then it hadn't been easy to find a place to move them *to*—Diomedes didn't have fancy accomodations as did the Roman and his Egyptian whore.

He'd finally managed all of that and was sitting

pensively before the tent, thinking that he'd just call
Helen out and walk with her behind the revetments,
and speak to her of things that mattered: of the
shame of fighting this war eternally, of the hearts
that had broken and would be broken again, of all
that was wrong and how they might fix it if she and
he could just act as one, when Caesar came riding by
on a great horse that might have been one of Achilles' Thessalians.

"Diomedes," said the Roman commander. "A moment, please."

He had an endless supply of moments, though not
all would be spent in light the color of finest wine.

He got up and went to the horse's side, absently
scratching that spot on a horse where neck meets
chest that all horses love scratched, so that Caesar's
steed stretched out its neck, half-closed its eyes, and
lolled its tongue in pleasure.

"Speak, then."

"The woman Helen, whom you have there, she's
part of what's keeping us rooted here like trees. Be
careful. Don't venture onto untested ground. Aeneas
thinks that, with her and Paris unharmed to present
as tokens of our good faith, we might be able to make
a change in all our fates."

"And that change would be?"

"Propose an exchange of places to the two armies—a
change of camps: put the Trojans in the citadel and
the Achaeans on the beach. Do you see?"

"Restore the balance? So the war can proceed as it
did before? No! *Never!*"

The last word, too loud and full of passion, hung
between them.

Caesar's slightly narrowed eyes and slightly tight-

ened mouth told Diomedes that the Roman had expected his reaction—it was an Achaean reaction, after
all: obvious, logical, and without thought behind it.

But the Roman was giving him time, time to think
again, to call back the words. And he took it: "See
this, Caesar. Achilles is lost to us, now. Alexander is
lost to us. Maccabee is lost to us. I cannot quit any
battlefield of this nature leaving so many soldiers
with their fates unknown. Here, you must have noticed, the Undertaker is slow to claim the bodies—
the Trojans on the walls lasted far too long. If our
missing were dead, we'd come upon their corpses.
We have not. I, for one, seek no end without resolution: I'm in no place to treat with Trojans, but were
I, I'd ask nothing—make no deal with anyone until
my missing were found."

"You're telling me you'll stay here until they're
found?"

"That's right."

"Then find them," said Julius Caesar, and kicked
his horse in the ribs so that it snorted and leapt away
from Diomedes' hand.

He stood there for a while watching the figure on
the white horse ride up a hillside to one of the
groundeffect tanks, tether his hose there, and climb
aboard the mighty physeter, where he sat looking
out over the plain where Scamander had writhed and
struck like a giant snake.

Hatshepsut was up there, Diomedes thought he'd
heard.

But one heard many rumors around this camp.

And he'd spoken his soul's plain truth to the
Roman—truth as he knew it. He could do no more.

He stooped into the tent: "Helen? Would you

come here—no, not you, Paris. I must speak with her
alone."

Maccabee was unsure of what he'd gained, when
they'd broken through the wall and seen Hektor, in
some ungodly peril, pinioned within a pillar that
wasn't entirely corporeal.

He was sure for a moment that all his troops would
break and run, that nothing would advance this
doomed enterprise.

And then Hektor's shade winked out, and there
was just Achilles and Menelaos there, jingling spent
brass and asking questions.

The cocky little chopper pilot didn't seem to understand when Maccabee explained about the maze
with its fewer and fewer exits, or about the hand that
wouldn't decompose, the woman's hand that was
always on the seat of the throne whenever they'd
returned there.

But he did seem to understand the lay of the
caverns.

For Achilles said, "If you just follow me, and we
can get back to the little chamber Menelaos and I
landed in, we can use those Germans of yours and all
this extra manpower to tunnel back up to the surface. I'm sure of it."

And when Achilles finished explaining how he'd
gotten down here, Maccabee was willing to give it a
try. He wasn't as sure as Achilles that it would work,
but he was sure enough to give it a try.

And they had rounds and rounds of spent brass to
mark their trail, to leave in their wake, so that they
could follow the brass back to this spot and make
sure they weren't walking in circles.

So much spent brass, in fact, that how it had gotten here began to weigh on his mind.

Some of the shells were Uzi shells, and Alexander had favored the Uzi.

But there were no bodies bobbing in the black water they followed, and the torches of the Romans blew wildly in a wind from somewhere, and so they followed Achilles and Menelaos, who at least seemed sure of their direction, while Maccabee, with the sight of Hektor's transluscent manifestation fresh in his mind's eye, was sure of nothing much at all.

"Caesar? Why not?" Welch said when the summons came, although Machiavelli was still enjoying the hospitality of the com truck and Nichols wouldn't be as gentle if Welch were not around. "I'll be right with you, Mouse."

Decius Mus was one of the few Romans that Welch would have liked to suborn, but he was hesitant to try it.

The Roman looked into the truck without fear, his sharp eyes seeing everything.

Welch could only hope the soldier didn't comprehend the significance of what he saw.

Right now, on Welch's private scoreboard, as indicated by his various telltales and surveillance electronics, the score was tied between the Devil and Caesar, who was definitely his own man.

Any minute, unless someone intervened, Alexander of Macedon, Zaki, and Gemayel's Maronites were going to come floating out on Scamander's currents into the early evening, realize where they were, and start yelling like blazes for help.

Then a number of items of information were going to come out into the open.

Welch didn't really care what happened here—not to the Trojans and Achaeans with their war—but he did care about his own skin.

He disdained a hand up into the jeep Mus had brought for him: he'd spent more time in jeeps than any of these skirted poofs.

But Julius Caesar—facing him was another thing. This wouldn't be happening if Caesar wasn't beginning to put pieces together and not liking puzzle as it took shape under his nose.

Oh well, you did the best you could.

And he had a hole card.

He always did.

This time, he was figuring as Mouse jounced the jeep up the hill toward one of the groundeffect tanks, it was Niccolo Machiavelli.

Almost immediately, Welch had to play it: for when they reached the tank, Caesar was sitting on its rear skirt, waiting.

Caesar said: "Welch, tell me how you and your truck and your subordinate came into my service—how you came to be among us."

"Sir," Welch said calmly, still sitting in the jeep. "I think we'd better talk about Niccolo Machiavelli first. We've been interrogating him in the truck—we found some discrepancies, you know. I'm not altogether sure you're going to like what I've got to tell you, sir, but here goes . . . ."

Alexander's party—himself, Zaki, Gemayel and his five Maronites—went straight to the tents of Julius Caesar.

The little group was muddy and wet and shivering, but triumphant. Even Zaki was smiling, and the Jew's hands upon his everpresent hat were still.

Alexander had cautioned the Maronites that they mustn't say a word about their adventures until he, Alexander, had conferred with Caesar.

But Kleopatra didn't know where Caesar was, she swore. "Out on the perimeter, somewhere," she said. "But come in, Basileus, and tell us what happened to your pants." She giggled, and she was warm and sloe-eyed and he was tired and in need of comfort.

He knew that there was no way to hush the news, whatever command he gave, no matter how Gemayel tried to control his Maronites.

Those soldiers had seen Aziru the Amurrite carried up to Heaven, had seen with their own eyes a man find his way out of Hell.

It was going to be all over the camp by morning, and whether Caesar could keep the Roman army from charging down into that maze en masse, to find the spot where the riverbank hosted a stalagmite that was really a pillar, was anyone's guess.

When Alexander heard that Maccabee was still missing, and believed to be in the maze, his heart lurched: had his friend found the magic door and, without Zaki there to open fire upon Minos, Judge of the Underworld, made good his escape?

Alexander dared not hope—or couldn't find it in his heart to hope. He'd be so lonely without Maccabee.

The question of the ravening Minotaur, and of what Minos (if there still was a Minos, if Zaki had not murdered the very Lord of this local patch of Hell and thus ruined all their chances) would demand as penance for being shot at, Alexander tried not wonder.

He pulled from under his shirt the mask of Agamemnon and offered it to Kleopatra: "A spoil of war, Pharaoh."

After that, he was very busy trying to find out from Kleopatra what had happened while he'd been gone, and what it meant that Aenaes was in camp, and that Achilles and Menelaos had been swallowed up by the river.

This, while avoiding Egypt's tempatations, in case Julius Caesar should come home to his tent unexpectedly.

Bishop's Move

The stench of sulphur was overwhelming about the pit, and there was no man of them that did not look doubtful at this hole that extended—perhaps into the next hell, perhaps to a deeper one, perhaps to a blind end—Scaevola ventured as far down it as indicated it was no mere pocket, and turned back again to face the mouth of the pit, where a cluster of silhouettes showed him the better part of two cohorts, human figures black against the ruddy sky, blacker still as a thick arc of fire heaved up behind them. Scaevola's heart clenched up as he thought it was coming down on them, and then he realized the size of it, saw the silhouetted soldiers turn and stare behind them at that horror of a river which heaved and lashed in its multiple beds like a headless snake.

"Advenite!" he yelled at them, beckoning, before they should lose their courage. And good men that they were, he saw them hesitate in the roaring no-sound of the river, saw some start down and others lay hands on the shoulders of men still watching, paralyzed by that sight; then those men moved and turned and came, bringing their rifles and their supplies on their backs. Last of all, the jeep, nosing down over the rim of the old lava track—damned well easier to walk than ride on this trek, Scaevola thought.

Camouflage helmets, black-face and field kits for

this one, no shields and no red cloaks and damned little flash. M-16s were the standard issue, every clip they could liberate without tipping off the Pentagram, that and the stuff the jeep carried.

He waited for them, till the first few legionaries had reached him and he knew that the jeep was going to make it onto the smoother ground below the lava pillows; then he got them sorted out, shouting an order to the second centurion to walk tail back there with the jeep and keep everyone in sight . . . while the jeep headlights jounced and flared on the walls toward them at the best pace it could manage.

Scaevola took point, himself with one of the third cohort to handle the flashlight, while he kept the Galil slung where he could use it to cover both of them. Forward right now was not the direction that gave him the cold sweats. It was the power that boomed and thundered in the rock walls around them and heated the rocks under their boots.

But if Phlegethon whipped their way and sent a part of its burning torrent rushing down this old tube, there was only a second's difference between the jeep at the rear and where he was walking.

Maybe they could still make it on down there, in that event, march right through hellfire and into Agamemnon's hall. But damn, they could still die, too. There was a terror in Scaevola's heart that did not have to do even with Phlegethon. Rather it was lost time, and directions, and whether these places led anywhere that they remotely wanted to go.

If the Devil knew what they were up to and if the Devil wanted them, while they came sneaking through this twisting gut, he could hail them all to the Undertaker with one crook of his finger.

*   *   *

It was long that Caesar delayed, and a Great King's patience frayed with waiting, frayed still more with the comings and goings of this and that soldier to the tent and the little queen going to speak with them in private, sometimes with a backward glance, secret-keeping by the turn of her head when she answered something or gave some order.

And there were his Germans, these giants who stood at the corners of the tent or hunkered there by the door, and diced and diced with now and again a glance his way, as if the game somehow signified something of him. Their eyes seemed reproachful; for Perfidy and Murder he had lost, with Maccabee, he thought; and he imagined them wondering questions they could not ask of him. Tyr, they called him, and he could not ask them what this was. Everything between them was confounded. Zaki had gone back to the Amerikanoi or somewhere, and in that desertion of the Jew who had saved his life and damned him, Alexander felt another reproach—

It had been very well for a while, this homecoming, all of them having bested the odds and their fates (but they had lost their hopes and Aziru would not come again).

There had been a welcome in camp (but these Romans and their lot were prudish as the Persians—he knew it now, and was outraged to understand why Kleopatra had laughed when first she had seen him; though nakedness was no shame to him, they plainly thought it was, and he must be patient of them, sitting here like a suppliant in Caesar's tent).

His Macedonians had cheered him when they saw him (but they had not known at first that he had left their comrades behind, and they fell into a hush and gave each other troubled looks and asked him in that blunt way his people and the Romans shared: "What will you do?")

"I will find them," he had said (but he did not know how he would do that, only that he was weary and the camp was rife with rumors which made everything uncertain. And he must talk with Caesar. Who delayed.)

He washed, he dressed himself in clothing syco-phants brought—such lost, slavish souls attended on the Romans, non-beings, which chittered and moaned and mourned, whose invisible hands touched his hair and laved his skin—("Away," he said, and brushed them off. And again: "Leave me—" with that tone he had used on mutiny and Persian courtiers alike. They left. So he tended his own needs and sat down to wait, in that way he had sat thrones for hours, with no linkage between face and soul—as well *his* face had been a mask: so in the end he and the queen Kleopatra Ptolmaiđes played this diplomatic game of statues opposite each other, his Zeus-Ammon to her Isis—or was it Bast?)

So by that she thwarted him again, and held him prisoner of his own pride.

"You will hear," he said at last, cutting through silence the way he had split a knot at Gordion (but now he was far, far less the youth, and more the king) "that Aziru has found escape from here. He will not, I think, be back. There is such a thing as Paradise, and he is there. We saw it. So did others. If Caesar *is* this other self and I am his,"—he remembered Achilles and flinched inwardly, "—his *hero*, then what of us, queen Kleopatra, what when one part of this triple soul—finds Paradise? Can it draw the others to heaven after it?"

He doubted all these things. He spoke to dislodge her from her scheming and her silence, this woman, this priestess-queen of a latter and alien age.

But: "Or one of the three being damned," Kleopatra said, "can anchor us all to this fate." She chilled him with that saying.

The failing of one dooms all. The flaw in one is the flaw in all of us.

It was fated that Zaki fire, that there be the Maronites to drive away the judge who might have opened the way for me—

One soul bound in hell, in three bodies?

Foolishness!

"Shadows of shadows," he said. "And lies." He thrust himself to his feet. "I am out of patience."

Achilles. Dead, and judged, and binding us all. Is he the flaw which damns us?

"There is no way," said Kleopatra, "from here to Paradise."

"I tell you I bought it for Hephaistion! And do not tell me your lie, woman, I will not be patient with it now! I have seen, I say, a man go up to Paradise, I have seen the judges, I have seen mine, and I say that I bought that way for my friend—do not *say* his name, woman. Do not you foul it with your priestess tricks. Only find me Caesar and two sane men will reason this out."

"Do you threaten me? You used to do that. And I would tell you that I would sit down and wait—"

He held back his fist. He was trembling.

(But it was true, it was what Hephaistion had said. Publicly as well as privately, his own Macedonians might have said it—there were ways she might have discovered it.)

It was surely his own imagination put the familiar soul behind those eyes, that way of looking at him, head tilted, a worry-line between the eyes—("You drink too much, you remember too much, Alexander, come, lie down, let me ease your shoulders—")

"There is no way," she said again, "for us to Paradise. You could not give it to me, then or now. You spend your years in the hills, avoiding your men till they have drifted away from you; those who would love you, you rage at, you choose loneliness because the men who love you demand too much, because you cannot help but give all or nothing, now. You did not send me to Paradise. You banished me."

"Woman," he said, cold and careful, so very careful. Beside the tent door the dice-throwing ceased. The Germans rose and stood, impassive. In the maze had been shadows. A dream of shadows. And blood. His whole vision was a wash of red. He would not strike her for this mummery. There was no wine in him and the god was quiet in him, his heart cold and dark as the maze. But he had had enough of women altogether, and trembled in a rage Hephaistion would have known and dealt with.

It is your daimon, Hephaistion would say—". . . *Alexander, hush, be still, come with me. We will reason through it together . . . ."*

"Alexander," she said, "it is your *daimon*—it has no place in reason. Listen to me—"

But he did not stay to hear the rest. He did not want to hear. "Come," he snarled at the Germans, turning, and stalked out of the tent, out into the camp which sprawled at the foot of the hill of Troy.

It was a long road up. A long climb afoot, searching like some damned foolish herdsman come to the city, applying here and there, bowing and scratching after fleas—ha' ye seen the *strategos*, good sirs . . . ?

His face burned. He rounded on the Roman guard at the door of the tent. "Fetch me a jeep."

The Roman's face did not change. The eyes flickered, left, right; and abruptly the man turned for the tent door, and other authority.

"*Damn* your impudence!" Alexander caught at the Roman's shoulder, jerked him round and grabbed at the rifle before the man could shove him off with it. Held there. Men had tried that with spears. Another shove. The Germans hovered, one put his hand out to separate them and urged something no one could understand, a hand the size of a man's head and a shaggy, fur-smelling presence compounded with oil and metal and sweat and woodsmoke. Germans were all about him, huge and ominous, wishing him to draw back, interposing their arms and their shoulders till he could not maintain the fight without fighting them all.

He shoved free, and they put their bodies in the way. Their icecolored eyes and bearded faces showed reproach—for failing them. For giving them back to a woman and deserting them. Gods knew. He had lost their leader and his brother along with Maccabee and many of his Macedonians with them, the others of his men who remained in camp gone off to themselves to mutter, surely, how much of honor he had lost before the Romans . . . and where was Diomedes, but snared by Helen? Diomedes himself, he had learned, had suffered, had been rescued, had betaken himself to his tent and his own counsel; while the Romans, and Caesar himself, Kleopatra had revealed to his profound dismay reckoned themselves descended of Trojans.

—of Trojans—and not of Hellenes at all. As if this mattered nothing to him or to this mad queen who claimed to be Hellene, who claimed—*Zeus!*—to be Hephaistion's ghost, and played the oracle to drive him mad as she, while Romans gave him barbaric guards and drove a wedge between him and all that was his.

He turned in a fury and shoved a German aside—it was Famine—or Grief, they both wore lynx-fur and he could not always tell them apart; he walked away, seeking the road, and the Germans did not come further with him. Perhaps they thought he had spurned them again. Perhaps they served a woman now. Or she had given them to Caesar instead, who knew?

He would not turn and ask them, not ask anything of Kleopatra and that crew. He knew the ways of courts and kings and queens, and that kings always slept with politics, no matter what its shape or the color of its eyes or skin. He had slept with this queen. And shared wine with her. But he would not be obligated and not play her mad games and not, not, and not—become her partisan in whatever it was she truly wanted of him, nor admit she had any part of Hephaistion's soul—that great spirit in that painted woman's tiny body, O Zeus, it was travesty! It was grotesque. He had slept with her. And there were times that a turn of her head, a way of standing— or touching. . . .

No.

Through the camp then. "Where's Caesar?" he

asked a knot of soldiers, in slow, deliberate Greek; and: "There," they said, one and the other, and pointed, without honorifies, without the *sir* a Greek would have added: but they were Romans and born rude.

Or they did not even know who he was. He flung his borrowed cloak about him against the chill wind and walked on the muddy track that the soldiers had worn among the tents, walked past cookfires and men sitting in groups and left the tents then, for the road that led up the windy heights of Troy.

A motor growled along behind, and overtook him. He heard it coming and tended over to the side of the road when he heard it take the turn behind him, lest he be run down by these Romans and their brute machines and their damnable haste to be somewhere.

It stopped beside him, squealing as such things would do. A Roman hardly more than a boy looked at him from under a bucket of a khaki-colored helmet. "You going uphill?" the youth asked, and blinked, and said: "General, sir."

The shock and the recognition in the young face was salve to wounds. Alexander stood there holding his cloak together and wondering whether it was Egypt who had put the boy up to it, but he did not think so. "I'm looking for your commander."

"He's up in the citadel, sir, I'm to run this stuff—" The Roman hooked a thumb back at the rear of the jeep, where boxes sat, and an Oracle of Litton. "—up to the lieutenant, same place, you want to get in, sir?"

"What's your name, boy?"

"Valerius, sir."

It was a handsome face. An innocent one, and guileless. In his own army—But the Romans would be horrified, the boy would be offended beyond words; different days, different ways, and a colder and lonelier world, it seemed to him. No wonder the Romans clung fast to machines and dealt death with such dispassion.

He climbed in and sat down, watched the boy's—Valerius'—fine hands as he shoved levers and did the expert things that put the jeep in motion, up the winding road. There was grace. And a good heart.

It was well to know such things had been born after him, even in a cold and foreign world.

"What was your age?" he asked.

"Eighteen, sir."

"No, I mean what year?"

"Seven oh eight, sir. A.U.C. Died in Spain." A bright, quick grin. "Never did know what of, but I reckon it was a bullet, the things was coming in like hail." A hand left the wheel to describe a thing half a finger long. "Bit of lead, the slingers threw 'em, come in just as mean as powder 'n ball would, them Spanish—" The boy took both hands to his business again as a drop swung into view and out again off the left side. Then he went abashedly quiet, as if he had reckoned his chatter unwanted.

"Go on," Alexander said, wanting such a voice and such ingenuousness. Here was a young soldier, not a diplomat, nor a queen with lies and motives, and the world seemed some little warmer. *Eighteen all these years. And no wiser. Or is he? Or am I?*—watching Valerius' hands on the wheel and the levers. "I never saw Spain."

"Well, I sure wish't I hadn't." Another grin, flung

sideways, as the jeep pulled in through the wrecked gate of Troy, and zigged for the sharp turn. "But I didn't get to see much of it, after all." Another turn round the corner, and into the wreckage the physeters had made of the city street.

"What would you rather, Valerius? A long life with no renown? Or a short one, with glory?"

Achilles' question. Thetis' question. His own, when he was young, at Aristotle's knee. The young face turned toward him, sensing something perilous, and away again, as peril turned up in a jagged slab of a fallen wall and the jeep veered and jolted.

"Which?" Alexander pursued him.

A second, panicked look. So the boy had heard that question before. Knew him, and knew whom he carried, and understood omens. A second correction of the erring jeep. "Dunno, sir. Down here—is there a difference?"

"Up there. In life. Which did you want?"

The boy did not look at him. Both hands were on the wheel. "I wanted the army. Wanted out of the Neapolis. Wasn't any living. My folks was dyers. I never found 'em here. But you wouldn't. Not here. They're all right somewheres. I know they are. My brother too. I figure he got the shop, dye all over him, till he was purple, that's what he wanted. Me, I wanted—I dunno, out of there. So I'm here."

"And here?"

"Shit—sir, begging y'r pardon—I just want to walk out of here, just damn well walk out of this one on my own legs, sir, that's the ambition I got." The jeep whined and complained, the last steep climb to the courtyard, among parked vehicles. "I got no fondness for the Trip, damn old man and that white room . . . gives me the shivers." Valerius pulled the jeep about and stopped, facing a guarded door. "I got you here, sir, they can show you the way."

"I'll find my own way." Alexander reached out, rested his hand on the youth's shoulder, squeezed hard, very hard. As if he touched the earth or the rocks or something of substance among so many shadows. For a moment he met the Roman's eyes. "Thank you. *Thank* you, soldier."

"Yessir. Thank *you*, sir."

He climbed down again, gathered his cloak at the neck against the gusting wind and walked on, while Roman sentries gave him a scrutiny; and wisely showed no disposition to stop him.

"Caesar is here," he said, question without question.

"King's hall, sir." Murmured and fast. "Straight on."

Mouse watched from within that hallway, stood in the shadows as the *basileus* headed toward the throne room with a deliberation and a look on his face that did not bode peace. Mouse's nerve endings twitched, instincts to be there, to get himself into that room, quickly. But it was Alexander, not just any angry man; this man was no personal danger to Julius; and in fact there was some hope in this arrival, the more so if Alexander did what Mouse believed he might do, and demanded privacy so that two of that uneasy triumvirate might come to an understanding. It was well, this time, to stay out of there.

It was another gut feeling that centered his eyes on a second interested watcher in that selfsame wake, a watcher in khaki and not her accustomed glowing pink—Alexander had brushed right past Hatshepsut,

who stood with one hand clenching and unclenching
ominously.

She turned and looked at Mouse then, and her
kohl-painted eyes with his.

So the gut feeling grew and gnawed at Mouse and
overwhelmed all reticence. "Pharaoh," he said, deliberately acknowledging that stare; and knew when
he spoke and waited that she would then ask to talk
to him. There was that take-action look in Pharaoh's
eyes, there was a conference about to take place, in
which she knew herself superfluous: so he offered
himself up in her path and met her eye to eye.
Desperately.

He is in trouble, Pharaoh.

And her look said: *Come with me, Mouse.*

She gave a jerk of her head, back toward a recess
and a stairway. He went, and she went behind him,
into shadows the lamps in the hallway dimly touched.
There was a fresco there of vines. Bullets had pocked
it and they stood on tiles powdered with fallen plaster.

"Mouse," said Pharaoh, "do you want to talk,
Mouse?"

"I will talk."

"There's a rumor going the rounds—it it true?"

"What rumor?"

"*What* rumor? Save me your advice then. I have
better sources in the kitchens."

"Pharaoh."

She turned her head to face him again, black hair
swinging; he did not forget that night, and lamplight,
and Pharaoh the woman—for a moment of true
panic he had lost his perspective, and his very memory of the good Roman wife who had wed him by fire
and water, who had borne him his son . . . rippled

like the unstable landscape, and left him in a cold
sweat, remembering instead the touch of perfumed
skin on skin, and the exotic arts his wife had never
had—

"Aziru," he said; and drew a deep breath, while
images of his wife and the Pharaoh meshed and
unfocussed in his heart. "Yes. Gemayel has been
here. And Zaki. Whatever he saw—" Another and
deeper breath. "—Julius—listened. There are too
many factions. There is danger inside this camp and
outside, too many weapons, too much at stake . . . .
Pharaoh, I said that at a time like this—I might
come to you."

"Ummnnn, with information? With the truth of
this? *Where are we going,* Mouse, what in hell does
Julius think he's doing up here?"

"Welch . . . has taken Niccolo. Niccolo has con-
fessed certain things . . . to the Americans." He
watched the flicker of Hatshepsut's eyes, the movement of dark in shadowed white. So there was another one with secrets at risk in Niccolo. Like Julius.
"Niccolo claims connections in the Pentagram, claims
one contact there that we know branches three ways
at least. He claims he's gotten orders for specific
moves and nothing more. He claims Achilles belongs
to Administration, that he's another operator, but he
fears Achilles is doubled— A faction war, in the Pentagram. It could even be the truth."

Another, flicker, white round the edges of Pharaoh's eyes. "Briar patch."

"What?"

"An American fable. Don't fling me into the briar
patch, the rabbit told the fox. *Doubt Achilles. Or*

wonder if I want him out. But what is Welch up to, telling Julius this, tell me that, Mouse."

"It *is* the truth . . . not the Achilles part. But you know and I know . . ."

"It always exists in the Pentagram. It's been worse, it's been better, and Julius doesn't play that game, not with his own hand, that's why he stays outside the high command—what in *hell* is he doing? Is he getting Niccolo out of there?"

Playing soldier, what else? It's his best camouflage. But it's not enough now . . . And aloud: "He's getting him out. Pharaoh, this faction-war . . . I think it's true. But not the old business, not the way it was. The rift is higher up. I am much afraid, Pharaoh . . . higher up than the Pentagram."

"Set and Typhon!"

"Something like."

Hatshepsut turned aside, a hand clasped to the back of her neck. Looked back again. "Is that what Julius thinks?"

"He's afraid, Pharaoh. He rarely is. Push and wait, push and wait, that's what he's doing: he's taken on a Power of Hell and doesn't know which one. He's trying to recognize it. Or decide how much noise to make. He doesn't know how far up the echelons this goes."

Pharaoh's eyes shone white-edged in the dark.

"Now he needs you," Mouse said. "I can protect him—physically, up to a point. But this is beyond my reach."

"Hell, Mouse!"

"He needs all of us of the Household. And some of them can't be told."

"Antonius."

"I didn't say it. I daren't go to Klea. Her personal interests blind her. You I trust."

Pharaoh's glance went hooded. Her face took on a masklike calm. "Oh, *thank* you, Mouse."

As well say it to Niccolo.

"I am no liar, Pharaoh." He said it with some small offense, but not a great deal of it: he had insulted Pharaoh, too.

"Come, you *are* a man, Mouse, I've had the proof." She came up against him and ran a fingernail down the front of his shirt. "You trust my self-interest; let's get it up front. Maybe we should have another one of these talks. Later. We'll *talk* about my interests."

There was not enough air to breath. Pharaoh smelled of dust and oil and still smelled of woman's sweat. It was an unguessedly erotic combination.

"Later," he said.

"Not all of them are in your charming self."

Of course they were not. He had lived with the Great Kings long enough to know the atmosphere they breathed, the force they exuded, and this one was no exception. They drank up souls and warped all ambitions around them. But his soul was already bartered and his ambitions were small ones, his possessions few. And no one in Hell would kill Mouse. That was the nature of his curse. So he smiled in her face, and saw her eyes looking up to his, read him to the depth, one honest soul having found another one.

"Watch Julius," she said then, pushing back from him.

"Where are you going?"

"To tell Curtius he has the Armored till I get back. You get the hell back to Julius. Now."

She walked down the hall, lithe khaki-clad figure that did not walk like a man. Mouse exhaled slowly. Then he left the alcove and walked down the hall in the other direction.

Pharaoh was not Julius. But she was the only other soul he knew in this who had no ties here, no preconceptions, no personal expectations and no orders to follow. The outsider. *He* dared not leave Julius, she was right; and he did not know where she was going. That gave him most hope in her . . . that she was older Dead than any of them and more modern than Achilles or Zaki or the Americans.

And doggedly resolved on her own survival.

Alexander shed his cloak and flung it into a chair. "I am done with patience," he said. And if front of him, Julius, who had left the table, the surface of which was deep in the kind of clutter that followed generals and kings, had his back turned, as he gazed toward the head of this dim hall, at the carved seat that sat in front of the dead firebowl. Light reached here from the sky, but it was a fading light, a treacherous light, that glanced about the frieze of tribute-bearers. The wonders of this place should have dazzled a Hellene's soul. But it seemed to Alexander only too dark and too shadowy and vague, like the man in front of him, who could not have been working when he walked in: there was an electric there, on the desk, and it had not been lit; was not now. Caesar stood in the twilight, alone in this place, excepting always his guards. And Alexander sensed unease everywhere, in the room, the vacant throne, the implications of empire that marched across the painted walls . . . a city which had won its own Hell and perished in it, again and again.

"Are you content to sit here?" Alexander asked again, of the man who claimed to be his senior and his completion. His voice echoed around the empty hall, behind the columns. "Do you understand what I have just told you?"

"I understand," Caesar's voice echoed back to him.

"Others saw him go, all those with me saw the Judges—they are in the camp. I told them it was well not to speak it, but men are men, and have hearts and mouths—Zeus blast you! look at me!"

Caesar turned. "I got your report. Klea sent it."

" 'Klea sent it.' Do you trust your cook with state documents and send your orderly to make treaties? Your horse groom to command a phalanx, perhaps?"

"They always said you couldn't delelgate," Caesar said wryly.

"Women in command!"

"Wherein they did in life, *basileus*, no different here. I assure you I am aware what happened down there. But that is not the only front. Down that hall, in the northeast quarter, we have Achaeans surviving. Not many of them. Yet. About three hundred of them holed up there. Welch is watching them via the com truck. But you've fought in Hell. You know how much a head count means."

He did now. An army once defeated, its numbers refilled when Hell did not want a conclusion. "Then get off this damned hill. Get out from these walls. I know the way we should go!"

Julius seemed dimmer still. Paradise light was fading from the square of sky above the firebowl. Vision strained the eyes. "Do you? Even Diomedes' counsel fails us. And him."

"What *of* Diomedes?"

"The man's had a rough trip. The Trojans. And Helen. You've missed a lot, friend. Been stuck down there longer than you may think. Thank gods we got you out. And him."

"Gemayel said as much; but we didn't know the rest till we reached camp. Diomedes tried something that didn't work, that's all; whatever happened, it was bad luck, not—"

"Like his taking Helen *and* Paris into his tent? Like a hairtrigger temper and no listening to reason? I could have stopped him. We'd have had to sit on him and tie him hand and foot, and I wasn't willing to do that. You reason with him. Or we *will* have to go after him. We've got an Achaean quarter out there we'll have to hammer to rubble—won't we? unless we have Diomedes to talk to them and persuade them off his hill. We don't have Achilles. We've lost Menelaos. We're going to have to break that news to the Achaeans, soon, if they haven't seen what happened down there, and I'm betting they have their spyholes in that wall down in that quarter. Now, I can deal with Diomedes by force. Or you can, with reason. I know which is easier."

"Persuade him to win the Achaeans? Or persuade him to surrender their interests? Your woman told me you're dealing with the Trojans. She named a name. An ancestor of yours. How many souls *have* you, Roman? Achilles, me, now this Aeneas—it's Proteus, I'd swear it's Shapeshifter blood you have: you change allegiance by the hour."

"This—" Caesar tapped himself on the chest. "The

blood and bone is Trojan, friend, and Latin, and
Sabine, and gods know, maybe Etruscan and even
Oscan and Greek; but if Achilles is you and I, then
we are one part lunatic. Beat down that temper and
listen to me: we're under attack, we have an embarrassment of hostages no one seems to want, and the
Trojans are damned well as confused as we are."

"Let me tell you first, since we name tribes, Roman, you are not dealing with *Achaioi*. Menelaos
and his lot are the only Achaeans out there; for the
rest you have Danaans, Inachids, Minyans. I, I am
Heraklid, desended of the Damaans—"

"That I know."

"You do not know it or you would not ask what
you do of Diomedes."

Caesar blinked, mute interrogatory.

"Diomedes is son of Tydeus son of Althaia daughter of Thestios son of Ares himself. Tydeus' sister was
Deianeira, wife to Herakles *my* ancestor, Roman;
and Althaia's sister was Leda queen of Sparta, whose
daughter was Helen . . . I am not telling you history,
Roman, I am telling you that Diomedes and I are kin
enough to count for a Hellene, and that Helen is my
remote kin and his cousin twice removed, which is
not far enough to ask him or me to treat her as a
hostage. Kill her he may; or free her. But hold her
prisoner he will not, not at any man's bidding or any
woman's either."

Caesar gazed at him a moment. "Damn *comitia
tributa* politics. You don't have to explain kinship to
a Roman, friend. I just wish I'd known that before
now."

"That's why we Hellenes ask ancestries of strangers we meet," Alexander said in a hushed and bitter

voice. "But you Romans know too much, it seems, to bother with obvious questions."

"Here's one. Where do you stand?"

"Among my enemies, possibly. Your guards are at the door. But if I walk beyond them I will go to the Hellenes and I will lead them out of here; I will take Diomedes and Helen. And Paris. And you may have your Trojans. Ask me and I may even give you back Priam's son."

"Don't you see what that sets up?"

"Or. Or—*you* are free to follow *me*, Caesar, with your physeters and your machines, and whatever you can gather. We may need them on the way to Paradise, but down there, down there, Minos is waiting for me and mine; and whatsoever Judge you Romans face; and one for these Trojans, whatever it is. Whatever came for Aziru was terrible; but he knew it; he welcomed it; he knew where he was going. If you had seen his face you would have no doubt of it. And I am going back."

"Zaki fired at what he saw. And could not remember, for me, what he saw. Yes, I talked to him. I told you I took the report. He told me he found you dazed and wandering and muttering something about snakes. There's a bite on your arm. Isn't there?"

Alexander looked, reflexively, and clasped his arm where the punctures showed red and angry. "You think that I was raving."

"I think that you saw something. I won't stop you if you want to take command of the Hellenes, the Danaans, whatever they are. Take them with my earnest good wishes. But before you go—I want you to meet someone from my side of the family."

* * *

Zaki made haste off the road where Antonius had
let him off on his way down, not toward the camp,
with its evening fires sending up a smoke haze and
glowing like so many embers down the rows of tents.

He took, instead, the goat track which led around
the curve of the hill, toward the post which the com
truck had lately taken, in its probing of the land and
the surrounds.

Zaki hurried, because he carried a dispatch by
hand, which Caesar had thrust on him, demanding
he take it and bring back Niccolo Machiavelli, who,
Caesar had said, might need some help. Discreetly,
Caesar had said. And sent him, who was not his
man, with an anger in his voice which might be for
him, might be for Machiavelli, and might be for the
Americans, who knew?

Perhaps Caesar had sent him precisely because he
was not his man, and it was political. But if Machiavelli
needed fetching-out, it had indicated Machiavelli had
serious troubles of his own, Zaki's sixth sense and
sharp ears had that much figured, inscrutable Romans and all. Welch and Nichols must have finally
caught the man at some proveable mischief, and
Caesar wanted him extricated, from Welch's keeping, which meant Welch had not rushed to turn
Machiavelli over to him. Hence this sealed message,
which Zaki had in his breast pocket, and this trek
across a hillside along the track the truck had made
getting to this isolated spot.

Ah. This isolated spot. Isolated from Romans. Isolated from knowledge. And overhearing. Indeed, Caesar did not send a Roman. Not even the silent Mouse.

And suddenly it made ominous sense, so that the
skin between Zaki's shoulders twitched, and he

scratched at the back of his neck as if something were crawling there.

Welcome back to civilization. It was Romans and it was Americans, and New Dead and Old, and the Romans sent the Jew to do the touchy job, not confiscate but liberate, quietly, without the official character of Mouse or others of Caesar's staff; without Romans noticing . . . Who saw the scruffy little Jew, eh? slogging along the hill on his ordinary contacts with the American foreigners? Or cared.

Quietly, Caesar had said. Zaki built a scenario involving Mouse and such confiscations, dour armed Roman and stubborn armed American, with waiting, official and noisy jeep.

He swatted his shapeless cap upon his leg as he headed up the last of the track. The men in that truck knew he was coming by now, absolutely had him spotted. Could Caesar know, perhaps, just how much that truck *could* know . . . and fear that the approach of a Roman might trigger some—mishap with the detainee?

Who knew what a Roman thought?

But that he was walking into politics Zaki well knew, and he crushed his hat with an anxious vengeance, sweating despite the wind that blasted and blew and rocked at him as he walked.

"Nichols," he sang out, in the case he *might* surprise a busy man. And rapped on the side door of the truck and stepped back in a hurry when the door opened and he stared into a gunbarrel in a large fist. "It's me," he said, wringing the hat, then put it on and fished after the message. "Is Welch here?"

Nichols backed up and waved him in with the barrel. Zaki climbed up into the dark and the green glow of the screens, where a second shadow-figure stood, with the wind blasting and rocking at the truck.

To that one Zaki offered the paper again, and saw the dark shape curled in the corner, the screen-light picking out a pale hand that told him what it was: his eyes focused instantly near, on the shadow that was Welch. "From Caesar."

"Yeah," Welch said. "He called down."

What message is that paper, then? "I, uh—" He took off the hat again and crushed it in his hand. "—have to pick up this man." A jerk of his shoulder, a shrug, a slide of the eyes. "Is he walking?"

"He'll walk," Welch said. "Nichols."

Nichols went over to that corner, and reached up on a counter and got something. An alcohol smell spread through the stink of bad air in the truck, pungent and brief. They were being sanitary. A man could get blood poisoning from dirty injections. Come down sick and become a problem.

No one was welcome in here, between these two. He was not. It was very dangerous. This man might have spilled things. Might say things even yet—

For that, had Caesar sent him? That he was expendable, and Caesar's Romans were not, or there were things Caesar did not want his Romans to know? Or had they both become a problem somehow, had one of Machiavelli's lies incriminated him from spite, and the Romans and the Americans believed it?

"Up," Nichols was saying, and gave the Italian a kick and pulled him by an arm.

Zaki moved in, edged past a counter and got Machiavelli at the other side before his ward took more damage. "I have him—here, I'm getting you out of here, all you have to do is walk."

Machiavelli said something, what, Zaki could not hear; and slumped and put weight on him as he stumbled, catching himself again.

"You got him from the Trojans," Welch said. "Hear?"

"Yeah," Zaki said, catching onto it, and put his hand in the middle of Machiavelli's chest. "Come on, man, walk. Fresh air in a minute."

Machiavelli moved, slowly, step by faltering step. Zaki's heart pounded. This was a set-up, perhaps: he did not see the edges of this thing, this man was not fit to walk, Caesar did not send a man of his own, messages had passed from the hill to this truck by radio and the Jew got the job of walking a drugged man out on this brushy trail—

"Come on," Zaki said, as Nichols opened the door again, and twilight and cold clean air hit them full on. Zaki stepped down. "Step, you have to step here—"

Between his bracing hand from the front and Nichols' grip behind, Machiavelli stumbled down into his support. "Come on, come on," Zaki murmured, sweating, and hauled on him, toward the track the tires had made, there among the rocks and brush.

He expected a sudden double shot from behind, a bullet into his head, a sound he would never hear; he could not say why, had no idea why, except that he knew he was the only one in this affair except Machiavelli himself who knew too much and not enough—down in the maze and out again, after his talk with Caesar himself—send the Jew, two birds with one stone. All you have to do is walk a corpse uphill, up the road, through the gates, the streets, past the Greek snipers. . . . Discreetly, Caesar had said. Where, then? Hide him among the rocks?

"Come on, come on, walk, damn you—" He was panting, his hands were cold. The wind rocked at them. Step after step. Each one was life.

The wind lessened. They were rounding the hill. Machiavelli stumbled and Zaki held him up, braced his shoulder under the lank Italian and shoved. "Come on. *Walk.*"

Less and less of the wind. They walked, the truck would be out of sight behind them, they were still alive, and Zaki understood less than before. He stumbled, exhausted under the weight, and they both nearly went down; stumbled again, the breath rasping and cold in his throat, and he found a boulder to prop the Italian against—"Stay on your feet, *stay on your feet,* I can't pick you up again."

Machiavelli stayed there a moment, leaning back, his face white in the twilight; and slowly his knees folded and he slumped bonelessly down against Zaki's resisting hands. "*Dove andiamo?*" he asked. *Where are we going?*

"Up the hill. To Caesar."

Machiavelli braced his legs under him again. His head fell back against the rock, crack! and he made a feeble wave of his hand. "*Prego,* let me go." He took his own weight, and Zaki took his hands away carefully as Machiavelli moulded himself against the rock surface and hung there like a black starfish, just breathing.

"Cesare sent you."

"Yes."

Dark eyes slitted open and fixed on him, cold and hazed. "Am I to get there?"

"By all that I can do. Yes. Let us move."

Machiavelli waved a pale, limp hand. His clothing was dusty. Bruises showed on his face, blood had dried on his upper lip and liquified again in beads of sweat. "A moment. A moment, *signore.*"

"They are back there." Zaki cast an anxious glance over his shoulder, grasped Machiavelli by the arm and pulled at him, but Machiavelli resisted him with a shift of his weight.

"No. *No.*"

"Then, man, I will leave you here. And you can make your own way."

Machiavelli's hand closed on the front of his jacket. "Then, *signore,* you truly *are* from him."

"I assure you." He pried the hand loose, cast an anguished look back to the curve, beyond which was the truck, and mouthed silently: *They can hear us.* "Do you want me to take you?"

"No." Machiavelli hitched his shoulders higher against the rock. The voice faded out in hoarseness and came back again. "I will find my way. In my own time."

"To the Undertaker, you'll find your way. Don't be a fool."

Machiavelli reached to his pocket, two questing fingers, his head back against the rock. "They took that. The means. Give me your arm. I will walk—"

Zaki gave it, offered his shoulder, and Machiavelli gripped it and leaned forward, his mouth to Zaki's ear. "I lead," Machiavelli said, illusory as the wind, and hanging his hand from Zaki's shoulder, thrust himself from the rock face and began, slowly, to walk.

A Roman would have followed orders, Zaki thought; and cold and swift on that thought's trail: *I am Caesar's message to this man—that I am not a Roman.*

Why do I not run?

Caesar has just put me on his side, that is what he has done. I dare not go back to that truck till the dust of this business settles. The Americans will ask me about Caesar. They will doubt me.

Maccabee is lost below and Alexander is with the Romans, and Caesar has compromised me with the Americans.

So I walk where this man tells me and am ready to kill him if he makes a false move.

But where would that put me with the Romans?

I might cut his throat now and say it was Nichols.

But where would that put me with the Americans?

I could kill him and say that he left me—me, the Jew, I tell this to the Roman, of course, and he will believe me.

God is shaking his head at me.

There was a stairway, a great wide terrace open to the evening sky, where Roman guards waited, by a row of doors, shuttered doorways all dark.

A man stood against the last illusory light of Paradise, a man leaning on the rim of the balcony and looking outward, over the wreck of the city, at the edge of night.

"Aeneas," Caesar said while Alexander waited, and the lone man turned, and straightened, and waited as they came to him—tall, and dark-haired, and with a nose that said East and not Greek; but Alexander, who had been prepared to hate this man, suffered something of the thing he had felt when first he met with Diomedes—the first that he met the man face to face, and saw one of the great heroes.

"This is Alexander," Caesar said, "king of Macedon, of Hellas and Persia."

The Trojan's eyes reacted to the *Hellas* part. Not fear. It seemed impossible that such calm could be shattered. The gaze only became less opaque, and more vulnerable. "A new king in Hellas," Aeneas said, and made a gesture at the darkening court about him. "Then perhaps you can tell me, king of Hellas, where—they are."

A chill went over Alexander's skin. It was so calm a voice, holding so much of anguish. *They.* It was the Women's Court they stood in. He saw the great upright loom, against the dim wall, weaving interrupted. He saw the scatter of children's toys.

"He doesn't know," Caesar said. There was compassion even in *his* voice. "But there are older Greeks. He will find them and ask them."

Caesar did not consult him in this. But one did not ask a man, whether he would do justice. One assumed, till a man proved a scoundrel and meanspirited.

"I will ask," Alexander said in this great quiet, only the wind howling about the eaves and the bullshorn-decorations of the parapets. "Is there someone—in particular?"

"My wife," the Trojan said. "Creusa. I know—she died down in the streets. But I died in Italy, and *I* am here. So many of us are here. We had hoped—so much—and feared—"

Tears glistened in the Trojan's eyes, and did not fall.

"Perhaps," Alexander said, clearing his own throat, "they found the way to Paradise."

"What way is that?" the Trojan asked. "Tell me what this Paradise is, Hellene. And we would go there."

Dark and the constant drip of water, the echo of steps coming back at them out of the maze . . . and cold that frosted the breath in the light of the flashlights, that made towering black ghosts of their column on the uneven walls and the stone pillars. Achilles kept walking, having shed the helmet, having the strap still in his hand, the way he carried the Galil—he did not drop equipment, had not shed the damned flak jacket, not so much for that as that the thought of working out of all that gear and getting it on again sent stabs of pain through his ribs. It was protection, it ached, but it might keep the jab of some damn rock out of what might be broken bone—he had had all the pain he could handle; and worst was the look the Romans gave him, the doubt and the curiosity: *Yes, dammit, I bleed, you damn great fools, I hurt like hell—what do you think?*

They were disappointed in him, were altogether disillusioned. People always were, once they knew the ordinary, mortal truth.

Damn you and your—

His foot hit a slick spot, one sickening, joint-wrenching flailing of his arm as the second foot hit the slime-coated stone and both feet went sliding out from under him—*Oh, damn, it's going to hurt!*

Splash! down on his back with the pain blinding him, and his head cracking against the water-cushioned rock, the wind knocked out of him. He gasped after breath, torn muscles contracting in a helpless spasm across his gut and his ribs. *Don't*, he tried to say when hands grabbed him, when damned fools hauled him up where he could not breathe and pulled him by arms and elbows, against the curl his body tried to make. He greyed out a moment, and came to as they were letting him down again. . . . "He hit his head," someone said, a wan distant sound, beyond the struggle he made with his own body, trying to expel air that wasn't there so he could suck in fresh.

One driving effort, that hurt like hell and sent tears to his eyes, and the air started coming in on the draw afterward. He breathed in what he could stand, gasped it out and got more while the world shimmered and resolved itself into a ring of staring, under-lit faces.

Gawking fools, fools, fools—

Someone hauled him up off the rock and held him. "He's all right," Menelaos' deep voice said, a rumble near his ear. "Peliadês, Peliadês—" A water-chilled hand wiped his face.

"I thought he was supposed to be—" a Greek voice said, with the disappointment he was so used to.

"He's just damned *good*," Achilles muttered between his teeth, and got his hand behind his butt where a sharp rock was, got his head up and pushed and clawed his way up to sit on his own, holding an arm across his ribs and trying not to throw up. "Where's my fucking rifle, somebody get my rifle."

"*Ecce*," a Roman said, and laid it down by him— Damn fools showed up without any ammunition left. Three rounds they had in the Galil, and a dozen fucking M-16s good for nothing but clubs. He groped after it and levered himself up with it, squeezing tears from his eyes till his sight glittered with them in the flashlights and the shadow. Hands steadied him. He shoved them off.

"Move, dammit." Another hand took his elbow, and he moved his arm and glared at the man who touched him. Menelaos. Menelaos who knew him— the old self, the prince from Thessaly, the young hothead with the charmed life, that the poets told lies about.

"Achilles," Menelaos hissed.

"I'm all right," he said, and jerked his arm back a second time, following after the Romans, the Germans, the Israelite who led them in his blind wandering. "That crazy Old Dead wants us to walk circles, we walk fucking circles till we drop, it's his party." He blinked and started moving, and steadying himself with a hand to the walls now and again as he worked his way to the fore, past the Macedonians and the Romans and the Germans.

He had seen his enemy in this place, Hektor Priamidês entrapped and frozen in stone like an insect in amber. He had seen the terms this place exacted; and he wanted the air again, wanted the winds and the light and the sky back. He had no faith in Maccabee or in Menelaos or in the rest of them, but sitting still and listening to the water drip was worse, was real hell.

So what did he do, he slipped and fell on his arse while he was trying to prove something, that was what he did, knocked himself stupid in front of all of them; and they followed Maccabee, who at least had not made a fool of himself, who could blame them?

He overtook the two Germans, and shouldered past, ducking down past a stone curtain, and into shadow again, walking just behind Maccabee. He

grabbed for support—a second heart-lurch as his feet
skidded on slimy stone; and there was a whisper of
waterfall up ahead, that grew as they walked.

"Hey," he said, his voice echoing away into dark.
He took a chance, balancing on slick rock to reach
Maccabee and yell at him over the water-rush. "We
have come in a circle, dammit, it's the chute up
ahead."

"No," Maccabee yelled back, and started walking
again, splashes echoing off the walls and drowning in
that whisper of waters.

The earth groaned, as it did from time to time,
and trembled. Achilles caught after his balance. "Shit!"
Maccabee was descending now, and Achilles followed,
using his free hand on the wall, testing for slimy
patches with every step. Their line was spread out
farther and farther when he glanced back. Their
shadows leaped and swung in the light of flashlights
behind.

The earth trembled and shook. Rock fell, splashing
about them. A mutter of oaths went up, in various
languages, and Achilles put his hand to the wall and
shifted his footing to dry ground, in Maccabee's track.
Maccabee's flashlight stabbed into the dark, and found
nothing, in this place where the waters whispered
louder and louder.

"You know, a cave can fill," a Roman legionary
said from behind him, "damned fast."

"Cheerful, real cheerful," Achilles said, with a glance
back, and gripped the wall again as the earth shivered.

On the slope above, a light whipped across the
ceiling like a lightning flash, a man yelled, and other
lights went crazy as a knot of men came tobogganing

down the slant in a gathering yell of dismay and terror.

"Oh, *shit!*" Achilles yelled, as the accident took all the men above him and rolled right over him in a hammer-blow of pain. He hit the watery rock, on his back, skidded into someone else and with the whole mass went flying off into black space, airborne. *"Damn you!"*

A trail of khaki led to the bath, the wretched little galvanized tub which was all the state Hatshepsut's four sycophants could come up with, and they were so harried they had not even retrieved the stinking clothes off the dirt floor of the tent. Hatshepsut laved her face in a double handful of tepid water, knees up to her chin—and tilted her head back, leaving her face to the feathery ministries of invisible hands, paintpots which whisked in and out of sight, while other hands combed her hair and still others held up a mirror. She saw her eyes lengthen in fuschia and mauve and lavenders, saw the tiara of mauve plastic and lights materialize above her head and settle into her hair, invisible fingers tucking a bit of its curious extension into her ear as other parts of it settled closely against her skull.

"Here," she said, tucking a knee up against her chest, thrust the foot out, whereupon a towel materialized in great haste and dried it.

She traveled in state, did Pharaoh, the Lord of the Two Lands, the Killer of Crocodiles, surely not what she had known in life, but life had never offered her the other benefits death did. Her eyes shone bright in the mirror she thrust away, her body arched lithe and hard out of the water as she seized invisible hands and sprang out to balance on one foot on a towel, while zealous hands toweled the other dry, rubbed her skin to warmth and quick fingers slipped transparent mauve silk stockings onto offered toes and tugged them up one leg and the other.

The fingers went a bit further, lightly, deft and quick . . . *that* sycophant, it was, who had improved over the years, her favorite. "Tsss," she hissed, and shrugged her hip, whereupon it made prudent haste, and her clothing appeared under her right foot and her left, and drew itself up in deft and quick hands which nevertheless managed to touch in a way very pleasant—as a mauve bracelet clasped her forearm, a flashing and busy flicker of lights till it adjusted itself, and a deft finger pressed a filament along her arm and her shoulder and down between her breasts and beneath the left one: she thrust that arm and the other into sleeves which smoothed up her arms as *that* sycophant smoothed the glimmering fabric and fastened it and fastened the belt which clasped low about her hips. Boots, then, the left one with its own concealments, smooth leather sliding onto silken feet— Pharaoh armed herself after her own fashion, tucking the disruptor into its clip at her belt, and there was no happier woman in Hell.

Now he needs you, Mouse had said. *I can protect him—physically, up to a point. But this is beyond my reach.*

And: *I daren't go to Klea. Her personal interests blind her. You I trust.*

Outside, in the camp, a stirring began, and Hatshepsut frowned, hearing that whisper, as if the wind which snapped and cracked at the tent had acquired human voices.

Ominously. It was not a sound any commander liked to hear in a camp.

"What the hell is that?" she asked the air; and:

Soldiers are moving, it said back, a sycophant's thin whisper.

They have heard, another said, *about Paradise.*

"Get around there," Antonius snapped, standing in front of the soldiery that was headed up the road his jeep was dead across. He put himself in the light of the headlights, saw familiar faces in the light that scattered onto the mob: one of them was the head centurion. "What kind of nonsense is this? What damned nonsense is this, *Bacule?* Where the *hell* do you think you're going?"

That got them quiet. Theater, it was. The Old Man's aide and the Tenth's favorite sergeant. The centurion came forward, set his hands on hips. "Question, *riumvir.* There's this rumor going round—the Macedonians and Gemayel's bunch, they say they *found* this hole they been talking about, they say they saw this guy go *out* it, is that true, *triumvir?*"

Voices rose up, drowning possible answers. The mob surged forward and Antony climbed up on the jeep, fast, and held his hand up. "You want to hear about it? I've talked to Caesar—" It was a damned lie, but it was the only one likely to work. The camp was emptying fast, not Romans only pouring out onto the road.

"They say it's this cave under the hill," someone yelled.

"They say those guys are alive down under there," someone else yelled from closer up. "The Macedonian walked out of them caves . . . where'd he leave them? What's going on down there?"

"Yes, he walked out!" Antonius yelled back. "Send these men back to their tents, centurions, and, *Bacule*, you and Lentulus come with me, if you want to ask the commander about it, what are you doing, you want a mess like this? We got a fucking army facing us out there, you remember that? You lose track of it? We got the Greeks up there—" He waved an arm up at the citadel. "We got the Trojans off there—" A wave of the same arm off toward the flat, where the revetments extended. "Any of you off that line out there? Any of you decide to take a walk off the revetments? *Pro di immortales*, if any of you sheeplovers took a hike off guard you damn well better get your butts *back* out on that line before the centurion starts counting heads or you'll be getting the fifty, *I'm not joking, son*, you get your arses turned round and think again. You got the centurions to speak for you, all you got to do is say. I'd listen, Curtius'd listen—"

"We don't want listening," an anonymous voice yelled out.

And someone else: *"Give 'im a drink, he'll go away."*

That stung. That hit like a thrown rock. "You tell me that when I was with you guys at the cliffs? You tell me that when I got three of you off the table, after the Korean mess? I risked my damn ass and I went down to the Hall and I *lied* your damn way out of that, *Paule*, I remember I did! You want to tell me who dragged you out of that damn swamp, *Caepio*? Go on, you want to tell me I don't care what happens to you guys?" He wept. He wiped at his eyes and waved his arm. "Damn. Damn. I'm trying to save your damn asses. I don't want the Old Man to see this. You want him to see this? You get back on that line, you get back out there."

Quiet grew on them, and a different kind of muttering.

"Look," he said, spreading his hands. "Look, I *know*. Don't you think I know? Caesar knows. We got the same rumor. You think we'd walk out of here alone? *Pro di*, the Legion goes together! These cohorts and the guys we left back there in New Hell, you think we go like some damn *rabble*? Hell, no, wherever we go, home or heaven or some hell below, dammit, we go in our ranks and with our Standards in front of us, no other way!"

A thready cheer went up, a brighter sound. Antonius raised both his arms. "Then, dammit, get the hell back where you need to be and let me and the centurions get up there and ask the questions. Who's leader on that line? Do I hear him here?"

No, triumvir, a muddled lot of voices yelled back.

"Well, damn, then get back there, he's standing watch alone, isn't he?"

Kleopatra drew a whole breath, in the shadows by the tents, as men filtered back. And let it go, shaking.

Two thousand years and more and he could still do it. Still played a mob like an artist. And they were true, the things he had told them. Every one was true.

Except the hope of heaven.

A step drew near her. A figure appeared, whose crown and wrist glittered with plastic surfaces, whose hair was bobbed and whose figure was not in any particular, male.

"Damned good," Hatshepsut said, stopping beside her. "He's *damned* good at it. But how long can he hold them? Tonight? Tomorrow?"

"They'll listen to Julius. Antonius can charm the fire out of them; Julius can have their firstborn and their next. Don't worry about it." But she was worried. She was shaking.

And Hatshepsut laid a hand on her shoulder.

"They could have killed him," Kleopatra said. And with a turn that dislodged the hand, pointed, where men still moved, where horses passed. "The Macedonians. O Zeus. He mustn't try with them. The Macedonians are going up there—"

"He's got better sense. Damn!" For a moment everything was in the balance, as Roman soldiers shouted after the horsemen, who were headed for the hill; but Antonius' voice rang out: *"Let their own commander handle them, hold it!"* And the horsemen thundered on, around the jeep and onto the road which led to the citadel.

"Diomedes might have stopped that," Kleopatra said, trembling with fury. 'But he's with *her*. Damn that woman! Damn all this wretched mess! It's all gone wrong!"

"Helen?"

"That *girl*. That damned, shortsighted jackal *bitch* and all her trouble! Nothing's been right since she came. Nothing!"

Hatshepsut's hand found her shoulder again. "Don't look at the light, dear Klea. It blinds. Look at the dark, look at what the light turns up, never, never, never be distracted: that's how she gets her way with the men, don't you know? We can handle Helen. Put her out of your mind. She's a sweetmeat, a

cloying little mouthful, *useful* if you want a man
distracted. There's not anything at home up there, is
there?"

"Or she's a damned good actor."

"Tssss. Get your hands on Paris if you want to see
her move."

Kleopatra looked at the faceless face, saw the min-
utest flickering of lights about Hatshepsut's jewelry.

"*I* haven't time for him," Hathsepsut said. "Besides, I never liked sugary things. It's something
serious I have in mind. Like that man of yours in
trouble."

"Antonius?" Her heart lurched. She thought of
riot, of mutiny redoubled.

"*Julius.*"

Kleopatra's heart turned over in her chest. For a
moment her breath would not come.

"Now, now, you're thinking," Hatshepsut hissed.
"Good. The word is, the Macedonian's found a way
out of here. Do you think the Powers are going to let
us go the way Antonius said? Marching out by rows?
Not so easily."

"No." She shook her head, colder and colder.
"There isn't one."

"*Isn't* one?"

"Isn't a way out. I've talked to Alexander. I heard
it all. That place is a trap, that's what it is. We're
held here, and she's the focus—it pulled Achilles
back, don't you see, this place drew Achilles back to
this plain and we came with him, that was what
happened, it's putting that soul together again and
Hell won't tolerate it."

"Mother Isis. You're not making profound sense,

Klea. We're talking about a way out of here. That's
what Hell isn't tolerating."

"*There is no way for us.* Get out of here, yes, get
shed of this woman and get ourselves out of this
abominable place, but not the way they're trying to
lure us to go! It was a trick, a wicked, cruel trick. I
don't know where Aziru is, I don't know what it's
done to him or where it's taken him—Don't you see
that the dead don't vanish here? The bodies lie on
the field and then they go all at once. I'm not sure
they go to the Undertaker. I have no idea what Aziru
went to—but it wasn't Paradise."

"You haven't been playing with that damned eight
ball, have you? Set *take* it, that thing's going to give
you the Devil's own answers! Talk about something
that'll lead you to the next hell, my friend, *that* thing
is not to trust! A dozen men saw Aziru go—smiling.
Does a man smile who's bound for the lower hells?"

"Is he smiling now? Do we know?"

"Doubts and dithering. We came here for a way
out, do you think you'll find it paved and marked like
a highway? Or in anything like plain sight?"

She shivered, drew her shoulders together, hug-
ging her arms against the chill inside and out.
"Hatshepsut. There is nothing friendly about this
land. Not that woman. Not this place. A judge for
Aziru, a judge for Alexander—shapeshifting again,
do you see, *everyone sees what they want to see.*
We're being *lured.*"

Hatshepsut was silent for moment. Wind cracked
the tent beside them. Voices came from the road,
from the men gathered in small knots out along it.

"Neither you nor I," Hatshepsut said, "was there

to see. Alexander was. And you say he wanted to follow."

"What would you see?" Kleopatra asked, a dagger thrust back, into the dark. "Ma'at and the feather on the one hand? The Devourer on the other?"

Again Hatshepsut was silent, a shape in the dark.

"Was there ever that?" Kleopatra pursued her. "Or was it only the House of the Dead . . . and the Undertaker and the white room?"

"Dammit, Klea—"

"So whence this business of judges?"

"Why should it not be?" Hatshepsut thrust out a hand to the side and lights flashed within her bracelet. "What is the law in one level of Hell, does it have to be the law here? We see what we expect to see. We shape our own destinies!"

"No. This land . . ." Bronze glanced in sunlight, weapons clashed, the body was weary to death and the citadel loomed overhead, the battle pressed to the very walls—

The pyre and the heaped-up dead—

The burning of flesh—

"Klea?"

She plunged her face into her hands. "There is no Paradise. Not all the offerings in the world could win it for me, then or now!"

The Egyptian's strong hands closed on her shoulders, arms folded her into a warm embrace, held her while she shivered, and for a while after, till Hatshepsut took her face between her hands and stooped to look her squarely in the eyes.

"Are you all right, kit?"

"No way out." Kleopatra's teeth chattered, and she clenched them and swallowed. "It is that woman, do you hear me? She was the beginning of this disaster, she is again. I know."

"Kit, you need some rest. You've been on your feet too long. Get a drink in you—We'll talk about this. After you've got the drink."

"A drink won't help. I have dreams. I have them wide awake—I know—I know *things*—I don't like. I know what I'm talking about. I've been here before— Twice. Twice!"

Hatshepsut's hands landed on her shoulders. Heavily. "Listen, kit, you take this whole souls business too damned much for real—"

"I know this place. I know Diomedes. And Helen. I was Achilles' partner, dammit; I was Alexander's— now Julius and Antonius both—too many people have loved me too damned much, too damned much—" She shoved the Egyptian away, but Hatshepsut caught her arm and pulled her round again.

"Klea. Klea. Come out of it. Shove it *out*—by Set, when you play oracle, woman, you've got to walk that path two ways, or lose yourself in it—It's this place, Klea, dammit, you're *right*, it's this place, it's got a new tactic—"

The words rolled around and made no sense, loops and turns until they slowly found a niche and rattled to a stop.

—Zeus, it's giving us each what we came to find.

That's how it draws us, isn't it? The hopes and the fears we can't turn loose of. It takes them and holds them up in front of us. . . .

Damn it, damn it, it doesn't mean it's not true.

That's the hell of it, isn't it—that we have to

disbelieve ourselves to doubt it; and then how do we believe again, ever?

"Myself, kit, I want to be alive again. I want to see the stars. I want to go there, where the world's gotten to. And it'll come up with that promise too, won't it, kit? Something for everyone."

Hatshepsut's voice trembled. That as much as anything shook her confidence.

"That damned *thing*," Hatshepsut said carefully, "has Mouse scared. It's working on Julius, do you see? It'll come at him from this side and that and he's *stopped*, he's well sitting still up there, and it's sent him one offer and another—you know him, longer even than Mouse. What does he want most—not on the outside: what are the things he wants that he wouldn't ever admit to?"

"I wouldn't tell you that."

A small silence. "Smart, Klea. That *is* smart. But watch him. Watch him the way you know how. And watch Diomedes."

"What are you going to do?"

"You wouldn't answer my question. I won't answer yours. Just hold the fort."

Hatshepsut went, a shadow treading back through the maze of dark tents. Klea shivered, turned for her own tent and gasped, confronting a living wall, a shadowy cluster of giants whose presence she had not known. The German Guard was with her, not letting her wander the dark alone and unprotected. She saw the sheen of reflected lanternlight on metal in their hands and about their persons.

"Fear," she said, her heart still beating in lurches and thumps. "Panic." Naming two of them. She pointed up, at an angle, toward the unseen citadel. "Caesar. Go."

They muttered and clashed their weapons in salute, and two of them left her, to take up their guard in the citadel.

Julius knew their nature. He would not reject them. And if she sent them to die, with glory—they were grateful for it, who had spent hell in Tiberius' filthy hands. They were not unaccustomed to women's direction: their wisewomen cast bones for prophecies and told them their fates on which their chiefs rose and fell. Julius had explained such things to her, how in their paradise they fought every day and feasted in the evenings with the dead risen and their wounds healed, to do it all again.

And did she not offer them Paradise?

Two, Famine and Grief, she sent to Alexander. Slaughter and Chance to Antonius. Two she would have sent to Hatshepsut, but she thought better of that: she had saved them from Tiberius, and well as she knew the Pharaoh might please them in one thing, she did not know what their sensibilities might be in the other. They had wept when Alexander had spurned them. These great tall men had stood there with tears on their faces, seeing he had turned his back on them. And the two she kept were anxious, but she walked close beside them and laid her hand on the rifle that Vengeance held. "Good," she said. "Come."

As she went to deal with the Other Woman.

Niccolo stumbled, caught himself between a rock and Zaki's arm, and grunted in pain, just kneeling against the hillside and breathing for a moment, one foot braced downslope. Close. Close. He had no wish to go rolling down to the stream down there— had not held out this long only to break his neck.

"This is crazy," Zaki said. "Sit. Sit down. Tell me who to go to."

Niccolo struck with the back of his hand, a weak blow. *Let me alone.* While the dizziness and the dark came and went.

Possibly it was a setup. He was supposed to betray himself to this man. Then there would be Nichols. And Welch, to pull him in, take him back, and continue the interview. Nichols had taken the needle he had; he had had the option to use it, and declined for his own reasons—

He was not a fool. A fool, in this case, would have used that needle and gone back to the Undertaker, a failure.

A fool would sit down on this hillside now as this New Dead wished, and coddle the pain in his gut, and wait on the intervention of people who would not listen to reason, and whose actions he could not answer for.

A fool would believe that this little Jew had no other motives in wearing himself to a panting wreck, carrying a madman through the brush and the rocks and the dark.

Do we reach a place, little Jew, when you have seen all you wish to see, and you are ready to ask your own questions—and sell Niccolo Machiavelli to the best bidder? But you know I know these things.

He straightened again, and walked on the dry, graveled slope, without the Jew's hand under his elbow for a few paces, with it again, as Zaki caught up and steadied him on a slippery place.

Down and down again, among the rocks where the small stream ran, and toward the ground where he had been before. Possibly Welch and Nichols knew where he was now. No, it was more than possible. They might have a locator on him, might have one on Zaki, if Zaki were not in deliberate contact with them. It did not matter.

Possibly—even possibly Zaki would go to Caesar. Possibly Caesar would intervene, but that was not the message he got. At times, with his mind wandering in and out of focus, he yearned to be on that upward road, as far in that direction as they were in this track toward the flat. But that was not what Julius expected of him. Julius gave him a chance, and did not know, *perdio*, what the game was, or how desperate.

Would Julius have sent this man if he were not under secure control?

Did Julius send him? back to that question again.

Niccolo held too many secrets, too many people's secrets, of too many dangerous agencies. . . . *Beware, Welch, beware. Cesare will take you in or Cesare will silence you now, barring my assurance I said nothing—but could I know, Welch? Or could he be sure?*

And if not Cesare himself, there are others who would take you now. Cesare is your protection, Welch. And if you are useful I will not kill you for this.

But Nichols I will remember. La vendetta, Nichols.

He blinked and squeezed his eyes shut, expelling the tears that hazed his sight, caught a breath on the chill wind and set his hands on the rocks which guided him down to the little stream, made it down with one skid and Zaki's saving grip on his bruised arm.

"Come," he said, and kept walking. His feet wandered, one too far to the left, the other recovering. But it was grass now. Two tall, slanted rocks, leaning on each other, which stood apart from the hill. He reached them, leaned panting against the larger, and rolled his shoulder against the stone to look at the Jew.

"You are alone with me," Niccolo said, between breaths. "Are you not to ask me questions?"

Zaki spread his hands. "Only the ones you want to answer."

"Cesare has put you in a position, my friend; he has a mind like yours and mine. He would never take a thing for granted. Like what I did not say to you. And he is a very hard target. Far harder than you or me."

"I am on your side." Zaki stood with hands visible in the afterglow of hellish night. "Do I carry you up and down mountains for nothing? Do you think Welch couldn't stop us if he were a fool?—which he is not; which, thank God, no one is being. You want help, ask. I'll think about it."

"*Perdio*, an honest man." Niccolo slid down to his knee and gave the Jew his unprotected back, reaching into the dark niche between the rocks. He found the leather case and pulled, gritted his teeth and dragged the Litton out into the light with an effort that brought tears to his eyes.

"Ah." The Jew squatted down beside him, hat in hands. "Hidden treasure, is it? About which your Cesare himself does not know? Or does he?"

"No matter," Niccolo said, and wiped the sweat from his face with a shaking hand and turned the unit on. "This is the last time I use it. One way or the other, no? It—"

There was a rumbling in the ground. He ignored it, desperately adjusted the set while the rumbling grew. *Dio, prego, a little more time, a little more time—*

"Machiavelli—" Zaki said, leaning onto one knee, hand on his shoulder. "Machiavelli, that's a chariot—"

"*Lo so, che sparco—*" He grabbed up the unit and thrust himself for his feet, hauling himself and it to the other side of the rock, but the thunder came up on them, chariots and more than one. He got down again as Zaki flattened himself against the rock; he keyed his code and sent, and sent again, without waiting.

Hatshepsut stopped still, well as she had schooled herself not to react to the inputs. There was panic in that sending. It was Niccolo: she knew that much; and it was repeated, dinning over and over into her ear.

She broke into a run, headed for the motorpool, while the rest of the camp went about its business unawares.

The computer in New Hell bleeped, and the monitor screen went black. Numbers started pouring across it, the drive went on, and Dante Alighieri, drowsing with his head on his arms, jerked, knocked a coffee cup full of pens off the desk and caught at the pill bottle that his jolt had toppled off the console. It fell over, and dropped a last tablet precisely in the crevice between the J and the H keys. "*Maledetto!*" he moaned, trying to fish it out with nails bitten to the quick, while pens rolled and the larger fragment of the coffee cup rocked to quiescence.

He bent over, got a pen, fished the pill out, and looked up again as the drive went quiescent and computer bleeped up a prompt.

He hit Enter; the drive whirred again and worked and worked.

Then a message filled the screen, and Dante gulped, threw himself to his feet, and ran for Augustus' office.

The chariots pulled up, to the ring of spear-wielding warriors who already had things under control.

A spear had taken care of the Litton, and Niccolo rested carefully where he was, beside Zaki, with several more Trojan bronze points pressing them back against the rock. It was too cruel. Gut wound was the worst and they were bound to do it. Niccolo just shut his eyes and rested, thinking that he had done his best, come damned near to heroics, which he had sworn he would never do—but it was only practicality, after all, not stupidity, and he was done. The damned Trojans would stick him in the gut, the next hour or so was going to be absolute hell, and then by another night he was going to be lying in his own clean bed, swimming in the villa's warm Olympic pool, having wine with Sargon in the garden room, telling Augustus—

Oh, God, no. It was not going to be like that. He would not have the chance to tell Augustus . . . to tell Augustus that he had lost Julius. . . .

There would be no villa. There would be no legions. Perhaps there would be nothing at all, only smoking ruin where New Hell had stood.

And win or lose then, there was no safety for those who had been on a side, and failed it.

Horses snorted, a chariot creaked on its axle, and a step whispered through the grass toward them. Niccolo looked, not wanting to look, and blinked at a white-bearded man in a robe, not armor, a man who made a small gesture, spoke a word, and took the spears back a degree.

"Are you of that camp?" the old man asked in Greek, with a broad gesture toward all the affair at Troy.

God, what answer? What answer ambivalent enough? Which side is he?

"We belong to Caesar," Niccolo said.

One of the warriors said something unintelligible, and shoved his spear into the wreckage of the Litton. It was not Greek, whatever it was, it was not Greek.

"Who is kin to Aeneas," Niccolo said, suddenly inspired, and drew a breath that hurt. "I am his herald. Is this a way to treat a herald?"

The old man spoke, and the spears lifted, the warriors aiming the points at the sky and setting them on their butts. Shields settled against the ground, and another man stepped forward and thumped a staff against the earth.

"Herald of Caesar son of Aeneas, I am herald of Priam son of Laomedon. My lord is here under truce. My lord asks: will you ransom his sons, living or dead?"

"Perdio." Niccolo drew a second breath that hurt, and grabbed Zaki by an arm, hard: *get me on my feet. Fast.*

Zaki moved, scrambled up and gave him a pull to get him up. Niccolo caught his breath and set himself to stand against the rock. "My lord is willing to talk," he said, on a breath well-modulated as he could manage. "Your lord has a safe-conduct." He knew his Greek and his *Iliad*. He knew everything a classical education could give him, and centuries of studying Caesar could show him. "My lord will meet with him face to face."

The old man said something in his own language, and turned and went back to his chariot.

"Will you ride with my lord?" the Trojan herald asked.

"Honored," Niccolo murmured, and resolutely went straight that direction as he could walk, and climbed aboard, with Zaki's help . . . caught the rail and caught his breath as the floor tilted under Zaki's step, then jolted again as the horses started to move.

Jolt and jolt and jolt—one got *used* to suspension in a vehicle, and Niccolo's head snapped and his hands cramped and sweated, holding the rim while the pain in his gut was sending the world in spinning spirals. Someone was behind him, pressing against his back and saving him from the worst of the shocks.

But he lost his grip and fetched up hard against the rail when the chariot slewed at a sudden crack of fire, and headlight glare came at them, sending the horses shying up in screaming panic.

He *knew* the female voice which shouted at them in garble and Greek over a loudhailer and told them to surrender. He held up his arm, desperately, as the chariot bounced and tilted with the charioteer fighting the reins; and winced when the light hit him full in the eyes.

"*Niccolo!*" Hatshepsut's voice thundered at him in

shock. He saw her standing up in the jeep, bright color behind the white glare of the lights.

Disappointed, he thought, sagging against the chariot wall. He brought her the king of Troy and there was no pleasing this woman. "The High King of the Aigyptoi," he murmured to the Trojans, with what wind he had left. "One never calls her queen. —*Hatshepsut! It's Priam, dammit, he's come to talk!*"

Silence for a moment. Then abruptly, without a word, Hatshepsut threw herself back into her seat, the driver threw the jeep into gear, and swung about to escort them in.

Niccolo wilted against the chariot wall, right down onto the floor, a humiliation he would have avoided, but his legs no longer held him, and Zaki and the king's herald held onto him while the damned chariot bounced and rattled his skull against the sidewall.

So he missed his triumphal entry into Troy. He only hoped to remain obscure, hoped that someone somehow would get him to a medic, without making a spectacle of him, and that somehow he would get to Caesar to advise him, and finally, having done his best, he believed. Or it made no difference.

Absent Friends

"If this level of Hell gives us all what we want, friend Diomedes," said the Egyptian woman, "then think back upon what's happened to you here—what you've done and what you've got to show for it, breaker of horses, beyond that nag you fondle."

Kleopatra's eyes were blazing more brightly than the cookfires set before the tents of Caesar's army or the torches up on the hill that marked the Achaean presence in ravaged Troy.

Diomedes, one hand on the velvet of his horse's muzzle, stroked its bright mane with the other and reminded himself that no one had listened when he'd counseled that women could bring only ill fortune on this endeavor into deeper hells.

Then he said, with temper rising in him that had flouted the very gods on Olympus (not from what Egypt had said, but because he'd taken a woman into his tent and she was Helen, his cousin, and she had burned herself into his heart so that it ached continually and that aching dulled his wits), "Leave off, twit. Take it where someone cares to listen to it—to your bedpartners, however many they may be, or to your fellow 'oracles.'"

The tiny woman, whose eyes were ringed with kohl to keep away the glaucoma that flies could bring (as if there were still such flies to fear, here where everything happened by Diabolical plan or the

287

Amerikanoi Murphy's Law or because men's souls
were their own final and furious curse, and it was
enough to loose their passions one upon the other,
enough for any Devil's pleasure or any Hell's design)
—this diminutive distaff "king" stamped her delicate
foot as if he must now tremble at her wrath, and
fairly spat at him like a cat with a trodden tail: "Fool.
Fool! From the others, one might expect obtuseness.
But from *you*, son of Tydeus? Did the poets lie so
fecklessly, then, that you are no better than an ani-
mated phallus, to be jerked hither and thither by
that gilt-haired slut?"

His cousin, she meant; Helen, she slandered.

But in the night behind her waited Germans, two
hulking things with only glimmers of sanity glazing
their minds like badly-made pottery, with lynx fur on
massive shoulders and intent watchfulness in their
eyes that beat back even Hell's untimely night.

So he spoke carefully in Greek, which these half-
wit guardians barely understood, and modulated his
tone because timbre, not content, would prompt
those murderous thews to wreak destruction. But
though the stamped foot of Egypt brought those
bodyguards to trembling eagerness, Diomedes did
not stay his words.

If Kleopatra sicced her hounds on him, he would
fight. For the honor and the freedom of Helen was at
stake and his own honor hung there in the air where
family obligation was concerned. Alexander had confided once, in a moment of drunken candor, that the
only way to deal with the threat of Kleopatra was to
bed her, but this was not the Argive's way.

He'd rather sleep with the horse he stroked than
with the snake she was.

But she *was* that snake, the very evil in the garden of Gemayel's faith, and so he must be cautious. She was Caesar; she was Hatshepsut; she was the Amerikanoi in their magic truck. For all Diomedes knew, she was the black bird of war, that same engine of destruction his vision had predicted, in which Achilles had come among them to confound an entire army and make these Great Ones small.

He could have grabbed her, snapped her in two before the Germans' slow brains could prompt their limbs to intervene.

He could have rid Alexander of her weight and Caesar of her miasma and every man in this camp who'd slept with her (Half? The entire Roman 10th? Surely every man who mattered, each poor prick with influence or weight to throw where she'd command.) —rid them all of the spell this witchling cast.

For Helen's honor and Helen's safety, he would do it if he must. None of these ageless antiques understood what Helen was, what she represented, the mantic honor and the Spartan glory that lived within a girlish, childlike form. They were "Old Dead" but not old enough—they'd read Homer but never understood the truth between the lines.

So he retorted finally, "Poets lie, of course. Achilles should have showed you the truth of that."

Then behind him he heard a rustle of tentflaps and his heart said, *Please no, priestess of my heart and of my blood, don't come out now. Don't face this thing who wants only supremacy over you, yet can never have it. This one thinks and proclaims herself a living goddess. You, are one. The end of that is clear enough, if snakes be snakes and women have their way.*

But prayers were to no avail here; they never worked; your worst fears always took hold in this foul soil and sprouted like a hardy vine. So he felt Helen's cool touch upon his arm and saw out of the corner of his eye her fine profile before she lay her cheek against his shoulder arm and peered past him at Kleopatra, the crocodile on this accursed shore.

He'd seen the Macedonians ride out, rag-tag, mutinous or worse. He'd heard loud arguments and turned from mixing in when the Roman troops embraced infernal rumors and only Antonius could stop them.

This wasn't their war; they didn't understand.

The fatalism that sustained him here, when he was worn past better thoughts and tired past caring, alighted on his shoulder like a bird.

Taking its counsel, he said, "Helen, this is Kleopatra, as you know. She wants—"

"I want," said the Egyptian, "an end to this—release for my people, even only if to go on to . . . another Hell . . . any other will do. If we must be entrapped, let it be in Upper and Lower Retenu, where civilization flourishes; not here, among the fleas and dogs."

Helen's cheek moved from his arm, and eyes like the Mediterranean tried to drown him when he met their gaze. And the mystic child whispered, "What does she want from us? Why does she torture me? Oh, Diomedes, I'm so afraid."

Wonderful timing, he thought as her Germans stomped in three full paces because of the tone in Pharaoh's voice.

If Kleopatra was going to come apart—to lose her mind or go hysterical—there would be no way to convince those non-literate barbarians that it had been none of his doing.

He couldn't help his cousin if he were dead. "Helen, go back inside. Stay with Paris. He'll be worried. I'll take care of— "

"You'll do nothing of the kind," decreed the Great King who was a woman. "It's her doing, so much of this. And her fate we're talking about. Men don't rule over women's—"

"My *fate?*" came the sweet, pure sound of Helen's voice, laced with becoming trepidation. "My fate is with my family, Queen. I want only what Diomedes wants for me, since he is the wisest of us—"

"The wisest of you all, pet? Then you're in deep trouble. Aeneas speaks with Caesar; Priam wants his sons back—what do you think your fine *man*-cousin's going to do? Give you up whatever way makes the army safest, child. And soon. Because he has no honorable alternative to . . ."

With a stifled wail, Helen sank to the ground and began her lamentations.

"Now look what you've done!" Diomedes heard himself cry out, and then was kneeling by the girl, enfolding her in his arms as it hurt him so to do. She had a husband; she'd spent centuries with the Trojans; they'd both lived and died apart. Why Athene in the hardness of her heart had decreed he feel like this, he could not fathom.

Speechless, bound up in the silken webs of two women so that he could barely think at all, he held the shivering body of Helen against him, hoping against hope her husband wouldn't come forth and take offense, yet hoping that he would: Paris was an easy kill, and overdue for it.

Kleopatra's fists balled on her hips. She spat: "Phaw. Fool you are. I say to you, Argive, that only you can put this mess on track. Give up the girl, give up this war, give up your memories of obligations that went to dust with your earthly bones. Or there'll be no saving us, any of us. Not until Achilles is in his tomb again and your war is over will any—"

"*It's not my war!*" he bellowed, surprising even himself, glaring up at Kleopatra with unexpected tears in his eyes.

Which terrified Helen, so that she broke from his embrace and scrambled toward the tent, where Paris (gods help them all) was standing, leaning against the centerpole, arms crossed and a dangerously thoughtful look on his pretty, vapid face.

But the Egyptian wouldn't leave off: "Not? *Not?* Tell that to Alexander, or to Achilles, or to Julius. Did you know Alexander is going up to the citadel to take the remaining Achaeans—your brothers, your responsibility if I understand this tangle one whit— under his protection? Pro*tec*tion, Argive—in the guise of command. And did you know he's lost his chance at Heaven, down in the maze? Or that Maccabee is still lost and he'd never leave a friend unfound? Or that—"

"Egypt," said a voice out of the dimness for which the Germans gave way, "It's not that bad. It's not that dour. It's merely war, a thing I'd thought you'd understand."

And the slight form of Alexander strode forth from the night.

Klea's voice rose: "Not that bad? Then where are Aeneas' women? And why doesn't he just assume that they'll turn up? Death is a mystery here, my friends. The Undertaker is a stranger to these folk. Where they go after they die here, I don't know. But *they don't come back here*. Or Aeneas wouldn't be so full of tears and fears. And the Undertaker would be the foul joke he is elsewhere."

"Not that bad," said Alexander smoothly (while the Germans cooed "Tyr, Tyr," with something like regret in gutteral voices). "*If* Diomedes will come with me, help me talk the Achaeans off that hill before Caesar's only recourse is to pound the Achaean quarter into rubble."

Alexander speared Diomedes with his ingenuous stare. "Will you? To save lives? Come with me, friend? Priam is with Julius—Helen and Paris will be safe with them. Hostages must be returned."

Helen gasped, "Oh, no," and Diomedes saw her hand stretch out, grasping for the distance as if there were some physical anchor she could grab to save herself.

The Argive said, "She's been a hostage too long. I've promised her that I'd return her to Sparta." He was lying, but he knew that was what she wanted. "It must be here somewhere, everything else is. As for Paris, I'll give him to his daddy, whenever—"

"Speak for me?" Paris burst out. "How dare you, a jilted suitor, make so obvious a play for my wife? You'll not—"

Helen gave a despairing little cry and, both hands spread over her ears, ran into the dark recesses of the tent.

A quiet fell upon the little group outside it, where her heartbroken sobs wrenched the very air.

"Admirable." Diomedes looked square at the coward who had no arrows or bushes around him tonight. "If you were worth it, I'd split your bones. But even your marrow's inferior. Get out of here. Comfort your 'wife,' boy. This is a council of adults. Children are not welcome here."

And Kleopatra echoed his words with some instruction in a gutteral tongue that made the Germans come forward, so that Paris retired hastily and closed the tentflap behind him.

And then there remained the three of them, in the Devil's darkest night, with only the Germans, who could not listen though they heard, to witness what was said.

"It is true, then, Basileus," Diomedes asked, pointedly ignoring Kleopatra, "that you saw a Judge in the maze, that Aziru went up to Heaven?"

"Aziru went . . . somewhere, with ancient gods, gods of the underworld he called the Anunnaki."

That name struck a chord with the Argive, not of recognition, exactly, but of appropriateness; he had traveled far and he predated both these arrogant kings confronting him.

"Because of this, you would have me surrender the Achaeans to Caesar?"

"Win them to me, to our cause. We will not travel with the Tenth and these creatures much longer. We will find Maccabee, and Achilles, and Menelaos. We will put these matters of kinship to rights, by logic or force of arms. Then we will depart—far from here, we can find peace. I have glimpsed it. And I am certain it is worth a try."

When Alexander spoke like that, Diomedes recognized how the world was won.

Even Kleopatra didn't gainsay him, but simply waited for what the Macedonian would say next.

But it was Diomedes who spoke first: "You cannot expect me to surrender Helen to the Italian. Or to the Trojans. She wants to go home. She is my—"

"I am of your blood, such things I understand as Zeus understands the thunderbolt. We will make peace here, I told you, by reason, by your good offices, or by my swords. And then she will come with us. Nothing is lost by making peace. In peace, everything can be regained."

It was a canny plan, and Diomedes knew it would salve both their hearts' pain.

But it was not right. And rightness was a factor, though he did not say it there and then, with the wily snake-woman from Egypt watching and listening. If it were true that the war could be ended by negotiation, then he'd be glad to lend his help to that.

But it hadn't been, and Diomedes saw a distorted mirror in this hell, like a face seen in badly-cast bronze: if they must replay the past, then how could they change it? If it must be as it was, then what were these strangers doing among them? It might be that only his fears and his knowledge guided this fated dream, as Klea had intimated.

If so, could the dream end before the dreamer waked? And what was waking, if sleep was life? Afterlife? Death? Would a death, or a few deaths, break the distorted pattern, the web of half-truths in which he struggled? Would a sacrifice do the trick?

Fear not to wake the dreamer, whispered something inside him—a something he always heeded.

But what did *that* mean? The others were waiting: Kleopatra, to go running to Caesar, her tail wagging, with tales of whatever deal he'd made; and Alexander, his eyes full of guile, to see if Diomedes understood.

He hoped he did; he hoped Alexander did. As with Odysseus on the night hunt, treachery was Diomedes' most trusted weapon now, and stealth, and trickery. Sweet deception. He would give Helen to Priam, for the moment.

And then, when imperiled men were safe, he would deal with the fates of women. If not for Achilles' sake (in aid of which he'd be loath to lift one finger), then for Maccabee, and for Menelaos, and for all the Achaeans Caesar threatened to snuff out with his physeters of war, Diomedes would play counselor to the king of Macedon, and Companion where all companions were lost, until the men in the citadel were safe and united with the Macedonian horse.

Then they would have an army, of a sort, of their own.

As he and Alexander were affirming their pact, determined, Kleopatra said, "And don't forget, boys, you must also keep alert for lost Hektor and the missing Trojan women. We'd like them back as well." Then with a giggle that made Alexander scowl and Diomedes want to sacrifice to Athene, the Great King turned on her heel and stomped off, her four Germans trailing behind.

Relief flooded Diomedes, until he returned his attention to Alexander and saw a stricken look there he didn't understand.

And then he fathomed that: Kleopatra had taken Alexander's Germans away; if he was a good boy, her twitching ass seemed to say as it winked away into darkness, maybe she'd let him have them back.

*   *   *

Maccabee was thrashing about in the water, banging against other bodies being washed helplessly downstream, then against rocks and dirt, submerged trees—

Trees. He opened his eyes the next time he surfaced, rather than just gasping for air, and saw that the darkness here was not so complete as the darkness in the maze had been.

And saw others, and yelled hoarsely: "Achilles, Menelaos, the shore! The shore!"

For it was there: the campsites, fires blazing; the hill of Troy, the ravaged citadel atop it.

And, closer on, two burning lights like idol's eyes, bright as halogen torches in a legionary's hand.

But larger, much larger.

He struck for that shore, personal survival obliterating, transiently, all concern for his men. And then remembered them, and hollered commands as loud as he could.

The Romans were good swimmers; the two Germans seemed to force the water away as, closest to shore, they tried to stand on their feet, were bowled over by the current, but tried and tried again.

Achilles had Menelaos in tow, one arm crooked around the Atreides' neck. Maccabee wasn't yet safe himself when he realized that Menelaos was dead weight and Achilles was unreasoning, hysterically stroking, his jaw clenched and his head a topography of huge bruises: Achilles was back-stroking, with an unconscious man in his grasp, toward the middle of the river and not to shore.

Maccabee trod water and considered whether he really owed Achilles enough to try to reach him: the Thessalian was beyond hearing a shouted command;

he was barely conscious. It was only the strength of
his will to survive that had brought the hero this far.

Hoarsely, Maccabee shouted for the Germans:
"*Agite. Agite,*" he demanded, not knowing if it was
the right word, but it was the only one he was sure
they understood that produced movement when you
yelled it at them. And "*Tyr! Tyr!*" He wasn't sure
what that meant, either, but it always got their
attention.

When shaggy blond heads turned toward him,
Maccabee pointed, then gestured urgently in the
direction of Achilles, stroking strongly away from
shore.

Then the Israelite went under himself, swallowing
water.

By the time he struggled back to the surface, the
Germans were headed into deeper water; three of
the Romans who'd accompanied him into the maze
were scrambling onto the shore, where two dark
figures waited; and a Macedonian was throwing
Maccabee a rope with knots in it, a rope that stretched
all the way to the lights that burned through the dark
and showed him a small cone of beach as clear as
day.

Maccabee grabbed the rope on the second try,
fancying that Alexander must have come down to
save him, and pulled himself shoreward hand over
hand.

By the time he could stand upright, Maccabee was
so certain he was saved that weakness was coming
upon him and thus he still needed the rope, over
which his hands pulled him, because his legs were
trembling so.

On the other end of the rope, beyond the dripping

legionaries and the Macedonians, were the two Americans, Welch and Nichols, dressed in dark fatigues, leaning upon the bumper of their insidious truck which had come, Maccabee knew, from the Devil's own armory of dirty tricks.

He stumbled up on the bank, taking one of the coarse green blankets piled there in the sand and blinking in the glow of the truck's headlights, meaning to walk back down to the water's edge and direct the rescue of the Germans who'd gone to rescue Achilles and Menelaos, if the giants needed mortal help.

But the two Americans, whom Zaki felt to be the most dangerous men in camp, unfolded their arms and forsook their truck and came toward him, something in their hands.

When the two reached him, the legionaries gave back.

The smaller man—Maccabee's size, but less massive than his friend who sucked on a burning weed—said, "Remember me, Maccabee? Welch is the name. Have a drink, buddy."

And he held out a glass (a glass!) and poured something into it, and into two others, and gave one to his companion also, then said, "To absent friends, then," and clinked his glass against the other American's, then held it out so that Maccabee could join in the ritual.

Since the second American had repeated the words and clinked his glass against Welch's, Maccabee followed suit:

"To absent friends." He repeated the formula, the American English unwieldy on his tongue.

And drank. Choked. Then sputtered as fire coursed into his guts.

"What—" *Cough.* "was—" *Choke.* ". . . *that?*" And: "Absent friends?" an afterthought, when he had time to realize what the words meant as the drink swirled through his brain like Phlegethon on the prowl.

"That? Kentucky mash, sort of—hard liquor, friend. You're old enough," answered the second American, Nichols. "Time you got a taste of the real thing."

And: "Absent friends, right now," said Welch, answering Maccabee's second question, "include . . ." Welch spread fingers in the headlights and began ticking off the missing, "Alexander and Diomedes, who've gone up to the citadel; Aziru, who's gone up to Heaven,"—a smirk writhed across Welch's features, full of something quite different from humor—"and a whole household full of Trojan women; Scaevola and Company. I think that's about the lot of them, for the moment. Oh yeah, and Hektor. Hektor's got missing, and Priam won't settle anything, Zaki says, until he's found. You wouldn't have run across anything we could call Hektor, in that maze? A piece of Agamemnon that wouldn't be recognizable, or some such?" A flash of white teeth accompanied this last; the Amerikanoi had big, white teeth, the best in camp.

"Hektor," said Maccabee slowly, with the mash cooking his brain. He took another drink and this time the fire was welcome; it chased the chills from him and seemed to dry the very water from his sopping flesh. "We saw something, at least Achilles did—something like Hektor's spirit, in the pillar; you see there was a pillar—"

And he began explaining to Welch about what

they'd seen in the maze. Then stopped, realizing that the Americans thought he was a hopeless fool, and turned to look where they were looking.

By now, Maccabee had emptied his glass and his limbs seemed to belong to some other fellow as he followed Welch, who was striding down toward the shore, a black shadow followed by a larger shadow that was Nichols.

And as he reached them, he realized why they had left him: the Germans had brought Menelaos and Achilles to shore.

The American called Nichols was astride Menelaos, pummeling him on the chest and kissing him obscenely.

Maccabee ran to intervene, to pull the American off Menelaos, when he realized that a scuffle had broken out between the Germans and the Romans for just that reason: the Germans were trying to get to the American to remove him bodily from the Greek, and the Romans were pushing the Germans back.

Withal, the Macedonians waited, their attention on Maccabee, hoping for some kind of signal as to which side of this brawl they should be on.

Through the fog of the liquor, Maccabee strove to reason things through.

And succeeded, and bawled to his Macedonians to break up the fight, while he himself stumbled to his knees, breathing hard, beside Nichols who was still on top of the prostrate Menelaos and demanded to know, "What sort of defilement is this?"

"I'm trying to save his goddamned life, mother-fucker. Now back off." Nichols mouth was dripping water from the kissing; there was water all over Menelaos; it was obscene; ghoulish.

Yet Maccabee's instinct was to trust this man whom no one in camp trusted.

He turned his head and saw Achilles then, stretched out in the sand beside Menelaos, and Welch had Achilles' head in his lap and was carefully pouring something down his throat, medicine from a small pouch.

The Thessalian coughed and spat. His breathing was labored; it rattled as if he'd swallowed an entire inland sea.

Achilles head was so bruised it seemed he had giant warts where the bruises swelled; his whole skull was misshapen from them.

But somehow, Maccabee knew that wasn't what caused the convulsions which started then, and ended so quickly—so quickly that Welch had no time even to scramble out from under Achilles' head before he gave up his spirit in one last, rattling breath and died.

Just like that, Achilles died on the beach, in the sand, soaking wet and ravaged from his toils. He lay limp; his chest no longer rose and fell; no breath came from his nostrils.

Welch put the battered skull of Achilles down gently in the sand, got up, and waded into the water without a word.

Maccabee, with a last shake of Achilles' still form to make sure he was really dead, then followed Welch.

They stood in water up to Welch's knees and Welch said, "So much for that," and threw the pouch of medicine out toward the middle of the river, as if in disgust.

Maccabee said gently, "It is not your fault. He was too badly hurt, too many times. It had to happen."

"It had to happen, all right," Welch said in a clipped way the Americans sometimes spoke. "Now maybe we can get the fuck out of here."

The American turned and trudged back toward the shore, where his friend and the evil truck waited, and Maccabee couldn't help feeling that he had missed some essential point here.

But a friend and comrade in arms had died, died after heroic labors and great travail, and Maccabee had led too many men to their deaths not to feel in some way responsible.

It was only when he got back to shore that he realized that Menelaos was dead too, and that the Macedonians had deserted their posts, looking for Alexander (or so Nichols said) and that Maccabee must take the angry Germans and Romans in hand, and see about preparing funeral rites (at least both men were from the same time) before there were no bodies to praise.

Nichols saw what he was doing, and called out of the com truck's open window as he began to drive away, toward higher ground, "Ain't no hurry with that, buddy. Those corpses'll last a good long while down here. Dead here, you're really dead. Or at least they don't pop right back. Let the right people know, is all. That's your end of it. Then come around later, up the hill, and we'll have another drink."

Welch had monitored Machiavelli's transmission, via some unaccounted-for Litton, and every move the American had made since then had been determined by events, not choice; set in motion by others.

He knew better than to proceed reactively; he just couldn't figure another way to handle things.

Until the chance had come to use Machiavelli's own poison on Achilles.

If these crazies understood their situation at all, pulling Achilles out of play was going to put Welch and those he represented back on the offensive.

Machiavelli wasn't going to like it, but he'd be Welch's man as soon as things shook out.

It was a small victory, as was Achilles' death—small if it didn't work. If Achilles was the magnet binding this mismatched army to a bottled piece of Hell's spacetime that ran by the rules of Minos and other Judges, and against the Devil's best interests, then at least they could get out now.

No one admitted to dispatching Achilles here— Welch had checked and rechecked.

Now, in the com truck with Nichols who was quietly getting soused and who wasn't the world's friendliest drunk, Welch had only minutes to decide on his next course of action.

He could go to Machiavelli, straightaway, and read him the riot act. Machiavelli was with Priam, however, accompanied by Zaki, and the lot of them were conferring with Caesar, who had Aeneas with him.

Nichols leaned one hand on the bumper of the console and slurred, "Let's blow the lot of 'em out of the water—remotes work good on the groundeffect tanks. We can call it an acident or blame it on that Hatshepsut bitch. No one'll get wise; they're too damned ignorant."

It wasn't a bad plan, it just wasn't the way Welch wanted to play it.

"I'll think about it," said Welch, taking the bottle that Nichols held out.

Nichols was becoming increasingly more expendable, but Welch was as fond of Nichols as he'd ever been of an operative. Nichols didn't understand the bigger picture, but that wasn't his fault. No one had expected him to, or prepared him to. Nichols was a weapon, as much as any of the heavy guns on the tanks or a Macedonian javelin.

But back in New Hell, a power struggle was escalating. The Agency that tried to split the Pentagram fought a cold war, manipulating the dissidents and even the denizens of this deeper underworld, where Minos and other Judges proclaimed autonomy.

And the problem of hubris in this deeper Hell was nothing compared to the meddling coming from the upper levels of Authority. This Agency who fought the Devil funneled power to the dissidents, as it funneled spoilers like Achilles into play wherever the Devil struck out to reestablish order.

Achilles might return to whomever sent him, once his body was burned. Welch sent a message alerting those who wanted very much to see just where, and to whom, the Achaean reverted.

But Mithridates and Tigellinus and those others who made up the Agency were so powerful that even Welch himself had occasionally hummed their tune: not to do so would be to expose his person to unsurvivable peril.

And Welch was a survivor.

He had his own loyalties, his Dark Cause; he had no interest in seeing this cold war break out into overt hostilities, not even the Higher Ups could command nukes, and proxies were a dime a dozen.

How much whatever happened here had to do with what went on back in New Hell, Welch couldn't be certain. But tentacles were reaching out to him, interests trying to work through him and too many others.

And Machiavelli was definitely working against Authority, which put him in the Agency camp, though he probably didn't know it. As a pawn of the Opposition, Machiavelli was more dangerous than he would have been had he, Caesar, Augustus, and their entire crew been actively engaged in subversion as were Mithridates' treacherous agitators.

Welch worried most of all that he'd never get these people out of here—that, even with Achilles gone, the Counterforce was sufficient to block the army's return to New Hell: that was what Achilles had been meant to do here, Welch was now reasonably certain.

So, Welch asked himself, what's the play? Go to Caesar, explain everything—or some things—and see if the Roman was capable of thinking like an operator? Caesar was too aware of him for Welch to count on ignorance as an ally, and a little information (plus evolving suspicion) was always dangerous.

Collar Machiavelli? Teach the little rat new tricks? Take away his field phone and his com privileges? Double him to Welch's service, where he ought to realize, by now, he should have been all along? Or let Caesar's doubts nullify the man, which soon they would if bad went to worse, as it surely must?

Welch sat back in his ergo chair and socked down one more shot of mash.

Nichols had ways of getting things nobody ought to be able to lay hands on—mash in this isolated piece of Hellish real estate, yet.

Aziru had found a Judge here, blast and damn; now the whole army wanted nothing so much as to trudge down those tunnels, sheep to the slaughter. Minos and a slew of ancient underworld gods that centuries of worship had created made this a sinkhole, a trap set by other than Demonic plan.

And Welch wanted nothing less than judgment; he wanted only to do his job and get back to the surface, where what he'd learned could do some good.

But since that was what he always wanted at this point in an operation, when things started to come together for him, he'd bide his time.

And take a chance. He was a betting man by nature.

Now he was betting that no one else had heard (or at least that whoever had heard had failed to understand) the implications of Machiavelli's message—not Caesar's command post on the hill; not Mettius Curtius in the tank designated Titan One up there beside the post; not any of the tank drivers along the lines; not even the commander of the fortifications facing the Trojan camp.

He wished he could hope that Dante and hence Augustus, and probably Agency ears as well, had failed to get that message, but he was a pragmatist: he never bet against a full house, and the Roman villa in New Hell was the fullest.

Welch got up, decided, stuffed a nine millimeter machine pistol with laser sights in his jacket pocket, and headed off toward Caesar's tent.

It was time to do some damn thing, *any*thing that would make things shake out so that he could see what was left, afterward.

He wanted to get the rest of these ancient types down into the maze before anything else went wrong; he'd bet on consolidation of forces, rather than the unlikely chance that anyone—even Julius Caesar—could hold this motley crew once the rumors solidified that there was a way to Paradise in the maze.

But getting Caesar to move wasn't going to be easy: that Old Dead was a canny commander, an intuitive man who'd had too many hard times not to be frozen into immobility, trying to figure out a safe course of action to nullify what was happening here. And Welch's bet was that Caesar wasn't liking what he saw before him: nobody who had any self-respect wanted to stay in this cesspool and yet there was no honorable way out of this mess, in Caesar's terms.

Slipping out of the com truck, he paused only long enough to make sure Nichols knew he was leaving, then sauntered among the jumble of men and armaments from many ages.

Damn fool mission, to begin with. Ill conceived and ill thought. Only somebody like Maccabee could really believe that a man could win Heaven by force of arms, or by guile, or by any way at all. Judgment wasn't withheld—they were here, all of them, because they'd fucked up in life.

It was a fait accompli that brought you here; this was no holding facility. Aziru had gotten through a loophole, a small one, one that wouldn't accomodate an army of Caesar's size.

There was some small chance of adjudication, of appeal. If you found the right moment and had the right bloodlines and met the right god of the right underworld in the right circumstances.

None of these here would be willing to understand that. Each would feel he had a shot at escape. And most of them wouldn't. So then, in the maze, you had to worry that those who were disappointed would turn on those who had a chance.

It was going to be real dicey in the tunnels, if any Judges were met.

It was going to be worse if he couldn't convince Caesar to *take* this army into the tunnels, because this particular patch of Hell was meant for Hellenes and their blood predecessors, for a certain mind-set, for the teaching of lessons about constancy and stubbornness and dehumanization.

It wasn't for Nam vets like Nichols and it wasn't for men like Welch, who didn't feel at home in any crevice of Hell they'd seen so far. And it certainly wasn't for the Romans, who'd squashed these people whose home ground this was.

There was a strong tendency of this turf to bring vengeance into play.

And Caesar had lots to answer for. Which was why he was the perfect pawn for the Counterforce Powers, for "Agency," as Welch liked to term it, because of a love/hate relationship he'd sustained with a similar covert organization or two in his lifetime.

Damned fools, bureaucrats and kings. Twice damned fools, those who acted out their orders.

Which foolishness had gotten Welch himself here.

The tents he passed were full of mutters—mostly Roman mutters—the Macedonians were almost fully absent, those not AWOL and down into the tunnels were following Alexander who, with Diomedes, was already in the Achaean quarter on the hill of Troy.

Damned Ilion. Welch's classicist's heart hardly believed this was happening to him. He'd loved the old poems so; they'd been his tranquilizers when he'd tried to hold his own in 20th century Athens, and do this and that for a government that didn't understand the Greek soul and didn't care to learn.

So it was probably fitting that he'd be here, stuck like these other flies in this particular piece of amber, trying to deal with a Roman (whose very epoch he despised) who in turn was trying to deal with his own devils.

If Welch had been calling the shots, he'd have come down on the side of the Macedonian and stayed there: Alexander was a man Welch could have helped without qualm.

But it was Caesar he'd have to deal with, and Caesar, when Welch finally got to his tent, was busy with Priam, Aeneas, and items of protocol which made Welch cross his arms and bawl: "Julius Caesar, Welch here. I need to talk to you a minute!"

The Roman guards immediately drew their swords, but Zaki ducked out of the tent in time to save face—and probably lives—all around.

In the torchlight, Welch was faced off against some reasonably sharp swords in some reasonably steady hands, his machine pistol cocked and ready.

He didn't want to hose down this crew, but he would without a second thought.

He simply waited while Zaki ran from man to man, wringing his cap, talking urgently to line commanders or guard captains that Welch couldn't have picked out by himself—defining targets, if things devolved further.

Welch marked each man Zaki spoke to, mentally, and held his ground.

In that tent, whatever was being discussed wasn't pertinent to events, as far as Welch could see. The only pertinent thing was getting these interlopers out of here, as soon as possible—while he still could.

There was a smoky breeze tinged with onion and garlic that tickled his nose; there was the smell of pungent sweat as Zaki came close and said, "He's coming, Welch. Hold your fire. Don't start a row, not now when we're so close . . ."

Welch would have said *"To what?"* if he'd cared to hear the answer.

He didn't. He wanted Caesar to know what the Roman's best next move was; beyond that, if Caesar didn't listen, was only the question of who among these Old Dead would assume command if Caesar died in the night, and how fast Nichols could get the job done.

Watching the tentflaps and listening for all he was worth, Welch realized that a lot of attention was going into funeral preparations for Menelaos and Achilles.

Which meant, of course, that he'd better get Caesar off alone to tell his tale.

And when, at last, the Roman came outside and approached him, Welch pointed his weapon skyward, saying, "Take a walk with me, Caesar?"

Zaki's face looked like someone had just stepped on his big toe, but Caesar nodded and walked beside Welch wordlessly until they were away from prying ears, in between tents where whispers wouldn't carry and no one could lurk unseen.

"So?" said Caesar with an arch of one eyebrow.

"So, Achilles is out of play, and you can get this army moving. Into the tunnels. Now. Tomorrow morning at the latest."

"This is your advice? Or your order? Or you think this is news to me? Which?"

Welch shifted his grip on the machine pistol he held. Caesar wasn't reacting properly. Nine millimeters were so damned loud.

Then he said, "Look, we used Machiavelli's poison on Achilles, let's not waste the advantage."

"*You what?*" Caesar's voice was harsh, like a backhanded slap across the face.

"Don't play dumb with me. What was that talk we had? You want to be Agency's pawn? You want to work with the rebel factions? Or you want to keep your special status? *Which* is it? Because if you play in this mud-puddle much longer, I'm not going to take responsibility for getting you out. You get your boys down those tunnels; use the maze as a rallying point—they'll go; they think salvation's down there. Leave the rest to me. Otherwise, you'll be here till Hell freezes over . . ."

"You murdered Achilles, in *my* behalf?" The Roman came up close, nose to nose, as if the gun Welch carried was a bunch of posies. "You've exceeded your authority, American. There is a punishment for such behavior by an officer."

"Yeah, I'm shaking in my boots."

"Your underling, your subordinate—he will bear the cost. It is his 'boots' we will discuss. Did he also kill Menelaos, then?"

"You'll have to ask him. Look, King, this isn't working out. You'd better admit it. You can't straighten out this Trojan War—it's been going on for thousands of years. Remember when we first came here, how so many of these ancients were frozen into statues, dead on their feet? That could happen to you and yours, if you start thinking about taking up residence in that citadel. Or worse—"

Julius Caesar said, "I've told you what will be," turned his back, and walked away.

"Caesar! Jesus . . ."

But the Roman was gone, and Welch didn't understand exactly what the Old Dead ruler had in mind until he got back to the com truck and realized that Nichols wasn't there.

Signs of struggle were, though.

When Welch found Nichols, his friend was at the funeral pyre of Achilles and Menelaos.

At least Nichol's head was, up on a pike.

Welch looked at the head awhile, fury rising in him, and then began to circulate among the men.

A mutiny isn't a tough thing to start, if you put your mind to it.

And Welch had a very good mind.

He was going to drive the com truck out of there, down into the maze if he had to use a tank to blast a way for him. And he was going to take the balance of these troops with him.

If he brought them home, and lost Caesar and a few others, he'd still have done his job.

Decided, he walked up to the head with its glassy stare and said, "Sorry, buddy. I should have realized it might go like this. Don't drink on the job next time, okay? See you, sometime."

And he was pretty sure he would—sometime. It took a little bit of effort to get your dead back to the Undertaker from here, but once Welch was in New Hell, there were lots of strings he could pull.

Right now, the single string he was interested in

was up in the Achaean quarter, attached to Alexander of Macedon.

Zaki took the message from Maccabee, who seemed dazed and somehow shrunken with sadness.

Outside Caesar's tents, the Israeli looked up into the eyes of the so-much-taller, beautiful Israelite, a walking page torn from the Bible, and was deeply troubled by what he saw there.

"Welch sent me," Maccabee was saying with a puzzlement that might have been suspicion if there were sufficient energy behind it. But there wasn't; there was only exhaustion.

"Welch sends us all, these days, here and there like Pharaoh's slaves," said Zaki bitterly, his trip to the com truck to retrieve Machiavelli still fresh in his mind. "What's the news, then?"

Maccabee rubbed his neck, his gaze focused over Zaki's head, and over the tent in which Caesar treated with Trojans, fixed on the distant mount of Troy. And then replied: "That Hektor is in the maze—we saw him; Achilles saw him. Now, I've got to go back to the funeral. . . ."

The funeral. That was it, Zaki realized: Maccabee mourned lost Achilles and Menelaos.

Mourned in a Jew's way, which never changed; which had not changed from Maccabee's days down to his own. Zaki looked behind him, at the tent in which Machiavelli sat with kings, and thought out loud, "What do they need me for? With you, I'll do more good. Let's go, friend. Two souls need Kadesh said and shiva sat, and around us are only goyim."

Zaki's smile was forced, but Maccabee knew it was an offering, and accepted.

With a qualification: "I must stop by Diomedes' tent, and what I do there must be kept secret."

Zaki agreed, and left with one backward glance and a feeling of immense relief: being the only Jew in that place was not comfortable.

Walking with Maccabee, Zaki felt as if he were walking through a temple, as if God were very near.

Even though Maccabee's questions were all about Alexander—where he was, who was with him, what his plans were, Zaki still felt this gentle awe as he paced the Sword of God through the Roman camp.

"The Macedonians," Zaki replied to one question, "are up there, too—the only way into the maze is through the throne room deep in the citadel. Alexander will have them back, and his honor with them, in good time. Do not worry about your friend. . . ."

"I worry," said the Israelite with the wind-blown curls, said this man of classical stature and finest form, this light unto the ages of Zaki's people, "about Diomedes, who is with him, taking offense at what must be done." He stopped, near the Argive's tent now, and peered at Zaki through the rufous dark of Hell's night.

Beyond, Zaki could see the flames of the funeral pyre licking skyward.

"No. No, I do not understand." Understanding was at a premium in Hell this season.

"Then listen, Jew." There was a seriousness in the tall Israelite, a quiet and an intensity that Zaki could associate only with matters bordering on those of faith and holy law.

"In Diomedes' tent," Maccabee continued, "is the shield of Herakles. They burn Achilles; they do not

bury him. Alexander once took Achilles' shield from
his tomb. Do you see?"

"A thief, you mean? The *basileus*?. No, I don't
see."

"The consonance must be satisfied. There is a
shared soul here—Caesar and Alexander, and Achilles . . . surely you've heard tell of it. Whatever
Achilles is—was—must be separated from the others. Diomedes began this enterprise when a vision
appeared to him. The shield of Herakles appeared to
him also. And he brought Alexander to meet with
Achilles, here. Now if I know the ways of men and
gods—and God—then there is a meaning in these
bits of fact. Achilles must have his shield returned to
him, and since the only shield which could substitute, the only one that came among us in a numinous
fashion is the shield of Herakles, which Diomedes
gave to Alexander but keeps for him, then that
shield will finish a pattern, complete a circle, break a
bond."

Zaki said, "But you're not going to *steal* it?"

"I am going to place it on Achilles' body—or ashes
if it takes that long. I am going to see it burn with
the body in order to sever whatever hellish bond is
between these men. It is the only way to see the
hand of God in these affairs, and you, Zaki, know
that the hand of God is everywhere—even here."

Zaki found his cap in his hands, and he mashed it.
"But they're not going to—"

"They will accept what I have done, for the sake of
single souls and lifted curses, for the sake of a fallen
hero and his peaceful rest."

"Yes, I suppose. . . ." Doubtful acquiescence was
the best that Zaki could do. He wouldn't argue with

the primitive, fabled creature. All Hell was torture, all learning, pain. If he must learn that this man he'd so revered was impenetrably primitive, it did not make Maccabee any less a creature of wonder.

But the pragmatist in Zaki wondered what would happen when Diomedes and Alexander found out what Maccabee was going to do—had done, by the time they heard about it.

Together they approached the tent and before it they halted: words were coming from it, loud and angry words, words between two women and a man.

"Kleopatra," Maccabee spoke the name with disgust.

"And Paris and Helen," Zaki added.

"Go in there for me, get the shield, and bring it hence," commanded Maccabee, crossing his arms, as he had commanded so many suicides in the past.

"But Klea—" Zaki bit off the protest. If he were the single comando left to this ancient leader, then that must be enough. Whether he understood or agreed with the objective did not matter: Zaki had served others here whose reasoning was more arcane and whose motives were more in doubt.

So in went the little Jew, hating that he must skulk and lie, with skulking and lying for a living Bible story whose wishes he could never refuse.

And there was Kleopatra, with two Germans hulking behind her, and Paris and Helen also.

Helen's face was swollen from weeping and Paris had her by the arm, saying, "She's right, woman. You're my wife, don't forget. And Priam is your father, by a marriage you cannot deny now, after so long. We will go to my father and we will do what we can for peace. Now!"

In so small a tent, Zaki should have been an obvious intruder, a person to be questioned, detained, or expelled.

But he was like an invisible man there, unnoticed, unnoticeable, a mote of dust in these ancient eyes.

And this made him angry enough that he simply grabbed the shield, which was under a blanket, and hefted it. It was as tall as he, and surely Kleopatra must have noticed him—he was only an arm's length from her.

But Egypt did not deign to recognize him, nor did the Spartan priestess or her husband, prince of Troy.

The Germans did not bat an eye when he hefted the huge shield and scuttled out with it like a crab, between their bulk.

Truth be known, no one cared what he did, not when such matters of blood boiled between these royal brats.

Outside, Maccabee waited, a pensive look on his face.

When Zaki brought him the shield, Maccabee slipped its straps over his forearm and said only, "Coming, brother?"

But it was enough.

Side by side, the Israelite and the Israeli went to perform a sacrifice to set Alexander free.

When Maccabee shoved his way through the crowd and, a few feet from the pyre, cast the shield upon Achilles' bones, sparks flew and the ground began to rumble.

Men retreated. Men called out to one another. Men turned their faces away from the bellows of smoke.

All but Maccabee were confounded.

But Maccabee merely raised his head and stared

up at the citadel, saying to Zaki, "Now, we join them. Soon, we will find our fates in the maze. Our judges. In a dream, I saw Alexander's Judge and it was Bucephalus. Look into your heart, Zaki, and decide who your judge might be. This opportunity, this path to heaven, is a test: it comes when it wills and it may not come again, if we do not recognize it when we see it."

Alexander's Judge was Bucephalus? It made no sense, but Zaki went anyway, agreeing to purloin a jeep with a machine gun mounted on it and drive Maccabee up to the citadel, where Alexander waited.

Where Diomedes was with the *basileus*, helping to recruit the Hellenes and attempt to unite them with the truant Macedonians, already making their way down into the maze.

Whatever the outcome, Zaki knew that he wanted to be there, with Maccabee; not here, with the Romans and the Americans—not here where Welch was finally making his move and Caesar about to learn lessons he would not like.

Klea's eight ball had told her what to do: flee. Flee before she ended up like Achilles, or like Nichols with her head on a pike.

Caesar's temper had slipped its traces and Hell had no fury like his when it was aroused.

Diomedes would not be pleased about Helen; he had left her in his tent on the assumption that honor would protect her. He was wrong.

Caesar was frightened. This terrified Kleopatra, as it did Hatshepsut on the hill with Curtius and Titan One and Mouse and every other one of them who orbited Julius like the stars the Earth.

Kleopatra wanted to behead the Spartan bitch, this Helen who was an albatross, as much an evil anchor as Achilles had been.

But it was just the fever of killing, and it was infecting the camp.

Nichols' head on a pike as an *object lesson?*

Caesar had said only that he was protecting Machiavelli from Welch. So now Welch was a great enemy, when before he'd been just an American with a handy piece of equipment.

And they were all thinking about New Hell, because another Transformation—another shift of the ground and of the rules and of their loyalties, and none would ever leave this place.

The kings were frightened, and the ranks felt it like they felt a cold wind whiten their breath or Phlegethon when he reared in fiery rage or Scamander when he surged beyond her banks.

This very ground was their enemy, and old souls who knew ancient curses, such as Hatshepsut, remembered them.

"Let the ground reach up and swallow you, let the mud mire your chariots so that they cannot get across, let the rocks open up and consume you," Hatshepsut had raged, when Klea doubted her ability to blast a way into the citadel's throneroom with her tanks.

If Klea could not enlist Caesar's willing aid, the army was going to go without him—if they had to drug him stuporous, if they had to tie him in his jeep.

Because it was *time*. Because Julius had lost his temper and with it all perspective, and the shadow of a young Roman lieutenant who could not walk away from a challenge, not to save himself or those he loved, loomed over them all.

The Trojan women and Hektor weren't their problem; weren't their concern. They didn't want to conquer this land, or make it safe for Rome, or loot it. Those days were long vanished.

They—the army and those who followed Caesar with a loyalty that surpassed all mortal bounds—wanted to get him home.

If they had to disobey him, to thwart him, to insult him in order to protect him, they would do it.

The question was, of course, whether he ever could forgive them. But to lose him . . . to have him die here and not reappear . . . that was intolerable.

And possible. This was a hungry land, an evil land.

A land they should quit as soon as cleverness allowed.

If he never forgave her, at least he would be alive to hold a grudge.

She brought Helen to Priam, Paris wound around her finger like a stalk of marsh grass.

And Priam was overwhelmed with joy to see his son.

Caesar was not. His countenance grew dark.

But the tanks were waiting and the army must be *led* up into the citadel, else they would lose it—there would be no army, only empty tanks and low-burning fires upon the plain.

To regain command, they must appear to command what otherwise would be a mutiny.

Antonius had held the troops, but he could not hold them forever.

So she said, "Caesar, I must see you outside. For a moment only."

And Aeneas watched them go, while Helen wept quietly in a corner and the open tentflap let in the smoky night.

There before his tent, Kleopatra said it brusquely: "It's time to go. After Alexander. Now. We can't hold them for you. If we stay, it's forever." And she waved a hand, pointing out the movement as the troops packed up.

Then closed her eyes and braced herself for the tempest of Julius Caesar's response to an insubordination verging on usurpation.

But it did not come.

So she opened her eyes and then Caesar, a sorrowful look on his face and a remembering look in his eyes, said, "Klea, I don't know how to fail. I never learned. . . ."

And Julius embraced her, while around them centurions began to gather.

Kings in Check

Hour upon hour of walking and the tunnel echoing with the jeep's laboring efforts, and there began to be a desperate look to the men's faces as Scaevola sat down with them at rest, white eyes staring back out of blackface, faces glistening with sweat and smeared with wiping it. The rocks were cool enough to sit on at least: weary legs had their rest; and the jeep ground and whined to a stop, squealed as the driver set the brake on this interminable incline.

They made their stop well past the last branching of the tunnel. The men had bitched and wanted to sit down to deliberate there, at the juncture of ways down and straight on, but it was a hell of a place to rest, to sit staring at the Devil's own choice of ways, at a reminder that they were without maps or knowledge and that Scaevola who led them had no idea where they were going, only a hope and a hunch.

Now the walls and floor were cooler, on this downward bent, the air had a clammy and fever-breeding chill, and Scaevola, wiping his face with his arm in lieu of hand on that side, and sitting with his back against the rock, had row upon row of silent, frightened eyes staring at him.

Volunteers all. But there was a limit to endurance, and a limit to how far the legionaries would follow a substitute commander, one who to their observation, made mistakes. No one was talking, hardly a word,

buddy to buddy, in the ranks, just those silent, exhausted stares and the accusations and the suspicions
they would not say aloud.

The loo'tenant took the wrong fork.

*Hell, who knows where the Old Man is, the lieu-
tenant come through the Undertaker, who knows
what he remembers?*

*Who knows, maybe they whispered this whole damn
plan in his ear, him lying there on that table, maybe
the Old Man's gone, really gone, and they ain't
saying. Divide the Legion, wouldn't that be the game?*

*Same's they played in Gaul, ain't it so—put us
under some damn fool lieutenant, keep us out on the
frontiers of the Empire, out of the Senate's hair—?*

There had been a call, a garbled and illusory call
which sputtered out of the field phone and for a
moment gave them soaring hope. For a while back
there, near the fork, there *had* been talk—*come on,*
the men had exhorted Scaevola, and their faces had
held despair when he had not been able to coax
clarity out of that transmission, or give them direction better than a guess.

He tried the Litton now, wondering in his heart of
hearts whether it had been the Devil's trick, or their
base-com trying to reach them with an emergency,
or truly what they hoped it was, a contact from the
lost cohorts of the 10th, from Caesar himself, seeking
some bridgehead back to New Hell and sanity. He
worked and fussed with the equipment, over which
effort the men came to hover and to hope.

But there was only sputter and static. Phlegethon's
magnetic flux played hob with transmissions; and
down in these tunnels which Phlegethon's naphtha
and lava had carved in solid rock, with the rock still

warm from those torrents, precisely *how* these tunnels had formed was not what Scaevola wanted to think about.

He shut down his efforts with a muttered, "Static, the damn river's in the way," and waved a gesture at the men to back up. "We'll try it farther down."

Then he wished he had not put it that way either. *Down*, in Hell, was not an altogether encouraging statement.

There was an eerie hush in the darkened streets, only, somewhere, the nervous hoof-falls of an abandoned horse, echoing off the walls beyond the headlights as the jeep came to a halt and Mettius Curtius used the loudhailer and his best antique (if heavily accented) Greek. *"Basileus! Diomedes! Caesar asks you to parley!"*

As the hoof-falls rang and the crests of the walls were aglare with the conflagration down the hill, the funeral pyre of a Hellene king and that of a Thessalian prince.

Helen's husband. Murdered. And the bitch had not shed a tear or come to throw a stick on the fire either, but stayed whimpering in her tent. Her sister Klytemnaistra hewn to bloody death with Agamemnon, her husband burning to ash, but no matter, Helen had one pretty prince in her toils and Diomedes on his knees— Better Hatshepsut, he thought with a shudder, better couch with the lioness who knew no shame in bed and brooked no dishonor out of it, than this beguiling, doe-eyed nymph who robbed sane men of their senses.

Keep an eye on the Pharaoh, Caesar had said, assigning Curtius to Hatshepsut and the Armored, an officer too high in the legion to be errand-boy for one of Caesar's imperial pains in the ass: but it began to look the other way around.

Hatshepsut had had qualms about sending him in here, *Hatshepsut* had argued with Caesar that they should simply knock a few walls flat and then hail the recalcitrant Achaeans out, *Hatshepsut* was in close consultation with Mouse, than whom there was no cooler head or wiser in all the legions; and *Hatshepsut* and Mouse together were sending frantic orders to Antonius, trying to keep the lid on rumors running the camp, while trying to keep an eye on the American Welch at the same time.

But Helen, the damned cause of so much blood and ill-omened murder, sat it out below; Kleopatra was gods-knew-where, and Mettius Curtius took it on himself to play herald, since it was Caesar's order not to use the tanks to hail Alexander and the Hellenes out.

Another damned hostage, he thought, *or another damned fool . . . isn't what we need.*

A man who had jumped his beloved horse to perdition—a sacrifice to the gods— Oh, he had learned, had Mettius Curtius, what rash gestures cost. In Hell he dreamed of falling. Dreamed of the horse screaming, so much that he forswore the mounted cavalry, and took to these things of metal, which he could love and tend without risk and without nightmares.

And now, a ghost in the haunted ruins, an echo among walls stained with funeral fires, he heard frantic hoofbeats on the pavings, among the walls, heard the fitful start and stop of a trapped animal above the whining engine.

Fool, he told himself. *Fool to go further. It's ambush. Alexander may be dead, you may gather yourself a Hellene arrow out of one of these windows—gods know what he ran into, or where they are—*

But the hoofbeats came near, echoing wildly, scraping on stone in the way of a horse which has lost its footing in its panic, over in the next street. It screamed, and that scream ached through his horseman's soul.

"Oh, *damn!*" he cried. He was not Mouse, he had never meant to come to Hell, had never bargained for his fate. He had thought of glory and gotten only death, and known an animal who trusted him was dying under him—

—he braked to a squealing halt, reckoning the motor itself was panicking the horse; killed it and leaped out and ran down a twisting, cobbled alley in the headlights, toward the clatter of hoofbeats.

It was a Macedonian horse, was a blaze-faced bay which had run as far as it could down the closed court, and which panicked again when it saw him, and raced and brought up again at the walls. He held out his hands to it, shaking, knowing himself a fool and derelict in his duty, which was to go back now, at once, and report calamity.

But the horse stood now in the reflected light in the dead end of the court, whuffing and throwing his head and straining with wide nostrils to pick out the scent of a man who smelled of oil and terrible machines.

"Come," he said, whispered to the bay, "come, boy, come, there's a lad—"

Closer then and closer. It threw its head and stamped and came up on its hindquarters, settled

again, sweating and scraped raw on a shoulder, and
hurting.

"Poor lad, come, I'll take you—" He snagged the
trailing reins, caught them up short near the bit and
kept the horse from rearing. "There." He patted it,
talked to it while it trembled, and he trembled in his
turn, with a great lump in his throat, which was in
part raw terror. "Oh, damn, let's get out of here. . . ."

The horse shied and rolled its eye, and Curtius
spun about to see the alley blocked by two men with
spears and rifles, two giant figures who hulked
toward him and had him dead, before he could unsling
his gun.

But they were not firing. Kleopatra's Germans,
they were, the giant northerners; and he held onto
the trembling horse and faced the men who came to
him mute and with hands held out.

"Tyr," they said, by which they meant Alexander;
and one gestured toward the ground. "Hell," the
other said. Or something like that. While, bewildering sight, they looked heartbroken. Curtius clung to
the bridle of the shivering horse and listened to a
torrent of German, from these giants who looked at
him as if he were their sole source of hope.

"Tyr," one said again, and gestured wide with his
spear, around all the citadel by implication, and reversed that spear and pointed at the ground.

*Fool Roman, Alexander has gone below, do you not
comprehend me yet? Gone and left us.*

The horse shivered at the omen, and backed and
jerked at the bit. Curtius turned and grasped its
mane and hurled himself up, onto warm and living
flesh. "*Graeci?*" he asked.

A second gesture with the spear. Blue eyes stared

up at him like ice in melt, suffused with rage and
tears. The German smote himself on the chest and
proclaimed something in a voice like thunder, and
the tears fell.

"Come on," Curtius said. "Come on." While the
horse danced and shied under him. "There's nothing
good here. The damned horse knows it. You know it.
Let's get out of here."

"Grief," that one identified himself, with another
thump on the chest, and gestured toward his comrade. "Famine. Go. Tyr. Freya give."

For the Germans it was a damned long speech.

"Yeah, go. Tyr."

Fast as they could. He felt the uneasiness of the
ground, felt it the way a Roman could, who had lived
his life on the quaking banks of the Tiber, at the
pleasure of the gods of earth and thunder. He knew
it in the panic of the horse, which trembled and
shivered when he stopped beside the jeep in the
alley.

But before he could get down, Grief climbed into
the driver's seat and hunted for the keys.

"Damn, can you drive?"

A huge hand reached out, Famine's. Expectant.
Curtius hesitated, flicked a glance at the modern
rifles, remembered whose service they had come
from, and surrendered the keys, not wanting to see
what happened to the fenders.

He wanted out, out of this place. Like the horse,
which had had its fill of terrors. He felt the very
ground pregnant with earthquakes—he, who had died
to still the shocks that ravaged Rome; he damned
well knew now, that the vacant windows about them
were vacant, that the streets held nothing living.

Behind him the jeep roared to life and followed; the horse ran for safety, and dust and bits of plaster shivered and fell in streamers from the riven walls, whether that the racket and the lumbering of the jeep disloged them, or that the whole land had reached its limits, and the gods below were not sated with the Hellenes.

A way out below the hill! They were mad, who thought so. The whole army had gone mad, and Curtius despaired of convincing even Caesar, who was snared like the rest. Only, gods help him, the Egyptian and Decius Mus, a foreigner woman and the only saint in Hell, both of whom were clear-eyed and sane as he was cursed to be. The Egyptian was no part of this. Mouse was part of nothing, but he was on their side, and nothing beyond Mouse's judgment did he trust.

The tents billowed down, the order having passed. The quartermaster's truck ground its way along the aisles and soldiers heaved up bundled canvas and poles and pegs, and smaller, personal kits, black figures against the white headlights of the trucks and the jeeps; and the redder, sullen glare of the funeral pyre.

It was defeat, though it was no rout. The 10th saved that much. They did not abandon their equipment (perhaps they would need it, against the gates of Paradise, which some thought to storm) or their discipline, once it was recalled to them. And Julius' eyes stung with tears and his heart ached, seeing it.

Alexander had said something of the like, turning from (he had believed it then) the sea; for his men, who could not endure more years of war, perhaps (secretly) for himself, who had taken too many wounds and endured too much. For Alexander's ambition, perhaps, had shrunk only to the desire to walk from sea to sea, and then, worn out, to think that he had brought the world to peace.

Young fool, Julius thought with hindsight, *you would have done everything and failed: and they would have remembered that of you, that great folly. There was no ending. There was no peace to win. Only more of war. I crossed my sea, I found Britain, and more and more of wars. Now it is another kind of sea, is it not, and it is the men who dream and I who know better than this. I can turn them—if we survive this. Follow them a space, and turn this stampede, and save them. If there is time.*

A quiet step came up on his right. He looked, saw Antonius there, a chastened and miserable Antonius. "The men are coming off the lines," Antonius said, "in good order. We have the tanks for cover over there, if we need them: the Armored's the only unit holding steady."

Gods, the damn woman. Who'd have thought?

"*Cai Iuli.*" Antonius cleared his throat. Bad news, then. Julius held himself still and let Antonius get it out. "The hill's clear. I mean—they've searched up there—Curtius—"

"*Pro di.*" Loneliness came over him like a cold wind. "Alexander's jumped the gun. That figures."

"Not like—" Antonius made a helpless, desperate gesture. "I mean he's just *gone.*"

"Dammit, man! He isn't just *gone,* he's damn well done what you can bet he'd—"

"Maccabee's here," Antonius said. "He's still here in camp. I checked."

Julius stared at him, his heart beating away in leaden cold. "You're sure."

"Checked. Absolutely."

"Damn! *Covering* for him?"

Antonius tilted his jaw up. Oldfashioned Med *no.*
Some things never died out of a man. The Americani
would not have understood, did not undestand so
damned many things. Julius had done Welch a favor.
And saved the damned non-expendable truck and its
chief operator—damned *fool* Americans; and now
they were not to call on, Nichols was beyond reach
and Welch . . . gods knew where the damned truck
was, somewhere off by the hill.

"Who knows?" Julius asked. Gods, limit the rumor, get it contained before it hit the lines the way
the other one hand—*Welch's* doing: Julius had had
that reported. "Who got the report?"

Antonius ticked off on his fingers. "Hatshepsut.
Mouse. The Armored. Anyone else with—"

"—the damn com truck."

"We should have taken them both out," Antonius
said. "The men—"

"Call the com truck. Tell Welch I want that hill
sounded. I want a report."

"He won't give it."

"The *hell* he won't give it. He knows damned well
what's going on. He spread the rumor. Gods know
what he's working for. Be civilized. Be *modern.* But
don't go there in person." He caught Antonius by
the arm. "Dammit, *Antoni,* this isn't a damned rabble. We're going in there, we're going to find an
answer if there is one. That much. Go."

Antonius left, fast. And Julius jammed his hands
into his pockets, feeling his back naked, for all that
two of Kleopatra's Germans stalked like giants wherever he went, armed and surly and quick to level

those rifles, no mucking about with spears and
ceremony—on men of the 10th, the way things were
going.

But he knew the legionaries. Knew them by name,
every one; and knew well enough that profound shame
would come after the panic; shame too dark and too
deep to bear, if he did not forgive them—so he
forgave them in advance, he gave in like Alexander
to his troops, even if they shamed him in front of the
Trojans, in front of Aeneas his ancestor, and all the
rest. Only that Welch had done it to them—that was
hard to forgive; a defilement, a shame that by military law meant blood, decimation . . . the cohorts
lined up by rollcall and every tenth man led off to
die. *That* was what the American had done to them,
that was why Julius did not stop them now, only
meant to lead them a little ways and pretend they
were following his orders all along; which being Roman, and subtle, they would finally guess, and know
what he had done, and come to him begging him to
relent and lead them the way that he truly chose.

It was, as revenge went, understandable that Welch
had done this. He kept reminding himself of this,
that Americans had difficulty thinking in the long term,
that their anger was extravagant and without calcula-
tion. But beware the rare one that broke the pattern.

Rifles rattled behind him. And it was Aeneas, no
attack—only his distant kinsman, in the face of whom
even the Germans seemed daunted, if only by the
quiet of this Dardan prince. "Iulius," Aeneas said in
his guttural, lisping Greek—his own lost son's name,
with a twist: surely it had some significance that
Aeneas chose that appellation instead of Caesar. He
came armed again; with his plumed helmet under his

arm. "I am going now. With the king and with Paris and Helen. Back to our lines. Never fear there will be a mistake. Only your Alexander will restrain the Ahhiyawans."

"It's not so simple," Julius said. And taking a breath: *father*, he should call this man. But like so many things out of joint in Hell, they were near the same age. *Brother?* That was too close and there were too many years between them, too much unspoken truth which, thank the gods for small mercies, the Trojan was too wise to ask: *What did my son become, how did he die, what fate did he find?*

A man in Hell long enough—grew careful of such questions. Especially the big ones.

"We're missing the Greeks," Julius said—it *had* to be said; dealing with an honest man, a deception was fatal. "We just got word. Alexander and Diomedes went up there, a man of mine went in there to find out why it was too quiet. They're gone, gone away, took the trail before us—only, Ancestor mine, Alexander's best friend is still here. In camp. I don't think they had a choice."

"The Greeks may have killed him, and gone."

"Possible. Possible. But they *have* gone. We don't know what we'll meet up there. If you want to change your minds—"

"To turn?" The Trojan shifted the plumed helmet in his hands: the white horsehair caught the stain of funeral fires, and the red light glittered off the bronze. "We will be with you." He spoke another word, his own tongue, too ancient for any Roman descendant to understand; and the sense of lapsed time and impossible gulfs grew worse and worse.

"*Vale,*" Julius bade him, in a language too new for

the Trojan to understand. And went and hailed a passing legionary. "Soldier. *Valeri*. This is Aeneas. See he gets safely to Priam."

He had the satisfaction of seeing a boy's eyes go wide and a living dream take the place of a poisoned one—"Yes, sir, *dictator*, sir, I will, sir—"

Aeneas walked away with a boy whose Greek was probably as rotten as his own; the hero put on his plumed helmet, and the Roman lad walked along holding his own WWII issue pot under his arm, the two of them silhouettes in the headlights of a truck inching nearer and nearer.

"Get that damn tent down," Julius yelled at his aides and dithering sycophants, wherever they were lurking. "Where in hell's Klea, does anyone know?" He stalked over to the communications desk, an island of a table in the midst of a flattening camp, and issued definite orders. Motion—any motion— was henceforth a relief.

Canvas was coming down apace, on all sides of them; and trucks growled and moved, devouring the camp. Niccolo sat still in a tent he would not permit them to demolish, and waited . . . waited till the little Jew came trailing in. There was the smell of smoke about Zaki. Zaki. Point. No other name. He blinked at the man and reached to the table beside him, to pour wine with his left hand. "Will you have a drink, friend? No? Do not drink with me? Or do not trust the cup?"

"It's not the night for it," Zaki said, and took off the hat . . . the wretched, shapeless hat, and wrung it in his hands. "Two men are dead. People are losing their minds. Should I sit here drinking? I said

I would come. I should get the ambulance for you. These Romans, who knows?"

"Nichols." Niccolo lifted the glass. "To Nichols. *Salve atque vale*. Hail and farewell." He drank a little of the wine, a red that had the raw, unpleasant tang of blood, and grimaced. "Soldier's red. The legionary, *signore*, has no taste. He *will* drink this abomination. And disdain good Bordeaux. Sit down. Sit down, *signore* Jew, my friend, my rescuer. Will you—truly—not share this execrable wine? I fear we are short of cups. The sycophants have filched everything off to the crates. Terrified, absolutely terrified. You think we have difficulties. Consider the lot of the sycophants."

"I should get the—"

"Drink from the bottle. I swear it is quite safe." He lifted his eyes to the Jew and gave a pained and rueful smile to see the suspicion there. "Ah, Zaki, Zaki, you doubt so much. Or is it the vintage you doubt? That, I should never blame you."

"The trucks are coming. They are breaking the camp." A gesture with the shapeless cap. "King Priam is going back with his son, with the Greek woman, this army is going into the maze, with *trucks* it's going into the maze. What do reasonable men do? No one is sane."

"Go to Welch."

"To Welch? This is a joke." Another punctuation with the hat. " 'So where is Machiavelli, eh? Where is Caesar, what side are you on, sit down, Zaki, have one of Nichols' cigarettes, he should care now—' Do I look stupid?"

"Ttttt. Can the American turn down help? It takes two to operate that truck. Keep him company. *Lie* to

him. I'm sure you can think of something." He looked
Zaki in the eyes, a difficult feat: Zaki's were seldom
direct. "This is important. Important. Do you understand me, Zaki?"

Zaki's dark gaze jerked aside, darted like something trapped; the hat suffered further abuse. "So, I
am a fool. All right, all right." The trucks squealed to
a halt outside, and Zaki went to yell at them: "A
minute, *minutum*, this is a sick man!"

Someone shouted outside. Cursed in Latin in a
soldierly, friendly way. Niccolo took a sip of the
wine. "I will manage them. *Prego, signore*, go on,
find Welch. Give him my regards."

Zaki stared back at him from the door.

"Go on," Niccolo said, lifting the glass. "A safe
trip, *signore*."

"The ambulance—"

"Ttt." And shaping the word soundlessly: *Go*.

The little Jew ducked his head and went, quickly,
out the door. There was more yelling with the legionaries outside, in English and Latin and mangled
soldierly Greek. *Later*, a legionary yelled in exas-
peration, in English. Latin had no convenient word
for the concept: nor understood its degrees.

So they would be back when they would be back,
when someone called their attention to a tent omitted. Then there would be remonstrations and shouted,
indignant denial of responsibility. Niccolo sipped the
raw wine and blinked at tears of pain as he set the
cup down.

So, well, there was little gratitude in the world.
Strange that it was the Jew who came to him, con-
cerned for his welfare. Who thought that Niccolo
Machavelli might need carrying, perhaps, publicly

through the camp, forgotten or abandoned by the Romans. Never. Cesare only expected him to give orders, that was all, demand what he needed, summon the ambulance if he wanted it—Cesare never saw to the little things, though when he found them omitted, Hell itself quaked in consequence. So Cesare expected that the necessary things were done. In the book that he was writing, Níccolo made a mental note, to add a chapter on the difference between princes and subordinates.

Zaki, for instance: he would himself, choose Zaki.

He drew the ivory-handled dagger at his back, and considered it, and without overmuch reflection sliced the veins of his left wrist. One hoped, earnestly, that his special privileges still held, even here, and that the strings which made Niccolo Machiavelli very, very hard to lose, were still intact. One hoped. He cut the veins of his right wrist, and leaned back in the chair—a sip of wine would be a comfort just now, and damned messy; he hated muss and mess, thank Nichols for this one, and it took so long and hurt like hell.

Let Nichols come through the Undertaker's office where he had influence. He and Nichols would have an interview then, with the situation very different. Very, very different.

To be friend to the powerful . . . cost so much, sometimes. This he did, for instance, because there was no choice. If it worked. If this was not the end of Niccolo Machiavelli's long career, here, in this tent, no dissolution and no return, only a body they could burn, added, for economy, to the pyre of two princes.

Poetic. But damned ugly.

Ah, now it stung. It ached. It hurt like very hell and it was very slow.

Kind of the man to have come. A thoughtful mind. A mind that filed problems away and somehow delved them to the surface again, thousands of details, little things one attended to amid the chaos, precisely the opposite of a Caesar—the Jew had the mind not of a prince, but of an excellent, a humane administrator, if he had not also the talents of the chameleon and the ferret, which made him far too dangerous in any structured organization. Well suited to the shadow world, the orbits about the princes. Well suited—

Zaki might have helped him to this. He should have asked. But his whole life was a pattern of reticences; he did not know how to let go of them.

As, for instance, one had to bid goodbye to friendships once the use for them was done. That was the characteristic of a wise man, not to cling to unuseful things . . . such a prince or such a man who served him . . . was doomed. . . .

"Pharaoh," the legionary-driver said, popping his head and arms up from within Titan One; "we got the world. . . ."

And Hatshepsut, Amon-Ra incarnate, Ruler of the Two Lands, turned her head and heard the confirmation by ordinary channels as she had heard the message come through that slender tendril of plastics that reached from her headdress to her ear: Marcus Antonius was calling out movements, and she turned to Mouse with triumph in her heart. "He's moving!" she said. "By Osiris my father, Julius is moving! *Marce!*" (This to the tank driver, hanging there on his elbows and waiting orders.) "Tell Curtius cut loose up there with number one. Tell him get my jeep down here!"

"I have to get to Caesar," Mouse said.

"Tell Curtius I need a driver!" she yelled up at the tank. "I'm losing mine. Tell him get through the throne room, we got a whole column coming!—Mouse." She stopped Decius Mus with a word, a look; and got one back from this silent, this strange and fatal man.

Mission accomplished.

For one dire moment she suffered a pang of doubt, who had used whom. She suspected then it was mutual. And suspected hard after that, that there was calamity in their further dealing with each other, an erosion of their personal defenses.

No more, Mouse. Not after this.

We would be fools. Would we not?

He turned, quickly, and walked away.

Up on the hill came the distant thump of fire. Curtius' acknowledgement was in her ear, small and distant voice, businesslike as all his kind.

Caesar was moving off dead center, breaking stasis. They had gotten that much. It was not the direction they wanted, but it was *a* direction, and with Curtius reporting faint tremors and siftings of plaster up there on the height of Troy, it was all they could hope for.

The striking of the camp was not merely precautionary now. It was up to the tanks to cut a way for them, and when they slammed this damned land in its stony gut, she and Mouse both agreed it would buck and kick, and maybe . . . *maybe* give her tanks a target worth the risk, and Caesar an enemy he could fight with overt action.

Trojans, the voices in her ear said, were coming in with them, joining the column: keep the tanks on the left flank on guard while the legionaries got off the lines, keep them there while the Trojans pulled up through that gap between Scamander and the hill to join their column, and then kick this land where it hurt, till it reacted, and reacted off-balance . . . or until some traitor in their midst showed her a target.

Even a Power, one could hope, could make a mis-step under fire.

"Niccolo," she muttered, hoping against all expectations that he might be near a radio. "Niccolo, do you hear me?"

Embers settled with a crash, sending a whirl of sparks up the wind; and a shift in that wind sent smoke drifting across the field, where very few lingered now, the guard of honor, a scattered few comrades who had come down the tunnel-trip. Romans, mostly, who stood around out of duty, and who looked up sharply when they saw the Old Man walk into the firelight, with his escort of Romans and two Germans.

Funeral stink. Different than other fires, even when the blaze was down to charred bone and there was nothing left but ash. Julius had smelled enough of it in his life, never looked (being dead) to have to smell it again, since bodies obligingly disposed of themselves in Hell and death here was not death.

Except here. Except on this damned plain, where bodies lingered until Something claimed them. And nothing had wanted Achilles or Menelaos, it seemed. Not even the woman they had contested for and one of them had married . . . had come to shed a tear over them. Just a few friends they had won in that fight of theirs and down in the tunnels. Now those

same friends were pulling out too fast even to gather
up the bones and put them in some kind of tomb.

Nichols watched, from the top of a pole.

And distant, very distant, like the thunder of the
gods, one could hear the tanks hammering away at
the hill, preparing the way neither Achilles nor
Menalaos would take.

Damn, damn, and damn.

Julius walked among the soldiers, touched one and
the other on the shoulder, ordered them away.

And found one man not his own, one man sitting
wrapped in a robe and with his head bowed, so that
at first glance Julius took him for a lump of stone in
the firelight, in the smoke and the unclean stench.

"Judean," he said, having come to stand between
this man and the light. "Time to move on."

Maccabee lifted his head. A sliver of light fell
aslant on his strong-boned features, cast a shadow of
curling hair, glistened on his cheeks.

The tears shocked him. But not. "You know,"
Julius said with acerbity, and he could not say why,
except that he sensed anger, and he ached, and
wanted to deal it out and not receive it, "Alexander
is among the missing. Vanished up there. He's in the
maze. Sooner we get up there the sooner we find
him."

The muscles in Maccabee's throat worked, his jaw
knotted and a muscle ticced there. No answer. Not a
one. Pain, Julius sensed it clear: *a quarrel, a part-
ing, a desertion?*

Sitting here in the smoke. "What in *hell* do you
owe Achilles?" Julius asked, unwilling to have it be
anything, unwilling to think that the young hothead
had inspired anything—senseless slaughter, sense-

less death, an expensive one, that had damned near brought the centurions to him in rage. Killing a comrade, even a damnfool bastard of a comrade, was serious business and Nichols had paid for it in Welch's stead. *He* had seen to that. But what was it brought the proud Maccabee to sit in the dust and the ashes, over a cursed, foul-mouthed little bastard of a Thessalian prince, who had done nothing for any of them?

Who had brought Maccabee back from the Undertaker, damn, yes. Who had been in Maccabee's party when he bought it, and Maccabee had reported the double murder with trembling outrage.

"He tried so hard," Maccabee said, in a voice thin and hard, "he tried so hard."

And heaved himself to his feet and turned away.

Julius caught his arm. A tall man himself, he had to look up a degree. "Where in hell did he come from? Who was he working for? For that matter, who sent *you*, Judean?"

The dark and shadowed gaze was surprisingly placid. Nothing he could get hold of. And it defied him. *Kill me*, it said. *Try it, Roman.*

Julius let him go without feeling him leave his grip. It was an instinctual thing, the confrontation was a fool's act, if it went further. The hate was too deep and too little reasoning.

He lifted his hand, preventing the Germans. And turned, walking off the other way, feeling the sting of the smoke. Stopped then, with an inexplicable sense of anger toward that smoke and that flame which had no substance to be cursed and shaken and questioned.

That this damned fool could bring such disparate mourners—

But *he* was here. The pain, he thought was for
Alexander, who was also a damned headstrong fool,
and probably in serious trouble—fool also, Judah
Maccabee, who thought that Alexander would desert
a friend of his own will: *murder one, yes, Judean,
and die a thousand deaths; to such things kings are
prone. But never walk away from one.*

The anger was for Achilles, who had been as trou-
blesome in his death as in life.

Whose slight form and cocky assurance and maddening, offensive manner he, dammit, would give a
great deal to see lounging in his tent or by the side of
his jeep—*Need an errand-boy, general, sir? Need a
miracle worked?*

He glanced back at the fire, at the dark heart of it.
And left as quickly as had Judah Maccabee.

The hammering of the guns echoed off the heights
and ran through the earth under Zaki's feet, and it
was with a feverish anxiety that he discovered the
elusive com truck where the legionaries had said it
would be, parked over against the hill, by the stream
that ran from it. Where Achilles and Menelaos had
died.

He was not, thank God, a thorough believer in
omens, not like the Romans. But he knew the poten-
tial for calamity, and the brooding silence of the
dark-camouflaged van there in the dark . . . offered
him no reassurances when he went up to it, in the
wan light of the funeral fires. "It's Zaki," he yelled at
the featureless lump. "I'm alone!"

That in itself had a forlorn sound, and got no
response at all from the van.

"I'm coming to the door!"

God forbid a volley should come through it. But
he went up to the sliding door and beat on it with his
fist. "Welch?"

He tried the handle. It was unlocked. Of couse it
was unlocked. It had just gone unlocked when he
came walking up; and now he had to open it, himself,
and Welch would not be in front of that door.

He jerked the door back and stepped back quickly,
not putting his head into that van. "Welch. Let me
come in."

"Come ahead," the American's voice muttered. "Real
slow. *Real* slow."

Zaki stepped up onto the tread, and climbed further into the truck full of green-figured screens and
little ticking troubles. This so-dangerous truck which,
he figured, could kill them all; with an armed American who could blow him to bloody rags into an
expendable storage cabinet, that was how he knew
which side of him Welch was on before he looked.

"Caesar sent me," Zaki said, and swallowed at the
lump in his throat. He held his hands up, classic
form, and saw the black shape of the American against
the glowing of screens and telltales. Lie, oh, yes, but
engage the man's curiosity: Machiavelli . . . Welch
might have less curiosity about, but madness from
Caesar himself, that would get his attention, that,
God willing, would make the little wedge in Welch's
defenses, after which he, Zaki, would have a chance.

He could also be wrong. This was equally possible,
equally balanced at the moment.

"Close the door," Welch said.

Perhaps he wanted to muffle the sound. *I could
bring you a grenade, American, have you thought of
that, do you think of it, do you imagine I have a*

reason to? I could hold it in my hand, deadman's trigger, so, if I had one. If I were willing to die for this, which I am not, God willing. I do this for reasons, I am not here to be a hero, look, both my hands are in plain sight.

"What did Caesar send you for?"

"The legionaries are marching, the Trojans are joining him, all the camp. Those sounds—"

"Say I know all this. What are you here for?"

"To help you—" Zaki ventured a small gesture, stopped as that silhouette reacted with a new tension. "Caesar is sorry. He is sorry, Welch. He says that."

"Does he. Tell it to Nichols."

"These are Romans! Someone had to die. Do you understand, Welch, it was Nichols or it was you, you killed their man, you killed a hostage, you brought him that news, what else could he do? He took Nichols. You he couldn't lose."

It was fabrication. It was possibly the truth. God knew, the Med was the Med, and the shores that sea washed were not the American's, no American could figure it. A smart one knew he could not figure it.

He is going to fire. Now I am responsible in his mind. I should have said the truth.

"Get over there," Welch said, and motioned with the shadow of a gun.

The earth shuddered again, out of time to the guns. The camp was down now, and a sycophant whispered frantically to Klea as she ran ahead of her German escort, her heart skittering faster than her feet, to the jeep that Mouse held waiting. Julius was in the passenger seat. Klea reached the jeep ahead of the Germans who guarded her, and climbed up the hard way, banging her knee in her distraction before they could help her. "*Cai*," she said to Julius, out of breath and desperate and terrified. "Niccolo is gone . . . he's *gone*—"

"I'm not amazed," Julius said, and snapped at her: "Get *in*, dammit!" as the ground shook again. "The tanks have broken through, we've moving in, *move it*, woman!"

She rolled into the back seat, instinctive: when Julius yelled like that under fire, muscles jumped and bodies went; and the lurch of the jeep as it started up flung her back against the seat, a second jolt, whereat she slumped back with a knot of terror in her throat which refused to work and say, *No*, mi Iuli, *dead, dead, he's deserted us*—

The earth lurched like a restless creature, the jeep swerved, and she yelled it out: "*Dead*, Iuli!"

As the jeep sped away and armies moved toward the hill of Troy.

The computer stared back, electronic cyclops, mantic with rippling green numbers, and Dante Alighieri bit a well-gnawed fingernail, pushed Enter, and wiped the sweat on his upper lip, while the computer consulted the drive, whirred and chuckled away. . . .

. . . and the house power glitched.

"*Dannazione!*" the poet gasped, and truly felt his heart spasm, under his clutching hand. He prayed, he wiped sweat and coded in his figures again. Such glitches were the rule in Hell, where city services were not the best, and where, lately, dissidents grew bold enough to have bombed a power station over in the Siberian annex. But one had to wonder, one

inevitably had to wonder, how many phone calls one
could make and how many numbers one could tweak
and meddle with—or who had talked or let something slip, or whether the Emperor had not answered that Infernal census amiss, or whether the
Hell phone company had not finally gotten into consultation with the wrong government department,
whereupon such glitches assumed a hellish import, a
Sign that someone was deliberately making life difficult. He had such a guilt. He had such a terror for
these things. Interventions came like thunderbolts,
and gave his heart irregular beats, and made his
stomach hurt.

He was not a spy. He was never cut out for intrigues. The Good God had only lost track of him,
that was what had happened, a computer (everything
in this strange age ran on computers) had glitched up
somewhere and his record had been misfiled, whereby
a virtuous and innocent! man ended up doing the
bidding of the powerful and the dangerous in Hell,
thank God for a beneficent prince and powerful pa-
trons, but, but, but! he had no skill to tread this
maze alone; and they had put so much on him and
asked such impossibilities—

The door opened, behind him. He saw the reflection, the light, the tall, unexpected shadow, and
turned his chair about with a squawk of wood-on-
wood, his over-burdened heart all but failing him as
he saw the lank, elegant man in a white bathrobe,
leaning there in his doorframe.

"My God!" he cried. "Niccolo! Where have you
come from?"

This was not a well man who left the support of
the doorway and closed it, who walked with un-

steady, feeble steps as far as his desk and his side, and leaned on his chair. Machiavelli's pale skin was ghostly against his black hair, he smelled of antiseptics, and the eyes that stared into his at close range were shadowed and very pits of hell. "I will give you the numbers," Machiavelli said, hard-breathing, "and you will not question, compatriot, you will not make a mistake in this. I have had a long trip and I am not patient. Begin. Now."

The legionaries did what legionaries did exremely well, and cursed every step of the way: they dug, with picks and shovels, in one shift and the other, where the battle tanks had blasted their way into the hollow hill, dug in the halogen light of the spots and floods and headlights, and proved what human muscle and Roman efficiency could accomplish without earthmoving equipment. Chink! a pick got under a rock, heave! it rolled, and several pairs of hands and sweating backs got it moved aside or passed to a wider spot, or whatever it took to clear a path. Foot by foot the cohorts made way for the jeeps and the trucks, while the battle tanks lumbered ahead, roaring and blasting on their air-cushions, and making the caverns echo like ten thousand Minotaurs. The horses did not like it, the chariotry of the Trojans plunging and neighing, led by their dismounted and terrified charioteers; and having, some of them, to be walked blindfold, while the fragile and empty chariots bumped and lurched over the rocks the legionaries had thought inconsequential to the trucks.

Caesar observed it all from the jeep with Klea and Mouse, between his own legionaries under Antonius' command, and the Trojans under Aeneas. In this slow going, the Germans had caught them up, and Perfidy and Murder as well, who muttered of Tyr and Freya and muttered things of death and Loki as they slogged along beside, at times reaching out to catch hold of the jeep or to lay hands on it. They had lost one of their wards, and the ten who clusterd about them now were doggedly determined not to lose another—gods knew what they thought or what they wanted: Grief and Famine had surrendered their jeep to a Lebanese driver, whereon Gemayel brought out three of his injured. The Germans walked along as a kind of living wall, a pale and otherly presence that rattled with weapons, muttered in their own tongue when they were stopped, and cast dice on the ground when the stop was long.

Klea, when Julius looked behind him, scryed their own futures, the eight ball cupped in her hands and its window glowing.

"What does it say?" he asked.

"Good luck," she answered, looking up, her small and piquant face all ghostly pale in the reflected light. "It says *Lots of Luck.*"

"Helpful," he said. Behind her, among the Trojans, he caught sight of Mettius Curtius, who led the horse he had come down from the hill with, among the Trojan charioteers, and walked as liaison back there. "*Metti!*" he yelled back. "How are we doing back there?"

"They say the last are inside!" Curtius' voice came back, hollow and thin above the noise of the motors. "If—"

The ground shook, rock sifted down, and horses reared and screamed in panic, charioteers and Trojan warriors fighting with all their strength to hold them.

Damn, we ought to leave them, turn them loose on the plain out there, if one of those damn teams get loose we'll have a hell of a mess.

The radio snapped and hissed. "Caesar," Mouse said, with both hands on the wheel. Julius grabbed after the radio.

". . . *something up here,*" an English, accented voice said. Zaki. The com truck was up ahead of Gemayel's jeep, a barely discernable shape against the reflected glare of the headlights on stone, "*. . . a kind of . . . with . . . a wide . . .*"

"Damn," Hatshepsut said, and stared at the vast cavern into which they had come, in which even the tanks were dwarfed. She stood in the jeep and held the mike in her hand. "Zaki, are you seeing this? Does this look like what you saw?"

"*No,*" the Israeli said via radio, while vehicle after vehicle labored and ground its way into this huge chamber. "*There was nothing like this.*"

"Where's our way out?" she asked. No. A man could raise his voice. A woman had to drop pitch to carry authority in this echoing madness. "Dammit to Set, com one, where's the passage gone?"

There was no quick answer. Not from the truck. And near it, afoot and alone, she saw Alexander's friend Maccabee. The big Israelite stood there with his hands at his sides, as if he walked dazed, and all the chaos of trucks and jeeps and tanks sorting themselves out—did not involve him.

Tall, and dark of hair, and bewildered in this chaos. Or beyond caring.

A truck lumbered beyond another, and Maccabee dodged a few steps, staring about him in the whirling lights and the noise.

The Ruler of the Two Lands, favored of Ra, knew the value of a jewel in the dust. But when she had gone to the trouble to rescue him, ordering her jeep across his path, he shook his head mutely and waved her off, waved a gesture toward the shadows. "There," he said hoarsely, "there—"

She twisted the mounted spotlight around where he pointed, where light glistened on wet stone, on the still surface of a pool that lay at the base of a vast pillar. Phallic and numinous beyond a doubt. The center of the quaking earth. Osiris and Isis conjoined.

"Tssss," she breathed, and: *"Pro di,"* her Roman driver, who had both hands clenched on the wheel, while the lost, uncomprehending voice of the com truck snapped and echoed.

Maccabee walked away from them, like a man bereft of will, toward that place. And Hatshepsut, Pharaoh, found nothing clear to answer to Zaki's query—glanced aside, as, close at hand, the com truck's sliding door opened and the little Israeli ran after the Israelite and caught him by the arm, arguing with him, restraining him by what terms and with what persuasions were beyond the competence of her personal devices, in this echoing and dangerous place.

A chariot rattled up, warriors holding the horses, among other chariots, others of the Trojans afoot and otherwise. And in that clatter and confusion a small woman in white dismounted from among the men, small golden figure walked among the plunging horses, the sweating and desperate men—

It is that woman, Kleopatra had said. *She was the beginning of this disaster, she is again. I know.*

We see what we expect to see. We shape our own destinies!

"Ra in heaven." Hatshepsut scrambled from the jeep, her hand on the disruptor she wore. She blinked and the very outlines of the pillar and the pool seemed to haze as if there were oil in her eyes: try as she would she could not see it. But if it should become the Judge Osiris and the River and the Devourer, then, dammit, there was an answer for it, was an answer which would blast the scales and damn her blackly, but she would not give way to so common and general a deception—*I do not go with the herd, Lord of the Dead, I do not go and plead in a babble of tongues and gods and Luwians and foreigners. I am not, my god, patient of such insults.*

"I see it, dammit!" Julius yelled into the mike, and bailed out, Mouse's protests notwithstanding, in this chaos of legionaries and jeeps and chariots and sighing and quiescent tanks. Order there was none, save where the centurions were cursing themselves deaf and hoarse and using their staffs to order the men into line. And close by him, white-plumed helmet beneath his arm, Aeneas walked among his men.

"Aeneas!" Julius called out. But the Trojan only glanced back, as in a dream, and turned and walked on, among his fellows. The horses were quiet now, the only noise the rumbling of the engines and the sigh and ping of the battle-tanks' exhaust, the noise of chariot-wheels, the sounds of hooves on stone.

Helen reached the edge of the pool and bent and dipped her hands there: and it was as if the water lay between them and the sight of her; she and all the vision forward rippled like bright water, and a gasp went up as she rose and held aloft a staff retrieved from the pool.

"Zeus, no!" Klea exclaimed, landing beside him; and drew her pistol and fired, as he struck her hand up. But he could not reach the Germans or their rifles: and Helen flew backward under the impact of that concentrated fire like a white rag flowered with red. "*No!*" Paris cried, a shriek of pain, as Helen hit the pool and the staff fell rattling amid the echoes of the gunfire. A belated gasp went from the army, a breath like a single entity; horses shied and reared and men cried out in despair.

"My gods, Klea—" Centuries of war had robbed Julius of overmuch shock at deaths. But he froze, his heart thumping and his knees gone weak for reasons he could not, in the thin, strange moment, define . . . as Klea lowered the gun, the Germans lowered their rifles, and the wreckage that had been Helen of Troy glowed, shimmered—

—spread something like wings and folded them together, a seam, a glowing line in the air that whisked like fire toward the pillar and poured into it. Paris cried out after it and rushed into the pool itself, but the only thing left was the staff, fallen unattended on the ground.

Julius moved, seeing that, moved with his Colt drawn, amid the tumult of the Trojans, some with spears ready, some fighting to hold the chariot teams, some behind the chariotry with arrows nocked.

But Aeneas was before him, Aeneas who bent and gathered up the staff and faced him with that thing deadlier than any armament they had. The cohorts knew. And Julius stood dead still, thinking wildly of Klea, of Mouse and the Germans and where he was in the line of fire. If he should fling himself flat Mouse at least would fire; Klea would—

But it was Aeneas he faced, Aeneas the gentle and generous, Aeneas the saint, whose eyes met his and said: *What shall we do, Julius, my kinsman?*

"Don't move," Julius said in Latin, and held up his hand. "Dammit, no one move. —Aeneas." In Greek. "We're not going to fire. Peace, Aeneas."

And Paris: "You have no right to it."

Shouting broke out among the Trojans. Somewhere shield clashed on shield.

Aeneas shouted at them in their own tongue. For a moment it was utter confusion, and worse as tank turrets hummed and turned.

"Hold it!" Julius yelled, not daring look away from Aeneas. But Aeneas called out toward his own, and offered the staff toward Priam, who came in a gathering silence, and laid his hands on it. For a moment the rival royal lines of Troy stood facing one another: then Aeneas let the staff pass to Priam's hands.

A step trod up close by Julius' side, others at his back, his own taking defensive positions, waiting a signal; but Aeneas held out his hands, between them and Priam.

"Peace," Aeneas said. "It is Paradise we aim at. Or Troy. Now we know we had descendants. It was not for nothing, Iulius, my son."

The old king touched the staff to the earth, once, twice, a third time; and the air shimmered and flowed like fire about the Trojans, about men and shields and chariots and horses, till they glowed like daybreak and flowed away, a quickening stream, into the pillar.

"*Prodi!*" someone murmured; and "*Hela,*" one of the Germans. "Damn," Julius said, and strode forward to the edge of the pool, before Klea and Mouse both got hold of him. But there was nothing to catch, no magical light to reach out to them.

Just a shimmering of the pool round about the pillar, and for a moment, a trick of the eyes as he looked down, the semblance not of their reflections, but of faces beneath the water, women's faces, grave-eyed and smiling.

"Back," Mouse said, and snatched him roughly from the brink—Mouse, afraid. Mouse who feared neither man nor devil. That in itself was worth sobriety. He found himself on the verge of shivering, looked about him and found only the legionaries, the Germans, the solid shapes of their jeeps and trucks and tanks, and Mettius Curtius clinging pale and doggedly to the cheekstrap of a lone and wild-eyed horse.

He walked back among them. "It was Paradise," someone said; and: "It was a trick," another said, "a damned trick, it was the Devil himself—"

"Shut it down," Julius yelled at them, his voice echoing. "Shut it down! None of us damn well know what it was, but we're still in one piece. Shut up and let's find out what our options are. *Antoni*, get a roll call, find out if we've lost anybody."

Give them a problem, keep them worried, keep them focussed—

"*Where's our recon, for the godsake? Mouse, is Welch asleep in there?*"

Focus the problem on departments, let them expect information forthcoming—

Gods, it had better be.

To Hell and Back

Alexander of Macedon had come this way before, yet familiarity didn't ease him.

The tunnels were deep and convoluted. The labyrinth was still curved in upon itself.

Somewhere they'd lost track of everything else—of the spent brass they'd been following, of the way back to the throne room in the citadel, of the Roman army and the Trojans and all their compatriots.

Now there was just Alexander and his Macedonians, supported by Diomedes and his Achaeans, and the pillar that had reared up before them in a geyser of water as black as the Devil's heart.

This was what he'd wanted, Alexander reminded himself: it was the only solution to the chaos—to the carnage—above.

None of the brilliant Old Dead with whom he'd travelled had seen it—not Caesar, nor the Egyptian pharaohs, nor the Amerikanoi.

No one but Alexander and Diomedes had realized that getting Hektor freed from the pillar was the only thing that would break stalemate—satisfy Priam, make an end to hostage taking and hostage trading, speak louder than words of good faith and honorable intentions.

Or so Diomedes had told him, while stroking his bright-maned horse and staring slit-eyed at the ravaged Achaean settlement around them.

Alexander's Macedonian horse had fared better—until it was time to get the cavalry's mounts to descend into storage magazines and negotiate palace stairs when secret passages were found.

Once behind the throne room, an eerie quiet had overtaken the nearly four hundred men of Alexander's army.

He counted it that way because Diomedes had pledged his men to Alexander.

And that had felt right.

To do it, with the Argive hero beside him and history awaiting the chisel of his spears—this felt completely right.

But in the deep maze, where silence overcame them as if their ears had been stuffed with golden fleece, things began to feel very different.

Dreamlike.

Fated.

Frightening.

Incomprehensible.

Alexander rubbed the snake bite on his arm and wondered if he were dreaming.

Dreaming was powerful, in this place. He'd found that out the last time.

The last time, when Zaki had opened fire on Minos, Judge of the Underworld.

The last time, when Alexander had been confronted with a chance at Paradise, and lost it.

Or so he thought.

Diomedes the Argive thought otherwise: "Alexander," the fair hero had said to him, when at last speech was possible, as the armies had merged and trod, in pairs and then single file, into this maze from which Alexander was not certain he would ever emerge.

"Alexander, the Judge must be the right Judge . . . the appropriate manumission from the appropriate Hell."

And Alexander had replied, "But Minos must hold it against me—the gunshots, the Minotaur's fate. I have lost my chance, eternally."

"So?" had said the Achaean with his far-seeing eyes, eyes that remembered the night hunt and all Odysseus' scheming. "How can you lose what you never had? You have an army of your own; you have my army. You have the hospitality due a guest-friend of my house. Do you see? You loved us so long and so well. It is not punishment, what happens to you here. Unless I misunderstand the gods as they work in the underworld."

With a quirk of his lips, Diomedes had fallen silent then, and his silence said: *Do you not trust me?*

But Alexander knew only that Aziru had gone up to Heaven and that Hektor was trapped in the pillar and that Caesar might languish on the battle plain forever if someone did not make things right here.

How he would make right the slaughter of the Minotaur, Alexander had no idea. But he had brought these men down here on (somewhat) false pretenses: he would sacrifice himself, gladly, to open the way that 20th-century bullets had closed.

The men were here—the Macedonians at least—for a shot at Paradise. Alexander was here for a shot in the heart.

Or a shot in the dark. Whatever revenge Minos would take upon him, it was upon him—and not these others—that vengeance should fall. King to king. Like meeting Darius on the battlefield, the necessity was clear to him; only the method remained in doubt.

Alexander would rescue Hektor, give the Trojan into Diomedes' care. And leave matters of Achaean preoccupation to the wisest Achaean of them all.

For himself, he would be content not to carry this burden.

It was for this reason he had snuck away without Maccabee. This was none of Maccabee's fight. Maccabee had suffered enough. Maccabee had his own life to live. Maccabee had offended no Judge of the Underworld, committed no sacrilege.

Alexander knew that his soul was the only thing he had worth saving.

He had seen Aziru triumph over the Devil.

Nothing less, now, would satisfy him.

All Diomedes' prattle of alternatives—that Alexander and his Macedonians could find a home here, where Diomedes was comfortable, a regent and a lord—was comfort as a man gives comfort to a wailing child.

Alexander knew his destiny when he saw it.

It was in the pillar, that stalagmite with its fiery edges before which he now hesitated.

In its midst he saw, as he knew he would, Hektor. A prisoner of fate. A hostage in need of release.

Alexander was about to walk up to that pillar, go down on his knees, and offer himself in exchange for Hektor when Diomedes came up behind him and grabbed him by the arm.

"Basileus, no. What is in your heart is laudable, but seeking after death or its sisters is not. Punishment is meted out by gods, not decreed by men. You must—"

"I must do what the heart in my breast demands," Alexander said, hardly knowing that he spoke, and shook off Diomedes' counsel with an irritable backward jab of his elbow.

And walked forward alone while, behind, the massed army of Macedonian cavalry and Achaean natives held its collective breath.

In that silence no horse snorted or fitting clanked. Every man held his breath and horse stood his ground.

As if with eyes in the back of his head, Alexander saw the scene.

And then saw the glow on the edges of the great stalagmite which was a pillar.

Before the pillar he saw a phantom Minotaur struggling on its knees.

Saw Minos' mask, his awful golden face.

The Minotaur disappeared.

Alexander stumbled.

The mask lay by his foot.

Where it had come from, or how it had gotten here, he could not have said.

He knelt to pick it up and touched it where it lay in a pool of blood.

Suddenly, as if from nowhere, Diomedes was beside him, and from behind him came a grating sound as an army unsheathed its swords like one man.

Diomedes whispered, "Put it down. Don't touch it. Wipe your fingers in the dust. Don't let the blood touch your face."

But the mask wanted to be picked up. It wanted to be put on.

And Alexander could hear the voice of Minos, far away and hardly discernable, urging him to do so.

"You'll take his place," Diomedes grated. "You'll become a player in an endless game with no winners. Minos is not your Judge. Don't let your sorrow blind you. Don't be a pawn. You are a *king*. Do not become a fool."

But in his head, Alexander could hear a song and see a vista—all that would be his if he picked up the mask.

And became the next Minos.

The future Agamemnon.

The wearer of the golden mask.

It was a kingship of sorts, a custodianship of this nether realm.

Slowly, so slowly because the mask wanted to be picked up and put on and Hektor was becoming more and more fully-formed within the pillar and a voice in his head was telling Alexander that he could decree justice as he willed if only he would don the mantle—the Macedonian turned his head to meet the Argive's eyes.

"Diomedes," he choked out, "what shall I do? Let it all go to Chaos? Leave you to fight this circle-war forever? When I could change it? Make it better?"

"It is you who would be changed. There is no *better* Hell. There are only more or less familiar Hells. And I am familiar enough with this one as it stands. If what we've shared means anything, I charge you: *walk away from this false kingship, while still you can!*"

Those words roared in Alexander's ears and his thighs began to tremble where he hunched over the mask.

Agamemnon, he remembered, had turned men into marble statues and destroyed everything he touched. The *last* Agamemnon had. And who had he been? Would Alexander be as mad?

Was Minos one and the same?

Could he decline what he'd come here to gain?

His fingers reached out of their own accord and nearly brushed the mask, when a woman's voice pierced the gloom:

"No!"

His head snapped up, and Diomedes rough shove pushed him backwards, so that he landed inelegantly on his rump.

There, beside the pillar, was a vision of loveliness with a phantom staff in hand.

"Deipyle!" whispered Diomedes, thinking he saw his mother, the goddess.

"Olympias!" gasped Alexander, thinking he saw *his* mother, the sorcerous queen.

"Helen," corrected the vision, and added: "You seek judgment, seek elsewhere, Alexander—you are welcome to bide in this Achaean dream, but not to control it. Kick away the mask, with your foot." She tapped the staff against the stone floor, a warning, a gentle tap, but the whole cavern rumbled and flared so that the rock walls and the high vault could transiently be seen, as if some New Dead shined his torch from wall to wall.

Alexander looked into the eyes of Helen and felt his whole body shiver as if from lightning's kiss.

And reached out with one foot, with a kick and a shove that sent the golden mask skittering across the stone.

It careened onward, as if with a life of its own, until it reached the bank of the black water. Then it teetered there, as if fighting its own fate.

It fell.

There was a splash.

Then nothing.

Until Diomedes said, "Cousin . . . Helen . . . what . . . ?"

And Alexander looked away from the place where the mask had disappeared to see Hektor, emerging from the pillar, full of hubris with a proud man's gait, rubbing his eyes as if awakening from sleep.

The woman—if woman she was, who was translucent—touched the Trojan on the brow with her staff and turned to them, tears like diamonds sparkling on her cheeks.

"So, it is done. Will you come with me, Heroes? All of you—your armies, yourselves, and make a place with us? All your retinue has gone onward, and you have only this choice, besides that of Evil—my world, or the unknown which lies at the end of these passages' turnings." Her eyes were as deep as heaven, as deep as the sky Alexander remembered from his youth.

He tore his gaze from her and turned to Diomedes, who was drawn up as tight as a nocked bow: "Your counsel, Diomedes, would be welcome."

The Argive shivered, glanced at his cousin who was no more than a manifestation of some greater power, and said, "Alexander, I am called home. This is not in doubt. Once before I asked if you would make your home with us. Now I plead it."

Diomedes, best of the Achaeans, held out his hand to Alexander of Macedon.

Almost bashfully, Alexander took it. Somehow, they would manage. He could not ask the Argive to come with him into unknown peril, and Diomedes would not leave Alexander to slog through this subterranean darkness alone.

All his life on Earth, Alexander had sought after heroism and honor as it was described in the Iliad.

If it were different here, this was because he was in Hell.

But a kinder Hell could no man of Alexander's temperament find than the citadel of Troy and the long ships, black ships on the beach.

So he said, "Until I find my Judge, if it takes eternity."

Alexander clasped the Argive's hand, and saw tears glittering unshed in Diomedes' eyes.

Somewhere in Heaven, Alexander hoped, Hephaistion was smiling.

Welch couldn't believe the mess they were in. Caesar was losing his grip, if he'd ever had one to lose.

Getting that damned army moving had been one of the hardest things Welch had ever done. It was as if the Counterforce was a palpable wall, invisible but physical, through which he couldn't get these crazy Old Dead to move.

He missed Nichols like hell, now with Zaki driving while he ran everything out of the back of the truck, snapping orders through his com station to Hatshepsut and anybody who had a Litton to listen with: Curtius, Gemayel, that lot.

As for Julius Caesar, they'd settle it soon enough.

The com truck jogged and bumped its way down into the tunnels, headlights trying valiantly to pierce a more-than-mortal gloom.

Damned mess. The Old Dead could pretend all

they wanted that this wasn't a retreat, but an advance to the rear was exactly what was going on here.

Horses and chariots and fucking executive tents and he didn't know what-all. Into a maze from which egress was unlikely, except for him.

And for his equipment.

One of the topo mapping screens was picking up other humans in the maze. It had been for a while, but now there were distinct groups.

One he'd long ago ID'd as Scaevola and party, and it was toward that lot that Welch was heading the Roman army. The second group of blips was behaving very badly: appearing and disappearing, multiplying and dividing itself, acting as though physical transit wasn't a necessary part of coming or going or being anywhere.

He didn't like that one bit.

If Zaki wasn't driving, he'd have had someone to chew out about it.

But Zaki *was* driving, and Welch was alone with his memories. And with his plans for the future, such as it might show itself to be.

He hadn't heard yet where Machiavelli had popped up, but he'd put out an alert. There was going to be some after-action shaking out, if he had anything to say about it.

He was aware that engaging in a vendetta with Niccolo Machiavelli wasn't smart; but it wasn't personal on his part—not like it was with Caesar, at any rate.

Caesar was going to find that New Hell (should they make it back there) wasn't what it used to be—not for him and his.

And if Welch couldn't reconstitute Nichols in the appropriate spacetime, then he was personally going to see this bunch of Romans evicted and Reassigned. Like to the polar Hell shared by certain Soviets and Eskimos.

Time was on his side.

An hour later, more or less, as the blips that were Scaevola's party began to separate into men and the column started to chatter, having got Scaevola's unit in sight, Welch was revved up to the point where he'd considered leaving the whole bunch in the lurch—it wasn't hard. Just push a particular button and speak an emergency retrieval code and see if his own side couldn't jerk him out of here, truck and all.

Leaving Caesar and his girls in this maze until Hell froze over.

It would make a nice memorial to Nichols' memory.

"All right," he spoke into his phone mike on an open channel that linked him to every player with com capacity, "your buddy Scaevola's up front. Let's not take too long with the reunion," and swivelled in his ergo chair.

Time for a shot of Nichols' mash whiskey.

Damn, it hurt to lose a good man.

Zaki put the truck in neutral and came back to see what was going on, so Welch said, "There's a bottle of mash under that console; fix us two, with water— it's Nichols' toast, and you ought to drink it with me."

The little Israeli who'd underperformed so consistently during the mission looked up at Welch appraisingly from under a jutting brow and said, "Yes? If it's your wish. But you are angry, this is so? And you knew this would happen—Scaevola, his men—all along. . . ."

"I'm not angry. I'm thinking about leaving this bunch of skirt-wearing psychos here where they belong, is all. Beats trying to play by their rules."

He wasn't watching Zaki as the little Israeli poured the drinks.

Maybe he should have been.

Lethe water, administered by an expert, is a very selective memory agent.

Welch had slugged half the mash before he realized that it was making him feel funny.

The next thing he knew, he was drinking the rest of it and wondering what all the fuss was about, and Zaki was telling him what orders Welch had given for the "safe return to New Hell's armory of the entire sortie party, and an end to all grudges, present and future. This is laudable, in an American. Authority will be pleased with the job we've done. See, I have written a detailed report."

And he was glad that Zaki had written that report, because Welch was so tired that he couldn't remember exactly what had happened . . . some of it, of course, but his memory was patchy.

They'd lost Nichols in the line of duty, he knew. And Machiavelli. And certain others.

But Zaki's written assessment of the valorous performance of all concerned made him feel a lot better. It was good to have somebody like Zaki around, to cover your ass, especially in Hell.

Diomedes brought the army through the pillar, as the Helen-apparition had decreed, without incident.

It felt strange walking through the numinous cavern that was so much more commodious than it appeared. His skin tingled and his mouth went dry.

But he was resigned to the meddling of supernatural forces. It wasn't birds winging up into the Italian sky, so he didn't complain.

Helen wouldn't hurt him, not ever. Blood was on the line.

And the Macedonian boy-king seemed resigned, at first, then transported with joy when, at the other end of the pillar—or portal, or whatever it was—happy Achaean and Trojan women threw blood-red blossoms at the army coming through.

When all the Macedonian cavalry and every Achaean stood on the "solid" ground of the beach below the citadel, and the procession had stopped before a dais on which Priam and Aeneas waited, Alexander found his way to Diomedes with shining eyes and said, "A parade of blood and blossoms . . . as I'd dreamed it. A triumph wrested from disaster."

And he clapped Diomedes on the shoulder.

But the Argive was looking up at the citadel, at a single horse picking its way down the rugged slope.

Closer to hand, Hektor was being hugged by his father and a physically substantial Helen (had she been here all along?) was casting come-hither looks at Diomedes.

If Hell was what Diomedes understood it to be, that promise in Helen's eyes was no lie.

He'd be careful not to start another war over her, but certain demands of destiny could not be eternally forestalled. Even if he'd wanted to forestall them.

All around were the men and women of his age; tortured souls, but souls nevertheless.

Diomedes gave a silent prayer of thanks to his mother, and to the fate that guided him. And he resolved to sacrifice a fat bull and an ox to the glory of Achilles, who'd died for this moment, but never seen it.

Even in Hell, a hero could find his way home.

"Alexander," Diomedes said gently, "there's someone looking for you." And pointed to the horse, the great black stallion with flagged mane and tail, now reaching the flat where he could take longer strides toward the man he loved.

Alexander looked where Diomedes pointed and a shudder coursed his small form.

Because it was a shudder of eagerness, not fear, Diomedes forebore saying to Alexander that Bucephalus was the Macedonian's Judge.

Between man and horse, love was a bond greater than time and death and Hell. Between those two, Diomedes knew without doubt as the mincing stallion with his arched crest picked his way through the crowd and Alexander left Diomedes' side to meet him, love would find a way.

Diomedes felt no surprise, and only a touch of sadness, when, without a word, Alexander took a handful of mane and swung up on Bucephalus' back.

But when the *basileus* called out, "Diomedes, thank you for everything. We'll be back soon," Diomedes shook his head.

Then Diomedes smiled, and waved as Helen came to stand beside him, at the retreating figure of the small man on the great horse: Alexander was allowed a small untruth, to save face and tears.

"Soon," called the boyish king again.

"Soon," Diomedes called back, "or late, you're always welcome."

Alexander of Macedon urged Bucephalus into a canter and man and horse disappeared, racing along the beach at Ilion, in a cloud of sand and ocean spray.

Epilogue

Maccabee had never thought to see the New Hell armory, with its chain-link fence and halogen spotlights and giant garage, again.

He knew it was the American called Welch who had done this magic—Welch was a creature of Authority, of the Pentagram, perhaps of the Devil himself.

Zaki was getting out of the com truck which had been first up the circular ramp that turned thirteen times before it ended at a metal door pleated like a rich lady's curtain—a door which no one of Caesar's army had known was a door until it raised itself up into the concrete and revealed the innards of the garage.

No one except Welch, perhaps.

Zaki had ridden with Welch to a deeper hell and back and Maccabee found himself drawn to that slight Israeli form, easy to miss in the chaos of horses and jeeps and chariots and men, all milling about their factional commanders.

Now that they were back in New Hell, command was dissolving, temporary alliances were being discarded: all was returning to what it had been before.

Except, of course, for Achilles, Menelaos, Nichols, Aziru, Diomedes and Alexander who, for all Maccabee knew, might never return anywhere at all.

The separation from Alexander was something he'd

dwelled long upon, on the journey back to New
Hell. It was this he wanted to discuss with Zaki, who
understood so much better the workings of Agency
and Administration.

But on his way through the crowd to the little Jew
he saw a black-clad, slight form—Niccolo Machiavelli,
already returned from the Undertaker's table and at
Caesar's elbow once more.

A murderous tension overcame Maccabee's flesh
for a moment, and then he shook it off with an effort
of will.

It was not Machiavelli's fault that Alexander had
been left behind, any more than it was the Italian's
fault that Achilles had died or that Maccabee was so
exceedingly lonely here in New Hell that he wishing
furiously that he'd found a way to stay behind.

But Gemayel had talked Maccabee out of it, and
Zaki had helped.

So, with Gemayel already melted into the shadows
with his commandos, gone as if he'd never been, it
was to Zaki that Maccabee must go, even if Machiavelli
saw him.

But the Italian did not—he was a part of the royal
retinue once more, sandwiched between two Egyptian pharaohs with luscious hips, nodding and listening to Caesar dispatch his officers: Decius Mus,
Mettius Curtius, Antonius and the rest.

When he reached Zaki, Maccabee stood towering
above the little Israeli, suddenly dumbstruck.

Zaki said with a soulful look, "I know, Judah. I
know it's hard. He'll be all right and so will you. We
always are."

A grip passed between them that had circulated in

the Med since ancient times and would have made Gemayel flash a rare smile.

"What will I do here, alone? Without him? Without . . . you?" Maccabee said, and flushed so hotly that in the headlights of the com truck, he realized miserably, Zaki could not fail to see it.

"Do? What you have always done. What you will always do. Learn. Remember. We will go for him, mark my words. Or he will come to us. Friendship and indebtedness . . . we understand that, don't we?"

There had been fears Maccabee wanted to discuss . . . possible retaliation from the Pentagram, from the various factions; repercussions of a dozen sorts.

But looking into the calm eyes of the little Israeli, so at home in New Hell, Maccabee said only, "You think it will be all right, then? For us all?"

"What's to worry? We have Welch on our side. And—ah, you don't know a good kosher house, is that it? You're staying with me, of course. You must. I have friends for you to meet, things for you to do. We need you, Judah Maccabee," and Zaki's voice fell to a whisper, "if we're ever to reach Heaven by force of arms."

Whatever Maccabee might have said in return was drowned out by the grating sound of the truck's side door sliding in its tracks.

Welch hopped down, a folio under his arm, gave Zaki a casual salute, nodded to Maccabee, and headed off into the shadows of the armory garage, whistling, one hand jammed into the hip pocket of his fatigues.

Julius and the Roman contingent turned up the driveway of the villa in as triumphant a homecoming as could be managed.

Kleopatra had seen to that.

They'd left the tanks behind, at the armory, and Hatshepsut's lower lip had trembled when she gave up her keys.

Machiavelli had visited with Caesar, then departed on an errand, the content of which Klea did not yet know. But she would find out, she always did.

There was a feeling of displacement upon returning, one that made her queasy and caused her heart to pound.

But they *had* returned. Returned to Sargon's comfort, to Dante's computers, to Augustus' politics and Tiberius' madness. . . .

"Set and Typhon!" she breathed, slapping her knee in the jeep. She'd forgotten all about Drusus . . . she'd promised Tiberius she'd find Drusus, in order to get the Germans from him. It seemed so long ago. . . .

So long ago. By now, mad Tiberius had probably forgotten too. She considered keeping the Germans, and decided that the time to decide was not now, but later, when she'd learned as much as possible about what had gone on in New Hell during her absence.

But then, on an impulse, she pulled the eight ball from the jeep's glove compartment, an act that made Mouse look at her askance as he wheeled the jeep up before the portico and brought it to the stop.

She concentrated, closing her eyes: *Eight ball, shall I return the Germans to Tiberius?*

And the eight ball in her lap, once inverted, replied: *Hell, no.*

Then she looked up and saw, as Julius' jeep pulled up behind hers, Brutus standing in the doorway, a painfully anxious look on his oh-so-young face as he searched among the returnees for his father.

Alexander sat his horse on a pinnacle overlooking a wine-dark sea. Stroking Bucephalus' trembling shoulder, he leaned down and buried his head in the horse's mane.

Below and behind, where there was not sea, there were clouds as deep and fresh and soft as a pleasant dream.

At that moment, Alexander ignored all the beauty around him: in his nose was the sweet smell of Bucephalus and in his heart was a joy so great that it threatened to overflow into tears.

If Alexander the Great cried in his horse's mane, Bucephalus would never tell.

Some time later, when the stallion under the boyish figure of the Macedonian raised its mighty head to let out a mighty bellow that rang out over the pinnacle and the sea below, the *basileus* was laughing.

**Rob a Pharaoh and you've made an enemy
not just for life . . . but for *all time*.**

FRED SABERHAGEN

PYRAMIDS

Tom Scheffler knew that his great uncle,
Montgomery Chapel, had worked as an Egyptologist
during the 1930s, and after that had become a
millionaire by selling artifacts no one else could
have obtained. Scheffler also knew that the old
man, fifty years later, was still afraid of some
man—some *entity*—known only as Pilgrim. But
what did that mean to Scheffler, an impoverished
student with the chance to spend a year "house-
sitting" a multi-million-dollar condo?

What Scheffler didn't know—and would learn
the hard way—was that Pilgrim was coming back,
aboard a ship that traveled both space and time,
headed for a confrontation in a weirdly changed
past where the monstrous gods of ancient Egypt
walked the Earth. And where Pharaoh Khufu,
builder of the greatest monument the world had
ever known, lay in wait for grave robbers from
out of time . . .

JANUARY 1987 • 65609-0 • 320 pp. • $3.50